Please
Come
Home

BOOKS BY ELAINE JOHNS

Please Come Home

Elaine Johns

bookouture

Published by Bookouture in 2023

An imprint of Storyfire Ltd.
Carmelite House
50 Victoria Embankment
London EC4Y 0DZ

www.bookouture.com

ISBN: 978-1-83790-565-2
eBook ISBN: 978-1-83790-564-5

For Anne and Tony with love

PART ONE

WATFORD, ENGLAND

JULY 1939

Anna's mother was dead. Her father might as well have been. He was a cold, unapproachable man – at least with her. She had heard him laugh with others, but he had never given his daughter a smile, let alone any affection. Ten years ago, when Anna was only eight years old, he had handed her over to the sole charge of his sister, Beatrice, a grim-faced woman who wore long, stiff black dresses with tight collars that looked as if they might choke her.

Her father, a wealthy businessman, had moved to Ireland, leaving Anna behind. He had sold the family home. The place where she was born. An impressive Manor house in Reigate with its retinue of servants. Then Anna had been callously thrust into the puritanical and church-going arms of Aunt Beatrice in Watford.

Her father's total indifference towards her had hurt and puzzled Anna as a child, until Aunt Beatrice had heartlessly explained exactly why her father could never love her.

Her mother had died in childbirth, giving birth to *her*. She had killed her mother.

The cruel thought that she was to blame made Anna wretched and a fog of sadness had followed her for weeks. It was her fault that her mother had died, although she didn't understand how.

Aunt Beatrice may have taken over Anna's care but any *care* that Beatrice had given had been applied with a heavy hand and a smack that left a mark for days. It seemed to Anna that her aunt was an unhappy woman, a tyrant who made it her business to make those around her unhappy too.

Anna always wished she had known her mother. She remembered her photograph, in pride of place on the grand piano in her father's drawing room. *Elizabeth Golding, her mother.* She had looked like a gentle woman; the kind of woman not afraid to smile, when most people looked so stiff and posed in photographs. The black, lustrous hair that framed her face in Marcel waves had the sheen of silk, unlike Anna's, which was like her father's: tough and wiry. But Anna's hazel eyes came from her mother, and she was glad of that, for her father's piercing blue eyes were ice-cold when they had trapped her in their unfriendly glare.

As she grew older, Anna became certain of one thing. That her father and Aunt Beatrice were wrong, and that a child, a baby in her mother's womb, was an innocent. Blameless. Now, in her late teens, Anna Golding was convinced that her strange upbringing had strengthened her, made her mentally tough. Self-reliant and resourceful. She had learned a valuable lesson from an early age: that love was not always freely given, or an automatic right. Her aunt had grudgingly provided food, clothing, and an education. Everything that a body needed to survive. But never love.

Not that she had been totally starved of affection. Ruby, the housekeeper in her aunt's large Watford townhouse, had taken pity on her and throughout the years had shown her small acts of kindness. And Ruby's daughter, Edna, had become a friend over the past three years since she'd been a housemaid there. Sunny and cheerful and funny, Edna could always pull a smile from Anna's lips.

Aunt Beatrice, who was hale and hearty, could easily have fended for herself. Yet she had four people looking after her, washing her clothes, cooking her food, and dusting the hideous vases in the drawing room. That was Edna's job – dusting, beating the rugs – but she never complained about her lot. Even managed to laugh about it.

Come the revolution. It was a secret joke between them.

And one day, things would change. Anna was sure of that. Maybe soon. A war was coming. Everybody said so. And wars always changed things. Disrupted the old order. People might find other jobs, might not want to work as domestic servants any more.

'Can you imagine Beatrice doing her own laundry?' she'd asked Edna when they'd talked about it.

'Her Highness? She wouldn't have a clue,' said Edna.

'And cooking her own food? Maybe she's got skills we never knew,' Anna said.

'Na, shouldn't think so. The old bat would starve.'

'Edna! That's disrespectful.' All the same, Anna smiled. 'She pays your wages,' she said.

'Yeah, but not very much. Think she could make her own bed? All those hospital corners she fusses me about? Like to see *her* try 'em.' Edna winked.

'Then there's the dusting, cleaning the house,' said Anna, 'and those horrible rugs.'

'She can 'ave 'em, I wouldn't be sorry never to beat them damn things again.'

'I imagine she'd struggle with those,' said Anna. The image

made her smile. Not that she intended to stay around and watch.

Anna Golding would be eighteen next month and she was ready to set out on her own.

She could do it.

Her core was strong. Maybe she had inherited that from her mother as well. Anna smiled as she conjured her mother's face in her mind. A woman in a photograph. A woman who had missed her chance at life. But now Anna would live her life for them both.

Soon, she would step out into the world, to face the challenges it would bring. Somewhere to live. A job. She didn't welcome the war waiting in the wings, but maybe she would find her freedom in it, a chance to throw off the shackles of a loveless childhood.

Her heart fluttered in anticipation as if a thousand butterflies had beat their fragile wings. Fear and excitement, in equal parts, fought each other for control as she thought about the future. A step into uncharted waters. What would her future hold? But she made herself a promise. *Anna Golding, you will try to be courageous and honest and fair to others who cross your path.*

How hard could it be?

2

AIR MINISTRY HEADQUARTERS, KINGSWAY, LONDON

28 SEPTEMBER 1939

There were thirty of them in the room. Anna had counted them. Large women. Small women. Young women, most of them. All with their suitcases. All of them waiting. None of them seemed to know what for. What the next step in the recruitment process would be. She imagined, like her, they'd been told to report here, after their initial interview. Many of the women looked anxious, but some were smiling, as if this was the most exciting thing that had happened in their lives so far. That was how Anna felt: as if this was what her life had been leading up to.

Everyone had filled in a complicated enlistment form. Anna had helped one young woman with hers. Dorothy (*call me Dot*, she'd told Anna) had been effusive in her thanks. The girl had been in 'service', just like Anna's friend Edna, and had been ashamed and embarrassed that her reading was a 'little slow'. She had learned to sign her name, but it seemed that her parents had pushed her into the life of a domestic servant before

she could finish her schooling. *One more kid off their hands,*
Dorothy had admitted sheepishly.

A middle-aged man wearing a Royal Air Force uniform
marched smartly into the room. He came to rest in front of
them, a picture of precision in air force blue. In a bellow that
shook the window frames, he called out six names. Said they
should follow him. Anna left her seat. Her name was on his list.

She ended up in an office, facing a small, fussy-looking man
in a pinstripe suit who pointed to the chair opposite without
looking up or taking his eyes off the form he was reading. Any
other time, Anna might have told him he was being rude but she
wanted to join the Women's Auxiliary Air Force – to be a
WAAF – and wouldn't give him a reason to reject her.

'Sit. Sit!' he said impatiently, and finally looked up.

'Sir,' said Anna, and took a seat.

'You don't need to *Sir* me, Miss... ah...' He looked back at
her form. 'Golding.'

'Oh.'

'I'm neither an officer, nor in the air force.'

'I see.'

'I doubt you do.'

A sigh popped out of Anna. He didn't know her. She wasn't
stupid. Maybe she really *did* see.

The man coughed and raised an eyebrow. 'Right, let's get
on,' he said. 'Much to do. And there's a war out there waiting.'

'I understand,' she said – and she did. That dreadful bully,
Hitler, had invaded Poland at the start of September and, two
days later, Britain had declared war on Germany, doing the
decent thing and coming to the aid of the underdog. It was why
she was proud of her country. Why she had wanted to sign up
for the WAAFs. To contribute, no matter how small. Everyone
would be needed now.

She heard the man clear his throat again.

'The first thing I should like to point out,' he said, his voice

clipped and haughty, 'is that you have not filled out your regis-
tration form correctly.'

'I haven't?' she said, surprised.

'No. Next of kin, you've left it blank. I take it you have
someone, somewhere. Some family?'

'Oh. I see. Well, I'm sorry, Mr...'

'Morrison.' The man pompously straightened his tie. Sat a
little higher in his chair.

'Yes,' said Anna. 'I have family.'

'I'm glad to hear it. Now if you could just fill out the appropriate section on your WAAF651/20, we'll be able to move on
and get you processed.' He handed her the paperwork. 'I'll leave
you to it,' he said, and left the room.

She gazed at the form for inspiration. Who was she to pick?
She didn't want to put her father's name on there. He had never
shown the slightest interest in her. And Aunt Beatrice had practically disowned her when Anna said she was leaving to join the
WAAF.

But there was no more family, or so she'd been told. She'd
quizzed her aunt about it once. Were there no grandparents?
No! All dead. Her aunt had been adamant and seemed a little
angry that Anna should ask. But what about her mother? Did
she have no brothers or sisters? Being an only child was rare, she
knew. Her aunt had looked away, become evasive. Spanish flu,
she'd finally said. There *was* a sister once, but she had died from
the Spanish flu. It had killed off more people than the war.

That's when Anna had gone looking for proof. She had felt
adventurous going through the bureau drawers when her aunt
had left the drawing room. And she'd found something hidden
in her aunt's Edwardian china cabinet. Secreted beneath a
lining of embossed wallpaper, grey, with blood-red roses and
green leaves and wicked-looking prickles. Not the lining paper
Anna would have chosen, but somehow it symbolised her aunt
perfectly. Anna had carefully peeled back a corner of the paper

and there it was. Another photograph of her mother. A younger version. One she had never seen before. It had taken Anna's breath away, the shock of it. Her mother, a beautiful young girl, standing tall, smiling. And the girl beside her. The same height. The same hair. *This* face was serious, a little haughty, trying to look regal, not smiling like her mother. But it was the same face. Her mother was – had been – a twin.

The doorknob rattled and Mr Morrison returned. 'All done then?'

Anna dragged herself back to the present and quickly filled in the name and address of her next of kin. Edna Evans – her special friend to whom she'd once sworn a solemn oath to be *friends for life*.

After that, everything seemed to happen at breakneck speed. The waiting women were hustled towards two canvas-covered lorries by the man in the RAF uniform. He seemed to be in charge of them, for he was harrying them all like a sheep-dog. Anna had no idea of his rank, but his voice was loud and meant to be frightening, she supposed. But she wasn't frightened. She had been forged in the furnace of her aunt's rebukes, had survived reprimands and criticism from the woman for ten long, wearisome years. There was nothing he could do that hadn't already been done to her.

She learned a new skill – jumping onto the tailboard of a truck. She didn't look that elegant but managed it without making a fool of herself. And the journey – that was far from luxurious. Four and a half hours of being thrown around in the back of the truck, the wind howling through the canvas, and sixteen women trying to keep warm, battling to stay perched on the hard, wooden benches. But Anna didn't mind. One wit complained she'd got a splinter in her backside and most of them laughed. Immediately, Anna felt a comradeship. It was strange, and didn't make sense, because she knew none of these women, but already she had a feeling of being *settled*. Of finally finding her place. Of coming home. Maybe even having a family of sorts. To make up for the one she'd never had.

'You seem happy.'

It was Dorothy, the girl she'd met before. They'd ended up sitting next to each other in the lorry.

'Do I?' said Anna. 'Yes, I suppose I am.' She smiled to confirm it.

'Not homesick then, like Mary?' Dorothy nodded at a young woman sitting opposite. 'She's been crying.'

'That's a shame. Maybe we can help her settle in,' said Anna.

Mary raised her head. Her eyes were bloodshot and the skin beneath them was swollen and blotchy. Her nose was a matching rosy colour, as if she had a cold. 'I'm sitting right here,' she said. 'I can hear you, I'm not an idiot. And you needn't sound so superior.'

'What? No. I didn't mean to offend you, Mary. I know what it's like to be talked down to,' said Anna. 'I wouldn't do that.' It was true. She could never treat anyone the way her aunt had treated *her*.

'Okay, just so's you know. I may not have a fancy accent like yours, but I've been to school. I'm not thick. And I'm sure I don't need *anybody*'s help.'

'Of course you're not stupid. Nobody said you were. But we all need somebody's help sometimes,' said Anna. She stretched her arm across the aisle. 'Pals?'

'I suppose so.' Mary shook hands. Then the miserable girl sniffed and wrestled in her pocket for a handkerchief. When she couldn't find one, Dorothy handed hers across. It was a small linen square with rosebuds embroidered in the corners.

'Can't take that,' said Mary. 'Looks like a fancy one.'

'Birthday present. Ma made it for me,' Dorothy told her. 'She embroidered the roses special, took her ages. But I want you to have it.'

Anna watched the interaction and the smile that replaced the wretched look on young Mary's face. And although it was something positive, Anna felt a little sadness touch her. She had *never* had anyone take ages to embroider something for her.

The three of them stuck together through the next few bewildering days at RAF Wilmslow in Cheshire. It was a huge place, a training camp south of Manchester, chock-full of new recruits, both men and women. It boasted several parade grounds and mess halls, a shooting range and, best of all, a cinema. Strangely, at least to Anna, there was no airfield, although a proud Spitfire stood at its gate, a reminder that the RAF was all about flying.

And now Anna Golding had a new title. She was no longer *Miss*, but ACW 2nd Class. An aircraftwoman like the others beside her. Newly enlisted and the lowest of the ranks. And, like all good ACW2s, Anna went where she was sent and did what she was told – mostly. She picked up her eating irons: knife, fork, spoon, and tin mug. Picked up her kit: regulation underwear – two roll-on girdles with suspenders, and two bras (described on her kit list as 'brassieres, white, serviceable'). No fancy lingerie here. The bras were hard, stiff cotton, but she figured they could be beaten into shape. A few washes would soften them up. Then there were six pairs of white knickers and six pairs of navy-blue passion-killers that came down to the knee, with tight elastic that bit in and left red marks. She decided to ditch the navy-blue ones. It was as close as she came to defiance. The lisle stockings were scratchy but once you'd immersed them in boiling water, they became softer and more humane. Anna was pleased, for that was her idea, and lots of the others had copied her.

Kitting her out in uniform had been a challenge for the

quartermaster stores. She was much taller and thinner than the other WAAFs in the intake. The ACW behind the counter had handed over the blue barathea service dress tunic and skirt without even checking Anna's size. But she hadn't moved to pick it up, had waited patiently, bravely holding up the line behind her. A WAAF sergeant had finally arrived, looked her over from head to foot, tutted and sighed. And finally picked up a uniform from a rack out back. The shoes were an impossibility. Her feet were large, far from regulation size. So, they'd sent her over to the men's section and Anna was the only new WAAF recruit wearing men's shoes. She took a lot of ribbing, but it was only friendly banter, stuff that made her laugh.

They laughed a lot in the barracks – draughty Nissen huts, made of corrugated steel. Anna's hut had the same sixteen girls from her long truck journey, all packed in like sardines in a tin. At night, before lights out, they would all squash up in one end of the hut around the coke-fired stove, tell stories and jokes, and eat Marmite sandwiches. The WAAFs from hut 27 bonded into a distinct group. They ate together, sat together in their hut polishing their brass cap badges, and listened to each other's grumbles when things got tough. There was a feeling of camaraderie, and friendships began to form as they came together in a sisterhood, helping each other out through the first confusing days of their new life. Nicknames were given to some of them. She wasn't surprised at hers since she was the tallest in her barracks. 'Lofty' seemed a natural fit and she wasn't upset by it, for it was said with gruff affection. The other two women in Anna's trio of pals got nicknames too. Dorothy became 'Dotty' and Mary had to get used to being called 'Mo'. But nobody complained.

They learned how to sort their living space. How to clean underneath the beds. And how to neatly 'stack' their bedding in a very particular way. That had to be done before going to breakfast. Anna was fine with all that. She found she liked the regimented order of the whole thing. It gave a certainty to her day, in a time when other things were uncertain. But there were some who struggled with it. That and the rules about hair, which wasn't allowed to touch your collar. But Anna had smiled at that. Finally, her black, short, wiry hair – that Aunt Beatrice had called unfeminine and ugly – was a plus, and not something to be defended.

And she felt relieved to be wearing the uniform. Not only because she was proud to do so, but it meant an end to the continual struggle of finding clothes that would fit her tall, gangling frame. Clothes that her aunt had considered ladylike enough and appropriate for their 'social standing'. Anna didn't care a hoot about social standing. And she had no interest in clothes or fashion or women's magazines, and if that made her unfeminine, then that was fine by her. There were far more important things out there for women to spend their time on. Equal rights with men would be a start. Even here, in the training camp, a few of the airmen resented the WAAFs being there, didn't want their jobs taken by women. A chap had fired an insult at her when she first arrived. *Skirts in the RAF?* he'd said. *Should never be allowed.*

As it was, Anna and the WAAFs around her were only being paid two-thirds of the wages the airmen were. Even those women on dangerous jobs like guiding barrage balloons. She wouldn't mind if men didn't tip their hats to her. Or open doors. Or give up their seats on the bus. It would be worth it for what you would get in exchange. Some kind of equality.

She wasn't sure how many of her friends there at RAF Wilmslow felt the same, though. Not many, she suspected. And certainly not her best friend, Edna Evans. Edna was always able to make her laugh, taking life head-on, fearless, finding fun in the smallest thing. She remembered the time they'd gone to Watford fair together and watched a man weave pink, sticky candyfloss.

'It's a miracle,' said Anna as he'd spun the sugar in his machine, into sweet, fluffy, gossamer clouds. 'I'll get us some.'

'Your face!' shrieked Edna.

'What's wrong with my face?' Anna asked, wrestling with the sticky candyfloss.

'You got red dye all round your mouth.' Edna giggled.

'You have too.' said Anna, 'it's not easy to eat.'

'But worth it. It melts when it hits your tongue. My ma says it's bad for you, for your teeth. You believe that?' asked Edna.

'Maybe, but sometimes it's fun to do things that aren't good for you.' Not that Anna was often a rebel, but at times Edna brought that out in her, made her more adventurous.

They'd used Anna's handkerchief to clean up their messy faces.

Then they'd bobbed for apples in a water barrel and got soaked and laughed until Anna had thought she might burst. Edna, who had no head for heights, had courageously soared skywards in a frightening contraption called the Octopus and, afterwards, had to be helped to the edge of the field, where she threw up her candyfloss.

Anna missed her, missed Edna's optimism and her sense of joy. She hoped to be able to meet up with her friend again soon, maybe when they were both given leave. Edna had joined the army, and was in the Auxiliary Territorial Service – the ATS – with their scratchy khaki uniforms. Anna had heard that even the underwear was khaki, not something her friend would be thrilled about, for Edna was fussy about her clothes and especially her underwear. She had saved up for months to buy a silk chemise. Anna smiled, remembering. Her friend's philosophy was 'always be prepared', especially in the underwear department, for you never knew who might be looking at it. Some chap, perhaps. She knew that Edna longed for that *perfect* chap. Had she finally found him? Anna suspected that such a man didn't exist; at least, not outside her friend's mind.

She herself was cynical about love. Especially 'romantic' love. It had its place in fiction and women's magazines, but Anna doubted it existed in the real world. She blamed her father for this tainted view. But then she blamed him for many things after the way he'd abandoned her when she was only eight years old and cut her from his life.

He deserved it.

3

Hut 27 became Anna's new home. Their Nissen hut was one of many in the WAAF section of the camp, not far from the guard gate and backing onto the perimeter fence. She was proud of her billet, of the way the floor shone, and they'd all tried to keep it that way together, taking their shoes off outside, sliding around it on dusters – it gleamed, and for their efforts they'd been judged best hut in inspections. Basic training had been hectic and at times both physically and mentally tiring, lots of PE and parade-ground-drilling and the lectures on RAF rules. Not to mention all those aptitude tests to discover which branch of WAAF training you would move onto next. But all the same, she'd enjoyed it, and the focus it gave her. And she thrived on the comradeship of the women in the barracks.

It wasn't all roses, of course: there were some thorns as well. Route marches in the pouring rain meant having to wash out grubby uniforms and shine shoes that were caked in mud. And cleaning out the ablutions in the freezing cold wasn't much fun, or measuring the grass with a ruler and cutting it with a pair of scissors.

Some of the airmen laughingly christened the WAAF quar-

ters 'the henhouse', and she'd also heard them called 'the
nunnery'. But the chaps had to laugh at something, and Anna
didn't get upset by it; not like some of the other WAAFs, who
found it disrespectful. Overall, she found that most of the
airmen treated them with an old-fashioned chivalry. Only a few
of the men resented them.

Anna learned another new skill, her, and the other recruits.
They spent hours on one of the parade grounds 'square-bashing'. Marching together, tallest on the right, shortest on the left,
trying to get it right without piling into each other. Some
couldn't get the hang of it. Dotty was one of those, and Anna
had tried to help her, but the poor girl seemed to end up on the
wrong foot most of the time. She was gone now, Dotty – had
dramatically disappeared. Mustered out of the WAAF. *Family
trouble.* That's all they were told at the time. But Anna had
made it her business to find out from one of the corporals,
because Dotty had been a friend, one of a trio of pals who had
helped each other out. Tragedy had taken Dotty back home as
her mother had died and she'd had to look after her two young
brothers. To be a 'mother' for them, to comfort them and see
them through their grief. It was something she would do well,
Anna thought.

They would miss her, especially Mary, who still had the
handkerchief with the rosebuds. But now she didn't need it, as
she didn't cry. For Mary Armstrong had changed since their
arrival in camp. Anna had watched her transform from a
nervous, homesick girl into a confident woman, and gradually
the two of them had become closer; drawn together by the many
interests they shared, not least their love of books and crossword
puzzles.

Anna and her new friend couldn't have looked any more
different if they'd tried: Anna, tall and slim with her dark
features and hazel eyes, and Mary, a whole lot shorter and
rounder, with sandy hair that fell into tight corkscrew curls all

over her head, and deep blue eyes, the colour of sapphires. They may have gone to different schools and come from contrasting backgrounds but when both women took their intelligence and aptitude tests, they got identical scores; and had each been given a further interview. And soon, there would be a mathematical exam to sit. Anna looked forward to it because if she passed, she would have the title 'Clerk, Special Duties' and be selected for specialised training as a plotter in an operations room somewhere. She imagined herself in front of a giant maptable, her plotting rod in hand, sliding counters across the table showing positions of planes, their height, and their numbers in her sector.

The job, to track the route of enemy planes on the large ops room map, was a responsible one and could be stressful. It also meant that those WAAFs selected would be sworn to secrecy. *Could she be cool under fire?* one of her examiners had asked. She had no idea. She had never been 'under fire'. But she would try her best.

Four weeks into her induction and training, Anna was looking forward to her first day of leave. She considered they'd all earned it.

Her excitement mounted the closer she got to Market Street. Today was a day of firsts. It was the first time she had been out of camp since they'd all been driven there in the back of that freezing truck. And she'd never been to Manchester before. It would be her first time at a real coffee shop, too. The Kardomah Café sounded like an exotic place. Probably why Edna had picked it. And, although Anna Golding had been on earth for over eighteen years, she had never been to anywhere you might call exotic. That, and the fact that Edna had managed to get a twenty-four-hour pass, made this visit to the

Kardomah a special treat. It would be grand to see her friend again, to talk about old times and catch up on Edna's romantic pursuits. There were sure to be some. It should prove to be a pleasant afternoon.

The outside of the café was a disappointment. Not anything like she'd been expecting. The hessian over the windows meant you couldn't even see inside, and she tripped over the sandbags by the entrance. But the war couldn't be ignored, and most shops already had their windows smothered in blast tape or wire mesh. The threat of bombing was real, although it hadn't happened yet. People were building Anderson shelters in their gardens and there were rumours that underground stations in London were to be used as massive public shelters.

Once inside, the disappointment gave way to awe. The interior of the Kardomah might have been transported from a Hollywood movie set. Lush, colourful Art Deco furnishings and huge central pillars reaching up to swirling rooftop lights. A magnificent staircase that flowed up to the next floor instead of simply arriving there. It struck Anna that someone in a ballgown would not look out of place gliding down it, though the small woman in drab wartime clothes who'd just descended certainly did.

A loud, familiar voice shrieked behind her, and Anna turned around to see her friend.

'Lord almighty, you came!' said Edna, and ran at Anna in an enthusiastic tackle.

'You'd make a decent rugby player,' said Anna, smiling at her friend's boisterous welcome and hugging her right back. 'And of course I came. Did you think I wouldn't?'

'Thought maybe you'd got too fancy for your old pals,' Edna joked. 'Look at you in your posh blue uniform. Bet the blokes are impressed with that. I'm jealous.'

'What?'

'You! You look stunning,' said Edna.

'Nonsense.' But she was pleased, all the same. Her service dress fitted well and emphasised her slim figure and long legs, and she'd shined up her cap badge until its brass crown gleamed. On the way there, she hadn't failed to notice the admiring glances that came her way. She wasn't used to it. Had always thought of herself as an ugly duckling. Maybe she'd turned into a swan.

Edna bustled them to a table. The only change that Anna could see in her friend was the short hair and the khaki uniform.

'You cut your hair,' she said.

'Gave in,' said Edna. 'Easier than taking grief from a sadistic bleedin' sergeant.'

'You like the army? I mean, even with the scratchy khaki and the orders?' asked Anna.

'Been taking orders all me bleedin' life. Don't give it no mind. Then there's the lads. Fallin' over theirselves they are, some of 'em.'

'Careful, Edna.' Anna frowned. 'If you get in trouble, it'll be you who pays the price. Not some chap who takes off once he's had his fun.'

Edna tapped the side of her nose. '*Careful*'s me middle name. Saving meself for the right one. An' I ain't no bloke's comfort blanket, ta very much!'

'Comfort blanket?' said Anna. 'Oh... I see. Well, I'm glad. Put a high price on yourself. If you don't think well of yourself, nobody else will. And you deserve somebody decent.'

'What about you?' Edna asked. 'Find yerself some fancy flyboy yet?'

'Not in the market for one,' said Anna. 'Someday, maybe. Depends on the chap.'

'Hand on your heart and tell me there ain't some gorgeous bloke in blue you've taken a shine to. Must be loads of them in that camp of yours,' said Edna.

'You know me,' said Anna. 'Never been drawn to a hand-some face. There'd need to be more to him than that.'

'Ain't that just what I'm saying?' said her friend. 'The fun's in tracking down the rest of it!'

Anna laughed and wondered if the massive beam spreading across Edna's face and the lively sparkle in her eyes meant something special. 'You getting ready to hook some new chap, then?' she asked.

'Might be,' said Edna. 'Something to be said for getting wed, having your own lovely bloke look after you. Treating you right.'

'Married? You're getting married?' asked Anna, astonished.

'Not yet, but I wouldn't mind settling down – one day. All nice and cosy and secure.'

'Not me,' said Anna.

'No?'

'What – have some man tell me what to do and where to go and what to think? Keep house for him? And look after his kids while he goes on the town? No, thanks!'

'But what will you do?' asked Edna, shocked. 'How will you live if you don't marry?'

'It's the twentieth century. An exciting world, full of possi-bilities,' said Anna and, reaching across, squeezed her friend's hand affectionately. 'I'll be an independent woman. A modern, independent woman. I'll work.'

'Doing what?'

'Who knows?' Anna said. 'I've done well in the aptitude tests they gave us. I always liked mathematics. Maybe I'll get a job as a bookkeeper, or a secretary, or work in a shop or drive a car when the war's over. It doesn't matter, don't you see? We can be anything we like.'

'We?'

'Sure. You. Me. *Women!*'

The two of them chatted and gossiped about old times while drinking coffee that was strong and covered in froth. Edna became sad when she spoke about her mother, Ruby. Anna was fond of the woman, but it seemed she wasn't well, but still kept on working as housekeeper for Aunt Beatrice in Watford just the same.

'What with me leaving,' said Edna, 'and now Cook's gone, there's only me ma to do all the work. It's too much for her. I've told her to finish with all that and I'll look out for her. Send her some of me wages. But she won't have it. You know Ma, she's right independent, don't like bothering folks. Which reminds me...' Edna reached into her kitbag, rummaged around inside, and came out with an envelope. 'Ma gave me this for you. Came a week ago. She didn't hand it over to *her highness*, didn't want it to disappear. Ma's on *your* side. Always has been.'

'I know,' said Anna. 'And she's always been kind to me. She's worth ten of Aunt Beatrice.'

'Come the revolution!' said Edna.

They both giggled.

Anna took the letter. Her name was written on the front, along with her old address in Watford.

'Very fancy,' said Edna.

'What?' asked Anna.

'The writing. Proper copperplate. Looks like it's from some-body posh.'

'Really? But my writing looks like that,' said Anna, amused. 'And *I'm* not posh.'

'You certainly are,' said Edna.

'Never!' said Anna.

'Not stuck-up like some of them upper-crust idiots used to come to your aunt's house, but you *talk* posh,' said Edna. 'I ain't saying that's bad!'

'Hope not.'

'We still pals?' asked Edna. 'You ain't upset?'

'Of course we're pals,' said Anna. '*Friends for life*, remember? Give your ma my love and tell her thanks for this.' Anna pointed to the letter. She took her canvas gas mask haversack from the back of her chair and put the envelope inside. The gas mask holdall was a sort of unofficial handbag. Although it was frowned on by some of the more officious NCOs, even WAAF officers had been known to keep their make-up and personal items in there.

'Not going to read it then?' asked Edna.

'Later,' she said. 'Don't want to waste our time together. I'm enjoying it.'

'Me, too,' said Edna. 'I have to go, though.'

'But you only just got here,' complained Anna.

Edna pointed at the clock. 'We been gassing for over an hour. An' I only had a twenty-four-hour pass. Bleedin' trains took up most of that. Don't want to be AWOL. Already spent enough time peeling spuds on *jankers*, ta very much.'

'Punishment detail? You've been up on a *charge*, already?' asked Anna.

'Twice!' Her friend laughed. 'Sloppy drilling – and forgetting me cap. Got two days of me pay docked.'

'Still, worse things out there,' said Anna. 'Just you take care.'

'Will do. And don't you go being no hero, neither,' said Edna, as the two of them stood and hugged.

It was a tearful goodbye, for who knew when the two pals would see each other again. It was wartime. Nothing was sure. Not even where you might get posted from one minute to the next. It all seemed a bit random when you thought about it. But Anna assumed that the people in charge were all doing their best. They'd hardly do less, would they? All the same, they must be learning as they went along. Just like her.

She picked up her cap, slung the holdall over her shoulder and made her way out to Market Street. She was lucky, and picked up one of the RAF transport trucks heading back to camp.

It dropped her at the gate; and just in front of the barrier she spotted her friend and hut-mate, Mary, sitting on the grass. Anna noted the young airman beside her pal and the pushbike lying on the embankment next to them. They were lounging on a blanket from the billet. Mary's, most likely. *She'd get in trouble for that, but maybe she didn't care.* She looked as if she didn't mind, Anna decided, for she was smiling and holding the chap's hand. They were both eating sandwiches. A sort of picnic. And both looked happy and comfortable in each other's company.

Mary spotted her and waved her over. Anna shook her head. Two was company, especially where a chap was involved. There was an etiquette to such things, and she didn't fancy playing gooseberry.

'Join us,' shouted Mary, and waved again. 'We're having a party.'

Anna reluctantly walked over, not wanting to seem rude.

'Not much of a party,' said the man when she arrived. 'Only sardine sandwiches, I'm afraid, but you're very welcome to one.' He handed one to her as he greeted her with a large, friendly smile.

Anna beamed back automatically. Which wasn't like her. She was usually quite reserved meeting strangers. But her face just fell into a silly grin as if it was operating by itself, separate from her brain.

Absentmindedly, Anna took a huge bite from the thick, chunky sandwich. Tasted the oily sardine on the back of her tongue. She raised the remainder of the sandwich in the air, as if she were making a toast. 'Thank you,' she said. 'It's good,' she told him, as her eyes took in his face: the liberal sprinkling of freckles across it; the small, neatly trimmed ginger moustache above his upper lip. His eyes were green with flecks of light in them, and he had a ginger head of hair; thick and unruly, like hers.

Not a particularly handsome face, Anna supposed some

would say. But then, she'd never been impressed by good-looking men. Her father had been called a handsome devil. Maybe that was why.

She looked away from him. Dropped her head in embarrassment. Felt a pulse of heat work its way up her neck and into her cheeks. Not a good idea, staring at your pal's boyfriend like that.

'You *like* the sandwich?' asked Mary.

'I do,' she said. And, of their own volition, her eyes sought the man's face again.

'But you *hate* sardines,' said Mary. 'Oh... I see.'

'What?' said Anna.

'Never mind. It doesn't matter. Plain as the nose on your face, though,' said Mary.

'What is?' asked Anna.

'Nothing for you to worry about. But I suppose if you're eating his sandwiches, you'd better be introduced,' said Mary. 'This great lanky drink of dishwater here is James Armstrong. Sometimes known as Ginger. *My brother.* My *older* brother,' she added as an afterthought, and laughed.

'Thanks for the big build-up, sis.'

'You're welcome.'

'Jimmy,' he said. 'You can call me Jimmy.' He wiped his hand on the grass and reached over to shake Anna's. 'And I'm not *that* old.'

And that was that. The start of something new and totally alien to Anna Golding. Something unexpected. Something wonderful. And, yes – finally exotic. The tilting of the world on its axis and something Anna had never come face to face with before.

The overwhelming feeling of attraction for a man.

Powerful enough to make her overcome her loathing of sardines.

4

No one had been expecting the gas mask drill.

Maybe that was a good thing, she thought, because no one would be expecting a real poison gas attack if it came. And, as the sergeant who had sprung the drill on them remarked, Hitler wouldn't give them any warning. But it was certainly inconvenient, just before breakfast like this. And now, Anna had to get rid of all the stuff in her gas mask holder/unofficial handbag and fit the mask in there. Otherwise, it would be a black mark for hut 27. It might even get their next pass cancelled and get her on a disciplinary charge.

That's when she found the letter. She'd forgotten all about it. But there was no time to read it now. Already, WAAFs were lined up on the parade ground waiting for the infamous gas drill. You were expected to hold your breath in case there really *was* gas in the air. Then pull the wretched rubber mask over your face and head and try to breathe through the thing for twenty minutes. Anna had to screw up all her courage for the exercise. She was claustrophobic and didn't want to panic. But she wasn't convinced she could make it for the twenty minutes needed for the infernal drill.

'Chins in! Pull side straps!' intoned the sergeant in front of them, in her best parade-ground bark. 'Don't be wet, ACW Golding. Stick your face in the damn thing. It won't bite.'

Anna tried to. Her chin went in, but the blasted straps got tangled up in her rebellious hair. She wrestled with it and finally got the evil-smelling rubber mask over her head. But by then, the breath she'd been holding onto came out in one long hiss that reverberated around the inside of the strange, alien-looking contraption. The strange eyeholes – two small glass inserts that bulged out, making them all look like weird insects – had already misted over, so she couldn't see properly through them. A sickening smell of disinfectant mingled with the rubber in the respirator to make her stomach churn. She tried to control the panic. It was an eerie feeling trying to breathe through the filter. Sucking a breath in wasn't easy or natural. And when she breathed out, Anna's whole mask moved away from her face, as if it had a life of its own.

That's when one bright spark made a discovery. Anna wasn't sure who. One of the unit's comediennes – and there were several of those. Not someone from her billet. A different hut, because the commotion came from behind her, farther down the parade ground.

Curiosity. It's what drives humans on to great heights. To *experiment.* In science. In sport. In music. Anna believed it was a good thing. But she doubted the WAAF behind would feel the same. Not when she'd been put on *jankers*. Made to peel sacks of spuds or clean the latrines with a toothbrush or stand outside on guard duty in the freezing cold. But who knows? Maybe she'd think it was worth it. And you had to laugh. So, most of them did. Fits of giggles could be heard inside lots of the gas masks. For the enterprising ACW, whoever she was, had discovered that if she blew out vigorously through her respirator the rubber made some alarming – and funny – rude noises. Bathroom noises. After that, other brave souls joined in. Blowing out raspberry after raspberry until the gas-mask drill collapsed into chaos.

The culprit was hauled off in disgrace. She was last seen heading towards the admin office in C Block, where some unfortunate WAAF officer would have to think up a suitable punishment. Anna was glad the officer wasn't her – she couldn't have done it without smiling.

They were all ordered back to their quarters and told to prepare for an inspection. Which didn't seem fair. Blaming all of them for someone else's transgression. But Anna understood why. Discipline. It was the cornerstone of the military. Without it, there would be anarchy. And that wouldn't do. Not while the country was at war.

On the way back to her hut, she saw a figure she recognised. He was riding slowly on an ancient bike, outside the perimeter wire. Keeping pace with her. A tall man with ginger hair sprouting from under his RAF cap. He wobbled slightly as he waved at her, and Anna heard the worn brakes squeal when Sergeant Jimmy Armstrong stopped and dismounted.

He took a small object from the breast pocket of his battle-dress tunic and waved his arms in the air in a mime. He shouted an instruction of some kind. But she couldn't make it out.

'You want me to *what*?' she said.

'Catch!'

Something came flying over the perimeter fence. She wasn't ready and it dug itself into the grass at her feet. By the time Anna had retrieved the package, Jimmy was gone. No explanation. No goodbye. Nothing.

She sat on the grass and unwrapped the brown paper. Inside was a small hand-painted tin box: blue with flecks of gold, and a red rose on the front. Anna remembered the rose buds on Dorothy's special handkerchief and a single tear made its way down her face. Not a sad tear, though. A happy one. This man had given her a gift. Not something showy or ostentatious, trying to impress, but a simple thing that made her want to cry. She ran her hand over the box in a gentle caress. Its effect on her was powerful, for no one had *ever* given her such a heart-felt gift before. Even though it was perfect, the small voice in her head issued a stern warning. *Hold back*, it said, as it wagged a finger at her. She'd only just met this man. *Was it wise to let him into her life so quickly?*

Even so, she opened the tin. Six pear drops nestled inside. Her favourite sweets. And a note.

'Jimmy wrote me a note,' she said.

'I know,' said Mary. 'He told me he would.'

'He wants to meet up. Says we could go for a drink some-where if I'd like to.'

'And would you?' asked Mary.

'What?'

'Like to go out with him?'

'Not sure.' She *was* sure. At least about the magnetic force that drew her towards the man.

She'd met young men before – not many, admittedly – but had never been out alone with one. Her aunt wouldn't have allowed it, not without a chaperone. They were young men Aunt Beatrice had vetted and invited to call. Eligible bachelors, suitors in the market for a wife, shopping around for a suitable mate from the correct social background. Anna had always felt like a piece of property, up for sale – and her aunt had hovered around making mental notes, scoring the men on some kind of scale, ticking them off her list of prospects.

Most had been dull-witted chaps, fond of their own impor-tance. The last one her aunt had thrown at her had been like a spoilt child. He'd reminded Anna of a stuffed peacock, a preening dandy who had stared at himself in the mirror when he'd entered the room. He had not once looked her in the eye, or listened to her conversation, but she had been expected to listen to his.

Anna had been bored and unimpressed by her aunt's candidates, appalled at the thought of having to spend a lifetime shackled to one of those shallow young men. Not one of them had the effect on her that James Armstrong had. *But was that logical? To act on such a random emotion? To go out alone with this man when she'd only just met him?*

'He bought you pear drops,' said Mary.

'I know,' said Anna. 'He seems sweet.'

'Whatever you do, don't tell him that,' said Mary.

'Why ever not?' asked Anna.

'Men like to be the ones in charge. The strong ones. Being called sweet? Not manly, is it?'

Anna wasn't convinced, at least not about men being the ones who should always be in charge. 'So...' she said. 'Think I should go, Mary?'

'Not for me to say. But my big brother's a decent bloke, if that's what you mean. He's no oil painting and those ears of his could be used as door stops. But he'll make you laugh. And he won't break your heart. He knows what *that's* like.'

'He's been hurt, then?' asked Anna.

'He has, but it's not my story to tell. Maybe he'll tell you himself – when he's ready.'

They had both missed breakfast thanks to the bizarre and memorable gas-mask drill, and the rest of the morning had been taken up with scrubbing the barracks floor, cleaning kit and bulling shoes with polish and spit until their faces reflected in their perfect glossy shine. But their hut had passed inspection and they'd made it to the WAAF mess in time for lunch before all the good stuff ran out. Now the mess hall was beginning to fill up, and four more WAAFs joined them at the large wooden trestle table. New recruits. Excited. Gabbling away about shoes that didn't fit and feet that had blisters from the continual

drilling. And the gruesome drill sergeant. A man with a reputation for instilling fear in new recruits.

Anna came to her decision. She would go. Meet Jimmy
Armstrong outside the gate on Saturday like he'd asked her to.
One step at a time. Maybe those steps would lead somewhere
and maybe they wouldn't. But she couldn't deny that she was
looking forward to the journey – wherever it led.

'Get some pudding, shall we? Jam roly-poly,' said Anna.
'Might even be some custard left if we're lucky.'

'How can you eat so much and stay slim?' asked Mary, who
was inches shorter than Anna and several pounds heavier.

'It's a gift,' said Anna. 'Besides, we need to stock up on
stodge. Brain food for our mathematics exam.'

'Thought brain food was fish.'

'And you know how I feel about that!' Anna laughed. She
got it now. The joke. The sardine joke. 'I need to ask you a
favour, Mary' she said, once they were in the line for pudding.

'All right. Long as it's not borrowing underwear. Down to
my last clean pair,' said Mary.

'It's nothing like that.' Anna smiled. 'I've had this peculiar
letter and I'd like you to read it. To tell me what you think.'

'From an admirer?'

'Shouldn't think so,' said Anna. 'It's from some mystery
woman I've never heard of. Says she's a long-lost relative. Wants
us to meet.'

'Strange.'

'Worse than that,' said Anna, 'it feels downright creepy.
Feels she knows me, that's what she said. But I don't have any
other relatives. Not living ones, at least.'

'A ghost, then,' said Mary. 'Exciting. And where does the
mystery woman want to meet?'

'She wants me to choose. Says she's in London, but it
doesn't have to be there. She works in Kingsway, Adastral
House,' said Anna.

'The Air Ministry? Spookier and spookier,' said Mary. 'Maybe she's a WAAF like us.'

'Maybe. I'm to write back and let her know a time and place.'

'Yeah? Well – if she's *that* keen, get her to come here. A pub or a restaurant nearby. She can pay the bill.'

'Cheeky,' said Anna.

'She have a name, this ghost?'

'She signed her letter *Jane Walker*, but I don't know anybody with that name.'

'A skeleton, then,' said Mary.

'What?'

'She's the skeleton in your family closet. Lots of families have them.'

'Not mine,' said Anna. 'Sounds far too exciting to be my family.'

'So, will you meet her?'

'I'll think about it.'

Anna had other things to focus on. The maths exam coming up. If she passed it, there would be specialised training to follow. And her future in the WAAF? Where would they send her? She might end up as one of the teleprinter operators passing on important information to Fighter or Bomber Command. Or doing the job that she imagined she would be best suited for – in a busy operations room somewhere, working on a plotting table where her mathematics skills would be put to the test.

Anna tried to concentrate her thoughts on the war and her place in it. Tried to picture herself in an ops room, headphones over her ears, confident, resilient, ready to do all her country asked of her. Ready to be brave. But the image kept fading.

And in its place was the face of Sergeant Jimmy Armstrong. Not a handsome face, it's true. But...

5

Intimacy. It wasn't something Anna was used to. Not something she was comfortable with – being as close to someone as she was now. Before meeting Jimmy, that was.

She was staring at the back of his head, at the muscles standing out on his neck, at his shoulders as they moved up and down, at his hips as they pumped with rhythm and energy, moving their tandem forward.

She sat on the back seat of the heavy bicycle and tried to concentrate on pedalling, tried to ignore the strange effect that watching the motion of his body had on her. And his closeness. Right in front of her like that. Not that he had been anything other than *proper*, or respectful.

Giving her trust to a man. That was another thing that was new to her. *Could she do it?*

Travelling on a tandem like this, you had to give your trust. That's what Jimmy had told her after he'd wheeled the strange-looking bike up to the front gate. And you couldn't just relax because you were on the rear seat. 'No putting your feet up and coasting, expecting me to do all the work,' he'd warned her. But he'd winked, as well.

The bicycle had been a surprise. Anna had expected them to take the bus into Stockport on their date; after all, it wasn't that far. Their date! *She was out on a date.* What would Edna have said? Anna Golding, aged eighteen, on her first date.

Enjoy it, she told herself. *Don't be anxious, or nervous. Just relax.* She'd tried to, but the excitement and anticipation had made her feel a little light-headed and queasy at first. She wondered if Jimmy felt the same. Probably not; he was a chap after all and, at twenty, he was two years older than she was. He'd have done it all before.

Starting off on the cumbersome bike hadn't been easy. She'd wobbled a bit before she'd found her balance. The hard part had been trying to synchronise her pedalling with his. It had been a while since Anna had been on a pushbike, never mind one made for two where the back-seat rider had no control over the brakes, or even where they were going. And the saddle was like a medieval torture device. No padding, and hard as concrete.

Still, she soon got the hang of it all. She wasn't stupid – could see that her job was to provide extra pedal-power. Although, if she'd known she'd been expected to cycle, she might have worn her battledress trousers instead of the uniform skirt. It would have made her athletic pursuits a little easier.

Anna had worn her service dress uniform – freshly ironed. The best blues fitted her well and she'd taken time with her make-up and hair, though sometimes her hair felt like a lost cause, trying to coral it into a reasonable style. He'd worn his service dress uniform as well and not his battledress. He looked good, she thought – at least eight out of ten. Like her, Jimmy had taken trouble with his thick, bushy hair. It wasn't sticking out from under his cap, like the last time she'd seen him. RAF personnel were sometimes called the 'Brylcreem boys' because of their reliance on the cream, slicking down their hair until it shone, and Anna could see that's what he'd done – been liberal with the Brylcreem. The thought had calmed her, taken away some of her initial nervousness. She wasn't the only one who'd made an effort, then.

'You're a VERY important part of our transport,' he shouted over his shoulder.

'What?'

'You're our tail-gunner,' said Jimmy. 'You're doing a good job back there. Just stay centred like that and keep us stable. And try not to steer, that's my job,' he added, and turned his head and smiled at her. 'I'm the captain and navigator.'

'Hey, keep your eyes on the road!' ordered Anna. 'Or you'll *navigate* us right into a ditch.'

'Certainly, ma'am,' he said, and took one hand off the handlebars, touched his cap in a mock salute.

She was pleased that he had a sense of humour, didn't take himself too seriously. Seeing the funny side of life, being able to laugh, was important, Anna thought. Especially in bad times, when the world wasn't always kind. Like now, when they all had this war to fight.

She noted his cheeky grin. His was a face that seemed to fall easily into a smile, something she'd noticed when she'd first met him. Maybe not all the time though, for she remembered what his sister Mary had said. That Jimmy had been hurt, had his heart broken, and that Anna would be safe with him; he wouldn't hurt her or break her heart – because he already knew what that was like.

'Not long now,' said Jimmy. 'You still okay, back there? Got a hill coming up. We'll need to increase the power. Chocks away!' he shouted eagerly, like a pilot about to take off. 'Ready?'

'Ready!' Anna shouted back. *If he could do it, so could she.* She gritted her teeth and pushed her pedals hard. She had strength and endurance; these last few weeks of square-bashing drill and route marches had hardened her up.

She was enjoying this, the freedom of the open road and the new experience of being this close to a chap, of laughing with him. Was it reckless? Maybe – but she didn't think so. Foolhardy and rash? No! It felt adventurous and daring. But safe.

True, she was naïve when it came to men. Had little experience of them and none at all of sharing her emotions with any of them. *Trust me*, he'd said. And she did. She trusted him not to run them into a ditch or pile them into a tree. And for some reason beyond her understanding, she also trusted him with her heart – even though it was much too early for that. She'd only just met the man, and falling in love took far more time than that – *well, didn't it?*

They made it up the hill. On the crest, Anna listened to his triumphal whoop of celebration, and added her own loud cheer.

'We made it,' she said. 'I knew we would.'

'A winning team,' said Jimmy. 'The captain and his tailgunner.'

She heard him start up a cheerful whistle. One of the old music hall songs, she thought, although she couldn't put a name to it. But she remembered the story of the song. Some chap proposing to his sweetheart, offering her a ride on the back of his fancy bicycle – *a bicycle made for two*. A tandem, she supposed, like the one she was on. The girl's name was Daisy, as she recalled.

She smiled. Felt curiously happy. Of course she'd been happy in her life before, but this felt a little different. More of a contentment, a feeling of ease; of being in exactly the place she was supposed to be. With a companion who made her feel good about herself. Who made her feel important to him. *His tailgunner*. Jimmy Armstrong made her want to whistle along with him, except she'd never been able to pitch a whistle. So, she hummed along with his tune instead.

· · ·

They ended up at an old-fashioned public house in the centre of town. The White Lion Hotel was the sort of place Anna imagined Shakespeare might have raised a tankard of ale – if he'd lived in Stockport. It was that kind of building: all black and white; Tudor style with black beams decorating the outside walls. She tilted her head back to take it all in. It was an odd, higgledy-piggledy sort of place, she thought. Definitely old and spread over many floors with small, ornate windows and frames, and topped off with an impressive, round turret affair that reminded her of a lighthouse.

She dismounted the ancient bicycle carefully, tried to do it gracefully, without her skirt getting caught in the chain or riding up over her knees. Didn't want to embarrass herself or look awkward in front of Jimmy.

Anna watched him freewheel the tandem and prop it against the wall, then casually take off his bicycle clips. He had a breezy, carefree manner. Confident, but relaxed. She liked that, and hoped that it was real and not something cultivated to impress women he took out. She had no idea how many of those there had been in Jimmy Armstrong's life. She knew little about him, except what Mary had told her, that he was training to be a navigator in the RAF. She was eager to find out more. He seemed sincere. A gentleman. Not a rogue.

'Shall we?' he said, and gestured towards the front door.

'What about our trusty steed?' asked Anna. 'We're leaving it here?' She thought the bike looked sad and abandoned.

'Trusty steed? Yes, you're right. I suppose it has been faithful and reliable. Though *we* did most of the work,' he said, smiling.

'Somebody might steal it,' she said.

'You think so?'

Anna watched him pause for a beat and tap out a rhythm on the handlebars. 'I'd say we're safe enough,' he said. 'Once they see those awful saddles, they'll change their mind. Besides, there's more rust on her than paint. I'm sure our *steed* will be perfectly fine.'

'Her?' asked Anna. 'Is our tandem a "she", then?'

'Ships, planes, automobiles – and bikes, I suppose – they're always female. Maybe you'd like to give her a name.'

'Why not?' she said. 'I've never christened anything before.' Her brow furrowed as she thought for a moment. 'I know. Why don't we call her Daisy?'

'Okay, Daisy it is. Now – can we leave Daisy here and get inside, before we both die of thirst?' he said.

She didn't protest when he took her hand. It felt natural, and good, so she allowed him to guide her through the door.

'Have you been here before?' she asked, when they were seated in the restaurant.

'My first time,' said Jimmy, 'but I hear they do a fine steak and kidney pie.'

'It looks ancient,' she said.

'What, the pie?' He laughed.

Was he making fun of her? Did he imagine she couldn't think for herself? Anna could feel the blush building in her face. She took a breath, told herself to relax. 'The place, of course,' she said. 'All the ornate woodwork in the hallway and that spiral staircase.'

'Just teasing,' said Jimmy. 'And you're right, of course. It *is* ancient. An old coaching inn, I believe. Now – what about that pie?'

'I think we've earned it after our exercise,' she said.

'Amen to that!' he agreed. 'I'll go and order – and something to drink?'

'Should we?' she asked. 'We've still got to get Daisy back home.'

'Just one glass. I'm sure Daisy will be safe enough in our hands.' Jimmy grinned.

'Okay.' Anna nodded. 'I'll have a glass of porter,' she said.

'Fine, porter it is,' said Jimmy. 'Back in a trice.'

When he'd gone, she looked around the room, at the two other couples sitting there, eating and drinking. Here she was, with a man she'd just met, laughing and joking with him, riding on the back of his bicycle – and about to drink porter.

Was that racy and slightly shocking of her? The ladylike choice would have been sherry, she supposed, served in a delicate glass. She knew her aunt believed that *real* ladies only drank sherry. Aunt Beatrice would have been scandalised at the thought of Anna with a glass of porter in her hand, for she called it the drink of the lower classes, more suitable for workers at Billingsgate Market than a refined young woman.

She pictured her aunt in that dreadful black outfit of hers and the ridiculous ostrich feather hat she often wore. A snobbish woman, haughty and arrogant and often angry. A tyrant who had treated her domestic servants like slaves. But they'd all abandoned her now, apart from Edna's mother. She tried to find sympathy for her aunt, left high and dry by the people around her who had cosseted her, catered for her every selfish whim. But she couldn't feel sorry for the woman. Even so, she decided to forgive Beatrice for her last spiteful words, for the malice in her final goodbye. Her aunt had banned her from the house. Told Anna that she could never return, that she was useless, would be a failure at whatever she tried – and that she was stupid to think they would ever allow her into the WAAF.

Yet here she was! A part of something truly special. A member of a whole new family – the Women's Auxiliary Air Force – sharing hopes and fears and, above all, comradeship. Something Anna had rarely had before. She smiled happily.

'You look as if you've lost a sixpence and found a pound,' said Jimmy, as he put the drinks down on their table. 'Definitely cheerful. Happy about something?' he asked.

'Happy? Yes, quite content,' she said.

'Hope the company has something to do with that,' said Jimmy.

'Might have,' said Anna. 'Or maybe it's the thought of that pie.'

'All sorted, ma'am! Your wish is my command. It'll be here in a tick. Now, shall we have a toast?'

'Why not?' asked Anna, and raised her glass of porter as he raised his glass of beer.

'Ladies first,' said Jimmy. 'You choose.'

'Okay. Let's toast to friends – old and new,' said Anna.

'To friends,' Jimmy agreed. '*Especially* new.'

Did she get that right? Was he talking about her? Her eyes held his gaze, unflinching. They were brazen and bold, as confident as his. She felt like a rebel. Drinking porter. She could feel the sticky tidemark settle around her lips as the dark brown beer clung to them. She winked at her companion and dabbed her mouth delicately with a paper serviette, her little finger crooked the way a lady of fine breeding might do when drinking tea. Jimmy joined her in the joke and wiped his lips too, in the same exaggerated way. *Had she found a kindred spirit?* She hoped so, was pleased at the thought.

Then the wonderful food arrived. He was right. The pie deserved its hallowed reputation. The delicate pastry crust melted on her tongue and the gravy was thick; it was definitely an improvement on the last one that she and Mary had eaten in the WAAF mess hall. They finished it off with strong cups of tea, and she listened while he spoke about his family. They were a close, happy bunch, it seemed. There was a brother, Tom, older than him, and another sister called Alice; both already left home and in the forces – doing their bit for their country. His mother and father alone now and missing them all. Family gatherings had always been a chaotic affair, with relatives packed into every corner and the old house in Peckham bulging at the seams.

Anna felt envious of this family that was bursting with life and affection. She could see why her friend Mary had been so upset and homesick when they'd first arrived, especially as she was the baby of the family. That's if you could still be a baby at eighteen.

Anna told Jimmy about her unusual upbringing. She didn't dramatise it or mention any of Aunt Beatrice's punishments. It didn't seem right, and Anna didn't want his pity. She wasn't a victim and she had come out of it with an inner strength, impatient to take on the challenges of her new life. She remembered the letter she'd had from the woman who called herself a relative, and told him about that too.

'So, you've no idea who this woman, Jane, might be?' he asked her.

'None at all,' said Anna. 'If it hadn't been addressed to me and sent to my old home in Watford, I'd have said it was a case of mistaken identity and that it was meant for somebody else.'

'But clearly it wasn't,' he said. 'So, what will you do?'

'I wasn't going to do anything,' said Anna.

'But aren't you in the least intrigued?' asked Jimmy.

'It's certainly a puzzle. Mary thinks it might be a skeleton in our family closet,' she said.

'Sounds like it to me,' said Jimmy.

'But do I really want to dig up the past? I mean, who knows what you'd find. I might not like it!'

'You know what I think?'

'Go on,' said Anna.

'That you are brave and resourceful and clever. Whatever you find, you'll deal with it,' he said.

'You can't possibly know all those things about me. We've only just met.'

'I just *know*,' said Jimmy, his tone serious.

'So, you think I should meet this woman?'

'It's not up to me, but I think that if you don't go and see her

– well, you'll always wonder. And that's never a good thing. Regrets are worse than trying something and making a mess of it.'

When they returned to the barracks that afternoon, Jimmy asked, 'Can Daisy and I come and see you again?'

'I'd like that,' said Anna. 'I'll miss the old girl.' She patted the bike saddle affectionately and nodded.

'And me, too?' he asked. 'Will you miss me as well?'

'Not as much as I'll miss Daisy!' Anna laughed.

Jimmy put on a theatrical frown. 'Oh.'

'Don't sulk,' she said and lifted his hand, held it in hers.

They stood there at the camp barrier, neither of them wanting to say goodbye.

'I'm not sure when I'll have another weekend pass,' said Jimmy, regretfully, 'but they're keeping us on a tight leash right now. Still, if we pass out of our course, my lot's been promised a whole week's leave. That's not for another three months, though.'

'That's quite a while,' she said. 'Don't know where I'll be in three months' time. Mary and I could be off on our own training soon. That's if we both pass the mathematics test.'

'You'll do it,' Jimmy said. 'I know you will.'

6

Jimmy Armstrong smiled and waved goodbye. He didn't want to part from Anna, and maybe she felt the same, because she'd lingered at the camp gate holding his hand. Nothing more, just their hands touching, connecting them, but he'd seen something in her eyes to make him want to stay. A warmth, he thought.

Understanding women wasn't easy, though. A tricky thing. And he'd been fooled before, had given his heart, had even set a wedding date. But he'd been manipulated and abandoned when a brighter prospect than him had come the woman's way. Still, he wasn't bitter. Just surprised at how easily he'd been taken in by a pretty face – and a little suspicious of women in general now. Until Anna, that was.

Meeting her had rekindled his trust. There was something special about her, a refreshing openness, a willingness to say what she thought. She was a conundrum, though; an enticing puzzle to him. Anna seemed a mix of contradictions – naïve but teamed with a strength of mind. Something to do with her upbringing, he assumed. He imagined she'd had obstacles to overcome and perhaps some sadness. Not that she had dwelt on such things or complained about her life, but he could sense it in the way she had spoken of her childhood.

She hadn't been slow to challenge him, and Jimmy suspected that Anna Golding would have firm ideas about a woman's place in the world. She'd hinted at it. Had talked about equality for all. He had no problem with that. Equality and freedom, they seemed like good things. Wasn't that what they were fighting a war for?

She'd told him she had fun, enjoyed his company, and he'd been pleased as Punch because he felt the same. They'd laughed a lot. There'd been a spark between them, he thought, a definite connection. He'd felt it from the beginning, hoped Anna had felt it too.

As he cycled away, he could still picture her eyes. That was the first thing he'd noticed about her – how her eyes had looked when she smiled, how the light caught them; he tried to remember their colour. At first he'd thought they were light brown, but when she'd turned her head suddenly, they seemed green with tiny flecks of gold. A combination of brown and green then, he decided. Or maybe they were tawny – was there even such a thing?

Jimmy pulled himself up short. Told himself to put a lid on his thoughts. Next thing he knew, he'd be writing poetry and taking up knitting. Thinking about her eyes and her hair and the way her brow wrinkled into tiny furrows when she laughed – well, it just wasn't on, was it? *Dangerous, too*, to get distracted by a woman, even such a fascinating puzzle as Anna. A navigator's job was intense, needed total concentration for hours at a time; he couldn't afford to think of other things. His mind must be clear to plot a course for the bomber crew to reach their targets and get back home safely. They were relying on him. His job was every bit as important as the pilot's.

He thought about the chaps he'd been training with. They'd only been crewed-up for a month, but already the blokes had been knitting into a unit, getting to know each other's strengths and weaknesses – what made them laugh, what made them angry. They'd been in the classroom together, learning about the principles of flight, and some had scratched their heads at the complicated mathematics. But not Jimmy – he had always been happy with the language of maths, found it exciting to work his way through.

So, he'd been selected for training as a navigator. Soon, they would all be posted to an operational training flight and, if that went well, Jimmy would find himself on a 'real' mission – finally contributing to his country's part in this war.

'Don't be too brave,' his sister Mary had warned when he first enlisted. 'Don't win the war all by yourself,' she'd said. Now look at her: she'd gone and joined the RAF as well. He didn't think himself a hero; not in the way she'd implied, anyway. Wasn't sure he was made of heroic stuff; but he would do his best, get done what was needed. When the time came to be brave, he hoped he would give a good account, not only for himself but for the rest of the crew. They were like family, and you had to look out for each other.

In a four-man bomber crew like Jimmy's, the navigator had another crucial duty. He was also the bomb-aimer, the man responsible for targeting and dropping the bomb. The man who held life and death in his hand, beneath his button. That was the only thought that disturbed him, sometimes invaded his sleep with horrific gory dreams. *Would he be able to press that button?* To release bombs on the unsuspecting people below?

He wasn't a natural warrior. Nor was he an angry man looking for retribution. But when your country was threatened by enemies, it was the only thing to do. The honourable thing, Jimmy supposed. To join the fight and be there in its hour of need. To follow the orders he was given.

7

RAF WILMSLOW, CHESHIRE

31 OCTOBER 1939

The rest of their hut mates threw a special celebration for them. Tea and sticky buns – a rare treat – smuggled in and eaten in a midnight feast with them all gathered around the stove. Anna could think of nothing more perfect in her life so far. Except finding Jimmy. That felt perfect too. And the smile on her face – like a cat who had found the cream – was on her friend Mary's as well.

They'd made it. They'd done it. Passed the exam. With flying colours, the officer had said; two of the highest sets of marks the station had ever had. Hours spent in the barracks, helping each other revise, had brought them both a reward. *Clerk, Special Duties.* How impressive that sounded, Anna thought.

'Enjoy it, Lofty,' said a voice from the back of the crowd. 'You've earned it. You've both worked hard. Though I, for one, have never been much good at sums.'

'Congratulations,' said another. 'Well done, you pair of clever clogs.'

'Thanks,' said Anna, still beaming. 'And for the treats too. Won't ask where they came from.'

'Best not,' said the girl. 'Just act all innocent if LACW Dutton comes around!'

'You stole them?' asked Anna. 'You did that for us? You're a gem. You all are!'

'Yeah, thanks, you crazy lot,' said Mary. 'You're the best.'

'Your secret's safe with us,' said Anna, and nodded at her friend. 'Isn't that right, Mary?'

'Dead right!' Mary agreed.

'And if Leading Aircraftwoman Dutton comes sniffing around,' said Anna, 'she can pull out my fingernails, or make me drink castor oil – I'll not say a word.'

They had all laughed at that. Which was strange to Anna. She'd never thought of herself as someone who could make people laugh. If anything, she had maybe been a little too serious in her life before. Determined to plot her own course instead of the one her callous father had foisted on her – and her Aunt Beatrice, with her rigid rules. So, perhaps this was the real Anna, the one that had been hiding beneath the sober and earnest woman intent on making her own way in life.

'So, when do you suppose they'll send us off?' asked Mary.

'Now that we've passed our exam and been promised places on a plotters' course, I should think we'll have our travel warrants any day now,' said Anna, cheerfully.

But she was wrong.

They waited for days, and nothing happened. A week later, they were both called in to see their WAAF section officer. Anna could read it in the woman's eyes, before a word was spoken. Bad news.

She watched the WAAF swallow hard. The junior officer was new – and young – and had most likely been given a task that no one else wanted. Anna knew how it went; they usually handed the mucky jobs to someone farther down the line.

'Congratulations, by the way,' the officer said. 'You both did an excellent job. To be heading for a technical school and a plotter's table, that's a big responsibility – very well done.'

'But—?' said Anna.

'Why should there be a *but*?' the officer said.

'With all due respect, ma'am, I just felt one coming on.'

The woman coughed and said, 'Despite your results, I'm afraid you're rather stuck with us here for a while...'

'What!' said Mary.

'Why?' said Anna.

'It's wartime, ACW Golding.' The WAAF's tone hardened. 'Things aren't always run for our enjoyment.' She raised a hand to ward off any more interruptions. 'And I realise it may be a disappointment, but these things are often sent to test our mettle.'

'What things exactly?' asked Anna. She knew she was pushing her luck. Her question might be bordering on what they called insubordination – enough to get your pay docked and you put on a punishment charge. But the officer didn't flinch, which Anna took as a good sign.

'Both you and ACW Armstrong have indeed been accepted on a plotters' course – unfortunately, these are all highly oversubscribed right now. But as soon as two places become available, we'll have you on your way. Meanwhile, you will stay here. Consider it a temporary posting and report for duty tomorrow morning, at oh-six-hundred hours.'

'Where?' asked Anna.

'Doing what?' asked Mary.

'Report to the cook in the airmen's mess. You will be clearing up tables and waitressing and cleaning up in the kitchen,' she said. 'Everything a mess-maid would do.'

'But KP? That's like a punishment detail!' complained Mary. 'And it's unfair. We just passed our...'

Anna grabbed her friend's arm in a warning. KP – the infamous Kitchen Patrol – meant having to peel buckets of spuds and cleaning out the slops, and it was certainly a punishment. But it wasn't the same as being a proper mess-maid. She held firmly onto Mary's arm: no point complaining and getting in trouble when it wouldn't make any difference anyway.

'You signed up to the WAAF, ACW Armstrong. You go where *we* tell you and do what you're instructed to do, and that includes kitchen duty. Dismissed!' bellowed the woman.

Anna noted that the young officer seemed to have found her authority – and her voice. It was done and dusted and nothing either she or Mary could do would change that. But unfair? Anna didn't agree with her friend. It was unfortunate, maybe, the fact that they would now be slaving in the kitchen, when they hadn't signed up to do so. But Anna didn't feel disappointed. They would get where they were supposed to go, eventually. Besides, she had already spotted a bonus in it: Jimmy was only a few miles down the road and he was going to be there for three whole months. Now, she had more time, and they could see each other for as long as fate was kind.

The new thought made her smile.

As it turned out, Anna didn't have long to wait for fate to reach out its golden hand. Jimmy and his crew managed to get a twenty-four-hour pass two weeks later. Mary was a treasure and switched shifts with her, but the favour cost Anna her one precious slice of bacon at breakfast. She figured it was worth twice that, though – to meet up with Jimmy again. Him and his freckles and his ready smile and his unruly ginger hair. He was sometimes known as *Ginger* – that's what Mary had said.

But Anna didn't want to call him that. 'You can call me

Jimmy,' he'd told her when they'd first met – not Jim or James, she noted. So that was how she thought of him. And *Jimmy* was a fine, no-nonsense name. Plain, not pretentious or swaggering, or conceited; living with Aunt Beatrice had taught her to hate such things. It had shown Anna that a simple life, with people who had compassion, was better than being surrounded by luxury and shallow people who cared only for themselves. But the most important thing Anna had learned was that it was better to be poor and kind than rich and tyrannical. The rich, like her father and Beatrice, always seemed to have misery written on their faces.

She remembered Jimmy's face with his pleasant smile and that easy-going way of his. The sudden, boisterous laugh. She hadn't been sure about the laugh, at first. But it seemed real, an expression of joy at what life turned up.

She was looking forward to seeing him again. A surprising and unexpected treat. Something to break up the monotony of the duty that she and Mary had been landed with. To be cycling through the countryside instead of juggling dirty dishes in the mess.

He hadn't come alone. Apart from Jimmy on the tandem waiting by the gate, two more airmen had arrived on bicycles, two members of his crew.

'Hope you don't mind us pushing in,' one of them said.

Jimmy gave her a small smile and shrugged philosophically.

'You're welcome,' said Anna. *No point being ungracious.* Besides, it was done now. Although his message last night had mentioned nothing about others joining in.

'Didn't know Ginger had any friends,' said the other airman, and laughed.

She studied the man's face, and especially his eyes. But it seemed like an innocent joke. Friendly banter among pals. Still, the thought was unsettling. A *friend*, the chap had called her. Is that *all* she was? She'd hoped it was more than that, especially as he'd wanted to see her again. *And why had he invited these other airmen along?* They seemed perfectly nice, but surely four was a crowd?

'You okay back there?' asked Jimmy, when they'd got underway.

'I'm fine,' she said.

'You're sure? Only you seem a little subdued to me,' he said. 'Have I done something wrong?' He turned his head around.

'Keep your eyes on the road,' said Anna. 'We'll be piling into the others. Poor old Daisy won't thank us for that.'

'No, this won't do,' said Jimmy. 'I'm putting the brakes on,' he warned, and they skidded to a messy halt.

'But why...?'

'Because,' he said, 'I suspect you're *not* fine – and I think it's my fault, because I fancy it isn't yours.'

'I don't follow,' said Anna.

'You've been very gracious and accepted Freddy and George being foisted on you like this.'

'I wasn't expecting them, it's true. I thought it would be just the two of us, like before,' said Anna, knowing she sounded disappointed.

'And I apologise,' he said. 'That's my fault for not checking with you when they asked themselves along.'

'It's difficult for you,' she said. 'I understand. They're important to you, like family. I was just surprised, that's all.'

'I shouldn't have agreed, but they were at a loose end and everyone else had gone. Still, I should have refused. It makes it awkward for you.'

'Nonsense,' she said, 'they're perfectly welcome and they seem like nice chaps.'

'Yes – they're decent blokes. So, you're truly fine?'

'Absolutely! Now, can we please get on as your pals will be wondering where we've got to. Where are we going, by the way?

It's important for a tail-gunner to know these things, don't you agree?' Anna said, and finally smiled.

'Wherever the wind takes us,' he said and laughed.

It took them to a quaint and pretty village with the unusual name of Great Budworth. She wondered if there was a Small Budworth somewhere around. Every house and building in the village seemed ancient, as if the patina of time had settled on it.

'Shall we stop for tea?' she asked, as she spotted an old-fashioned tearoom. They'd cycled a fair few miles and there was only so much punishment she could take at one time from the torture chamber that was Daisy's saddle. She'd be properly sore tomorrow.

'Good idea,' said Jimmy. 'Tea and cakes, a very British pursuit. Important to keep up tradition, don't you think?'

'I do,' said Anna, eagerly. 'We'd only be doing our duty.'

All four of them agreed that doing one's duty was an important thing, especially if it meant a rest for the old posterior and a decent cup of tea.

Despite her initial disappointment at not being alone with Jimmy, she enjoyed the day. The others included her in their conversation and their camaraderie. Her uniform made her one of them and she was treated as an equal. It wasn't always that way back at camp. There were still men who felt threatened by the presence of so many WAAFs, felt that the RAF was no place for women. But Anna had tried to ignore them. It did no good to argue with those kinds of men. Actions spoke much louder than words would ever do. At least that's how she saw it. Courage was not an exclusively male domain. Women could stand up and be counted for their bravery too. She was sure of that.

'These scones,' said Freddy, energetically licking the jam from his luxurious handlebar moustache. 'They're a bloody good show.'

Anna tried not to laugh. Jimmy had introduced Freddy as

the brains of the team and they'd all grinned like it was a private joke. It turned out that he was the court jester, but they all seemed fine with that – Freddy too.

'Freddy's our tame public-school mascot,' said Jimmy, 'one of the upper crust, but he won't let them make him an officer – will you, Freddy?' he asked and laughed.

'Not bloody likely,' said Freddy. 'I'd rather be one of the chaps.'

'So, you're the whole crew?' asked Anna.

'Us and the old man,' said Jimmy.

'The old man?' she asked.

'The old man's gone off to spend the day with his boss,' said Freddy. He winked at the others.

'Oh?' she said.

'Our pilot. The skipper – he's an old hand, nearly thirty. That's why we call him the old man. But he knows his stuff,' Freddy explained. 'Not a bad bloke for an officer. He's gone off for the day with his missus.'

Jimmy coughed. 'Maybe we should change the subject. Idle talk and all that!' He nodded to an elderly couple at one of the nearby tables.

Anna looked across at the pair. They seemed creaking and ancient, but they were still holding hands. Their faces, although wrinkled by the traces of time, had sparks of life written on them, especially the eyes. They smiled at each other and nodded, and the man squeezed the woman's hand. It made them both beautiful, she thought. *Love*, she decided, *didn't have an age limit*. She dropped her gaze, for it felt like an intrusion.

She understood the need to steer away from talk that might help the enemy, but the pair didn't strike her as German spies! Still, she could see why Jimmy was being careful and that wasn't a bad thing. They would all need to keep their share of secrets from now on. She hoped Jimmy would be just as careful when his plane took to dangerous skies with German fighters buzzing around it, trying to shoot it down. Anna scrubbed the image from her mind. She didn't want to think of him being hurt or his name appearing on some missing-in-action list.

She watched him put down his cup. He'd have been more at home with a tin mug, she thought, than a delicate china teacup. He had large hands and had already given up the struggle to get his fingers through the tiny handle, more suited to Victorian ladies than a tall man like him. *What was it Mary had called him?* A great lanky drink of dishwater. Which was pretty unfair. Jimmy was tall, it was true, but he didn't resemble dishwater in any way – and Anna should know, for she'd been up to her elbows in the stuff lately.

She saw his eyes move from her hands to her face, to her lips. Anna felt a tightening in her jaw and imagined there would be a warm glow on her face. She forced herself to breathe, but only shallow breaths escaped through the tight tunnel of her throat. She felt a little queasy, shouldn't have had that extra scone, perhaps – the blackberry jam had been rich and a little sickly.

'That skeleton of yours, did you sort it out?' Jimmy said suddenly.

'What?' said Anna, surprised by the change of direction.

'What's this?' asked Freddy, his curiosity piqued.

'Anna's acquired a relative she never knew about – a skeleton in the family closet.'

'Nothing like that,' she said, tersely. 'Just someone who thinks she knows me. Probably mistaken identity.'

'So, you've not written back then?' asked Jimmy, surprised.

'I wrote,' she said, sharply.

'That's great!'

'Maybe,' said Anna. 'We'll see...' She took a deep breath, wished she could take back her blunt comments. She hadn't meant to snap, or be unkind, it was just that at times she felt vulnerable, as if she were waiting for the worst to happen.

The others said goodbye and left, but Jimmy stayed with her at the table. He didn't seem bothered by her replies about the letter.

It happened so quickly – the kiss – it took her by surprise. The pressure of his mouth on hers, his lips warm and moist, sent a small jolt of excitement through her that delighted and unnerved her at the same time. She liked it, *really* liked it, wanted it to go on forever. But was that right? The thought made her blush. Their mouths, joined together like this, seemed to pulse with a life of their own. Her lips felt on fire, and she could hear her rapid heartbeat racing in her ears, as if it might overwhelm her.

And then it was over. Her first kiss. An incredible milestone every bit as miraculous as she'd imagined it might be. She felt intoxicated, as if wine instead of blood filled her veins.

His expression when they were finished surprised her too. His face held an earnest, thoughtful look, as if he wanted her to know that it wasn't a spur-of-the-moment notion, this kiss. That it meant something. A promise of some kind. Then, he finally smiled, a smile that took over his whole face, his mouth, his cheeks – but especially his eyes. She watched them crinkle up at the corners into tiny, wrinkled lines. She longed to trace them with the tip of her finger. But maybe that was too forward. Too much, too soon.

She heard herself sigh, then watched him squeeze her hand. He seemed to understand. That hers was a happy sigh, a sign of complete contentment.

8

'So, he kissed you then?'

'It was so sudden, it took me by surprise,' Anna said, and smiled. Even so, she remembered everything about it. It had lasted longer than she imagined it would and had sent a small, delicious shiver along her spine.

'So, was it a *pleasant* surprise? I'm thinking it was, by the look on your face.' Mary grinned.

'We-ll...'

'Don't tell me you've never been kissed before!' said Mary.

Anna ignored the jibe. But it *was* a new experience to be kissed on the lips by a man. And yes, she'd liked it. It had excited her, but in a way, it was also a little frightening. If you enjoyed something too much, had too many expectations – didn't that make you vulnerable? Especially if that thing was taken away.

That kiss – it had seemed like the most intimate and personal thing a chap could do; but it wasn't, of course. She may still be a virgin, but she wasn't stupid; she knew things, had made it her business to find out. What might a husband expect of his wife? What intimate moments might a couple share?

Some of Anna's knowledge had come second-hand from her friends working *below-stairs* in Aunt Beatrice's house. But Edna's version of romantic bliss had been coloured by fiction she'd read, and Anna had wanted facts. So, she'd read Marie Stopes' book on sex in marriage. *Married Love* had made her blush in several places, but she had forced herself to read it, to find out about birth control. It was something a woman needed to know.

Anna agreed with Stopes – that marriage should be an equal partnership between men and women. It seemed quite a normal idea to her, though some men still thought it radical and that they should be the ones with the power, the ones in charge in a marriage. Some used that power, she suspected, making their wives pregnant time and again – ignoring abstinence or birth control. Women were easier to dominate, she supposed, when they were tied to a house and had an army of children to look after.

Still, although Anna had armed herself with some idea of the intimate dealings of man and wife, her knowledge was only theoretical. There had been no experience to back it up. Some might have called her unworldly and naïve and she might even have agreed. Until that kiss.

Absentmindedly, she touched her lips, right where they'd met Jimmy's. She remembered the warmth his mouth had left behind and the small thrill of anticipation that had moved through her. It was a feeling that was new to her. She had never felt anything remotely like it before. Certainly not in the presence of those young men her aunt had wheeled out in front of her. Evidence – in her mind at least – that it was solely to do with the effect Jimmy had on her.

She swallowed hard. Forced her mind back to where it should be. 'Yes,' she said. 'It was a special kiss, not the kiss of a friend. I think maybe he likes me. We seem to fit each other well.'

'He *likes* you?' said Mary, with a hint of a snort. 'Oh, I think you'll find it's a little more than that!'

Anna watched her friend grin. Tried to decode the things Mary had said. Jimmy, on the other hand, had said nothing. Just that kiss and a lovely smile to top it off.

'Right,' said Mary, all business-like again. 'You missed mail call and Corporal Bunting says there's a letter for you. I offered to take it, but you know how high-handed she can be. You'll need to pick it up yourself.'

'NAAFI canteen's still open,' said Anna. 'Why don't I pick up my post and meet you over there? We'll have a cup of tea and a natter before we start our evening shift.'

'Fair enough, and if your letter's from that mystery woman, you can read it out to me,' said Mary.

'Maybe,' said Anna. 'But you'll have to buy the tea.'

'Cheek!' Mary said. 'We're pals, ain't we?'

'Proper chums.' Anna smiled. 'But you'll still have to buy the char – I paid last time.'

Anna went to pick up her mail. She'd been expecting a letter from Edna, for she hadn't had a reply in a while. Maybe Anna's last letter hadn't caught up with her yet. She could hear her old friend's voice in her mind. *Ruddy war*, Edna had complained. *Moves people round like soddin' draughts on a board. Ain't no rhyme nor sense to it.*

She hoped her friend hadn't got into too much trouble or had her pay docked again. Edna was an important part of her life. Anna sighed and hoped her friend had not been too reckless in her search for an ideal man. She didn't want her having to pay the ultimate price. But she believed Edna more sensible and worldly than that – she wouldn't let a man take advantage of her.

There were many she knew already – WAAFs in her

barracks – who'd been taken in by a handsome face. When the results of their 'adventures' started to show in tightened uniforms, they were asked to leave. It was a time of war, of confusion, of people living life intensely, as if there wasn't enough of it left – as if the consequences of their romantic interludes didn't matter.

But they did, of course. To the woman – *and to the baby* – who would be left behind while the chap moved on. *And many would*, Anna thought.

Sex before marriage was becoming more common now: Anna had heard the innuendos, the conversations about who exactly should take the blame. A newspaper article she'd read some weeks before had incensed her. She guessed the author had been a man because it put all the blame for this new 'loose' attitude firmly at the woman's door. Women had joined the military and were now taking a far more liberal approach to interaction with the opposite sex. At least that's what the author argued. He complained that it was hard on men to ignore the sins of the flesh if these girls enticed them. He came down especially hard on girls who had joined the ATS – they'd been nicknamed 'officer's groundsheets' – saying many were in the army for one reason alone: to indulge themselves and their questionable morality.

Anna had wanted to throttle the writer for his ignorant and narrow-minded bigotry.

She picked up her mail from Corporal Bunting. Nothing from Edna, but there was a letter from a Miss Jane Walker – a reply to the one Anna had sent to London.

It was a pleasant enough letter, full of the sort of polite social etiquette that Anna herself had been taught to follow in letter-writing.

Was it a good idea to see this Miss Walker? She supposed she would have to, now that she'd replied to that first strange letter and agreed to meet.

The meeting place had been Anna's idea. She had enjoyed her time out in Stockport with Jimmy. Her letter to Jane Walker had suggested that they meet at the White Lion Hotel. If nothing else, at least she could sample more of that luscious steak and kidney pie.

~

28 NOVEMBER 1939

Anna and her intake of WAAFs marched smartly to the parade ground for a solemn and moving passing-out parade. They had made it through training and were all proud of themselves, but no one was prouder than Anna at that moment.

She'd polished her buttons and cap badge to a mirrorlike shine with Brasso, a rag and a button stick. It had taken ages, dedication, and lots of elbow grease. She'd thought the button stick a novel idea when she first picked it up as part of her WAAF kit. The air force seemed to think of everything. Or maybe the other services had them as well. And all those fancy brass buttons on Aunt Beatrice's black velvet coat – were they cleaned using a button stick too? It was something she'd never considered before. Perhaps she'd ask Edna next time she saw her. What a clever idea it seemed, simple and ingenious: a long, thin strip of metal that slotted behind the buttons, so they could be polished with Brasso without getting any of the metal polish on the material below. She applauded whoever had invented it.

The camp commander took the salute at the reviewing stand as they all marched past, an important and imperious-looking man with a huge handlebar moustache. He saluted but didn't smile. Their WAAF officer was standing next to him. Anna wondered if the officer was proud of her latest recruits. *She should be,* Anna thought. Their ability to march was impressive, the formation showed discipline and the precision was meticulous. Nothing short of miraculous, she felt. Especially when you thought about the same bunch of women weeks before. It seemed the hours of 'square-bashing' had made their mark, turning them into a well-tuned marching machine, shoes striking the parade ground at a regulation 140 beats a minute. Anna remembered back to a few months before, when they'd first arrived and been shouted at by a cranky drill sergeant on their very first day. He'd claimed they all had two left feet, and had made them stand perfectly still and repeat the words *left, right, left, right* until everyone was hoarse. And then there were those recruits, in those first few weeks, who had always started off marching on the wrong foot. Others found it hard to swing their arms.

She remembered Dotty fondly, and her struggles to march at the beginning. Anna wondered how the girl was now, back looking after her brothers and her family.

The parade went well, and they were told to 'stand at ease'; an order that Anna had always wondered about because really, when you stood there like that, you were never particularly at your ease. They'd had to learn it off by heart: '*Body braced... legs braced... knees braced...* (everything blooming-well braced...) *arms straight and extended behind your back... Back of your right hand in the palm of your left...*' And so it went on: '*No talking, no slouching...*'

She made a point not to slouch. Stood up tall, even though it put her head well above most of the others in the parade. She let her eyes wander over the WAAFs beside her and felt enormous pride in herself and her friends and the things they'd accomplished in a short space of time. They'd shared a special bond after these weeks of training and going on route marches in the rain. They had survived. And now they were all proper WAAFs, members of the Royal Air Force. Ready to strive for their country. To do whatever was needed, all kinds of jobs, to release the men to go to war.

The sad part was that most of Anna and Mary's compatriots and friends would be moving on now, going to different camps and technical schools to learn their allotted trades. Soon, Anna and Mary would be the only ones left in hut 27 who remembered how it was – the midnight feasts and the ghost stories told sitting on each other's beds, and trying to get warm by the foul-smelling coke stove. It had been wonderful, the comradeship. But now, only they would be left, with new recruits joining their hut.

A loud voice bellowed 'Dismissed!' and the women broke up into small groups on the parade ground. The low murmur of excited chatter drifted over the place. There were smiles on some faces. Others looked relieved. But there was sadness too, for it meant that pals who'd teamed up during basic training must now go their separate ways. There were tears from some as the bond of the Wilmslow sisterhood would soon be broken up, to become a memory.

Anna went over to Mary and hugged her. They were lucky they'd be staying together, even if it meant that for the time being they'd be slaving away over dirty pots in the kitchen and starting duty at six in the morning so they could stir massive vats of porridge with wooden broom handles.

'We did it!' said Mary. 'Made it through basic and covered ourselves in glory on the parade ground.'

'We surely did. Can't believe everybody managed a salute and an "Eyes right" without piling into each other, like the first time we tried,' said Anna.

'We should celebrate. Maybe we could swing a weekend pass.'

'Need to keep my head down,' said Anna. 'I've already put in for a twenty-four for the week after next. That woman, Jane Walker, is coming to see me. Though now that I think about it, do I really want to use up a precious pass on her? Feels like a total waste of time.'

'When you could be spending it with Jimmy, you mean?'

'Exactly,' said Anna.

She felt more relaxed now talking about him with his sister. It had been hard at first, even though they were hut mates and friends. Anna wasn't used to having a man in her life. But that's *exactly* what he had become – her man.

9

Jimmy relaxed back on his bunk and read the letter one more time. He held the flimsy pages carefully, like a precious artifact. It surprised him that something as simple as a letter from Anna could have such an effect on him. This was the second time he'd read it and he could hear her voice behind the words. He smiled and tried to picture her passing-out parade. He could feel her joy that she'd at last been accepted on a plotters' course. He was happy for her – and for his sister Mary too. They were both intelligent, hard-working women filled with dedication and ambition. They deserved to succeed, and of course he wanted them to.

And yet now, when he read that they had both been assigned a temporary posting at Wilmslow, he gave a silent cheer. *Selfish*, he knew. But now he had found this amazing woman, he didn't want her to move on. He was loath to let her go.

Tom, his older brother, a man he respected and looked up to, had once told him that you never knew how much you loved something until you were forced to let it go. *Love. Is that what this was?* Surely not. He'd only known Anna Golding for a short time. Was it possible that love could capture your senses this easily? If so, it had been a gentle invasion, starting with the day he'd first seen her and the way she'd laughed and waved that silly sardine sandwich in the air. It was a feeling of being happy in her company; a feeling that had grown, was getting stronger every day. So, not something indefinable like love at first sight. Or the fascination of romance. And he knew all about infatuation, had experienced it before. This was nothing like that. Far gentler, but powerful just the same.

Jimmy had bought her something special. One of the chaps in the mess had been selling a silver sweetheart brooch and, on a whim, he'd bought it. Although when he thought about it now, it had been more than just an impulse, surely it was fate. As if it was meant to be.

He looked at it now, taking it from the box it had come in and holding it up to the light. It was a pin with a pair of silver wings and a crown on top, and the RAF motto in a circle around the edges – *Per ardua ad astra*. 'Through adversity to the stars,' he whispered, as he read.

He was sure she would understand, because he felt that Anna had gone through adversity, even if he didn't yet know exactly what kind.

He hoped she wouldn't think it arrogant of him, to imagine she would agree to be his sweetheart, to accept the pin. He would give it to her the very next time he saw her. He would be brave. There was always the chance of rejection, but his hopes were high. She seemed happy when they were together, and they made each other laugh. Laughter was important; Jimmy had always thought so. There was a connection between them, as if destiny had made their separate worlds collide. He shook his head. That was a strange, fanciful thought and he didn't know why such a notion had popped into his head. He had never believed in destiny or fate before. His was a world where science and mathematics ruled. A practical place with things you could see and prove and trust, not some odd fantasy about something that threw people into each other's path.

Even so, the more he thought about her, the more convinced he became that they complemented each other well, like two halves of a whole.

But how did she feel about him? Did she like him simply as a friend, or was there more to it than that? He hadn't dared to ask. Didn't want to frighten her away. Then again, there was that kiss. He'd watched her eyes, had seen the surprise in them, but she hadn't pulled away or slapped his face. Neither of them had said a word, but he hoped she understood – that it was more than just a moment's flirtation on his part, that it was something deeper than that.

They had talked about love. No, that wasn't exactly true – Anna was the one who'd mentioned love when they'd spoken of their families. He recalled the expression on her face, the hint of sadness there. Although she hadn't said so, or complained, he imagined her family had not been as loving, kind and protective as his. Her words came back to him now: that love was not always freely given, or an automatic right. He thought that sad. *Love had to be earned*, she'd told him.

Perhaps that much was right. If so, what must he do to earn hers?

He wanted to ask her that right now. To go see her this very minute. To hand her the precious sweetheart pin, tell her what it meant to him – that she was the *only* woman who could wear it and that he would be true to her. He wanted to tell her how clever she was for passing her exam. But how could he tell her the most important thing? That he missed her when she wasn't there. That he loved the colour of her eyes and her hair, and the way her face lit up when she laughed. And the small frown that arrived when she was thinking.

He knew what he wanted to say, but when she was close to him, would these thoughts – that seemed so perfect in his head

– come out the right way? Not that there was much chance of meeting Anna for a while. Weekend passes were like gold dust now and between study and duty rosters, time was getting tight.

Jimmy got up slowly, as if the weight of his thoughts was pressing him down. Love was complicated, wasn't it? Had to be nurtured if it were to survive. But how was that possible in the middle of a war when people had so many important things to think about and vital jobs to do? *Country first, self last.* It was something the RAF recruiter had told him when he'd signed up. It had been only words, said glibly, Jimmy thought at the time. He hadn't given them too much thought, until now. To put your country first and yourself last – well, that was a definite sacrifice.

Perhaps he would write back to her; try to put his thoughts on paper, tell Anna how he felt about her. That might be easier than face to face. Not that he was a poet, but surely the words would come.

He folded the precious letter, put it carefully into his locker and sighed.

10

RAF WILMSLOW

17 DECEMBER 1939

'Sure you don't want me to come with you?' asked Mary.

'You're a good pal,' said Anna. 'But it shouldn't take long. I'll get the bus out there to meet her and we'll go to the camp cinema when I get back. Let's have a treat, eh?'

'It's only *Pygmalion*, a soppy love story with Wendy Hiller and Leslie Howard,' said Mary. 'The blokes'll be in there whistling and stamping and making a racket – but whatever you think.'

'Makes a change from sitting in the hut doing mending and bulling shoes,' said Anna. 'Besides, what's wrong with a bit of romance?'

'Depends on who it's with – wouldn't you say?' asked Mary.

'Absolutely!' said Anna, with a very large grin on her face.

'Okay, then,' said her friend, 'off you go or you'll miss your bus. And you needn't look quite so superior – just 'cause *you've* found a nice bloke. Don't forget who introduced you.'

'Fine.' Anna laughed. 'I'll put you down in my will.'

'Shoo! If you don't get on, we'll miss the flick.'

.   .   .

Anna sat on the bus and watched the countryside glide by. It was cold, but then it always was in winter in these double-deckers. The buses had no doors, just an open platform at the back for climbing onboard and a vertical pole to hold on to. *Like a wind tunnel*, she thought, and wished now that she'd worn her uniform greatcoat. At least then she would have been warm.

She forced her mind away from the cold and let it wander to this stranger she was about to meet. A woman who signed herself Jane Walker and claimed to be a relative, which was absurd, for Anna knew no one of that name. She'd only agreed to come to put an end to the mystery and satisfy her curiosity. One puzzle that needed to be answered quickly was how some random stranger knew her old address. It felt uncomfortable, like an invasion into her life. But it was also plain that, even though this Jane person had known to write to Aunt Beatrice's house in Watford, she'd no idea that Anna had moved on. It was a tangle that needed unravelling. And another thing, why would some stranger say they felt they *knew* her when the two of them had never met? She hoped she would soon have the answer.

She closed her eyes and thought of Jimmy. He had been on her mind for days now, ever since she'd read his letter. It was a declaration of love, although he hadn't used the word, but that's what she'd decided to call it. Not a love letter, exactly. His words were a little too stilted and clumsy for that, but they struck her as honest and sincere.

He wanted to be with her, he'd written. In good times and bad. If she agreed to be his sweetheart, then he promised to be true to her. *Always*, his letter said. It was happening a little fast, she thought, and how could anyone say such things as 'always' – especially now, when the future was so unsure. Except, he seemed sure, and he'd even bought her a special sweetheart pin, had asked her to wear it and think of him. A commitment to him, like the one he had obviously made to her in his heart. The thought was exciting, but also a little daunting: two people coming together, vowing to be more than just friends – to be sweethearts.

Love could bring happiness, Anna knew, but it opened you up to sadness as well. With love could come pain, especially the pain of loss. One day soon, Jimmy would be flying into hostile skies and his life would be in danger.

Even so, she decided that the chance of happiness was worth taking.

She thought about the pin he'd asked her to wear. One of her friends in the barracks wore a sweetheart pin on her great-coat – an army pin from her boyfriend in the Royal Artillery. It was a brass brooch with a cannon modelled at its centre and a fancy royal crown. She tried to picture *her* pin. Jimmy was in the air force, so instead of a cannon, perhaps hers would have a plane or maybe wings. It didn't matter. She had made up her mind to accept it. To wear it on her greatcoat with pride, what-ever it was.

He couldn't get away for a while, he'd said. Weekend passes were impossible right now, but as soon as he was able he would be there, would bring her pin with him and ask her properly.

She drifted into a perfect daydream, imagining her and Jimmy on a bright summer's day, the sun overhead warming them as they sat on a blanket together. They'd been riding the tandem and had stopped along the way for a picnic. She watched him move closer to her, cradling her face in his hands. Anna smiled and nodded, giving her consent, for she knew he was about to kiss her. She waited eagerly, but there was no kiss this time – instead, she was jolted out of her idyllic daydream when the bus came to a sudden halt.

Her heart raced as she forced herself back to the real world. The warm sun retreated, and once again she shivered in the cold. The driver started up the bus again and a glance out of the window told her she was nearly there.

Stockport looked the same as last time; maybe a few more shops had blast tape on the windows, but that hadn't stopped people from coming out, trying to get on with life. A new life for most. There were quite a few different uniforms dotted around.

They were coming up to the town centre and Anna looked at her watch. She was already late, but the bus hadn't come on time. Buses always seemed to be late these days; some blamed it on the war. Up ahead, she saw the distinctive turret and Tudor front of the White Lion Hotel and got out of her seat, made her way to the back of the bus, ready to step off the platform. She pressed the bell, but the bus didn't stop right away. She pressed it again, but still the bus carried on.

The clippie who'd taken her money and given her the ticket came up to her. 'Next stop's in front of the market,' the woman bus conductor said, in a high-handed tone.

'But I need to get off here,' said Anna.

'Can't stop here,' the clippie said, stiffly. 'We got rules and next stop's not till the market.'

'But we're going slowly – the driver could easily stop. I could jump off.'

'Rules is rules. We can't change them, it's the war.' The woman shrugged her shoulders and walked away.

Anna hung on to the platform pole and stared out from the bus in frustration. The hotel was right there and now she'd have to walk all the way back and arrive even later still. That's when she spotted the young woman, standing on the pavement in front of the hotel.

The image imprinted itself on Anna's brain along with the shock, so that at first she questioned exactly what she saw. The woman was tall, slim, wearing a dark grey suit. The kind of suit she imagined a secretary would wear. Anna watched her look up at the hotel as if she were about to go in and then suddenly shake her head and hurriedly walk away.

She replayed the scene in her head again. The images were clear and in any other time and place they might have been normal and unremarkable – but now they were incredible, and even shocking. A tall woman, her face as familiar as Anna's own, and the hair – a mirror of Anna's.

Shaken, she held on tightly to the pole as if her knees might buckle beneath her.

When the bus finally stopped, she was the first one off and she ran as fast as she was able, back the way they had come. Still in shock. Still trying to work it out. To make sense of what she'd seen.

She would need to be quick to catch up with the stranger. A stranger who all Anna's instincts told her was Jane Walker, the woman she was meant to meet. She didn't know why this woman had changed her mind and had not gone into the hotel as her letter had promised she would, but Anna knew only one thing – she had to find her. Ask her who she was and why she hadn't waited. Did she get cold feet? Wasn't she brave enough?

The pavements were full of people strolling and queueing at shops and getting in her way. She jostled through them, following the direction the stranger had taken. But it was useless, there was no sign of the young woman. She must have melted into the crowds. Or maybe she had caught a bus somewhere.

After half an hour's fruitless search, she finally decided to give it one last try and doubled back to the White Lion. Perhaps Jane Walker had changed her mind after all and was waiting in there. Anna hoped so. Because she needed to find out just who was this mysterious woman who seemed to be almost a copy of *her*.

She had always considered herself rational, someone who thought things through without letting emotion get in the way.

Sensible, logical, clear-headed and courageous – not someone who got flustered and anxious when something disturbing came their way. But what if she'd been wrong? Anna looked down at her hands and they were shaking. She willed her head to stop them. She needed time to take this in.

Perhaps a brandy would calm her shattered nerves. Her feet took over from her head and she found herself walking through the front door of the hotel. It wasn't often she drank, and she'd certainly never been in a bar on her own before. A woman alone, drinking? It wasn't a good idea. It sent out a signal that you weren't as proper as a young, well-brought-up lady should be.

But now her legs were shaking too. So, she carried on into the bar. There was no brandy, but she bought herself a sherry. There was nobody else there apart from the woman behind the bar.

'We're just closing up,' the barmaid told her. 'But you can take your drink into the restaurant with you, if you're having lunch.'

'I will,' said Anna. 'Thank you.' She remembered the pie that Jimmy had bought them, and she finally calmed down. She could sit and have lunch and consider this thing calmly, no drama, no shock. There must be a sensible explanation. Everyone, it was said, had a *doppelgänger* somewhere – a double who looked like a twin.

The restaurant was an impressive space. She'd thought so the last time she'd been there. Plush red velvet chairs and dark wooden beams gave it a luxurious, old-world elegance and the decorative horse brasses that hung on the wall made Anna think that maybe this really had been an ancient coaching inn just like Jimmy had said.

The place was crowded. People were crammed in and there seemed to be far more tables now than she remembered. She looked around for an empty one, but they were all occupied.

Her eyes scanned the customers: there was no mysterious woman waiting for her.

Her glance returned quickly to the back of the room. Something about the couple at the far table drew her eye towards them, something familiar. They were both in uniform, like many others eating in the restaurant that afternoon. The young woman was an attractive redhead in the navy-blue uniform of a WREN, the Women's Royal Naval Service.

She must be happy, Anna thought, for she kept on smiling. And although Anna couldn't see the man's face, she imagined that he was smiling too. She had no idea who the woman was, had never seen her before and yet there was *something* about the pair that made her want to watch. It was rude, of course: they were probably in love. Catching a few hurried moments together. That's what it looked like. She knew that she should look away. It was none of her business, she told herself. How would *she* feel if someone was watching her and Jimmy as they looked into each other's eyes and held hands like this pair?

That's when she realised. When she knew exactly why her brain had tugged her glance towards them. It was thinking about Jimmy that did it.

The man was in air force blue. And although she could only see his back, it was one that she knew. She would know that head, that ginger hair, that neck anywhere. She had gazed at it for a long time from the back seat of a tandem. She was his tail-gunner!

Anna gasped, tried to suck in air. Tried not to howl out in pain. Or scream at them both. Or call him a traitor. She heard the woman laugh now. He must have told her one of his jokes.

Oh, yes, she thought cynically. Jimmy was a joker all right. And now, the joke was on her.

She rushed from the place in a dream. But not a daydream, this time. A nightmare. The man who would never break her heart had broken it. Had betrayed her.

Anna forgot all about why she had come to Stockport that day. She caught the bus back to camp, feeling numb. It was hard to block the tears from her eyes; to hide her misery from others.

But she was strong, and stubborn, and would not allow his deceit to make her break down.

11

The hardest part was facing Mary. Mary was her friend and Anna didn't want to lose her. Neither would she abandon her just because her brother was a cheat and a swine.

'But I don't understand,' said Mary. 'You mean you didn't even speak to him?'

'I already told you,' Anna replied. 'I left when I saw him there with *her*!'

'So how do you know it was Jimmy, then?'

'It was him all right. I'd know that man anywhere.'

'I'm not convinced,' said Mary. 'It's not like him. He wouldn't lead you on. I mean, he said he loved you and he was coming to bring you his sweetheart pin.'

'Except he went to see *her* first,' said Anna.

'So, you're sure? It was definitely him?'

'Of course it was,' she said, feeling weary now, wanting to forget it, to purge him from her mind.

'I'm not saying you're wrong, but maybe there's more to it than that,' offered Mary.

'Like what? He's a cheating fraud, Mary – and no one's sorrier than me. I was falling in love with the man.'

'I know,' she said, 'and if he's taken up with somebody else, I'll be the first to go over there and wring his damn neck.'

Anna couldn't help herself. She smiled for the first time since that first miserable second when she'd spotted them together in the restaurant. 'You're a good friend, Mary, but I don't want you to fall out with your brother over me. Let's leave it.'

Her friend nodded. 'Well, if you say so.' She looked at her watch. 'Right, we've just got time to make that flick.'

'*Now?* You think I still want to go and watch some romantic slush when I've just been betrayed, thrown over for some fancy floozy!' said Anna.

'Very dramatic, I'm sure. And I doubt very much that you've been thrown over. Certainly not for some floozy. But we'll just have to wait and see.'

It didn't matter that the film was a total waste of time, that the projector kept breaking down, or that the cinema echoed to the sound of raucous airmen booing – Anna wouldn't have enjoyed it anyway. She didn't even notice the hard bench seats or the icy cold hanger that passed for a cinema, with everyone wearing their greatcoats inside. Or the way her warm breath came out in a cloud-forming fog each time she breathed. All she could think of was Jimmy and how he had deceived her. Had it truly been that easy? Was she such a naïve, simple-minded fool? She didn't think so. She had trusted him because he'd *seemed* trustworthy, a decent sort of chap and funny too – easy to get on with. But what did that say about her judgement? Still, what did it matter now? It was all gone. Along with his blasted sweetheart pin.

When Anna and Mary were heading back to their hut, they met Section Officer Jones, the woman who had given them their new assignments some weeks ago.

'I've been looking for you,' she told them, as she returned

their salutes. 'You're to come to the office tomorrow morning and pick up new orders and travel warrants.' The woman marched smartly away before either of them could reply or ask where they were going and why.

'It's the military,' Anna said, resigned. 'We were sure to be moved on sometime.'

'And you really don't mind?' asked Mary.

'There's nothing to stay here for,' she said. 'Maybe before, but not now.'

'I don't care what you say. There's more to this thing with Jimmy than you suppose. I'll write to him when we're settled. He'll have had a very good reason for meeting this woman. I'll ask him, get him to write to you.'

'I wish you wouldn't, Mary. I don't want him to write. I won't listen to his excuses, and I won't beg for his affection. I've still got my self-respect; I won't let him take that away from me as well.'

'I don't think my brother would do anything to make you sad.'

'Really?' asked Anna. *How she wished that were true.*

'Really!' said Mary. 'It's clear he loves you. And I think you love him too. And my brother may be daft at times, but he's not insane. He wouldn't do anything to spoil that.'

12

CHRISTMAS EVE 1939

Anna had gone, left RAF Wilmslow, and moved on. Jimmy struggled with the loss and the dark shadow that had settled on him. He'd been looking forward to the holidays, hoping she would join him in the mess for Christmas Day, but now, Christmas felt more like something to be survived than a celebration. All he could think about was the hole left in his life where she had once been.

She'd left with no warning, but he understood that it wasn't her fault. She was in the RAF, had to go where she was ordered, do what she was told to do. *Orders*: they all had to follow them, men and women alike, and mostly they were happy to. It kept your country safe from enemies. So, of course, he understood. But it had been so sudden that he hadn't even had a chance to say goodbye. He'd heard the news of their new posting in a letter from his sister. A harsh, surprising letter, full of outrage. If words on a page could kill, he would have been dead by now.

Jimmy read his sister's angry letter again. It was hard to take in, even harder to believe. It accused him of breaking Anna's heart. Something he would never do. Women were strange, alien beings who spoke a different language to him, a language he was trying hard to understand. But they did things differently and seemed to take offence at the very slightest thing. He felt he would never see things the way they did, no matter how hard he tried. Why would his sister Mary get this upset with him? He was totally in the dark. She'd accused him of playing around with other women. Had asked him to explain himself. And all because he'd been doing a good deed for his sister Alice. Was that fair?

Sisters! Both of his sisters had pushed his patience to its limit. First, Alice, dramatically insisting he drop everything and rush urgently to her side. So, he'd gone to meet her at the hotel restaurant that day. Now here was Mary, ordering him to explain, as if he'd done something wrong.

Sometimes the world just punched you in the eye, even when you'd done nothing to deserve it.

Mary had ordered him to apologise. Apologise? For what? For being kind? His little sister should have more trust in him, should know him better. How could she accuse him of having an affair? An affair with a WREN, that's what she'd said. If it wasn't so ludicrous, it would be funny. But it seems that Anna believed it too, had *seen it with her own eyes*. He was surprised she thought so little of him, of his promise to be true to her. Why would she throw him aside without a fair hearing? It seemed she was willing to condemn him without knowing the facts. He was confused because it didn't seem like her.

She was hurt, his sister wrote, didn't want to hear from him. Nothing, it seemed, would change her mind. What! Not even the truth?

He made up his mind. He would write to Mary. Maybe not straight away, for she'd made him angry. And not an apology or an excuse: he'd done nothing wrong that needed either. But he would write to Anna immediately. Explain about the WREN he'd met in the restaurant that day.

It was his older sister, Alice. There was a family crisis and she'd insisted he meet her urgently. Their mother's health was failing, Alice claimed; she'd noticed it on her last leave and soon *someone* would need to go back home and look after her. She hadn't mentioned involving Mary in their meeting, but he'd understood why. Alice and Mary could be like oil and water. Typical sisters, he'd always thought – sometimes they didn't get along, yet they would move heaven and earth to help each other if one was in trouble.

He'd agreed to meet Alice at the White Lion Hotel. He had happy memories of being there with Anna and it seemed like a good idea, to give his sister lunch and try to calm her. He wasn't convinced there was a crisis for Alice could be dramatic at times, was apt to exaggerate. Building huge mountains where only small molehills lived. Jimmy didn't believe their mother was getting frail. The woman was like the Rock of Gibraltar, the backbone of the family. She was kind, loving, always there. And she'd looked fine to him the last time he'd seen her, robust and fit as a flea.

All the same, Alice had decided to apply for some compassionate leave and check on things at home. If help was needed, she would take on the job, she'd told Jimmy. Both their parents were getting older now and it was time for them to slow down.

'And what's my job in this?' Jimmy had asked. He could always tell when Alice was lining him up for some sort of job, for something she didn't fancy herself.

'You're my heavy artillery,' she'd said. 'Mother always listens to you. Persuade her I'm right and the time's come when she can't do things all by herself.'

'So, I'm to tell her she's feeble? Ready to be put out to grass? Even if I don't think it's true?'

Families were every bit as complicated as war at times. Maybe even more so.

The two of them had argued for a while. But, in the end Jimmy had agreed – if it turned out that his mother really was sick, he would write to her. He knew Ma would hate the idea of someone else doing her work, of being waited on or giving up her independence. And she would especially hate the idea of Alice leaving the navy.

Besides, Alice liked being a WREN, she'd told him so, and he suspected she was a good one, that service life agreed with her. Jimmy had warned her not to rush into anything. All the same, he wondered if he might end up as referee, stuck between Alice and his mother, for they were both strong women. Resolute, spirited women – his family was known for them.

He thought back to Mary's fiery letter. All these feisty women in his life, but in a way he was glad. Even though he didn't always understand what went on in their heads, he was happy they were there. The world would be a duller and sadder place without them.

Jimmy got out his pen, pulled his thoughts together. Writing to Anna wouldn't be easy, but it was something he needed to do. He couldn't bear to think he'd hurt her or made her feel unhappy. So, he would try his best to sort this out. It wasn't a perfect world, but the notion that he had somehow let her down, or that she had lost faith in him, made it a much less perfect place than it had once been.

13

LEIGHTON BUZZARD, BEDFORDSHIRE

2 JANUARY 1940

Anna's new home was a bleak Victorian workhouse, somewhere just outside the town of Leighton Buzzard. A grim and eerie building, its ancient, blackened brick crumbling in places and they had to get to their dormitory on the first floor by climbing up an old iron staircase attached to an outside wall.

Some of the other WAAFs claimed it was haunted.

'They don't believe in spoiling us,' was Mary's verdict when they'd first arrived.

'Better than nothing, I suppose, and at least we've got proper beds this time. Don't expect we'll be here long anyway, not if we're just training,' Anna had said.

It turned out she was wrong. Their training as plotters would take at least twelve weeks, ending with the inevitable exams. And the strict secrecy was something neither of them had expected. Letters home would be censored, they were told.

They'd arrived at the train station in the dark and been met by RAF lorries to take them to their destination, so had seen little of their new surroundings. Jumping onto the tailboard of the transport and sitting in the freezing lorry with its flapping canvas had reminded Anna of the time she, Mary and Dot had been driven to their basic training camp. They'd been naïve recruits, had known nothing of what lay ahead.

Now, how things had changed. It felt like a different and new exciting phase of her military life, something that caused those butterflies in Anna's stomach to beat their wings again.

All new trainees were confined to their dormitories when they weren't studying in the huge building next door – an equally uninspiring place covered with camouflage netting. They had been marched there on their first day, and all twenty of them on the course had been provided with pens by an RAF sergeant who'd given them copies of the Official Secrets Act to sign. Then they'd been made to swear on a bible that they would never divulge any information they were about to hear, or speak to anyone about their work.

Afterwards, the sergeant had taken the pens away, as they weren't allowed to keep diaries or take course notes; it all had to be done in their heads. For the first month, the trainee plotters were expected to study every day – with no weekends off. *There are no weekends in war*, an instructor had told them. No one complained.

Their classroom was a huge, draughty room filled with maps and telephones, with two large metal tables for them all to sit at and listen to the many lectures. They learned about map coordinates, grids, vectors, and compass bearings, and how to plot aircraft movements on an exact copy of a Fighter Command plotting table.

The importance of her job had become clear to Anna from their very first day. And why there was such a need for secrecy.

The training was confusing at times, the teaching intensive, and all the information they had to take in was challenging, but Anna found it exciting too, even though she sometimes went to bed with a headache.

They had been there for two weeks now, and both Anna and Mary had learned they were to be part of a unique and highly secret and sensitive radar system. Her country was the first nation in the world to have a working early warning radar network; something to be proud of, she thought. A string of radar stations, known as Chain Home, had been built by the RAF and set up along the coast. It could detect enemy aircraft as they massed over the Channel, even up to a hundred miles away. But it was a system their enemies would go to any lengths to find out about, and sabotage.

It was a kind of modern miracle, Anna decided – and her part in it would be to take information provided by the radar stations and Observer Corps' posts and transfer it onto the huge map in the centre of an operations room. She might be a small cog in a large wheel, but her job would be a crucial one.

She was anxious to get on with the real work and move on to her proper posting. That would only happen if she passed her exams, of course, but she was determined to study hard and make sure she was successful. Then she would be a fully-fledged plotter. An *official* Clerk, Special Duties.

She was feeling positive, getting into the swing of studying and enjoying the company and banter of the WAAFs in the dorm. They were a friendly bunch who shared each other's hopes and frustrations, and helped each other out – especially those who were struggling to keep up with the vast amounts of detail they were expected to take in. One thing that had bound them together in those first few difficult weeks had been their shared hatred of the food. Right now, there were all sat around their trestle table staring at the curled-up sandwiches that passed for lunch. Anna inspected hers, examining the filling inside.

'Cabbage,' she said in surprise. 'Have you ever heard of such a thing?'

'Maybe they think we're rabbits,' said Mary.

'Rabbit would be nice. My ma used to make a lovely rabbit stew,' said a WAAF called Jessica, who gave a wistful sigh.

Several heads nodded in agreement. But Anna imagined the huge, sad eyes of a beautiful furry bunny and didn't think she could bring herself to eat one. She ate the cabbage sandwich. They all did and only grumbled afterwards.

'Let's make a pact,' said Mary.

'What kind of pact?' Anna asked.

'When the war's over, let's all come back and take vengeance on the cook,' suggested Jessica, a blood-thirsty look on her face.

'I know what,' said Anna, 'let's make her eat one of her cabbage sandwiches.'

Everybody laughed.

∼

That night Anna hummed as she changed into her striped winceyette pyjamas. Her cheerfulness had been fuelled lately by the letter she'd had from Jimmy.

She sat on her bed and curled her feet under her, and turned to Mary beside her. Mary was having her nightly tug-of-war with her hair but she seemed to be winning, for Anna noted a look of satisfaction on her friend's face.

'Let's test each other again tonight,' Anna said.

'You're a glutton for punishment,' said Mary. 'Haven't you had enough all day?'

'You heard what the officer said – in two weeks we're due our first exam. If we pass, we get weekend leave.' Anna smiled. 'I can't fail,' she said. 'I need that leave.'

'I see. And where might you be spending it? As if I didn't know,' said Mary.

'Thought I would go and see Jimmy.'

'You've forgiven him, then. Thought you'd been a mite more cheery since his letter arrived.'

'Nothing to forgive, was there? And now he's only got a few more weeks till he gets posted to goodness knows where. Who knows when we'll be able to see each other again,' said Anna. She couldn't bear to think of not seeing him again. Her fault in a way for ever doubting him. She should have had more faith in him instead of throwing away her chance to see him before she left Wilmslow, and worse still, what if Jimmy's plane was shot down? That was her greatest fear, but she wouldn't mention that to Mary.

'You can always write,' Mary said.

'I know – and I will, but it's not the same. I've *got* to see him!' she said, her voice hoarse, choked with feeling.

'I see that,' said Mary.

'And I hope he wants to see me,' she said.

'Oh, he'll want to,' said Mary. 'You can be sure of that.'

Anna searched her friend's face, hoping for a sign that it was true – that Jimmy was that unique 'someone' meant for her. That he felt the same way she did. That she hadn't gone and ruined everything by being a jealous, impetuous fool.

'I hope so,' Anna said. 'I hope I didn't throw something special away. I was maybe too quick to blame him, but I mean to apologise. Think he'll forgive me, Mary?'

'He'd forgive you if you stabbed him in the eye with a fork.'

'What!'

'You know what I mean. The man loves you,' said Mary.

It felt strange for Anna – to think of the 'love' word. To use it. To try to understand exactly what it meant. But she wanted to find out.

She had finally admitted to herself that the way she viewed people was a complicated affair. Trust wasn't easy for her. She'd always blamed that on her father, and the way he'd abandoned her, but she'd been thinking of him lately, had come to realise that nobody was *all* bad. He seemed to have truly loved her mother. Besides, he had disappeared from her life a long time ago, so perhaps it was time to be an adult and stop blaming him for anything that went wrong in her life.

Now, it was up to her. She'd worked hard, and with motivation she would pass her exam and get that weekend leave.

She and Mary tested each other on that day's lessons until they were both exhausted. Then their overbearing corporal arrived and called *lights out*. How good it would be, she thought, just for once to keep the lights on as long as you wanted to and stay up for as long as you fancied. Even better, to get up in the morning when you felt like it and not at six thirty, when you were ordered to. Better still would be to wake up to a lovely warm dormitory with the coke stove *already* lit, and to have your morning wash in hot water instead of icy cold.

But the war demanded sacrifices. And her sacrifice, she told herself, was much less than that of some others. Dressing under the bedclothes in the morning to keep warm, and cleaning condensation from the windows of her dorm, eating cabbage sandwiches; those things weren't ideal, but Anna was happy to go along with it all.

So far there had been no danger, although she had a feeling that would change. She remembered the words of her examiner months before – *Can you be cool under fire?* Fire was coming; how or when, she didn't know. But it would be here.

She thought herself a realist – accepting whatever came and getting on with it. The war was here, that couldn't be changed, and those people who said *It'll all be over by Christmas* had been wishful thinkers, burying their heads in the sand. Christmas had come and gone, and the war hadn't disappeared.

She fell asleep dreaming of Jimmy and the time they'd spent together, and the fun they'd had. She knew it had been real and that, soon, she'd get to see him again and this time... well, who knew? She was a grown woman. A woman who knew her own mind. A woman of her time, her generation. Women were taking power into their hands and believing in themselves and in their equality. They were equal to men. They could make decisions about who they loved and how they loved and *what they would do about it.*

14

JIMMY

She couldn't wait to see him. That's what her letter said, and it bubbled with expectation. She had wangled a weekend pass and the best thing was that she was going to use it to travel to Cheshire to meet him. Her turn to come to *him*, she'd said.

Jimmy could feel her happiness and excitement leaping off the page and he tried to keep his anticipation in check. To focus on the vital job in hand. They'd been doing simulated bombing runs all day – paper runs in a classroom, but important all the same. His head was still buzzing with it all. He was getting so close to the end of his ground training now, he couldn't afford to let up if he was to succeed and not let the others in the crew down. Chaps who relied on him to get them safely home after a raid.

The standards of his navigational training were rigorous. Fifty hours a week in a classroom, sometimes ten hours a day, if they were allowed a weekend free. But he had worked hard and felt confident he would make the grade. His instructors seemed to think so too. Other navigators on his course hadn't. After the last set of exams, two of his friends had been tapped on the shoulder by the commanding officer and had quietly packed up their gear. He'd heard they'd been deployed to another station and retrained as ground crew.

He went back to Anna's letter, picturing her face as she wrote it. She was writing it under the bedclothes, she said, after lights out, using her torch. The notion gave it an exciting clandestine edge, and it gave him a thrill to imagine her there. Anna and him under the bedclothes together – nothing improper, of course, for he was only there in spirit. Not that he expected anything more and he wouldn't ask it of her. Part of him wanted to – he was only human – with all the urges a caveman was born with, he supposed. But he wouldn't ask it of Anna. Not yet. He hoped that one day there might be more, at the proper time, when he could offer her a ring. She had never been with a man before. She hadn't told him that, but he could tell. And she wasn't just any woman. She was *the* woman. A true lady, too, due his respect as well as his love.

She'd need somewhere to stay, a hotel or boarding house nearby. He'd book her a room at the White Lion; he thought she would be happy there. She liked the place, and he heard that the rooms were fine – a bit old-fashioned, but comfortable. Maybe he could even get himself a sleeping-out pass. Then he could spend more precious time with her. He decided to try. He could get a room there as well. Separate to hers, of course. They could have dinner in the hotel or take in a show. One of the chaps had told him there was a good variety show on at Stockport Theatre Royal. *You Shall have Laughter*, or something like that. Anna might like it. And who didn't like laughter?

They could make it a bit of a holiday, although it would be a short one. Her letter said she would use up several hours of her weekend pass just getting to Cheshire by train. He had no idea where she was coming from. She wasn't allowed to say in letters out, and Jimmy had sent his letters to a central military post office box. Sometimes it was like that – very hush-hush, especially if your job was a secret one.

He thought about her sitting there on the train. Timetables were a thing of the past. Train travel was a gamble nowadays, waiting in sidings for hours to let goods trains with important war resources through, waiting for connecting trains that never arrived. Journeys that used to take hours now took a whole day, and fortune had truly smiled if you managed to bag a seat instead of standing in draughty corridors. But there weren't too many grumbles. Most folk accepted it as part of the new reality that came with war, like the kind of food you had to eat. Jimmy and his crew had eaten some bizarre meals in the mess lately and real eggs seemed to have vanished into thin air, replaced by an odd, powdered affair. And Spam. The pale processed meat came in huge tins that were piled up like building blocks in the camp store. It had been a novelty at first when the Americans had sent it, but Jimmy wondered how many more ways you could cook the damn stuff. They'd had it chopped, fried, and mixed with powdered potato in what the cooks called 'cowboy hash'. The exotic label hadn't made it any more palatable.

Anna's letter had been a mixture of passion and remorse. She apologised and asked for his forgiveness for not trusting him. For condemning him so quickly, and for a crime he didn't commit. She had obviously been at the hotel in Stockport that day. But one thing that puzzled him was *why*. She hadn't mentioned it in her letter. It couldn't have been to see him: there was no way she could have known he would be there. He hadn't known himself until a few hours before. He must remember to ask her when she came.

In her letter she'd called him *honourable*, said that she could see his intention had only been to help his sister, Alice. Fine words that made him feel a little guilty. He wasn't being noble or any other of those chivalrous things. He'd met with Alice simply to calm her down and keep things in the family running the same way they always had. Jimmy didn't like disruption, wasn't keen on change. He loved his family exactly the way it was: comforting, reassuring, always there. With their mother at the helm.

Anna had said nothing about her work, although he knew that she and his sister had both wanted to be plotters. He assumed they were in training, like him. Men and women everywhere were being trained for wartime jobs, learning skills they may never have thought about before.

All were necessary skills right now, but some would have been too terrible to contemplate in peacetime. What would become of those men who had had to learn how to do the unthinkable, when the need was over? How could they come back from that? Could you 'unlearn' such a skill? That was a question in the back of Jimmy's mind. A question for another day.

All over Britain, it was a hive of activity, but at the same time the nation seemed to be holding its collective breath for what was to come. The Phoney War, newspapers were calling it, because so far not too much had happened. Everyone seemed to be waiting for Hitler and what he would do next, which country he would choose to invade.

Jimmy hoped it wasn't Britain, but if it was, he would be ready. They all would. Soon, he'd be posted somewhere for his training with an OTU – an operational training unit. No more classroom! He would finally get into the air. None of them knew where yet, but there was a rumour going around that Cornwall would be a likely spot.

Freddy had put a half-crown on it. And Freddy might be a bit of a joker at times, but everybody knew that he only ever bet on a sure thing.

15

The journey had made her grumpy. She'd started off fine, feeling positive and cheerful, full of smiles and hope. But Anna's patience was tested when the train slowed down to a crawl yet again. They'd just gone through a station, but she couldn't tell where; all station signposts had been removed, making the land a place of mystery. At least that was the idea – no point in making the geography easier for foreign spies.

It seemed a bizarre notion, that even now there could be enemy spies trying to gather intelligence or plotting sabotage. She tried to imagine them, blundering around in the blackouts. People were still getting used to those; pedestrians trying to find their way home in the dark were having a hard time. Some had been hit by cars and others had fallen in canals; though Anna suspected that those who had ended up taking an unexpected swim might have downed a few glasses beforehand. There had been lots of grumbles about the blackouts; neighbours complaining to each other over the garden fence, people writing letters to *The Times*, but they were part of everyday life now.

But saboteurs would know all about the blackouts and other changes already. They were clever people, she assumed, who'd been trained to act normally, to fit in like one of the crowd. Sitting on a train like this one, travelling to Stockport. They would need patience and luck, for there were far fewer passenger trains now and travellers were shoe-horned tightly into freezing carriages. There was no heating in this one – easy to understand, but not so simple to get along with. Cold water, cold trains, saving wartime energy and resources, it was something that good citizens took for granted now. Like church bells being melted down and people giving up their iron railings and front gates to the war effort. It showed loyalty to your country.

Anna sighed. It drew a look of sympathy from the woman sitting opposite.

'It's the war, dearie,' the woman said, and smiled as she offered Anna one of her last carrot scones.

Anna nodded in solidarity. 'Thanks,' she said. 'You're very kind.'

'Never hurts to be kind,' the woman said.

That was a funny thing about the war, thought Anna. In many ways it seemed to bring people together, allowed them to understand each other better. But war also encouraged cruelty and man's savagery. It was a strange and puzzling contradiction.

'Travelling home, dear?' the friendly woman asked.

Anna studied her face. It could just be an innocent question, she thought, and the old woman didn't look like a spy. But then how could you tell? Better to be safe than sorry and she'd signed the Official Secrets Act. All the same, she could still be civil without giving away anything about her job.

'Not home – no,' she replied. 'I'm going to meet someone.'

'Ah – someone very special, then.'

'Yes, how did you know?'

'It's written on your face,' the woman said, 'and in your eyes.'

'It is?' she asked, surprised.

'Yes, of course, dearie. The eyes... it's hard for the eyes to lie.'

'You came,' said Jimmy. 'I wasn't *absolutely* sure you would.'

'I promised I would – and I'm a woman of my word,' said Anna.

'I see that,' he said, and gave her a playful wink to make her laugh.

She allowed him to take her hand and guide her to the end of the platform. 'This is a lovely surprise,' she said. 'I didn't expect you at the station. How did you know when I'd get in?'

'I didn't,' said Jimmy. 'I've been waiting for three hours. But you're worth it. And I brought a sandwich with me.'

He laughed. She'd missed the boisterous sound.

'Sardine?' she asked, and added a laugh of her own.

'Not sardine,' he said. 'Are you hungry?' he asked suddenly. 'I've booked us a table in the hotel restaurant, if that's okay? It's a bit of a hike, what with the blackout, but I think we'll be all right. There's a moon out tonight.'

A moon, she thought. *It couldn't have been better if it had been planned.* Not that she was impressed by all that fluffy romantic stuff, but, even so, it might easily have been a sign... What was she thinking? Had she suddenly turned into Edna? Her heart ruling her head? She laughed to herself at this thought of her friend, wondering what she'd say if she saw Anna right then.

They walked out of the station entrance arm in arm and into the night. A figure loomed out of the darkness and stood beside them.

'Enjoy your leave, dear,' a voice said.

She recognised it: it was the friendly woman from the train. 'I will,' said Anna, 'and thank you. You've been really kind.'

'Who was that?' Jimmy asked, when the woman had hurried away.

'Just a nice woman I met on the train.'

'Well, we'll have to make sure you do. Enjoy your leave, that is,' he said.

'You know, I believe I will,' she said, smiling.

'How about we make a start, right now?' said Jimmy, and he stopped them in their tracks.

She watched him take something from the pocket of his greatcoat.

'Open it,' he said, 'and put me out of my misery.'

'Misery – you're miserable?'

'Tormented,' he said. 'And only you can free me.'

She understood him better now. Was getting used to his ways. A laugh and a joke to help him through something serious. At first, she'd thought it glib and flippant, the way he had of reducing things that were important to him to something smaller and trifling. But it was a way of keeping himself safe from hurt, she could see that now. Someone who had been hurt before would do that, especially a chap who needed to seem strong. Anna didn't mind. She found it made him more endearing, vulnerable and human, like the rest of them. Feet of clay, she supposed. Everybody had them, in one way or another. Falling in love was a gamble. She knew that much. It gave the person you were in love with the power to hurt you when you put your heart into their hands.

She fiddled with the brown paper wrapping and it reminded her of something else, a memory that made her happy. *What was it now?* Oh, yes. The day when they'd had that awful gas mask drill and he'd wobbled up to the perimeter wire on his ancient bicycle. He'd looked dishevelled, that bright ginger hair sticking out rebelliously from under his cap. That was probably the moment when he'd won her over. Well, that and the thoughtful gift he'd thrown over the wire. Not jewels, but something very simple, a tiny painted box with her favourite sweets inside. How had he known they were her favourites? She hadn't thought of that until now, but of course he must have taken the trouble to ask his sister – Mary had known all about Anna's love of pear drops.

The brown paper finally gave way and underneath there was a box, smaller than the painted one had been, but important just the same, because when she opened the lid, the tiny object inside made her head reel.

She held it up high, trying to make out the details in the dim light. It was the sweetheart brooch he had promised, had asked her to wear, and she would wear it with pride. His commitment to her was real, she could tell that. After all, he'd waited for three whole hours on a cold, draughty station platform for her to arrive.

The silver pin twinkled in the moonlight, the wings outstretched, the colourful, enamelled crown above it and the RAF motto around the edge, something about 'making it to the stars' if she remembered rightly. Now the night seemed magical.

'Can I pin it on for you?' he said. 'If you'll wear it, that is?'

'I'd be happy to,' Anna said, as the dry lump in her throat tried to catch her out.

'You know what I mean by it?' he asked.

'I do.'

'That I want you to be my girl,' said Jimmy. 'My *only* girl.'

She felt him move closer, felt the brush of his hand on her chest as he pinned the precious brooch to her greatcoat lapel. His touch made her shiver. But then the night was cold, she told herself.

His kiss when it came was different from before. Not such a surprise to her this time, and not so tentative, she thought. As if he already knew she would return it.

And so she did. They stood like a fixed tableau in the moonlight, two bodies entwined, linked in a loving embrace. His lips were cold in the winter air, and they tasted of something that she knew, but couldn't for the moment pin down.

People coming from the station passed them by on the pavement and still the pair of them didn't move, but clung to each other, hands touching, bodies touching, faces touching, and lips joined together as one. Even their breathing seemed to be like one person, Anna thought. And the tingling sensation that was moving through her in the place that her friend Edna delicately described as 'down below' – *was that normal?*

An unsettling feeling took hold of her, a panic that told Anna she must break away, break out of this physical embrace. Heat soared through her, even though the night held an icy chill.

She was the first to pull away, frightened by her feelings, their intensity.

'Sorry,' said Jimmy. 'Did I overstep the mark?'

'What?' she asked, trying to rally her flustered brain into order.

'Did I go over the line?' he asked.

'The line? Oh, I see.' She squeezed his hand. 'No, the line's still there,' she answered, quickly. 'No need to apologise. That was nice.'

'*Nice?*' asked Jimmy.

'Well – more than nice really,' she said, groping for words. 'Exceptional.'

'Ten out of ten?' he asked and laughed.

'Easily,' said Anna.

'Excellent. As long as I haven't upset you. I thought maybe I'd put you off with my Spam sandwich.' He rubbed his mouth with the back of his hand.

'Spam!' she said. 'I thought I recognised the taste. Good to see you don't mind sharing.' And now it was her turn to laugh.

'Let's see if we can dig up something a bit more exciting than Spam, shall we? At least the restaurant should be warm,' said Jimmy, and gave a long, dramatic shiver. 'And I've booked you a room at the hotel.'

'You have? That was thoughtful,' she said.

'Me too,' said Jimmy.

'You too what?' Anna asked.

'I managed to bag a sleeping-out pass and I've got a room there as well. A *separate* room,' he said.

'Ah – you're worried about my virtue?'

'Not a bit. Your honour is quite safe with me.'

She nodded, understood that he didn't want to compromise her reputation. And it was sweet. She didn't say that, though. She remembered what Mary had said – that men didn't like to be thought of as sweet. Somehow it presumed a weakness in them. But Anna didn't think so; she thought the opposite. It showed a strength.

She took his arm as the sky darkened, the moon disappearing behind a bank of grey clouds. They walked side by side, fastened together like an old married pair, two sets of footsteps, in tandem, walking to the same rhythm. Snuggled up so close to him like this, she felt herself in a kind of heady dream. It reminded her of the daydream she'd had once before, but this was real. And comforting. He made her feel cosy and safe, miles away from the fear of war. As if danger could never reach them.

The night folded in around them, and when she looked up, the moon had reappeared from behind its blanket of clouds to join the myriad stars in a vast purple sky. Neither of them spoke for the rest of the way, as if some outside hand had taken charge and orchestrated their silence, until the only sound Anna could hear was their footsteps on the pavement.

'Here we are,' said Jimmy, breaking the spell. 'We've arrived.'

'We have? Sorry,' she said. 'I was somewhere else then. Off in a dream.' Anna laughed.

'Well – I hope I was there, too,' he said wryly.

'Certainly, you were. I wouldn't start a dream without you.'

'I'm very glad. You like your pin?' he asked.

'It's beautiful.'

They walked into the hotel and Anna felt the warmth of his hand in hers. People looked up as they made their way to the restaurant table and she wondered what they saw. A carefree couple dressed in their country's uniform, stealing a few precious hours of happiness before they returned to the business of war? Or some sort of immoral liaison? A clandestine meeting at a hotel and a room shared and neither of them with a wedding band. Is that what this seemed? *Anyway*, she chastised herself, *what did it matter what people thought? She was an adult, could make her own decisions and it was nobody's business but hers.*

The restaurant was warm; the log fire had been lit. She hadn't noticed that before. The blackout curtains were drawn and the glow from the lights and flickering candles on tables made shadows dance on the sparkling white walls. It all gave the room an aura of romance. The deep red velvet seemed richer now and the brass shone, and the white lace tablecloths seemed to come from another, grander age. An age of elegance, a gilded age, long gone.

They laughed and joked and ordered wine, started drinking it before the food arrived. It seemed perfect to her. Only one thing was off-key – the food, but even that gave Anna a reason to smile.

'It's funny,' she said.

'Oh? What's that?'

'I'd been looking forward to our pie,' she said slowly, carefully sorting out the words in her head before they reached her mouth. She'd only been sipping the wine, but, even so, between the wine and the journey, her head felt a little soggy. Yes, that was the word, *soggy*. And *mushy* – that was another good word. She was having to concentrate hard to get past the alcohol.

'Though we're still having pie,' he said. 'Lord Woolton would no doubt be impressed.'

'Pish!' she said. 'What does the minister of food know about cooking? I bet the man has never eaten his *Woolton* pies. Nothing but vegetables in there.'

'Pish?' said Jimmy.

'Rubbish,' she explained.

'Ah – well, it was between that and those awful corned-beef fritters. We get enough of those in the mess.'

'You too? But at least you don't have to choke down cabbage sandwiches,' said Anna.

'Don't let's talk about that, not when there are other more exciting things,' said Jimmy.

'Oh, like what?' she teased him.

'Like us. And how much I've missed you.'

'How much?' asked Anna.

'This much,' he said, and opened his arms wide like a fisherman exaggerating his mythical catch.

'Impressive. I've missed you too,' said Anna, suddenly serious. 'I don't know what I'll do when you move on, I'll be miserable.' Already she felt sad thinking about it – about the pain of separation. He'd been posted to Cornwall, which wasn't the other side of the world and didn't seem like a very dangerous place, but then again, anywhere with an RAF station was a target for the German Luftwaffe.

'I'll be miserable too,' said Jimmy. 'Maybe you could put in for a posting to Cornwall. We could see each other more often.'

'I haven't even passed my course yet,' she said, smiling, 'and already you've got me a job.'

'You'll do it,' he said confidently, 'I'm sure of that. You've been working hard, and you'll make an excellent plotter.'

'I hope so,' said Anna.

'Meanwhile, we'll write,' said Jimmy. 'I'll expect a letter

every week. Though I think your letters will be far more interesting than mine. Which reminds me...'

'What?' she asked.

'Speaking of letters – that mystery woman who wrote, did you hear any more from her? You said you were going to agree to meet.'

'I came here to meet her, actually,' said Anna. 'I remembered how good I felt the first time you brought me here.' Her eyes left his face and travelled around the beautiful room. So elegant, she thought, when everything seemed drab and colourless with the war.

'What? You're saying that's what you were doing that day...'

'Yes, that was the time I saw you with Alice; although I didn't know it was your sister, of course.'

'The day I made you so unhappy,' he said, and frowned.

'That's all done now,' said Anna. She reached over and took his hand.

'So – what did this woman want, the one you came to see? Was she a skeleton, after all? I'm intrigued.'

'I think maybe I've got a twin,' said Anna. She tried to keep her voice flat and calm, as if the thought was unremarkable, the kind of thing you discovered every day. Instead, her words shook with emotion. It was the first time she'd said it aloud. Or told anyone else about her fears. Her hopes, too. Because, if it were true, it meant she finally had family. True family, not Aunt Beatrice, who had never tried to love her, or her father who had done his best to wipe her from his life.

'You've what...!'

'Got a twin. Someone who looks like me... same age, I think – and her face and hair, it was uncanny.'

'But surely that's impossible?' said Jimmy. 'Didn't you tell me you were an only child, that your mother died giving birth to you?'

'It's what Aunt Beatrice told me, but then maybe she lied.'

'It's incredible. If it's true, I'm thrilled for you. It's great having brothers and sisters. I should know – I've got bucketloads,' he said, grinning. 'Christmas in our place is a free-for-all, and you need to have a loud voice to make yourself heard.'

'I'd love that,' she said, wistfully. 'A proper home and family.'

Even so, the more time went by, the more Anna doubted exactly what she'd seen. *The resemblance between them – was it only in her head, just something she'd wanted to see? Besides, she'd only seen the woman for a fleeting glance.*

'But what did this woman – what's-her-name – say?'

'Jane – she writes that her name is Jane Walker. Other than that, I've no idea.'

'She didn't speak?'

'We didn't meet. She was waiting outside the hotel, but then she changed her mind and ran away. I couldn't find her.'

'But you've written again?'

'Not yet,' Anna said. 'I've been busy with study and our exams. And writing to you,' she added, boldly.

'I'm glad. I love your letters, they keep me going,' said Jimmy.

'I'm pleased. But I'll write to her again when I get a chance. Still, I don't know what good it'll do.'

'Why not?' he asked, confused.

'She clearly changed her mind. She didn't want to see me.'

'Well then, why would she come in the first place?'

'Maybe she got cold feet. Whatever the reason, she ran away,' she said.

'Anybody who runs away from you must be mad,' said Jimmy. And he winked.

'Flatterer!' said Anna. But she didn't mind – it was good to have somebody compliment you once in a while.

The food arrived and at the same time as the waiter put it

down, a young man in an air force uniform rushed up to their table.

'George! You remember George,' said Jimmy.

'I do,' said Anna. 'I hope you're well.'

'Thank you, miss,' said George awkwardly, and removed his uniform cap. 'Sorry for interrupting your supper, but we've got a situation.'

'This had better be good,' said Jimmy. 'We're just about to eat this wonderful pie.'

'It's Freddy,' said the airman, an apologetic look on his face. 'He's gone AWOL. If we don't get him back in another twenty-four hours, they'll charge him with desertion.'

'Desertion?' said Anna. 'But I thought Freddy loved the air force.'

'Freddy's a card,' explained George, 'but he's just had a *Dear John* letter from his sweetheart. She's thrown him over for somebody else and now he's on his way to London to have it out. He'll get himself in all kinds of trouble, we need to get him back.'

'It's okay, he won't find a train,' said Jimmy. 'Not this time of night.'

'He's stolen Corporal Meadowcroft's motorbike. You need to come – he'll listen to you, Ginger.'

'And how will that work?' asked Jimmy, frustrated.

'I've borrowed a car. He'll not have gone that far. There's not much petrol in the bike.' He looked at Anna. 'Sorry, miss,' he said again, 'for dragging him away.'

She studied Jimmy's bleak face, saw his look of helplessness, the fatalistic shrug of his shoulders. His sigh of resignation was no surprise. She knew he would go, that he had made his choice between his friend and her. *That was unfair of her. She would try not to be bitter or blame him. Or burden him with guilt.* He really had no choice. She was here, safe, warm, about to eat;

Freddy was in danger of throwing his whole career away – or, even worse, he could end up in jail for desertion.

Anna gave a resigned sigh herself. 'Go on,' she told him. 'Go and find Freddy. He needs you.'

She watched Jimmy's shoulders droop in defeat. He didn't want to leave, was full of regret, she could see that.

He wasn't the only one.

She took his hand in hers as he stood to go, gave him a smile of reassurance. And in return, he kissed her lightly on the forehead.

She'd imagined an entirely different end to the evening.

16

Anna's weekend leave was almost over, and it hadn't turned out as she'd expected. But then life had a way of taking you down a different route to the one you'd planned.

She'd spent some of it in a hotel room by herself. The room Jimmy had booked for her was pretty and she'd had the luxury of a bath, but she wished he hadn't paid for it. She could have done that for herself, and it made it harder to be angry with him – not that she *was*. Disappointed, maybe, and a little hurt that he had left so soon. Still, she couldn't find it in her heart to be upset with him, not when she pictured the dismal look on his face when he'd had to leave. And when she thought back to those few hours they'd had together, she could feel herself smile. There had been moments of joy, times when she'd felt elated: that long lingering embrace in the moonlight was one, and when he'd pinned on her sweetheart brooch. And the pair of them drinking wine and laughing and joking together in the restaurant. Those were pleasures she'd remember and take back with her to the bleak, grim building she now called home.

The station platform was crowded, with people pushing to the front, ready to make a dash for any empty seats when the train finally pulled in. It was already half an hour past its timetabled arrival. Stockport was an important station for people taking onward connections, but the hold-ups could make changing trains a trial. On the way there, Anna had seen a soldier jump from one train as it slowed down and hurtle wildly towards another at full speed. *Who said the war didn't have its funny side?*

Not that it was funny right now. The cold was beginning to seep through her, despite her greatcoat. Her eyes moved down to her sweetheart pin on the lapel. It was still there. She touched it and reminded herself exactly what it meant – why Jimmy had pinned it on. He had called her his girl. His *only* girl, although why he felt the need to tell her that, she wasn't sure. Unless he was trying to reassure her after that business with his sister Alice.

'Train's on its way,' she heard the station guard shout. It seemed to Anna there was relief in the man's voice, for he'd been in the firing line, an easy target for complaints.

There was a general shuffling in the crowd as people picked up suitcases and shouldered kit bags; folks like her, grateful for having had a spell of leave or a weekend pass.

That's when she spotted him, making his way towards her, a look of hope on his face.

'Thank God I'm not too late,' Jimmy said, breathlessly.

'You made it,' she said, relieved. 'I'm so happy you did. I'd have hated to go without saying goodbye but we're lucky the train was delayed.'

'Then I'm lucky and grateful, too,' he said.

'Oh? And why might that be?' she gently teased him.

'Because I've got an incredible girl like you.'

'Incredible? Yes, that's true,' she agreed. 'And under-standing and patient and long-suffering. You left me on my own last night with that awful pie.'

'I know and I'm sorry. If it helps, I was miserable, too. Forgive me?'

She wrinkled her brow, plastering a stern look on her face as if she was thinking it over, although she'd already made up her mind. 'You're forgiven,' she said and finally smiled, pulling him in closer and wrapping her arms around him tightly. She kissed him lightly on the cheek before she let him go.

'You *are* still my girl, then? I was worried I'd lost you. That I'd never see you again. I'm moving on, you see. We'll be heading out soon,' he said, suddenly serious.

'I'm still your girl.' She pointed to the twinkling brooch on her lapel. 'Unless you've changed your mind.'

'Why would I do that when I've got the best woman in the world?'

'And Freddy?' she asked.

'Freddy can get his own girl,' he said, and laughed.

'But is he okay? Did you get to him in time?'

'Freddy's an arse, pardon my French. He came off the bike, got a few scratches – less than he deserved – but he'll be fine. And we managed to keep him out of the guardhouse.'

'So, my sacrifice wasn't in vain,' Anna said.

She didn't hear his reply. It was drowned out by the sound of a train whistle and a loud hiss of steam and billowing coal smoke as the train pulled in with a rush of air and brakes.

'Keep back from the edge of the platform, please,' the guard shouted, trying to stem the inevitable rush towards the train.

She shouldered her bag and gas mask and followed Jimmy as he pushed a way through the throng of anxious passengers. He spread his arms wide, creating a corridor for her to get to the front of the platform as he nudged people aside. *Like Moses*, she thought, bizarrely, *clearing a passage through the Red Sea.*

Before they could even kiss goodbye, she was carried in through the open carriage door on a wave of jostling bodies. She got a window seat in the nearest compartment, a small miracle, and it was all down to him. *My hero*, she thought, and looked at him out there. Standing strong. Smiling. Being brave, as if it was just another day and not a sad departure. He blew her an extravagant kiss as Anna waved a final goodbye.

'Your young man, is it?' asked the woman squashed in next to her.

'He is,' Anna said, feeling proud. 'He's in the air force.'

'You too, from what I can see. WAAF, ain't you? Must be nice.'

'What must be?' asked Anna, distracted. She didn't want to chat. Didn't want to waste a single minute; time when she could be looking at Jimmy, greedily savouring the last glimpses before the journey robbed her of him.

'Being together, like. 'Spect that's really nice. Having a bloke what understands you. You're lucky, 'cause they ain't *all* like that,' the woman said, with feeling. As if she'd had first-hand knowledge of the other kind.

'You're right,' Anna admitted. 'I *am* lucky.' Her tone was much softer now, as her sympathy for the older woman came to the fore. She studied the face beside her with its lines of worry, and perhaps even sadness, etched into it. Some people had a life touched by hardship and woe, and yet somehow managed to face trouble cheerfully. Struggled on without much complaint. It said a lot for the courage of the human spirit. It was a humbling notion, Anna thought, and optimistic. *With people like this woman around, Hitler and his cronies didn't stand a chance.*

Her gaze returned to Jimmy, still standing doggedly on the platform to the very last minute, waiting for her train to leave. She saw his wonderful smile, watched his lips move, but she couldn't hear what he said and he did a strange mime, moving his hands quickly through the air.

'I think he wants you to put the window down,' the woman beside her said.

Anna pulled hard on the brown leather strap and lowered the window all the way, holding it down by pushing the hole in the strap over the metal stud at the bottom of the frame. A sign warned her about the danger of leaning out of an open window, but she didn't care: she wanted to know what he'd said.

The guard blew his whistle and waved his green flag, and the train began to slowly move forward. Coal smoke belched out, some of it drifted into her eyes, until they stung and watered, but still she didn't retreat.

'We should get married,' Jimmy called again.

'What?' She watched as he ran to keep up with her carriage. She could hardly believe what she'd heard. And why now—? At the very last minute when she was on her way back. When she didn't have time to think it through.

'Marry me!' he shouted at the top of his lungs.

'I'll write to you,' said Anna.

'I will too, and I'll get you a proper ring,' he promised. 'So...?'

The train finally picked up speed and the last glimpse she had of him was an anxious face and a flash of ginger hair.

She pulled the window up again and collapsed into the seat. She was exhausted, her body aching and her jelly-like legs shaking as if they'd been on a route march. But it wasn't just physical; her emotions were all over the place. She took a deep breath and fought hard to bring them under control. *She should feel happy, elated even – well, shouldn't she? He'd just asked her to marry him.* Perhaps it was the suddenness, she told herself. Coming out of the blue like that. It was a leap, an unexpected step up from wearing his pin and being *his girl* – to being a wife.

She felt a little as if she was becoming someone else's property.

'It ain't my place, I don't suppose,' whispered the woman beside her, 'but you didn't say yes.'

'No,' she said, 'I didn't.'

'But you pair look right fond of each other. Not that's it's my business.'

'What's your name?' Anna asked, kindly.

'Ida – Ida Norman. Very pleased to meet you, I'm sure.' She stuck out her hand and Anna shook it.

'I'm Anna Golding, and the pleasure's all mine,' she said, warmly. 'And you're wrong, you know.'

'I am?' said Ida, surprised.

'*Fond*, you said. But it's more than that. I believe I'm in love, and he said he is too. You see this?' Anna asked, touching the brooch on her lapel.

'Very pretty,' said Ida, eyeing the sweetheart pin.

'It means I'm his girl – and it makes me proud. He's a fine chap.'

'Well then, what's the problem? If you're in love with him, why can't you get married?'

'It's not that we *can't* get married,' Anna replied, still struggling to understand her feelings, 'but he didn't give me time to think. He caught me off guard, and you heard how he said it!'

'How's that?'

'He said "we should get married" – *should*, like he only asked because that's what he's expected to do,' she explained.

'So? He ain't good with words,' said Ida. 'Not many blokes are.'

Anna thought about that. And in a way it was true. Finding the right words didn't come easily to him. But that was part of who he was, she thought: his charm, his honest character; surely she couldn't blame him for that?

Anna patted the older woman's hand. 'You're right, of course. Chaps have to hide their feelings. I suppose we do that to them – women. Maybe they need to seem strong because that's what we expect of them.'

A loud, exaggerated cough came from the corner of the compartment, and she looked across to see a man in an army uniform raise his eyebrows at her. He wasn't the only one staring at her, and she felt herself blush when she realised that she'd been sitting there discussing her private life in front of all these strangers.

She remembered something Ruby, Edna's mother, had told her. Anna had been sad and lonely and terribly unhappy when she'd first arrived in Watford. She'd been cast aside by her father and ended up at Aunt Beatrice's house among strangers. Ruby had been kind; had explained all about strangers. *Strangers*, she'd said, *are only friends we haven't yet met*. It was a phrase she'd heard often since then, and, while it might not always be true, Anna thought, at least it made her smile.

17

PECKHAM, LONDON

15 MARCH 1940

The ordeal of the final exam was over. Anna had been expecting something different; that it would be her and her friends together in their familiar classroom, taking comfort from each other during the last, crucial test. But it had been far more nerve-wracking than that.

She'd been the first of them to take it, which had sent her stomach into a queasy spin. She'd been marched to an unfamiliar place, had to face a serious-looking panel of senior WAAF officers who'd fired questions at her, their faces stony. She'd imagined she'd sit at a desk, read an exam paper and have time to think about her answers, but it all had to be done in her head, nothing written down, thinking on the spot. Standing to attention the whole time while the officers sat.

The examiners had quizzed her on the procedures she'd been taught over the last three months. It seemed to Anna that they were out to trip her up, to make her panic. But she stayed calm. They suggested scenarios where things went wrong in some mythical operations room where Anna was a plotter – and then waited expectantly for her to come up with solutions.

She couldn't remember much about her replies, or even if she'd directed some poor pilot into the sea instead of guiding him safely to land. But she must have done well, because at the end of the ordeal, one of the officers had finally smiled and told her she had passed. Mary had passed, as well. But only eight of the other WAAFs had made it through. Ten of them out of their class of twenty would go on to be plotters at RAF stations. It made her realise how tough the standards were and grateful that the hard work and study both she and Mary had put in had paid off.

'You're very quiet – though I can hear your brain knocking from here,' Mary said now, walking beside her.

'Just wondered how much farther it was,' Anna lied.

'Nearly there,' said her friend, cheerfully.

After the pressure of the last weeks, Anna thought this leave might have been some sort of relief; but it wasn't. It put her on edge. It was being back in London again, she supposed; a place that held memories – good and bad. And she didn't feel right about pushing in at Mary's house, although that had been her friend's idea. They were to have a week of enjoying themselves for a change, Mary had said – going to the cinema, visiting a restaurant that served real food... It had sounded enticing, and they had to report to Adastral House in London, anyway, to pick up the paperwork for a new posting, so it was practical as well.

Neither of them had a clue where they might end up, but Anna hoped they'd still be together.

'I still feel bad – barging in like this,' Anna said.

'Well, I wasn't going to let you mope on your own in some dingy hostel for your whole leave,' said Mary.

'I'm a big girl, Mary,' Anna said and smiled. 'I'd have been okay. And I wouldn't have moped.'

'I know, but...'

'Your mother and father have been incredibly kind to invite me, but this is a family time, and they don't even know me.' *All the same, she was very grateful that her friend had asked her to stay.*

'Never mind all that – they'll be thrilled to see you.'

'Yes, but it's *you* they want to see. They'll be celebrating that you've passed your exams,' she said.

'You too! Imagine that,' said Mary. 'Both of us plotters now.'

Anna smiled. Of course she was thrilled that she'd passed her final exam, but no one would be celebrating *her* achievement. She tried to imagine Aunt Beatrice congratulating her on her success. Not that she'd planned to go back there. She'd been banned from returning, after all.

'You'll love my ma,' said Mary, 'and she'll love you too.'

'Will she, though – when she finds out I broke her son's heart?' Anna asked.

'Thought we'd finished with all that. And you hardly broke his heart, did you? He's still writing to you. You're still his girl.'

'He seemed fine,' Anna agreed.

Secretly, she thought that maybe Jimmy was relieved she hadn't said yes right away. His proposal had struck her as a spur-of-the-moment notion on his part. Her train had been pulling out and perhaps he'd felt sad. Maybe a little guilty too, for leaving her the night before. She'd written, tried to explain. Told him that, although she hadn't said YES, she hadn't rejected him. If she were to marry anyone, then it would be him, she'd said – *just not yet*. She wasn't convinced wartime marriages were a good thing, when no one knew what would happen next.

She felt Mary tug at her hand. 'Look over there.' Her friend's words were breathless, excited.

'What am I looking at?'

'The steeple. See that great steeple in the distance—? That's St Luke's church, and it's practically in our back garden.'

Anna rushed to keep up as Mary picked up the pace. She tried to imagine how she'd feel if it was Aunt Beatrice's large house in Watford they had spotted, instead of a modest home in Peckham, where a boisterous, loving family lived. If the situation had been reversed, would Beatrice have opened her home and her heart as readily to a friend of Anna's; especially one she would surely have considered working-class and beneath her? The answer was obvious to Anna. Her aunt *had* no heart or humanity. It made her feel ashamed.

'You can call me Glad,' said Mary's mother, as she welcomed Anna with a beaming grin.

'If you're sure, Mrs Armstrong,' Anna said.

''Course I am. You been good to my Mary, I'm glad to have you here.'

'Glad's *glad*,' sniggered Mary.

'Oh, very sharp, I'm sure,' Gladys Armstrong told her daughter.

But Anna noted the woman laughed all the same. As far as she could tell, Mary's mother was the power behind the door of 21, Lidgate Street. The woman was a bundle of energy, tall and thin, like a whippet, she thought, ready to spring into action. With a pleasant, kind face too, marked with a sprinkling of life's troubles, perhaps, but eyes that still sparked with fun. She reminded Anna of Jimmy – her hair was the same ginger colour, except his mother's had a few liberal streaks of grey salted throughout. And when Anna watched the cheeky grin on Glad's face, she could see where Jimmy got his humour from.

'Now, you girls go and get settled in. I've sorted out Alice's old bedroom for you, Anna.'

'*Girls?* You know we two *ladies* practically run the air force, don't you, Ma?' said Mary, smugly.

'Is that so? Well, in this house there's only one *lady* in charge, and that's me. So, get yerself up them stairs, Mary Armstrong. You ain't too big to be put over me knee,' said Gladys.

Anna watched her friend smile but, even so, they both headed smartly for the stairs.

Her room was homely, and very different to the bedroom Anna had grown up in. But she would happily have swapped her room in Aunt Beatrice's fancy townhouse for this one any day. There was a homemade knotted rug on the floor, made from all kinds of random odds and ends of colourful material and a crocheted bedspread that looked to Anna like a labour of love. It must have taken a long time to make. The wallpaper was covered in massive, cabbage roses, so pretty that she went over and touched them. A matching porcelain set of washing bowl and jug stood on the sideboard – she wondered if it was some kind of family heirloom.

When she'd unpacked her few belongings, she went along the hall to Mary's room. It was smaller than the one she had.

'I love your mother, you were right,' Anna said.

'Said so, didn't I?' said Mary.

'She looks well, full of life. Not a bit frail,' she added.

'Frail? Oh, you mean that thing with Alice when she told Jimmy that Ma was getting feeble?' Mary smiled. 'If you met my sister, you'd understand that Alice can be dramatic – and she likes to be in charge. There's not a thing wrong with Ma, I'm glad to say.'

'That's brilliant news. And why did I get a bedroom all to myself when you've got two beds squeezed in here?' Anna asked.

'Alice isn't coming for the party, so I guess Ma thought she'd give you a bit of space.'

'Party?' Anna said. 'There's a party planned?'

'Tomorrow night. Ma loves to put on a party and now I've

passed my exams, she's got an excuse. Not that she's ever needed one, mind. So – what now?' asked Mary.

'I was hoping we could sort out our new orders first. Get this stuff at the Air Ministry out of the way, then we'll have the rest of our leave free. Maybe we could get a bus to Kingsway. They still have buses running here, I suppose,' said Anna.

'If you could get a bus in Stockport, we should be able to catch one here.'

As they left the streets of Peckham for the bustling West End, Anna had another thought in mind: to take a shot at two birds with the same stone. The Air Ministry at Adastral House was where they had to pick up their papers and travel warrants, and it was also where Jane Walker worked. Or at least where Anna had been told to send her letter. She'd try to track down the woman and put an end to this unnerving mystery. Her mind needed to be free to concentrate on more important things. Her new job was one – and the man who filled her mind, as well as her heart: Jimmy Armstrong. A very special man, a man whose pin she wore. She thought about him constantly, about his marriage proposal and what it would mean to be with him every day, taking whatever life threw at them. She remembered one of his letters when he'd said that he would always be true to her in both good times and bad. It was the closest he'd come to a love letter and she cherished it. 'He could think of nothing that would make him happier than to have her by his side,' he'd told her. She felt exactly the same and the only thing that was holding her back was the thought of marrying in the middle of a war – when everything felt so temporary, and no one could be sure what the future held.

But when this grim war was over, she'd be happy to marry him, for them to be joined together. Hand in hand through life. If she were to be *anybody*'s wife, it would be his. Jimmy under- stood her. When she looked in his eyes, she could see his heart written there. It said he loved her. He wouldn't want to own her, not like some chaps might. Theirs would be a marriage of equals.

18

They leaned on each other for support. It was what friends did when things went wrong – when the news was bad.

Anna had argued with the RAF clerk who'd handed them their orders, had pointed out that a mistake had been made. It was wartime, things were done in haste, mistakes were a normal part of life. *She wasn't blaming anyone*, she'd told the young man. But she would stay there in his office until he got it sorted out.

The pair of them had passed the same plotters' course, no one could argue with that – it was written in their records. The RAF was split into three sections: Fighter Command, Bomber Command and Coastal Command. But while Anna had been assigned to a high-profile Fighter Command station called Biggin Hill, close to London, Mary was posted to a Bomber Command aerodrome up in Lincolnshire, almost two hundred miles away.

Anna had read the tiredness and resignation in the young airman's face. He'd left them sitting in the tiny office cubicle and had gone to make tea. A peace offering, she realised, but tea couldn't fix everything in life. Still, it was a start.

When she looked at Mary, she could see the shock on her friend's white face and reached out to take her hand.

'They'll have to change it,' said Mary, her voice tense with emotion. 'We can't be separated like this. I need you here beside me, or I won't survive.'

Anna put a comforting arm around her friend. 'You're a strong, determined woman, Mary Armstrong,' she said. 'Of course you'll survive. Just look at what you've done so far.'

'You don't think he'll change it, do you?'

'He seems like a nice young chap, but I don't think he can. He probably won't even try – he knows how these things work,' said Anna.

'God, no! What will we do?'

Anna smiled. 'We'll be the same skilled and extraordinary women that we've always been. Cheerful, confident. We'll stay calm and carry on. We're in the WAAF. It's what we do!'

They didn't wait for the tea. Anna felt a little shabby about leaving the poor young airman in the lurch, but it wasn't helping, staying there. Mary needed a distraction, so Anna linked arms with her friend and marched them both out of the building, their heads held high.

'Where we off to?' asked Mary, as they walked briskly through the busy London streets.

'We're heading for the Strand. I'm taking you to lunch – my treat,' Anna said.

'We're eating at The Savoy?' asked Mary, perking up.

'The Savoy Hotel!' spluttered Anna. 'Do you think I'm made of money? Lyons Corner House awaits your pleasure, ma'am.' She removed her cap and gestured towards the end of Kingsway and the treasures that lay ahead. Steak and kidney pie, *if they were lucky*, or real bangers and mash. Or maybe just the same old Spam, Anna thought. Or, if they turned out to be truly unlucky, that awful rubbery whale meat the Ministry of Food was encouraging people to buy. Either way, it didn't matter, because her friend beside her had finally smiled. That was worth even giving whale meat a try.

Ten minutes later, they were both tucking into a magnificent leek and potato pie, made from real potatoes – and there was even some cheese in there, Anna noted, though how the cooks managed it was a puzzle when everybody you spoke to complained about rationing starting to bite.

'You never asked in there about that woman, Jane wots-her-name,' said Mary.

'Forgot – with the shock we both had. It went right out of my head,' Anna replied. It wasn't quite true. She'd thought a speedy retreat better for her friend, but she didn't want Mary to feel guilty on top of everything else. Finding out about Jane Walker would just have to wait – it had waited this long already.

'It was a shock for you as well?' asked Mary, surprised.

'I wasn't expecting Biggin Hill. I'd swap it for your RAF Binbrook any day,' she said.

'But so close to London – you can travel in on your leave.'

'Too close for comfort to...' She trailed off.

'To what – or whom?' Mary asked.

'Never mind, it's not important,' said Anna.

'One favour you could do for me, if you don't mind, is to keep an eye on Ma. You'll be much nearer to my family than I'll be now.'

'Absolutely. If she won't mind me getting in the way,' said Mary.

'Told you before, she thinks you're great.'

'Even though I wouldn't marry her son.' Anna frowned.

'Don't suppose she even knows he asked you. Jimmy won't have told her. Talking about which – there's something you should know.'

．　．　．

The *something* turned out to be special. Jimmy was coming home for tomorrow night's party – or as Glad Armstrong had called it, *a proper shindig*, like the good old days when the family had all got together.

Anna thought about the surprise her friend had planned for her ma and she was glad. The family would be happy, she knew.

She was happy too, to have a chance to see Jimmy again after their last hasty goodbye at the station. But she worried a little that she would spoil the celebration with a drama, or maybe even tears. Jimmy could bring out powerful feelings in her and she didn't want to make an idiot of herself. Not in front of his family.

Excited and happy and carefree, that's how he often made her feel. And, sometimes, there were those intense moments – like when he touched her or put his lips on hers. That's when her body felt truly alive, shivers of anticipation moving through it in ripples that seemed to vibrate every nerve. *Passion*, she supposed. It had been a new sensation, like visiting an unknown land. She remembered pulling away from his embrace that night in the moonlight, but promised herself that next time she wouldn't let fear get in the way.

She imagined his voice in her head, warm and friendly, with that edge of his London roots still fiercely clinging to it. She liked his voice. She pictured the unruly red hair, his wide grin, and the laugh that made strangers stare. She loved that laugh and how he could make her laugh as well with his silly jokes and stories.

It was the simple things they'd done together that she especially loved. She'd never been happier than the times they'd cycled on the tandem. Pedalling through the countryside, the sun on her face, trusting the man in front of her to steer them safely. Their captain, that's what he'd said, and she was their tail-gunner. An important job. She kept them grounded and balanced. Maybe that was how it would always be. She liked the idea.

She wondered what had happened to Daisy, their trusty and loyal steed, when Jimmy had moved on to his new posting. She hated to think of their quirky old bike rusting away. Not that much was allowed to sit and rust now. There wasn't an ounce of scrap metal going to waste. Poor old Daisy might already have been on her way to a collection centre somewhere. It was strange to think that, just like her and Jimmy, Daisy might too be doing her bit for the war effort.

'Hey, you still in there?' Mary shouted through the bedroom door.

Anna looked around Alice's old room. She'd been sitting on the bed, reminiscing about pleasant times, and had forgotten her promise to Mary that she'd come down to the parlour 'in a jiff'. More than a jiff had passed.

'On my way,' she said. 'See you in a jiff.'

She could hear Mary's laugh. 'You said that before! Come down now. Ma's doing toast and her famous blackberry and apple pie. You'll not want to miss it, it's scrummy. And then we're playing games.'

Anna pulled on a jumper and opened the door. 'You're doing what?' she asked.

'Playing board games or card games. We all have to join in – you too. No one escapes.'

Anna smiled. 'And I wouldn't want to.' She couldn't stop smiling, a massive grin fixing itself to her face. *How brilliant. What a wonderful place to be!*

They played Ludo: Anna, Mary and Glad, making up comical new rules as they went along and giggling together like giddy schoolgirls. Then Mary's father, Harry, arrived home from his training with the Red Cross volunteers. His manner was gruff, but Anna suspected there was more to him than that, for she noticed the way he smiled at his wife and patted her hand in thanks when she gave him his tea.

'Ma, let's have a bit of a sing-song,' Harry said, his mouth still crammed full of pie.

'Like we used to,' said Glad, delighted.

'Ma – you wouldn't!' said Mary, squirming with embarrassment.

'Why not? Time we had some fun again.'

'Yes, but we got company!' Mary said.

'Anna ain't company – she's one of us,' said Glad, 'and I expect she'd enjoy a bit of a singalong. And Da's got such a fine, bass voice. Pity to let it go to waste.'

Anna watched Harry nod and smile. Whether that was because of the compliment or he just loved to sing, it was hard to tell. She guessed Mary's father was much older than his wife. They looked like opposites, but they seemed to fit together fine. There was deep affection between them, she could tell. Something in the way they looked at each other, in the way Gladys held her husband's hand with a fondness that spoke of a lifetime together. She imagined how that life might have been, with good times and hard times, built on a foundation of love – quiet and steady, not dramatic maybe, but always there.

And a singalong – who'd have guessed? Then she remembered what Jimmy had told her about all those rowdy, chaotic celebrations with this old house packed to the rafters. They seemed the kind of family who could happily make their own fun and enjoy themselves by doing simple things. Anna could understand. It was the sort of family life she had longed to have. Being accepted as one of their own brought a film of tears to her eyes: sentimental, happy tears – the very best kind.

At first, the only voices raised in song were those of Harry and Glad. Mary's mother was right, Anna thought, Harry certainly had a booming bass voice, powerful and robust for a small, rotund man who looked on the elderly side. Glad's voice was high, with a tremulous vibrato that rattled the teacups on the shelf.

Anna was enthralled and although she didn't think herself a singer, their enthusiasm was catching, and she found herself joining in. Even her friend finally gave way, adding a wobbly contralto to the mix. It got louder in the small parlour, the noise swelling to a crescendo, the walls echoing to the cheerful songs until everyone was smiling.

The impromptu concert had already moved through a repertoire of World War One songs when there was a very loud knock on the front door. In a way it was a relief for Anna when Harry Armstrong went to open it. She'd enjoyed the sing-song, of course, but now that they were singing 'Wish Me Luck As You Wave Me Goodbye', she'd found it hard to stop her lip from trembling. Next thing, she'd be blubbing away, for she'd immediately thought of Jimmy going off to war and the danger his job would put him in. She felt suddenly ice-cold as an unreasonable fear took hold of her and an image of him falling from a burning plane and spiralling into the ocean repeated over and over in her head.

'Well, you lot seem to be enjoying yourselves,' said Jimmy himself, as he bowled through the door.

'My lovely boy!' Glad said, clapping her hands. 'What a terrific surprise.'

'Didn't tell you, Ma,' said Mary, 'in case he couldn't make it.'

'Well, this calls for a real celebration. Get the sherry out, Da,' ordered Glad.

'You're just in time to join us for a song,' said Harry.

'Now you know I've got a voice like a bullfrog with a head cold,' Jimmy said, looking over at Anna with a wide grin on his face.

'A cinder trapped under a door,' Mary confirmed.

Anna stared at him, tears suddenly streaming down her face. That horrific image of him tumbling from the sky was still lodged in her mind. She couldn't seem to shift it.

'Here, here, what's this now?' Jimmy asked, rushing to her side.

She tried to smile, to talk, but all she could do was sob in this pathetic way. She took a deep, shuddering breath as he picked her up in his arms and hugged her closely.

'I'm sorry,' she whispered at last.

'What for?' he asked.

'For being so feeble. It's just that I thought you were gone,' Anna said.

'Gone? Of course I'm not gone, you silly goose! You're still wearing my pin, aren't you?'

'I am,' she assured him, and managed a wistful smile.

'Well, I never! Fancy that. You two already know each other,' said Gladys Armstrong. She folded her thin arms across her best pinny, looked at her hubby and winked.

Anna drank more of the sherry than she should have done but she wasn't the only one to get merry. Mary's mother had taken a glass or two as well and was helped upstairs to bed while singing some sentimental tune that Anna hadn't heard before.

Soon it was just her and Jimmy alone in the parlour, snuggling up together on the threadbare sofa. The dim light from the standard lamp sent a soft glow across the room. It was warm and cosy with the fire still in, and although she felt drowsy, she couldn't bear to drag herself away to go to bed. The bedroom had been cold, but it wasn't just that; she didn't want to break the romantic mood.

She could see that Jimmy felt the same. She wanted his arms around her like this forever, to never let go. The outside world was far off now, and Anna wanted to keep it like that as he gently stroked her face. Then he kissed her in a way he had never kissed her until now: not just on the lips this time, like before, but with his tongue tenderly exploring inside her mouth. It felt strange, at first, but then it seemed to tap into something primitive and raw in her, something waiting to be released – an urge hidden deep. So, she answered it, meeting his probing tongue with hers. She heard a small moan of pleasure, wasn't sure if it came from Jimmy or from her.

It was her.

Was this love, or romance, or was it simply lust? She was confused, but she wanted to find out. To see what happened next. Her head reeled when she realised this could be the night when she fully became a woman.

That's when the ceiling light came on and she saw Mary standing in the doorway.

'Sorry,' said Mary, looking flustered.

Anna wrestled with her jumper, while Jimmy straightened his tousled hair.

'Yes?' asked Jimmy.

'Thought I left my book in here,' Mary said, 'though maybe I was wrong.'

'This it, sis?' he asked, pulling it out from behind a cushion.

When his sister had fled and closed the door, Jimmy said, 'Maybe it's for the best.'

'What's that mean?' asked Anna, thrown off balance.

'What it means is – I love you, and maybe we should save this for another time when we haven't been drinking and we're absolutely sure.'

'I *am* sure,' said Anna.

'I know you think that now, in the heat of passion, but I don't want to force you into something you might regret, and I don't want you to get into trouble.'

'Trouble – what trouble?' she asked.

'You know,' he said, embarrassed now. 'Unforeseen circumstances.'

'Unforeseen... ah. The patter of little feet, you mean.'

'Exactly. I know you love the WAAF, and I wouldn't want you to have to leave because of me,' said Jimmy.

'Don't you think that's my decision as well as yours?' said Anna.

'Of course, but...'

'Still, maybe you're right and your mother's parlour may not be the ideal place,' she said. She smiled, took his hand in hers. 'We'll save it for the perfect time,' she promised.

'Have I told you how incredible you are?' asked Jimmy.

'Not for a while.' She laughed.

'Well, you are. But we should get to bed now, I suppose. Big day tomorrow. What with Ma's celebration shindig. And Anna...?'

'What?' she asked him.

'Promise me you'll think about what I said before – at least about getting a transfer down to Cornwall. We'd be closer to each other, we could meet.'

'I'd like that, though I can hardly put in for a transfer the minute I get to Biggin Hill. You know how it goes, it doesn't work that way. But I'll try.'

'And the other thing?' he asked.

'Getting married, you mean?' said Anna.

'I won't rush you into anything. I understand how you feel about wartime marriages, but we could have a long engagement. And one thing I promise...'

'What's that?' she asked. *People promised lots of things, but they didn't always come true.*

'I promise I will always, *always* be faithful – and treasure you,' he said, earnestly.

She looked deep into his eyes, remembered what the

woman on the train had told her – that it was hard for the eyes to lie. She believed in his fidelity – that his promise was real.

'But I'm already your girl and I'm wearing your pin.'

'I really do love you, you know. I want to spend my life with you. But I need you to be sure and I'll wait for you, no matter how long it takes. Whenever you're ready, you only have to say. I've already got a ring,' he said.

'I love you too. But let's wait and see – about the ring,' she said.

'The woman says she loves me!' Jimmy shouted at the top of his voice.

'Shush! You'll wake everybody in the house,' she said, and put a finger to his lips.

'I don't care. She loves me!' he shouted again.

'Of course I love you. What did you think?' she whispered.

'I think it's a wonderful world,' said Jimmy, as he scooped her up in his arms, planted a hungry kiss on her lips and carried her gallantly up the stairs.

PART TWO

19

RAF BIGGIN HILL, BROMLEY

23 JUNE 1940

Anna had fallen into bed at the end of her shift, exhausted. But she hadn't been able to sleep. There was far too much going on in her head. Soon, she would report for duty again in the operations room, but before that, all WAAFs had been told to assemble in front of one of the hangers. Some kind of pep talk, she supposed.

But that was still half an hour away, so there was time to read Jimmy's letter again. To hold it close to her face and breathe in the scent of him. She could swear she smelled his musk – an earthy, manly, and sometimes woody smell. It was a comfort to her, made her feel closer to him.

Months had gone by since she'd seen him, since they'd lain together in each other's arms. She missed him with a terrible ache that often consumed her, even though she tried to ignore it. The war wasn't going well; she needed to concentrate on her job. Just like him.

Jimmy's letters had become less cheerful than they used to be and she could see that he was losing heart. He was still at the same RAF station he'd been posted to in Cornwall, a place called St Eval. He couldn't say what he was doing there, but she could read between the lines, could sense his frustration – with the war and his part in it, but also with their separation.

Being wrenched apart from that one special person in your life was a profound pain, a kind of grief, she thought. And they shared it, but they weren't the only ones. One of the WAAFs in her section had married her boyfriend last week before he was posted overseas. The wedding had been arranged in a day and the girl had moved swiftly from girlfriend to wife, with a marriage in the morning and a honeymoon in the afternoon. The pair had no idea how long their parting would be, yet the WAAF seemed supremely happy. It had given Anna pause for thought – and several sleepless nights.

She came to an important conclusion: she'd been *wrong*. Of course Jimmy and she should be married as soon as they were able. She would write and tell him so, tell him to keep that ring safe for her. She'd been lucky enough to find a man who loved her, and she loved him in return. The longer she thought about becoming his wife, the more sense it made to her. It was an investment in their love. Something positive – *especially* in times like these, when nothing else was sure.

She'd thought the opposite before, believed that with the uncertainty of war it was foolish to make long-term plans. But that wasn't true: when everything looked bad, that's *exactly* when you needed to be optimistic about the future – to plan for it, make commitments and be ready for whatever challenge came your way.

Challenges had been coming from every direction lately. The Phoney War was over now, and at the start of May, Hitler's army had begun its invasion of the Low Countries – Holland, Belgium and Luxembourg, before moving on to France. The very same day, the prime minister, Neville Chamberlain, had resigned, and Winston Churchill had taken over. He seemed a better choice, at least in Anna's mind. Strong, determined, fearless – a British bulldog, and he would need to be. Things were looking grim, with the British Expeditionary Force across the Channel barely holding on. Thousands of them had been trapped at a place in northern France; but what had started out a disaster had turned into a magnificent display of courage, when hundreds of small boats crewed by civilian volunteers had sailed across the Channel; had ferried the soldiers out from the beaches of Dunkirk to larger ships. Over 330,000 Allied troops had been evacuated. Saved. Torn from Hitler's greedy grasp.

Anna was so proud of her country, of the bravery and fortitude of her fellow countrymen and women. Even in some of their darkest hours they could still stand up and fight. At Biggin Hill, the pace had been frantic and unrelenting during those days in May and the Dunkirk evacuation. None of them had slept for days, whether they were fighter pilots constantly patrolling over the Dunkirk beaches, or WAAFs, like her, in Biggin's sector operations room. They'd all been exhausted, but gratified, that so many of the weary and battered soldiers had been lifted to safety, were now home on their native soil. She had played her own small part in that.

Anna had learned a lot during that harsh week. Mostly, that she was far too busy to be frightened and could just get on with the job in hand, relaying radar plots that came in over her headphones onto plaques that she would move across the huge ops room map. Her hand didn't even shake as she moved her plotting rod across the board to plot all the aircraft in her particular sector. Mostly they were *friendlies*, often even pilots she knew from the base. But sometimes they were *hostiles*, what the controller – up in the gallery high above the giant map – called *bandits*. That seemed a better name for those enemy fliers, Anna felt. The controller would read the information represented on the plotters' map below him and phone through warnings of the impending attacks to the different towns and airfields. They all worked together as a team in the ops room, but the plotters' jobs were vital.

Because of its closeness to important targets in London, Biggin was a crucial aerodrome – a controlling station for number 11 group, Fighter Command. If the German Luftwaffe decided to bomb British cities, as they had with other places like Poland and poor old Rotterdam, then a frontline station like Biggin Hill would be in a perfect place for the defence of London. Though it might also be a dangerous place to be.

But that was in the future, thought Anna, and you couldn't worry about things that hadn't happened yet, not when there was something else to concentrate on. Like being on time for this pep talk from their fastidious WAAF leader, Flight Officer Kemp. *She who must be obeyed.* That's what the WAAFs had nicknamed her, but only behind her back, of course. F/O Kemp was a stickler for spit and polish and doing things the 'air force way'. If any WAAFs should talk on parade, they'd end up getting lots of practice peeling spuds in the cookhouse. One of the WAAFs had giggled once and ended up cleaning latrines for a week. Still, Anna had a sneaking respect for the woman, an officer who did her job professionally and wasn't afraid to speak her mind in front of her male colleagues.

Reluctantly, she put down Jimmy's latest letter and got dressed, checking her uniform was spic and span, and that her cap badge shone. War or no war, F/O Kemp made no exceptions for WAAFs who were improperly dressed.

Anna was one of the first to arrive at the hanger and she watched as the officer ran an expert eye over her charges lined up outside in the freezing cold, inspecting their uniforms. Anna hadn't put her greatcoat on and neither had any of the others. The officer liked to see correct uniforms, wouldn't allow her WAAFs to hide shabby or improper dress under the camouflage of a greatcoat. Hopefully, they wouldn't have to stay out in the cold too long. It was June and you'd think it would be warm, but

Biggin was perched on a plateau on top of the North Downs and there always seemed to be a wind blowing.

Anna had been surprised when she arrived at her first proper posting. She wasn't sure exactly what she'd been expecting. Something neat and orderly and perfect, she supposed. Instead, it was a sprawl of huts and offices, messes and barracks, and hangers painted with camouflage beside the concrete runway. It wasn't pretty, but it was a serious place with skilled, determined people prepared to do their duty and protect their country from any enemy who threatened its skies. Not just pilots, but squads of mechanics, riggers and ground crew, radar operators, medical teams and of course WAAFs of every description and trade.

Her attention turned to Flight Officer Kemp, who had just cleared her throat.

''Ten-shun!' the officer ordered.

Anna and the rest of the waiting WAAFs immediately came to attention, standing tall. Silence fell among their ranks.

'I have here an announcement from the station commander, Wing Commander Heath, which I will read. Please pay close attention: this is important information, especially for those of you working in the operations block. Our ops room will be operating around the clock from now on.'

Anna looked at some of her ops room colleagues – they seemed as mystified as she was.

'As most of you will already know, our French allies declared Paris an open city and the German army took control of it on the fourteenth of June.' Flight Officer Kemp looked out into the ranks of women in front of her and carried on. 'What you may *not* know is that yesterday, the twenty-second of June, France capitulated and signed an armistice with Germany. The war is over for our French allies, who have now been occupied. In essence, what this means is that we presently stand alone. *Britain is alone* – and must prepare for an invasion.'

Anna could hear nervous murmurs coming from those around her. An invasion? It was a frightening thought. To be alone! But then, they'd been alone before, she thought. She looked back at the officer. Wondered what the immediate effect on them all here at this frontline aerodrome would be.

'There will be those of you who are expecting twenty-four-hour passes. Some who have already booked leave, and of course you'll be disappointed when I tell you that, for now, all leave and passes are cancelled. But I know you will all do your duty courageously as befits a member of this country's air force. Should any of you require a pass for compassionate reasons, then you may come and see me. My door is open. Now, ladies, return to your duties. Dismissed,' said the officer.

As the gathering broke up, the grumbling began. 'No leave! For how long?' Anna heard someone ask. But it didn't matter, did it?

She had been expecting a twenty-four-hour pass at the end of her shift block that week. Had promised Mary's mother, Glad, that she would visit again soon. Gladys was a fine, good-hearted woman. She'd been kind to Anna, treated her like another daughter, knitted Anna a hat and gloves and made her one of those famous blackberry and apple pies of hers. Anna had carried it back to the barracks as if it were made of glass, delicate and fragile. Her barrack mates had helped devour it.

Glad would be disappointed. Anna felt the same, for she enjoyed the older woman's company – her cheerfulness, the way she'd opened her home and her heart with no thought of anything in return. Yes, she would miss the old lady too. The same way she missed Mary. They'd been through a lot together. Survived those first difficult weeks when they'd joined the WAAF and the hardships of basic training. They'd pulled each other through and grown closer, sat on each other's beds and shared laughs and tears, helped each other study for their exams, and both eaten those awful cabbage sandwiches. They understood each other well. She hoped they could get together soon.

War had a way of scything through friendships, but it was important to keep them alive. She often wondered what had happened to her old friend Edna: she'd written to her several times but not had a single reply in months. She hoped no harm had come to her. Now she and Mary had been parted as well.

But the worst separation of them all was the one that pulled at her heart every time she thought of Jimmy. Except now her heart was in a tug of war – for how could she push for a transfer after that lecture from her commanding officer and the importance of their jobs at Biggin Hill, when the defence of the country would rely on them all? Her country needed her. But Jimmy also needed her. And she needed him.

Whatever it took to keep their love alive through the trials of war, she would do it. Because no one on earth meant more to her than him.

20

RAF ST EVAL, COASTAL COMMAND, CORNWALL

JULY 1940

Jimmy raised his tin mug jovially and smiled. The tea in the mess was good and strong. 'Cheers, come and join the fun,' he said.

'You're chirpy today. Somebody die and leave you a fortune?' asked Freddy.

'I'm always cheerful,' said Jimmy.

'You've been a grumpy beggar since we got here. What's changed?'

'I'm in love,' Jimmy said.

'You've *always* been in love. Far as I can tell, it doesn't do a chap much good. Not if it makes him miserable, like you.'

'I'm not miserable,' he said.

'So, what's happened now?'

'I'm getting married. Anna's finally said yes, and we'll get it done the minute she gets down here.'

'She's coming here? She's got a transfer, then?' Freddy asked.

'I've asked her to, and she's promised she'll try. Any day now I'll be a married man,' he said.

'A mad man!' said Freddy – but he smiled just the same.

'Mad with love. I'm living in a place called ecstasy,' replied Jimmy, with a laugh.

'So long as you don't take us all there with you, old bean,' Freddy said.

'You could do worse. Look at the old man, he's been happily married for years,' said Jimmy.

And it was true, he thought. Andrew, their pilot and the captain of their crew, seemed happy enough, although he never spoke much about his wife. He hadn't brought her with him to St Eval, even though there was decent married housing on the station. He kept that part of his life separate from his job. Maybe it was a survival skill you needed to learn when you tied the knot, Jimmy thought – none of them could afford to be distracted.

He looked at Freddy. Freddy may have been a joker at times, but he was reliable, good at his job. A gunner. The thought brought him back to Anna, his personal – perfectly wonderful – tail-gunner. How he missed those bike rides.

'So...' said Freddy.

'What?'

'You're engaged. Soon to be a married man, eh? The old noose planted firmly around your neck.' Freddy laughed.

'That's me and happy for it.'

'So you said! Just keep your mind on the job. Wouldn't want you getting us lost and having to ditch in the drink. Remember, I can't swim.'

'I remember,' Jimmy said. 'And there's fat chance of us getting lost. Any rookie out of flight school could have plotted the course we've been plodding along up and down the coast. Same old thing every day.'

'Anti-submarine patrols – important all the same,' said

Freddy.

'Yeah, and how many U-boats have we spotted so far? How many torpedoes have we managed to drop? Still, I've a feeling all that's about to change,' Jimmy said.

Freddy changed the subject. 'So – you'll be buying the beers in the mess, tonight?'

'Why not? It's a celebration after all.'

For the first time in months, Jimmy felt himself relax. Once Anna got her transfer to Cornwall, they could get moving on the wedding. It was great news. He thought of how excited his mother would be. She'd want them to organise a proper wedding with all the family joining in, but he wasn't sure how easy that would be. Quickie weddings with everything done and dusted in an hour were all anyone seemed to manage now – with the war banging on their door. His ma would understand. Still, maybe he wouldn't tell her just yet, not till the date was fixed. She seemed to like Anna. But then, who wouldn't? She had a gentle, loving nature as well as that independent feistiness he loved in her. And a sense of humour that matched his. Yes, he'd been lucky: a chance meeting outside RAF Wilmslow had changed his life.

He wondered where Anna might get her new posting. It would be great if she ended up right here at St Eval with Coastal Command, like him. They could see each other every day. But then, maybe that would be hard on them both. She, watching him take off, and worrying that he might not make it back. Out of sight, out of mind might be less stressful. And they'd both need to concentrate on their work; like Freddy had said – anything less could be dangerous.

It was a large, busy station, with three runways constantly in use – although the airfield had been rushed into service so quickly that the place hadn't been levelled off properly, and the main runway rose sharply for its first two hundred yards. The result was the notorious St Eval 'hump', but the pilots soon got used to it and some saw it as a good luck charm, to see them on their way and bring them safely home. An impressive Norman church on the northern edge of the airfield had become a land-mark for returning planes. Jimmy always breathed a sigh of relief when he spotted its friendly tower – a beacon to welcome them back after a mission.

Though it was mainly Coastal Command, St Eval was home to an assortment of squadrons and aircraft. Most of the RAF was represented there. Fighters and bombers used it, and anti-submarine patrols, and photographic and reconnaissance planes took off from its runways, along with meteorological flights. They all worked side by side. But most important of all those, at least to the many aircrew who used the station, were the air-sea rescue crews. Jimmy knew chaps felt easier in their minds knowing that if their kite landed in the Channel or the North Sea and they had to ditch, there'd be a friendly face up there throwing you a life raft or transmitting your position to a rescue launch.

But if Anna didn't end up working at St Eval, there were lots of other aerodromes in Cornwall close by: several Fighter Commands and some bomber stations. She was already working for Fighter Command, so maybe her transfer would take her to Portreath or Perranporth, which were practically on his doorstep.

He thought she would like the county. Cornwall was a beautiful place, so picturesque with its beaches and dramatic cliffs and crystal-clear waters. It was somewhere to make perfect memories, he thought. He could take her to visit Newquay, an enchanting place on the coast, only six miles away. Maybe they could even swim in the sea. Did she swim? Strange he didn't know that, had never asked her – but then they'd talked of other things. He supposed there was lots he didn't know about Anna, the woman he loved. But he would have a lifetime to find out. A lifetime of discovery. What a marvellous thought.

21

RAF BIGGIN HILL

She woke up cold and shaking after a nightmare-ridden sleep; the scream that had been trapped in her head leaking slowly from her throat in a mournful sound. She knew she was awake, but still the terror of the spine-chilling dream had her firmly in its grip. The nightmare was always the same: Jimmy frantically calling her name as he tumbled through the air like a rag doll and plunged into the icy sea below.

She stumbled to the bathroom, locked the door, collapsed to her knees with her head hanging low over the bath. She thought she might be sick, but there was only a dry unproductive heave that left her feeling weak. *She was strong, wasn't she?* Determined and resilient. Fearless! She'd hoped she was all those things. Maybe she was, she told herself, but this fear wasn't for herself, it was for him.

It was the vivid dream that had done it: she'd convinced herself he was off flying into dark, perilous skies, being a hero; that, right now, he was in the gravest danger. Heading for a catastrophe that would take him away from her and his family, from

the people who loved him. Was it too late? Could such a catastrophe be averted?

She bowed her head, clasped her hands tightly in front of
her, their grip rigid to quell the tremor. It had been some time
since she'd prayed, but she threw her heart, head and soul into
it. A plea. She could feel the power of it streaming through her
and reaching out to Jimmy, wherever he might be, whatever the
danger.

'I love you,' she whispered, 'more than my very own life.
Please,' she implored him, her voice growing stronger now, like a
powerful, magical incantation, 'JIMMY, PLEASE – PLEASE
STAY SAFE.'

She raised her head slowly. Her body felt heavy and sluggish as
she pulled herself to her feet and splashed her face with ice-cold
water. Reality tumbled in on top of her. She was on duty today, and
if she didn't get dressed quickly, she'd be late for her shift. It was
sure to be another busy one, for already she could hear squadrons
of fighters taking off and landing. Their crews were exhausted, but
then so too were most of the airmen and airwomen at Biggin Hill,
straining every fibre of their being to do their best, not to give in to
pessimism. Victory was never easy, and it had to be fought hard for.
Spitfires from Biggin had been relentless in their pursuit of the
German bombers and Messerschmitt fighters. Her country was in
a fight for its life now that France had fallen. They were calling it
the Battle of Britain, and it would be fought in the air.

Anna had suspected that all along. Airfields and RAF
stations like Biggin Hill were being attacked daily. It had been
nerve-wracking at first, deep in the operations room, hearing the
scream of enemy aircraft overhead, wondering where the next
bomb would fall. Listening to the fury as runways and hangers
were strafed. Still, Anna had sucked in the fear, done her job
tenaciously and stayed at her post.

Now, once again, she made her way to her place in the ops

room. The ops room was underground. There was one set of stairs to get to the surface. Nothing but ordinary brick walls surrounded them, and should one bomber have a lucky strike, then the operations block and the ops room were as vulnerable a target as any other on the station. It was something she tried not to dwell on; any anxiety of being trapped, unable to make it up the stairs into daylight and fresh air, had to be dismissed, put to the back of her mind. Otherwise, it would be impossible to stay here and work in what the controller affectionately nicknamed 'the hole'.

She forced herself to be calm and listened intently to the stream of numbers coming in over her headphones from the Observer Corps and the WAAFs in their radar station filter rooms. She transferred the numbers and locations of *bandits* and their *friendly* aircraft onto her sector of the giant map in front of her, worked out the vectors and tried not to think about the young pilots behind those numbers. Young men from *both* sides of the war with their lives ahead of them. But some of them wouldn't make it through the day.

Only for a second did she allow herself one small indulgence as she thought again of Jimmy. Conjuring his face in her mind, Anna breathed deeply and prayed with all her will that whatever gods were in charge would keep him in the palm of their hands and bring him safely home.

Anna's morning shift in the ops room had finished two hours ago, but she hadn't gone back to her quarters to sleep. How could you sleep when your nerves jangled from the action and the noise of the screeching planes overhead, and the terrifying crump of bombs when they landed on the runway and buildings exploded around you? They all prayed, sending up secret prayers that the next bomb wouldn't have their name carved on it.

Now, like some of the others on the station who were currently off duty, she was helping to fill in potholes on the runway. Potholes made by Luftwaffe bombers as they tried to obliterate the fighter station. There were gaping, smouldering bomb craters everywhere and some buildings had been completely destroyed. But the thing the bombers had been hoping for – to catch the British fighter planes on the ground before take-off – hadn't happened. Thanks to the miracle of radar, all the pilots had been scrambled in time and had managed to get safely into the air. But, unless the runway craters could be fixed quickly, the planes couldn't return to land and would have to be diverted elsewhere.

She was halfway along the runway when she saw it. At first, she couldn't make out what it was – the pothole was deep, more like a pit, filled with foul-smelling water and debris. But when Anna jumped in to investigate, she saw part of a gas mask holder and a WAAF's cap. That's when she pulled herself out, stumbled over to the grass verge and threw up.

Two of the ground crew jumped into the large hole and started digging frantically, urgently pulling out sharp fragments of stone and rubble with their hands.

'There's somebody down here!' one of them said.

Anna went back to help and was just in time to see one of the chaps shake his head. 'No good,' the man said.

'Don't come any farther,' the other one told her.

'Why not? If it's a WAAF, then I probably know her. I need to make sure,' Anna said, and climbed down, covering her mouth with her hand. The smell was appalling: rancid water mixed with petrol and that other awful metallic smell. She wondered if it might be blood and wanted to leave and be sick again. But she stayed. She needed to know exactly who it was. If this was a WAAF then it could easily be one of her barrack mates. They'd all been instructed to make their way to the bunkers when there was a raid on and they were off duty.

It was Elizabeth. Anna didn't know her well, didn't even know the young girl's second name, but they'd smiled at each other from time to time as they'd made their way to the operations block. The girl was a telephonist, Anna remembered, passing information about squadron readiness to different places in the station, including the wing commander, who made it his business to see off each flight from up in the control tower. The wingco knew the names of all his airmen and WAAFs, so it was said. Took it personally if anyone came to harm. *He would be sick at heart today*, Anna thought. She was too: as she was helped out of the crater by one of the airmen, her body began to tremble with shock.

'Get yourself a cuppa,' a corporal told her and pointed to the NAAFI van set up on the edge of the field.

She gave him a weak smile. He seemed like a decent sort, and he was trying to be kind, but she needed to deal with this in her own way. And doing something was better than standing by drinking tea while others got on with the work.

'No, I'll carry on. We'll be needing all the bodies we can get right now,' she said.

It was a bad choice of words: she hadn't meant to say *body*; it had just come out, been triggered by the horrific sight she'd just seen. *Her first dead body*. But then, they were all in shock, right then, women and men alike – you could see some people staring off into space with it, others wandering around confused, wondering what to do next. The entire airfield had been pulverised. How did they even start to make it whole again?

But thoughts like that wouldn't help. She pulled herself up to her full height, stiffened her resolve and tried to wipe the image of Elizabeth – battered and broken – out of her mind. She walked the perimeter of the field, looking for ways to be useful. To show Hitler that whatever he threw at their airfield, he wouldn't stop them. The RAF could not be bullied! Its determination would win the day and Anna was proud to be one of its ranks. Today had been a baptism of fire for them all, a truly hard and bitter day she wouldn't forget. But one thing was true – the WAAFs had proved themselves equal to the task, every bit as hard-working and courageous as the men.

22

RAF BIGGIN HILL

31 AUGUST 1940

It was a small miracle, she thought. The aerodrome was still operational despite the pounding it had taken over the last few days, and the amount of damage caused by the enemy air attacks. Two squadrons were able to fly from it, which was surprising, but that was due to the massive and exhausting effort of every single person working there. No matter how many times the Luftwaffe had torn up Biggin Hill's runways, lots of tired but determined men and women of the RAF had made overnight repairs. So, maybe not just a small miracle, but a huge one, brought about by ordinary people who had become extraordinary.

War seemed to do that.

Anna hadn't been to bed for what seemed like days. It was hard to remember the last time she had slept, or even ate, to separate the hours out in her head. Everything seemed to be mixed into one long nightmare. She'd been in the ops room that day, even when she wasn't on duty. Not that there was anywhere to go. The WAAF quarters had been destroyed, the windows blown out and their beds strafed with machine-gun fire. A terrifying thought, for she might easily have been in there trying to get some rest.

That morning's raid had demolished two workshops and damaged hangers, and the cookhouse had taken a hit. There was blast damage everywhere you looked. Very little of the station seemed to have escaped, and this time two Spitfires had been caught just as they were about to take off.

Right now, it was quiet again. Peace after the storm. WAAF cooks and mess maids were making soup outside in two giant cauldrons and ground crews were still busy filling in new bomb craters from the Luftwaffe's daily visit.

The worst part of all was the morning's casualties – some of them people she knew. One of the air raid shelters had taken a direct hit and been turned into a tomb for thirty-nine airmen. It should have been a place of safety, but instead it became a smouldering crater, packed with debris and bodies. Men who had eaten breakfast that morning, but who wouldn't eat dinner that night.

Anna had cried when she heard, found it incredibly sad. An explosion had also blown out the entrance to the airwomen's trench and the walls had caved in. Many were injured, and she could only imagine the horror as the women buried inside waited in the dark to be dug out. Anna thought she might have panicked and screamed if it was her, what with her claustrophobia. She couldn't be sure how brave she would have been, feeling the earth packed in around her, the thought of being trapped underground, of fighting for breath. Nobody knew if their courage would hold. Not until it was tested.

She'd been sent out of the operations block on a NAAFI run and ferried back tin mugs of tea for the controller and his staff up in the gallery. The tea was strong like bark but laced with sugar, and they'd all been grateful. Then Anna went back to her post below and got ready to report for her duty shift. She hung up her cap and gas mask on a hook, collected her headset from a row of them and plugged in next to the WAAF she was about to take over from. She picked up her speaking tube, hung it around her neck, checked that the fit was comfortable and plugged that in as well. It was called 'plotting in rhythm', a seamless handover – one shift of WAAFs replacing another in the ops room.

She studied the huge map in front of her, listening to the information coming in fast over her headphones. It was good to have a proper job to do again, something important to focus on. It looked like there was to be little respite for the aerodrome as a massive build-up of enemy planes had been spotted on radar coming in over the coast. Vast numbers of the enemy. Far more than Anna had ever seen before, outnumbering the RAF planes on the giant board in front of her by around five to one. It seemed they were about to be hit yet again.

It was a serious, frightening thought, and she had to hold her plotting rod with both hands to stop herself from shaking. She felt the fear trying to take her over, panic just seconds away, and imagined everyone around her could hear the alarming sound of her heart hammering in her chest as if it was about to break out through her skin. She took a deep, shuddering breath, made herself think of those brave young men fighting in the sky above her head, wondered how many of them could possibly survive such frightening odds. Five to one!

She managed to pull herself back from the brink of fear. She was angry with herself, felt ashamed. Her job was much less dangerous than theirs. Here she was – safe – while they were out there in the thick of it with nowhere to hide, courageously facing tracer rounds, flying out day after day with no complaints.

That's when the voice of the controller sparked into life in her headphones. He had a calm voice, and with a touch of humour, she heard him say that five bandits to one British fighter plane meant only one thing: that today the Luftwaffe would lose five times as many planes. Anna smiled.

This present raid was the worst she could remember. Although she stayed focused on her work, it was hard to ignore the muffled noise of bombs landing, not knowing where they would hit next and not being able to see when they did.

Suddenly, everything in Anna's world changed. The floor beneath her feet seemed to vibrate, sending a tremor pulsing through her like an electrical shock, and the walls around her shook as if they were no longer solid. Then the noise reached her, a shrill, piercing sound that grew into a deafening thunderclap.

It felt as if the explosion had turned the whole room upside down. The force of it ripped the plotting rod from her grip, and the table, which shuddered at first, then just disappeared, disintegrating in the blast. Plaster rained from the ceiling and she was blown off her feet, thrown onto the floor beneath what remained of the ops room gallery.

Mere moments later, there was a terrible rushing sound in her ears, and her eyes and mouth were filled with choking dust.

Slowly, disorientated, she dragged herself from the rubble, shook her head and watched white plaster dust fall from her hair. Feelings of dread and a sudden panic invaded her mind. *How would they all escape?* But she pushed down the fear and a strange calm settled on her. She knew she could do this. Whatever it took, she would carry on, do the job she was trained for. Although her head hurt like mad, there didn't seem to be any blood anywhere and once her ears had popped, she could hear normally again. She'd been spared, had no injuries as far as she could tell. But she could hear the soft moans of others around her who hadn't been so lucky. She needed to help them.

Then a chilling scream pierced the air. She followed the sound to the corner of the room, stumbling across the debris-strewn floor, squinting painfully in the dim emergency lighting.

She found a WAAF trapped under a wooden balustrade, part of the ruined balcony. Anna marvelled at how easily she managed to pull away the wreckage, as if some Herculean strength had been allotted to her when it was needed.

The young airwoman, released, stopped screaming but then began to cry incoherently. Anna wrapped a comforting arm around her and tried to calm her. 'Can you walk?' she asked.

'I think my arm's broken,' the girl said, her desperate cries turning to sobs.

'But your legs are okay?'

'I think so, maybe... I don't know.'

'Right. Put your good arm around my neck and I'll get you up the stairs,' said Anna. She hauled the young woman up on her feet and half carried, half dragged her all the way up to the ops room entrance and daylight.

Then she went back down to the devastation, to the twisted carcass of the control room, to the swirling dust and smell of destruction and the cries for help. She found two more people and helped them to safety. One was a leading aircraftwoman called Mabel, her eyes large and staring, without focus. The WAAF still had her headphones on, and Anna gently removed them and guided her to the stairs. She watched the woman's lips move, although no sound came out. Shock, she supposed. There would be lots of that today.

And she returned again, to the moans and whimpers of casualties and the overpowering smell that made her dry heave. She helped a man to his feet. He brushed the plaster from his uniform and winked at her. She'd seen him before: he was one of the gallery liaison officers and together, they pulled a WAAF telephonist out of the rubble. They each put an arm around the girl and helped her hobble up the stairs. That's when Anna noticed that the officer himself was bleeding from wounds to his head and chest. She took him by the hand and led him outside. Anna was surprised to see the bright sunlight. It felt bizarre after the dim light below. It hurt her eyes and made her head reel. The officer's face was grey, a mixture of plaster dust and pain. But he didn't complain, just smiled his thanks as she handed him over to a WAAF nurse, who had arrived at the operations block.

'Get yourself to the aid station,' the nurse told Anna, and pointed to a spot that looked miles away.

She nodded, which made her feel sick again and engulfed her in a searing pain. Her legs too felt strange – a little like trying to walk on springy rubber. Just the shock, she surmised, catching up with her.

An airman rushed past. 'You okay?' he asked.

She recognised him. He was a rigger, one of the ground crew from 610 Squadron.

'I'm fine, just a bit wobbly,' she said.

'Can you walk, do you need some help?' he asked, a quizzical look on his face.

'Of course I can walk! Why?'

'You look a bit pale, that's all,' the man said. 'And there's blood on your face.'

'It's okay, it's not mine. Besides, none of us look our best right now,' said Anna, and tried to smile. It hurt her head.

'Right, well, if you're sure you're okay, maybe you could help them peg out the runway.'

'Peg out?' she asked.

'They're pegging out with red flags. Marking unexploded bombs. 'Spect they could use you over there.'

'Fair enough. I'm on my way,' she said.

'Right. Well, take it slowly. Try not to be a hero, eh?'

She watched him grin as he walked away. Was he making fun of her? She couldn't tell. *Take it slowly?* Didn't these airmen realise by now that the WAAFs were every bit as good as them? Some of the chaps joked that WAAFs wouldn't be able to take the strain, would buckle under attack, more interested in keeping their make-up fresh than getting on with the job like the men. But that wasn't true. And the wing commander had already made a point of congratulating his WAAFs on their steadiness and quiet dedication to duty. Of praising their coolness and professionalism under fire.

Can you be cool under fire? She remembered the examiner who had asked her that at her basic training camp. It seemed so long ago now, so far in the past that it felt like somebody else's life. She couldn't have known then what being under fire really meant. None of them could, she supposed. But she did now, and, miracle of miracles, she had survived and had managed to do her job. The trick, she decided, was just not to think too much about what was happening around you. *Don't think, just do*, she told herself.

So, with that in mind, Anna picked up the red flags from the bucket and joined in with the rest of them. But after only ten minutes she felt so exhausted and dizzy that she had to sit down on the grass. That's when she felt herself go. She toppled over gently, a red flag still gripped in her hand. It was a graceful sort of thing. Hardly dramatic. One minute she could see the grass and the next she was looking up at sky.

After that, there was nothing – only darkness and falling head over heels into a black pit that seemed to have no bottom to it. But she wasn't frightened, because tumbling right beside her was Jimmy. He took her hand and told her she'd be fine. Then, side by side, they fell through the darkness together.

She could even feel herself smile.

23

'You're awake. That's wonderful!' said a nurse at the foot of Anna's bed.

Anna opened her eyes all the way, took in the strangeness of her surroundings, everything white and clinical, with an anti-septic smell. It was a hospital, but how on earth had she got there and how long had she been wasting time sleeping like this?

'Yes, I'm awake,' she said.

'We've been thinking of calling you Rip Van Winkle.' The nurse laughed.

'So, I've been sleeping a while then? But I should be at work.' She hauled herself further up the bed. A tube was attached to her hand, dripping some kind of liquid into her. She looked at it, puzzled.

'You just rest a bit longer. You've been lucky, you lost a lot of blood from your head wound and that concussion was a serious affair. You'll need to recuperate here for a while.'

'I was wounded?' she said.

'A large chunk out of the back of your head but they

patched you up – they're good at that around here,' the nurse said and smiled.

'I didn't know I was bleeding,' said Anna, surprised.

'Adrenaline, it carried you through. We find that a lot. People do what they must to survive and often help others, like you did, without even noticing their own injuries.'

'I helped others? I don't remember that.'

'A little amnesia's normal after a bad concussion. You may remember things as you improve. But, right now, somebody wants to see you. Are you up to visitors, do you think?'

'A visitor? Is it my Jimmy?' she asked, excited now.

The nurse looked confused. 'Sorry, dear. It's not a chap. In the RAF is he – your sweetheart, perhaps?'

'He's my fiancé. We're going to be married.'

'Congratulations. But I'm sorry to disappoint you, he isn't here. It's your WAAF commanding officer – Flight Officer Kemp. She's been here every day to check on you. She seemed rather concerned.'

'Every day?'

The nurse smiled. 'The bombing was three days ago, my dear.'

Three days? Anna couldn't believe it. Then she panicked: 'Flight Office Kemp mustn't see me looking like this. Have you got a comb? I must be all dishevelled. She's a stickler for spit and polish.'

'I don't think she'll be upset, dear. She's seen you much worse, and she seems a nice lady to me. I'm sure she'll be pleased you're getting better.'

What the nurse had said was true: F/O Kemp was very kind and friendly and seemed relieved that Anna was finally awake.

'Everyone sends their best wishes, and if there's anyone you want me to contact, do say. Family, next of kin?' the officer said.

'Next of kin?' Anna asked, confused. Surely she wasn't

dying? Didn't they only do that when you were dying? Her heart rate soared, and she swallowed hard.

'Maybe you'd like to let someone know you're fine. We've got your next of kin down as a Miss Edna Evans...'

'Edna – that's right. That's what I put on my enlistment form, but I haven't heard from Edna for a long time. I'm not even sure where she's stationed now, but she's with the ATS, a lady soldier.' She smiled, remembering her friend. She hoped Edna was safe and well.

'Right. So, if not Miss Evans, is there anyone else? Someone you'd like to visit you here? Family? I'll get right on it,' the officer said.

'Family?'

'Yes – is there anyone...'

'Where are we – the hospital, I mean?' She had no idea where she was or how she had got there. But, like the nurse had promised, maybe eventually she would remember, and it would all become clear.

'RAF Uxbridge Hospital. A few from Biggin have ended up here,' said the officer.

'If that's the case, then there *is* someone you could contact for me. *Family*,' said Anna. Not real family, of course. But Mary and Jimmy's mother Gladys had been like a mother to her, better than her own flesh and blood had ever been.

She watched F/O Kemp take down the address and promise to get in touch with the Armstrongs. She hoped they could visit and that they wouldn't mind the trip. It wasn't too far. She found herself looking forward to seeing them. She wouldn't ask Jimmy to come; she didn't want to worry him, and it would be unfair, taking him away from his duty. The air battle was so fierce right now, he must be involved in it somehow. She longed to see him again, but fate had a way of intervening sometimes. Maybe there would be a way for her to get to him instead.

'There's something else you should know,' the officer told her.

'Nothing bad, I hope, ma'am,' said Anna.

'Lots of bad and sad things have happened at the station in these last few weeks. But no, I don't think you'd call this bad, Anna.'

'No?' *How odd.* It was the first time her WAAF leader had ever called her by her first name. Normally it was ACW Golding, or plain Golding. It felt strange.

'That last attack left us in a bad position. They've had to move the operations room to an emergency ops room in the village. And, sadly, we lost some good people. People whose families will be in mourning right now. But sometimes good things come out of bad.'

'I don't understand,' said Anna.

'The station has been christened "the strongest link" by Fighter Command Headquarters – and several airmen and airwomen have shown gallantry beyond the call of duty. Fighter Command has recommended three Military Medals be awarded for courage shown on that last terrible day.'

'I see,' Anna said.

'An officer from the ops room has put your name forward for one of those MMs. You should be very proud.'

'What?! But I didn't do anything other than my duty shift in the ops room.'

'Apparently you did, even though you may not remember all of it. The officer says you rescued some people after the explosion and helped him as well.'

'I did?'

'What can you remember?'

'I remember walking the perimeter and the runway, posting red warning flags. Everything else is blank.'

'I'm very proud of you, ACW Golding. But I'll leave you to catch up on your rest now. Later on, we'll talk about what you want to do. About your future. When you've recovered, and provided the doctor passes you fit for duty, we'd be glad to have you back at Biggin Hill.'

'Of course I'm coming back,' said Anna.

'Don't rush into anything before you're well. You've done your duty here – you may decide to put in for a transfer, that a quieter station may suit you better for a while. It's up to you. Recover your health first and then take some well-deserved leave. Meanwhile, I shall let your family in Peckham know where you are and invite them to visit.'

Anna didn't correct the officer. *Her family in Peckham!* How she wished that was true. Hopefully it would be soon.

Two weeks into Anna's hospital stay, a letter arrived – an unexpected treat. She scanned the envelope impatiently. *Jimmy*, she thought, and her heart gave a tiny jolt of joy, but the writing wasn't his and she swallowed her disappointment. Still, there was something familiar in it that she recognised. To her surprise, it came from Edna. Finally, she'd heard from her. The large, looping letters sprawled their way across the page, almost falling off the edge. She wanted to laugh. *So typically Edna!* she thought. Everything her old pal did was larger than life and to excess.

Yet the more she read, the more worried she became. It was a rambling, muddled and disjointed letter, its meaning unclear. It asked for Anna's forgiveness, but didn't say what for.

You always knew, you warned me. I should have listened to you – I've let you down, the letter said. *But I was lonely. He was lonely too and he was very kind.*

A man, then, thought Anna. But she could only guess at the size of the problem, because her friend never put that into words. The word *pregnant* wasn't written anywhere, still it seemed to be implied. But even when she'd read the whole three pages through, she was still unsure what her friend was asking of her, other than forgiveness, and she could see no reason for that. Edna was a grown woman, could do whatever she wanted to, no matter how foolish that turned out to be. She didn't need permission from Anna. It was the most troubling and confusing letter she'd had – apart from the one from that woman, Jane Walker, of course. But that had simply been a mystery, and hadn't made her sad. Not like this.

She must write to Edna. The return address was a hostel in Liverpool, close to the munitions factory in Kirkby, where her friend had told her she was working now. She was no longer in the ATS, which seemed to answer one part of the puzzle – at least in Anna's mind. Either Edna had become pregnant and been forced to leave the army, or she'd already had a baby and was trying to bring the poor little mite up on her own. She did a quick calculation in her head. If that was the case, then Edna might have been pregnant the last time they'd met, as far back as that trip to the Kardomah.

Her friend's letter gripped her in its grief. There was an air of hopelessness about it that seemed at odds with the cheerful, optimistic woman Anna knew, the one with no fear, who had ridden the Octopus at the Watford fair even though she had no head for heights. But what could *she* possibly say or do that would help? How could she offer advice when nothing like that had ever happened to her? Still, an encouraging reply would be a start, she supposed, to let her friend know she wasn't alone. Maybe then Edna would find the words that she needed to say. Would feel able to explain what had happened – what was happening now.

One of the volunteers came in with a cup of tea for Anna and smiled. 'A letter, that's nice,' the young girl said.

'Yes, a letter is always a treat,' Anna lied. She smiled back and thanked her for the tea and the fact that she cared.

The girl looked tired but still managed to stay cheerful. Anna had noticed that a lot about these volunteers, as well as the WAAF nursing staff: no matter how weary they seemed, they always went the extra mile. Heroines, all of them. The war made heroes, big and small – and silent ones, like these women, quietly working away with no thought of medals or fame. The backbone of the country.

Flight Officer Kemp had kept her word, had contacted Gladys and Harry Armstrong, and invited them to visit. Only Gladys had been able to come, and her natural breeziness, along with the pie she brought, had raised Anna's spirits, made her feel more like her old self again. She imagined the journey Glad must have made to get there, and the precious rations used up to bake the pie. Such selfless generosity was a beacon of light in the midst of the darkness of war, Anna thought. And once she'd been discharged from hospital, she had agreed she would go and stay with them. 'An open invitation,' Glad had told her. 'Come anytime – we'll be pleased to see you.'

But when would that be? Anna longed to get on with her life and her work again. As far as she could tell, there'd been no long-term effects from her injuries, apart from the slight memory loss. Her brain was functioning perfectly normally, at least that's what the doctor said. Occasionally she'd wake up in the middle of the night in a sweat. A new nightmare had taken hold – where the crushed body of a WAAF named Elizabeth lay in the bottom of a rancid bomb crater. The poor girl would reach out her arms, pleading for help, and Anna would try to pull her to the surface. But it always finished in failure and that's when the nightmare would end, and she'd wake. Sometimes, she had to press her lips tightly together to hold in a scream.

Still, that was normal, she supposed, when you'd seen your first dead body.

She'd been in hospital for three whole weeks now and was getting impatient to leave. There'd been lots of time to think. She'd surprised herself with some of those thoughts. Maybe F/O Kemp was right, perhaps it was time for a change of station. Another Fighter Command aerodrome somewhere else, a little less fraught than Biggin, still doing a valuable job in an ops room, still doing her bit for her country. It could be the perfect time to put in for that magical transfer that would hopefully take her closer to Jimmy. The next time her WAAF officer came to visit, Anna would ask for her help with a posting to somewhere in Cornwall. But would anywhere need an extra plotter?

She hadn't written that letter to Edna yet. She knew she owed it to her friend, but the more she'd thought about what she might say, the harder getting started had become. Finding the right words wouldn't be easy, but she hoped that whatever she wrote would show Edna she wasn't alone, that she had a good friend to rely on. Friends for life. It was a pledge they'd made to each other – and friends shared each other's pain. And Edna had sounded in pain. Her letter felt like a cry for help, and Anna would do all in her power to answer that cry, whatever it took.

24

LONDON

She lifted up the medal once more and gazed at it in wonder. There'd been a small, informal ceremony in the dayroom when it was pinned to her uniform. She kept checking that it was real. But that was the odd thing; it felt like a dream, a bit surreal, mainly because she couldn't recall what she'd done to deserve it. Still, it would be ungrateful not to feel a little proud, not to accept it gracefully, especially when she read the inscription on the back – *For bravery in the field.*

The Military Medal was a round silver medal – real silver, she supposed – with her name, service number and details impressed on the rim and the stately head of King George on the front. Something to be treasured, and of course, she would. But in a way it made her feel embarrassed, like a fraud. So, she put it back in its box and added it to her waiting kitbag. She wouldn't wear it, for it felt too much like bragging.

She was nearly ready now.

She'd said goodbye to some of the hospital staff and, although Anna was glad to be leaving at last, she felt weepy and emotional. It wasn't like her. She'd always prided herself on being strong. But maybe concussion could do that to you.

The hospital had finally signed her off after almost four weeks and she was going on leave. 'Go home for a couple of weeks and we'll see about your posting after that,' her commanding officer had told her.

Home-leave, that's what it was called. It seemed presumptuous to call Gladys and Harry Armstrong's house in Peckham her home but they'd invited her there for these two weeks and she didn't want to disappoint them. Besides, it was beginning to feel like home. A cheerful, friendly place filled with warmth and affection, where family life was built on respect, love and understanding. The contrast was stark between the Armstrong home and her childhood memories of home life. Aunt Beatrice had ruled by fear, whereas Gladys and Harry Armstrong believed in kindness.

She'd been given RAF transport to get there. It seemed unusual, a car and a driver all to herself to take her to Peckham. Maybe it was true that she had done something special, was some kind of hero, or should that be heroine? But the idea was an uncomfortable one. She wanted to be like everyone else and get on with her job – wherever that would be. But at least the car wasn't a fancy staff car, and the WAAF driver was an ordinary ACW2, just like her.

'Going on leave, you lucky tyke!' the driver said.

'Yes. But it feels strange,' said Anna.

'Oh, why's that?' the young woman asked.

'I'm still getting used to winding down after the action on the station.'

'I heard you all took a pounding at Biggin. Still, live to fight another day, eh?' the WAAF said cheerfully.

'Absolutely!' Anna agreed. That's when it truly sank in – just how fortunate she'd been. Luck had been on her side. The line between life and death was thin and definitely influenced by luck, she thought, but somehow, she'd survived. Maybe it was for a reason, and fate had given her another chance at life, a chance for something special. A life with Jimmy and a family of their own one day – the kind of loving family he'd grown up in, and which she had always craved.

'You've got yourself some breathing time. Go dancing. Get yourself a bloke. Wish I was in your shoes, but we've had all leave cancelled,' the driver added a sigh.

Anna had been shocked by the latest war news. Recuperating in the hospital, she'd felt removed from it all, but now as they drove through countryside and built-up areas alike, the bomb damage was plain to see. That madman Hitler had changed his tactics, was trying to wear Britain down with waves of bombers dropping their lethal cargo on innocent civilians, instead of airfields. They were calling it the Blitz and it was a monstrous plan, to bomb people out of their homes. Still, she imagined that some senior ranks at Bentley Priory – the headquarters of Fighter Command – wouldn't be sorry that the Luftwaffe were leaving their aerodromes alone.

She thought about Gladys Armstrong and how she'd said nothing about the bombing when she'd come to visit. Had been her usual, cheerful self. Talking about her family and the parlour games they'd played each Christmas and how they'd all do that again. But then Glad was stoic, a gutsy warrior – she seemed to take most things on the chin without complaining.

If Hitler thought people like her would easily give in, then he had a nasty surprise in store.

When Anna finally arrived in Lidgate Street, she was relieved that the place looked just the same as before. No sign of bomb damage. No rubble anywhere or houses ripped apart or ruptured gas and water mains. On the way there, they'd been forced to make several detours, avoiding roads pockmarked with

bomb craters, but her young WAAF driver had been unruffled
by it all. The girl was resourceful and bold – nothing seemed to
put her off – and chatty and friendly too.

Anna thanked her for the trip and got a smile in return.

'Cheerio, then, and you keep safe,' the driver said.

'You too, good luck,' Anna replied. She stood in the street
and watched the young WAAF wave a friendly goodbye as the
car drove slowly away.

People! she thought. They were amazing at times. The way
they could still smile and look out for each other. The way they
adapted even when life was tough. Their optimism and determination to see this war through, despite the sad loss of lives,
whether airmen or soldiers or sailors – or civilians, whose battle
seemed to have only just begun with this terrifying Blitz. How
long would they be able to take the strain of constant bombing?
Of hearing the sirens wail their warnings and rushing to shelters
and listening for the whistle of high explosive bombs as they
fell. Wondering how close the next one might be. She remembered how that felt.

The *Blitzkrieg* could be a fearful thing. It might push some
people to the brink of terror. Eat away at morale, maybe even
undermine that cheerful British optimism. The RAF had an
enormous task on its hands, stopping the Luftwaffe bombers
getting through. But she believed in her country's air force, in
the pilots and the airmen and the WAAFs working away in
stations all over the land. Right then, she wanted to be with
them. If she could do that, and at the same time be close to
Jimmy, then she would ask for nothing more.

'Ain't you a sight for sore eyes! Da's not here just now or he'd
give you a hug too,' said Glad, as she clutched Anna tightly.

She felt tears build up behind her eyes and hugged Gladys

Armstrong right back. 'It's great to be here, and kind of you both to put yourselves out like this.'

'Kind? It ain't *kind*, just natural. You're like family. Da feels the same,' said Glad.

'Is he well?' She'd wondered when he hadn't come to the hospital if Harry was poorly.

'The man's strong as an oak. Off doing important war work,' Glad said, proudly.

'That's grand,' Anna said.

'He's a corporal now.'

'He's in the army?' asked Anna, confused.

'The Home Guard. One of his duties here in Peckham is to guard the canal. Can't have them Jerries sneaking in the back door.'

'No, that wouldn't do,' said Anna, as she tried to keep from smiling.

'Now, what about you? Gave me quite a scare, you did, looking all weak and pasty. Nothing some good grub can't put right, mind. Put some weight back on those bones of yours – and colour in your cheeks.'

'I'm fine, Glad. Really I am. Bit tired, that's all. And I mean to pull my weight,' said Anna.

'We'll see. Da'll be back soon. So, we'll have us a celebration. Got some scrag end of mutton stew for his tea. His favourite – and I don't suppose you'd turn your nose up at stew?'

'Sounds wonderful,' she said.

The last time she'd eaten anything that sounded so good had been that incredible steak and kidney pie that she and Jimmy had devoured at the White Lion Hotel, back at the start of the war. Almost a year ago now. She couldn't believe that so much time had gone by. Coming up to an anniversary of sorts – when they'd first met. She wondered if the same thought had struck him. Not that chaps took note of such things. And maybe it was better if he didn't. She didn't want him to be distracted from his present job. She had no idea where his crew flew, only that he was stationed at somewhere called St Eval. The name sounded a little romantic and medieval to her. Other than that, she knew nothing about his present posting. His letters never mentioned his job. It was safer that way, and nobody understood that better than she did: careless talk could cost lives. It was written on posters now, but she didn't need a poster to tell her that any scrap of information floating around could help the enemy. Help them to destroy the most important man in her life.

She hoped that someone was listening as she sent up another silent prayer: *Keep him safe. Bring him home.*

25

RAF ST EVAL

28 SEPTEMBER 1940

The whole thing was a nightmare. Here he was, an adult, a grown man, and yet he felt as powerless as a babe in arms. It seemed that all the precious people he cared about, the ones he loved, had to be thrown aside. Sacrificed to a higher kind of love, the loyalty and devotion you needed to serve your country.

Country first, self last – once again the words of his RAF recruiter rang harshly in his ears. Putting yourself last? he thought. That was the easy part. But his cherished Anna, injured and in pain – how could he possibly ignore her? And his poor mother stuck up in London in the middle of the Blitz? He should be able to go to them. To protect them. To keep them safe.

Just two days, it was all he'd asked his squadron leader for. A measly forty-eight-hour compassionate pass. *Patriotism, loyalty*, those were the weapons that S/L Blake had used to refuse Jimmy's request. And, of course, he was a patriot: duty to his country was something Sergeant Jimmy Armstrong took seriously. But it wasn't his only love, or even his first love; that was a clever, strong, independent and beautiful woman who could make him laugh. And, right now, he needed to be with her, to hold Anna in his arms and soothe her, help her to get well again.

She hadn't asked him to come, hadn't even told him she'd been caught in a blast. His mother had written, explained about the hospital visit and Anna's injuries, told him about the medal. They didn't hand those MMs out for nothing, so she'd have done something courageous and extraordinary. Which didn't surprise him. Now she was staying with his family, getting better, according to Ma. But still having nightmares.

He should be there.

He took his ma's letter from the breast pocket of his tunic. Not that he needed to read it again: he knew practically every word that was there, but it was a link to home. The paper his mother had used came from one of his old school jotters and her large, oval handwriting, almost childlike, came from a different age. A simpler life that he remembered with affection. He ran his hand over the page. It felt good just to touch it. To smell the scent of home.

He was getting sentimental and maybe even maudlin, giving way to self-pity. How would that help? It was the beer that had done it. He'd been drinking far too much tonight; couldn't remember how long he'd been sitting here in the sergeants' mess, drowning his sorrows. But the airman behind the bar had given him a few strange looks, as all the others had left now. Everybody drank, it was part of service life. But not this much when they were on standby, and could be called to readiness anytime. Time to pull it together, he supposed. Act like a grown-up and get himself off to bed.

He squinted at the clock behind the bar, but the numbers swam around in his beer-swamped head. He felt a hand on his shoulder.

'I've been sent to collect you, old bean,' said Freddy, 'before you drink the place dry.'

'Have I been a bad boy?' Jimmy chuckled. He wasn't often a bad boy. Maybe that was the problem, perhaps he should let his hair down a little more.

'*Very* bad, old thing. You'll need to get a night's sleep before we fly out in the morning. You've not forgotten we're on standby?'

'Right at the front of my brain, old chap.' He tapped his forehead hard with two fingers. 'Right in here.'

'I see,' Freddy said. 'Hope that's not the only thing in there.'

'Quite right. I'm sure there's lots more stuff in there – floating around, you know. Like things do.' Jimmy smiled, and then laughed a rowdy, beery laugh.

'Now, why don't you be a good chap and put that letter away? I'll give you a hand back to barracks.'

'I'm thinking *strategies*,' Jimmy said. At least that's what he'd hoped to say, but the word came out slurred.

'You're thinking what?' asked Freddy.

'You know – what to do. A plan.'

'Well, I suppose you've always been the most sensible one amongst us,' said Freddy, tongue in cheek.

'It's true.' Jimmy burped.

'If you're after a plan, a good one would be to sleep it off.'

'No, no... listen! This is a better one. Remember that time you went AWOL...?'

'Whoa there! Galloping off into the night like some sort of knight on his white charger, that just won't do. That's one of the most ludicrous ideas you've had. It didn't work for me, did it? You saved me from doing something stupid. And this is even worse – Absent Without Leave when you're tagged for a mission, that'll get you thrown behind bars and they'll toss away the key. None of that'll help your fiancée, will it?'

'It might,' said Jimmy.

'You know it won't. At least you would, if you weren't so pickled in booze.'

'Oops!' Jimmy put a large hand up to his mouth, but a drunken hiccough made its way through on a gust of beery breath.

'You smell like a brewery! You'll need to have a shower before the skipper sees you.'

Before he could do anything, Jimmy was led away by his friend.

What kind of a chump had he been? Jimmy sat on his bed, nursing his head in his hands. He'd been up for most of the night; between the headache and sickness and the dizziness of a Force-10 hangover, he hadn't been able to sleep. He was still thirsty, as if he'd trekked in the desert for days. Now his tongue seemed to have doubled in size so that it didn't fit comfortably in his mouth any more.

But despite it all, he was slowly – painfully – returning to his normal, sane self. He could see that Freddy had rescued him, stopped him from making a fool of himself. It wouldn't have done any good rushing to Anna's side. He'd wanted to protect her, but he knew what Anna would have said about that – that it was his male pride. She didn't need protection. Maybe some women needed a man to cosset them, to be in charge, but that wasn't Anna. She was a strong, independent woman. She'd have been angry with him for putting his freedom and career at risk. Going absent without leave in wartime was a serious offence, he knew that. *But sometimes your heart just overruled your head.*

They were on standby. The old man would probably already be waiting out on the apron. Jimmy doubted the skipper ever slept. From newbies who'd first arrived at RAF St Eval just months ago, Jimmy's aircrew had turned into blue-eyed boys – the golden, lucky crew, who other crews treated with a new respect.

Suddenly, it seemed, they'd become a valuable asset, too valuable to be given even a two-day pass. At first, their Beaufort had been assigned to easy 'milk runs', the kind of sorties Coastal Command threw at inexperienced bomber crews like them: patrolling the southwest coast looking for enemy targets; providing anti-submarine cover. It had been repetitive, boring stuff and frustrating too, as if they were just marking time while others got on with the real war. He knew they had all felt the same way, even Andrew, their skipper, but orders were orders.

But then they had risen in Command's estimation. It had been a matter of luck, Jimmy thought. Maybe that was how it went in war. He remembered back to that day when they spotted the U-boat on the surface. He hadn't been sure how he would react once they'd got an actual target in their sights: Jimmy was responsible for getting the torpedo to its target, as well as firing it. Even now, he could still remember the feeling – the perspiration trickling down the back of his neck and rubbing his hands, slick with sweat, on his trouser legs. It wasn't that he had been afraid, or if he was, it was simply the fear of failing. They were all relying on him, and dummy runs and paper exercises were all very well, *in theory*. But in practice... getting a torpedo smack on target was much harder to achieve.

Aerial torpedoes were tricky weapons, easily damaged when landing on water if you didn't get it exactly right. The math was complicated. Speed, altitude and distance all had to be spot on. But then Jimmy had always been happy with maths, and his calculations had been precise. He'd called the numbers through to the skipper, who'd brought them in at the crucial height, had kept them level for the long bombing run. The man was a magician, Jimmy thought, with ice water in his veins.

Jimmy had lined up to the U-boat and launched his torpedo.

A waterspout had erupted below them, and then a fireworks display as ammunition exploded everywhere and yellow, orange, and purple flames – diesel maybe, he couldn't be sure – sent a colourful inferno into the air.

'It's a kill!' someone had shouted excitedly.

'We got the bastard,' he'd heard Freddy scream.

They'd done their job. It was what they'd been trained to do. *How many men in a German sub?* he wondered.

'Any survivors?' Jimmy had asked.

'Survivors?' queried Andrew. 'Shouldn't think so. You did a proper job on them, Ginger.'

'You sure did. Sent them down to Davy Jones's locker,' Freddy agreed.

'But what if there are survivors? Shouldn't we alert Coastal Command search and rescue?' Jimmy said.

'You did your job,' George answered wearily. 'Forget it, it's war. Could just as easily have been us as them.'

Jimmy had tried to forget it. But, sometimes, when he struggled to sleep, he imagined himself back in the plane flying over the waves and could hear terrible screams from the water below.

Luck! he'd told himself. *Our luck was good. Their luck was bad.*

26

PECKHAM

1 OCTOBER 1940

The Armstrongs' kitchen was a warm, welcoming space, and when Anna walked in that morning, Gladys was already bustling about, a pot of porridge bubbling gently on the stove top. After a week of being there, Anna felt at home in this wonderful kitchen. It wrapped around her comfortably, naturally, as if she'd always lived there. It was the heart of the house, a cosy place where, despite the rationing, miracles happened daily: Glad producing food from meagre wartime supplies like a magician. Anna still wasn't sure how she did it. A lifetime of cooking for a family, she supposed. She marvelled at how Glad never seemed to weigh things in her cooking and claimed that any successful result was due to the hand of God. But Anna was beginning to understand that Glad was modest and felt no need to take credit for her meals. As long as her family was fed and the house was a safe haven, she was content to be the anchor of the ship while her husband Harry did the steering. They both seemed supremely happy with how their lives dove-tailed into each other's; the way they cherished what they had.

It was exactly what she hoped for her and Jimmy.

She and Gladys exchanged smiles. The smile that pulled at Glad's eyes, and the way her mouth lifted – it was so much like Jimmy.

The two women went about their separate jobs. Anna set the table with the crockery and spoons from the kitchen dresser, while Gladys carried the porridge to the table and spooned it into her and Anna's bowls.

'Blimey, what you call this then?' asked Harry, his sudden arrival prompting Glad to ladle out his breakfast as well.

'Call what?' asked Glad.

'My two best girls starting without me. Ain't I the head of this house?' said Harry, winking at Anna.

'Well, you're the loudest one in it,' said Glad, 'if that's what you mean.'

'See how it goes, Anna? When a bloke don't get no respect in his own home.' But Harry smiled at his wife.

The innocent expression on Harry's round, dimpled face was almost angelic, Anna thought, making him look like a cherub from a painting. She watched him rush through his breakfast as if there was a time limit on it. Then he kissed his wife on top of her head and patted Anna's hand by way of good-bye. She found him a kind man. A man whose family was important to him. He also took his wartime job and his obligations to his neighbours seriously, she thought.

'Just mind you're home in time,' said Glad. 'Anna's got something special planned for tea. And if you're back at the canal, leave them boots in the hall this time before you muddy *all* my floors.'

When he'd gone, Anna poured her and Glad more tea.

'So,' Glad said, 'today's the day. You haven't changed your mind? Still want to learn a bit about cooking?'

'I'm looking forward to it. Excited, though I'm a novice at

cooking and I appreciate you taking me in hand. I can boil water and fry an egg, but as for anything else...'

'Don't worry, we all have to start somewhere,' Glad said kindly.

'I thought about what you said the other day about Harry,' said Anna. 'How his love for you began in his stomach and made its way up to his heart.'

'That's what they say.' Glad laughed. 'That the way to a man's heart is through his stomach – but then you've already captured my Jimmy's heart.'

'He's told you everything, then?' asked Anna.

'You know him, he finds some things hard to put into words, but he feels them just the same. I could see you pair were in love with each other the minute he arrived for the party. I hoped something would come of it.'

'But you didn't say,' Anna said, smiling now.

'Not my place to interfere. I know my Mary asked you to visit, to keep an eye on us two, but I hoped it was more than that,' said Glad. She reached across the table, took Anna's hand in her wrinkled one.

'You made me so welcome. Part of your family. I've never had that before. You've been good to me, kind and under-standing – like a mother would be. And soon now you *will* be,' she said, the words tumbling out from her, her smile growing wider. 'I'm sure Jimmy wouldn't mind if I tell you...'

'You mean, you're to be my daughter-in-law?'

'We're engaged,' Anna said. 'And you're invited to the wedding, of course, though it may not be for a while.'

'He's given you a ring?' asked Gladys.

Anna looked down at her hands, to the place where her absent ring would be. 'He's keeping it safe for me,' she said.

She wouldn't have been surprised if Glad's enormous shriek of joy could have been heard throughout the whole of Peckham.

~

Anna looked out the window of the train, at the countryside, at the cows in a distant field. The sight was cheering, so different from the greyness of London and the fabric of war that seemed to engulf the city.

She longed to open a window, to breathe in the air and smells of the land. She looked around the compartment at her fellow travellers. None of them would thank her for making the place even colder. There had already been complaints about the lack of heating and the endless hold-ups when the train had crawled along like a snail.

But neither the cold nor the slowness of the train could invade her happiness. Not today. Today she felt better than she had in a long time: rejuvenated. And excited. Every mile was taking her closer to Jimmy. Today, at last, she was on her way to him – heading for Cornwall to somewhere on the coast called Perranporth. Near the sea! She couldn't believe her luck – that after the grim landscape of the city with its bomb-scarred buildings she would soon be looking at the ocean.

Jimmy had described it to her; the colours that changed with the light, its water sometimes blue, sometimes turquoise, often tumultuous waves pounding the shoreline. The beautiful bays and majestic cliffs that looked carved by a giant's hand. She'd been quite moved by the images he'd painted. The closest he'd ever come to poetry. Well, if Jimmy liked the place, she knew she would love it too.

She didn't know much about her new aerodrome, only that it was a small satellite of a much larger station, and part of Fighter Command. There were other WAAFs there, she'd been told, and she'd be working as a plotter in the ops room. She would be useful once more, something that filled her with optimism. But more exciting than that was the thought that she would finally get to see Jimmy again. There'd been no time to let him know that her transfer had come through, that she was on her way, but she imagined he would be just as excited as she was. They could pick up where they'd left off that night in the parlour when Mary had interrupted them. A shudder went through her – and it wasn't the cold.

Everything had happened quickly once notice of her new posting had arrived. But she would always remember the kindness of the family who'd taken her to their hearts, made her feel loved and safe and *wanted* – that was the most incredible thing.

Last night had been her final one in a place she'd come to think of as her real home; they'd given her what Glad had called a bit of a send-off, bringing out the precious sherry bottle.

By the end of the day, Anna's optimism and excitement had been a little drained. There was no train to get her into Perranporth as she'd been told there would be. The guard at Truro had shaken his head: 'It's the war,' he'd told her, when she showed him her travel warrant.

She shrugged her shoulders in defeat, wondered how she would get to her new post.

'You one of the WAAFs from RAF Trevellas?' the guard asked. He was old, probably around Harry's age, she guessed. Maybe he was in the Home Guard too.

'I'm going to the RAF station at Perranporth,' Anna said, eagerly.

'Ah – well, we locals calls it RAF Trevellas, but 'tis the same place, right enough – up on Cligga cliffs above Perranporth.'

'And is it far? Could I walk there?' she asked.

'Bless you, my bird! 'Tis a fair mile as the crow flies and you ain't no crow, if you don't mind me saying so.' The guard laughed.

'No,' admitted Anna, 'I'm no crow.' She gave the man a friendly smile. She'd been feeling weary and slightly pessimistic, but now she cheered up. The old Cornishman seemed kind, if a little eccentric, but maybe that's how the Cornish were. She didn't know, this was the first time she'd been here.

'Right, my bird – you just hang on there. Old Pop Truscott 'av got 'is van outside. He'll be off to the cookhouse at Trevellas *dreckly* with a delivery.'

'You mean he'll give me a lift?'

'He's a bleddy good bloke, should think he'd be pleased to help out one of our girls in blue. Can't leave you out here all night.'

'Brilliant. Thanks so much, Mr...?'

'T'int Mister anything. The name's Jago Penrose. Friends calls me Jago,' the guard said, and offered his hand. 'And you'd be...?'

'Anna – Anna Golding,' she said, and shook his hand warmly.

'Well now, miss. Let's get 'ee on yer way.'

Anna decided right then that whatever else came her way during this new posting of hers, if all of the Cornish were like this chap, it was a place where she could feel happy. He seemed kind-hearted and welcoming – although she might need a translator to understand the finer points of his dialect. The language was almost like English, but not quite. Still, the accent was a warm, friendly sound. And what did *dreckly* mean? she wondered. It sounded like *directly*, she supposed, which would make it a measurement of time. Something that might happen any minute now.

The guard let her sit in his room, next to an old coke stove, which was just as well, because it seemed that 'dreckly' was a flexible sort of time. It turned out that Old Pop Truscott hadn't even started to load his van.

Half an hour later, when Anna had drowsily nodded off in a comfortable chair, Jago Penrose coughed discreetly, and she followed him out to the station car park.

'You'll be fine with 'ee, don't you worry none, my bird. You take care now,' said the guard as he waved them off.

Anna strained her eyes in the blackout, but with only a sliver of light from the thin crescent moon, it was impossible to get any sense of the countryside they were travelling through. The road was a narrow black ribbon, straight in places, but mostly twisting its way through sharp bends and constantly climbing over hills. The journey was like a fairground ride and her queasy stomach reminded her that she hadn't eaten since breakfast time. The van pitched and heaved through every new turn, but the man beside her didn't seem alarmed as he whistled a jaunty tune. He was a cheerful sort of chap, she thought, and ancient – like the van that he tried to coax some speed from.

Pop Truscott gave Anna a reassuring smile. 'She may be old but she's willing, and she ain't let me down yet,' he said, patting the steering wheel fondly.

'She's a fine vehicle,' Anna said, because she felt she had to say something. And positive things were always better.

'That she is. Now you'll need to hold on to that hat of yours. This is the tricky bit. St George's Hill 'av always been a struggle for the old girl, but she'll get us there.'

The climb up out of Perranporth towards the airfield felt practically vertical and Anna could hear the van's struggles and wheezes, its gears grinding as if the poor old thing was taking its very last breath. She remembered what she'd heard about the airfield, that it had been built in a most unusual and inhospitable place, on a plateau right on the edge of high cliffs, looming above the sea. She wondered how easy it was for the pilots who had to take off and land from there.

'Hope I haven't taken you out of your way,' she said, holding on grimly to the dashboard of the old boneshaker.

'I were coming anyway. 'T'int nothing more than I'd do every day, and kindness to your fella man – seems only natural, don't you think?'

'I do,' she said, earnestly, 'I really *do*.'

She got out at the barrier of the airfield while he turned the car around and went on his way. She waved him off, could hear him whistling the same cheery tune again.

The gate sentry challenged her, shone a torch into her face. She handed over her orders and he nodded his head and grinned.

'Good to see a new face,' he said. 'Especially such a pretty one,' he added, with a wink.

Anna didn't rise to the bait, ignoring both the compliment and the wink. Some chaps saw themselves as Romeos, expected WAAFs to fall into their arms and be grateful for the flattery. She'd seen it all before. But she didn't need a chap to flatter her with false praise. She already had a man – a good, honest man. Someone she trusted to speak his mind.

Still, she was courteous and polite. It never hurt. 'Good to be here,' she said. 'It's taken a while.' A tired sigh left her lips.

She'd finally arrived, and she'd managed to travel these last few difficult miles from the station in the blackout, thanks to the kindness of a couple of fine men. They hadn't complained or made a fuss or asked for anything in return. And she couldn't even remember if she'd thanked them properly.

The kindness of strangers, she thought. If everybody were to be as kind as those two old Cornish chaps, wouldn't the world be a much happier, gentler place? Maybe then people wouldn't have to go to war.

27

RAF PERRANPORTH, TREVELLAS DOWNS, CORNWALL

Anna's first night at RAF Perranporth had been a revelation. She'd had to stand her ground in front of a grumpy and unfriendly WAAF officer who'd been hastily hauled out of bed. She hoped that was the reason for the woman's sour mood. And the officer's face – not to be too unkind, and Anna always tried *not* to be – well, it was hardly an oil painting. Her voice was practically a growl as she'd complained that it was far too late to get Anna to her assigned billet in the village of Trevellas. She hadn't been expected for at least another twenty-four hours, and it seemed that the cottage she was to live in was some miles away. They'd be providing a bicycle for her, but she couldn't cycle there in the dark and the blackout without knowing where she was going. That would be too dangerous, the officer had said.

Section Officer Garvey had huffed and puffed in front of her, but Anna wasn't deterred. She'd stood silently, a perfect model of military precision and attention, in front of the woman. Waited patiently, eyes front, staring at a spot above the older woman's head. Anna was a good deal taller than the officer, who reminded her of her friend Mary, small and round. But Mary was better-looking. And her scowl wasn't half as bad.

It wasn't a promising start to her new posting but, eventually, she'd been given bedding and a hurricane lamp and pointed in the direction of a storeroom, where she could sleep for the night. The floor was concrete and cold, and she slept with her greatcoat on, but at least in the morning, her WAAF leader had come to check on her and brought her a tin mug of tea.

The tea was cold, but Anna accepted it as a peace offering all the same, as Officer Garvey smiled when she handed it across. Anna smiled in reply: she wasn't one to hold a grudge. Besides, the woman could make her life hard if she wanted to – she was the one with the fancy braid on her sleeves. The one in charge.

'We're a fairly small crew, we WAAF. Myself, a sergeant, a couple of corporals and six aircraftwomen like yourself. Different from what you've been used to at Biggin Hill, but you'll find them all a friendly bunch,' the officer said.

'Thank you, ma'am, for giving me the tour.'

'It's quite an unusual set-up for a busy aerodrome, 320 feet above the sea like this. Some might call it an unsuitable and hazardous location – but we've had surprisingly few accidents.'

'And is it mainly Spits, ma'am?'

'We've had the odd Hurricane, but mostly Spitfires, as you say. The runways are short, hardly suitable for bombers or anything large.'

'So just ten of us WAAF?'

'Eleven now with you, ACW Golding. I'm in accommodation here at the field, along with the sergeant and Corporal Landry. Everyone else is in billets elsewhere. I'll get Landry to show you yours. Take the day to get settled in. You won't be in the ops room until the morning shift tomorrow – starts at seven. Six thirty sharp at the cookhouse, just over the main road. Be prompt or there won't be anything left, I warn you now. Oh, and Golding...'

'Yes, ma'am?'

'You'll know by now how some of these young airmen can be—?'

'Ma'am?'

'A new WAAF. Some of the chaps will be out to impress, will want to – well, you know...'

'Understood, ma'am! And don't worry, I'm not looking for a chap. I'm just interested in doing my job.'

'Excellent, well, good luck and I'll leave Corporal Landry to sort you out with your bicycle and show you the cookhouse. Welcome to RAF Perranporth,' she said.

Anna gave her best salute and waited for the corporal to pick her up and point her towards the cookhouse. Her rumbling stomach reminded her that it hadn't seen food since yesterday and was ready to mutiny if nothing came its way soon. She wondered what the food was like there and what kind of supplies Old Pop Truscott had delivered to the cookhouse last night. Right now, anything would do – as long as it wasn't those awful cabbage sandwiches, of course. The memory made her a little sad and sentimental. She missed Mary. They'd been a good team and seemed at times to know what was in each other's minds. But that was the war for you – separation was part of the sacrifice.

She heard the distant sound of waves crashing to the shore; the cry of gulls, saw them whirling in the air. She breathed in the smell of the ocean, of the cold fresh air, its sharpness stinging her nostrils. Her mind returned to her tour of the station, the aerodrome that was to be her new workplace. Her WAAF officer was right, it was certainly smaller than Biggin, but it had all the same elements, everything that was needed to get Spitfires into the air.

Three proper tarmacked runways were laid out in an A-shape and linked to a perimeter track for the dispersal of planes. There were two squadrons of fighters, twelve in each, and blast pens to keep the aircraft safe in case of attack. Anti-aircraft guns stood ready to be manned, which made her feel safe, as well as the substantial air raid shelter. But many buildings had to double up, like the flight office – used for planning operations – which was also the officers' mess. There was a small ops room and control tower and accommodation huts for the pilots. Nothing was lacking, it was just on a much smaller scale than what she was used to.

But one thing it had that Biggin didn't was its incredible location, built on dramatic, rugged cliffs with a spectacular view of the ocean. She was staring at it now and holding her breath – and she could see exactly what Jimmy had meant about the scenery in Cornwall. Majestic, he'd called the cliffs. They were certainly monumental and impressive. The last place you'd think anyone would pick to put an airfield, on the edge of a 300-foot drop – and it must have been difficult to build. Yet here it was. It said a lot for the determination and ingenuity of her countrymen. An airfield had been needed to tackle the German navy and air force, and the threat they posed to Britain's crucial Western Approaches to the English Channel. So, an airfield had been built – along with several others in the West Country.

'You'll be the new girl, I suppose,' said a plummy voice from behind her.

She hadn't heard anyone arrive, had been too busy gazing out to sea and imagining how many people before her had stared at the same amazing view.

'Yes, I'm new,' she said. *But girl?* As far as she was concerned, a girl was a child and it had been years since she'd been one. Even then, her childhood had been strange and cut short. *What was she, the new girl in some fancy girls' boarding school?* That's how this Corporal Landry had made it sound, she decided. But maybe the corporal didn't mean anything by it. Anna let it go, although the look on the young woman's face was a little haughty and superior. Still, it was too easy to jump to conclusions and make hasty judgements about people before you knew them. She would need to get the feel of her new posting first, and the men and women she would be working with.

'Right, I'm to show you the ropes. So, chop-chop, then! Hurry up, we need to get going if we're to bag any breakfast.'

Anna didn't have time to reply since Corporal Landry, who hadn't introduced herself, took off as if it was a race.

When they finally arrived at the cookhouse, she understood why. *Just over the main road from the airfield*, her section officer had said, but it turned out to be at least a couple of miles away. No wonder the corporal had hurried off, for they were both walking, and it seemed like everyone else was riding bikes.

There were scores of different ones, many of them ancient contraptions, some already rusting and with saddles every bit as torturous-looking as Daisy's had been. Most were standing upright, parked neatly in bicycle racks, while others appeared abandoned, lying carelessly on the grass.

The cookhouse itself was a ramshackle affair – three wooden huts joined together by a flimsy tin roof – but the thing that interested Anna most was the glorious smell coming from it. She warned her stomach to get ready.

Breakfast was a feast. Eggs, two slices of bacon, fried tomatoes, and huge slices of bread. It seemed inconceivable to her that the aircraftwomen and men sitting at the rows of trestle tables were all tucking in to such a banquet. At Biggin they'd been lucky to have Marmite sandwiches, but then they'd all been far too busy and weary to think about food, she supposed.

One of the WAAF cooks had noticed her surprise and

explained that, although rationing was still a pain, food was a little easier to come by in the countryside. Most folk kept chickens, which meant eggs were in good supply, and there was sometimes the odd pig or two that slipped through the *official* net. Pig clubs were formed, with locals buying a share. When a number of pigs were slaughtered, some of the pork had to go to government sources for rationing, but the people from the clubs enjoyed the rest. Still, not all pigs were declared to the authorities and the Ministry of Food, so that illicit – under-the-counter – meat was just one of the perks of living close to the land.

'So, you see,' the cook told her, 'we're lucky to be stationed where we are.'

'Seems so. I can't remember the last time I had more than one slice of bacon,' Anna replied, happily.

After breakfast, she followed the corporal back to camp.

'We'll pick up your bicycle and I'll get you a map of the village. Your billet's only a few miles up the road, that way.'

The woman pointed vaguely ahead, and Anna's eyes followed the direction of her hand.

'Is this the main road, then?' she asked.

'As main as you get *here*, I'm afraid. We're in the back of beyond,' said Corporal Landry, her tone dismissive, an eyebrow raised in scorn.

Anna wondered why the other WAAF didn't seem to like the place, wasn't bowled over by the magic of it, like *she* already was. She picked up her bike and pocketed the map. 'I've got the rest of the day to get acclimatised, so the officer said,' she told her guide.

'Acclimatised, is it? Well, aren't you the lucky one! But you'd be wise to be on time for your shift tomorrow. Our glorious leader can be a mite tetchy if things don't go as planned. Just a word to the wise. It's the Irish in her,' Landry said, as if that explained it.

'Thanks for the warning,' said Anna. 'I appreciate it. I'm looking forward to being here.'

'No accounting for taste, I suppose. By the way, you'll be sharing that billet of yours with a few civilians, and the last girl that was billeted there said it was the coldest house on earth. You'll be wearing your greatcoat to bed,' the corporal said with a smirk.

'I'm used to that,' Anna said cheerfully, and wheeled her bike out to the perimeter track.

It seemed, for some reason, the other WAAF wanted to make others around her unhappy. Anna had noticed it in the cookhouse too, had thought how much like Aunt Beatrice the woman seemed. She felt a little sorry for Corporal Landry, but whatever the reason for the woman's lack of joy, she would not allow her own optimism to be diluted by it. She was happy and she had every right to be. Once she had cycled to her new billet, she would get organised and the first thing she would do, she decided, would be to write to Jimmy. Even if she had to do it sat in a freezing house – with her gloves and greatcoat on.

28

8 NOVEMBER 1940

It surprised Anna how many things about her life were perfect. She'd never known anything like it.

Her billet in an old stone cottage was like something from a storybook, set in a small dingle – or was it a dell? She was never really sure of the difference; either way, both of those small, wooded valleys looked as if they belonged in a fairy tale. The house was a few miles from the entrance to the airfield and across the road from the end of the runway. The sound of planes taking off and landing was easy to hear, but Anna didn't mind that. In its way, it was a comforting sound, one she was used to, but it made the windows rattle in the ancient house.

Beautiful trees surrounded the cottage, their dramatic evergreen foliage standing out against the stark grey Cornish granite. In spring the place would be covered with snowdrops, bluebells and daffodils. She hadn't seen them yet, of course, but Lowenna Trevorrow, who lived in the cottage with her two small children, had told her about them. Just picturing all those brilliant colours and their heady scent made Anna feel glad to have ended up there. It was true that the walls were stone, but they were thick and kept out most of the cold. And Mrs Trevorrow always kept in a good supply of wood from the trees around to use in the Cornish range. It was usual for Anna to cycle home at night and arrive in time for a supper of bread and cheese and a warm and cheery kitchen to sit in.

She enjoyed her work in the ops room, as well; found her job exhilarating. The station was a busy place, often as challenging as Biggin, but the difference was that – so far at least – no bombs had been dropped on this airfield. The Luftwaffe was too busy elsewhere, it seemed, so no attacks had taken place. Not that any of them on the station were complacent.

She often worked on the plot table alongside her WAAF officer, Eileen Garvey, who was quite vocal about her dislike of the German air force and enthusiastic about her job. 'We plotters are the eyes and ears of Fighter Command,' she would say, and Anna thought that an excellent description of what they did. She kept it in mind as she plotted the movements of incoming enemy planes.

Another perfect part of her new life was the joy of riding her bike through the luscious Cornish countryside. Sometimes, she'd gone farther afield than Trevellas. She was proud of herself – an intrepid explorer – cycling up so many hills that her leg muscles screeched in fatigue and her heart hammered in her chest. Once, she'd gone as far as the small village of St Agnes and had cycled down to the sea, to a place called Trevaunance Cove. The beach was closed off on both sides with barbed wire, but a narrow pathway ran in between – for anyone brave enough to go swimming, she assumed. It was surrounded by high, jagged cliffs and full of rock pools, but these disappeared at high tide along with the beach – eaten up by the ocean. She imagined the barbed wire was to keep the enemy away, to discourage them from attempting a landing. But the Germans would get their feet wet if they tried to come ashore at Trevaunance.

Her air force-issue bike was like a passport to freedom. It wasn't pretty or sleek, but a heavy, obstinate old thing, hard to steer, with a mind of its own and mudguards that were slowly rusting away. But the bike had become a friend and in the dark of the blackout, she relied on it to find the way home. She'd christened it 'The Beast'. She had thought about calling it 'Daisy Two', but that would have been too sad. And it was sad enough already, the thought of pedalling away and not seeing Jimmy in the saddle in front of her.

So, her life would have been truly perfect if it hadn't been for one thing. One gaping hole at the centre of it. She'd been there for almost a month and still Jimmy and she had been unable to meet: when he'd been free, she'd been on the duty roster and the same in reverse. Meanwhile, they were both growing more frustrated as time slipped from their grasp. It was supposed to be easier to see each other, that had been the plan. The whole idea of her transfer. But plans sometimes went awry.

They'd written letters, but it wasn't the same, for no matter how passionate or tender the words on a page, they were no substitute for a loving touch. It seemed a simple thing to ask, to throw herself into his arms, to smother his mouth with her kisses until both of them had to struggle for air. To touch each other in places that made her shiver with delight. A *lover's touch* – was there anything more powerful? she wondered.

In desperation one day, she'd set off to cycle the twenty-five miles to his station at St Eval. But she'd only got halfway there and abandoned the idea. She had no pass, and it was a large and important station, almost 2,000 personnel, with tight security, Jimmy had said. She could try to sneak in but had no idea where he would be; he might even be flying. Besides, if she were caught, it could get her in serious trouble. Jimmy too, maybe. She couldn't do that to him, no matter how disappointed she felt, or how much she missed him. There would be a time when both their schedules would coincide. Surely fate would step in and rescue them, but right then, it felt as if the universe was conspiring against them, keeping them apart.

She tried to keep her frustration at bay, concentrated on her work, took the occasional trip into Perranporth, and wrote copious letters to him. Every night before going to bed, she would pray for his safety and for Mary, Gladys, Harry and her old friend, Edna. *Protect them all*, she'd implore, as if someone was listening and cared – as if the very mention of the names was an antidote to the perils of war. It was superstition, she supposed, going through the names on her list. It would hardly keep them out of danger. Then again, it couldn't hurt.

Afterwards she would add a few more lines to her letters to Jimmy, telling him about her day, as if he were a part of it. Sometimes, those letters had so many pages that it was hard to get them in the envelope. But he'd told her that he treasured every line.

Writing letters became an important part of her time. She wrote to Mary and Edna. She even composed a letter to that woman, Jane Walker, inviting her to come and visit, describing the countryside and her billet and the changing colours of the ocean that crashed its way to shore. When she reread it, she felt a little embarrassed by that one – letting her guard down, getting personal – after all, she knew nothing of this woman. She thought twice about posting it but in the end, she sent it winging off with the rest. What could it hurt, anyway?

NEWQUAY, CORNWALL

14 NOVEMBER 1940

Anna couldn't believe his face, how much it had changed. It was thinner now from the one she remembered and cherished – sharper, and more angular. And what had happened to that luxurious ginger moustache? It had disappeared. Instead, deep lines tugged at his mouth and his lips were tight, less generous than she recalled. He looked tired, with dark shadows surrounding those amazing green eyes of his.

He'd smiled at her as soon as they met and for a second Jimmy's eyes had lit up the way she remembered they could, but then the light seemed to fade, as if he'd turned off a switch. He seemed anxious and edgy, although he'd tried to hide it from her. But she knew, for this was a face that she saw in her dreams. She could trace every contour of it with her eyes closed. And now it was deeply troubled.

The man she knew seemed to have retreated into this thin, joyless version of himself and she wanted to cry. Where was his laugh – and that excitement and passion he used to exude? She'd been excited about today, hadn't been able to sleep last night, thinking about it. Imagining. Playing out a fantasy in her mind. Flinging herself into his waiting arms. She'd made up her mind that it was the perfect time to consummate the love they'd vowed. They weren't married, it was true, but she had never needed a wedding to prove how she felt about this man. A wedding would come in its own good time.

Yet, he'd been so quiet and subdued when he'd picked her up from the station in Newquay. If she didn't know him better, she'd have called him shy – the way he took her hand as if for the first time. They hadn't seen each other for so long, not since that last night in Peckham. A whole eight months had passed by since then. Maybe that was it, the absence. But it felt like something more, something deeper and more serious. Wasn't absence meant to make a heart grow fonder? Maybe it had done the opposite, made them grow apart.

'You look good, better than I thought you might. I was worried about you,' he said.

'You were?' she asked.

'Of course, I was in despair. You know that, right? But they wouldn't let me go to the hospital.'

'That's what love does,' she said.

'What?'

'You share each other's pain. As well as the joy. But it's worth it,' she said, and searched his face for a clue that he understood what she was trying to say – that she could tell he was in pain now.

'I tried to go AWOL, but Freddy stopped me.'

'I should think so too. It wouldn't have done me any good if you'd ended up in the guardhouse. Or you either,' she said.

'No. But you're definitely well? You're not just being brave?' he said.

'I promise not to be brave *ever* again. Now, what about this place you've promised to take me to?'

'It's not far. We can walk there, and it's right by the ocean. We'll go to Towan beach first and we can climb up to it from there,' he said, and finally smiled.

'If I'd known we were mountaineering, I'd have worn different shoes.'

'No mountains, I promise. You'll see!' he said, with gusto.

She stroked his hand lovingly and gave him a massive grin. He seemed more relaxed now, as if the man that she knew and loved was beginning to come back to her. She suspected it was to do with his job, with the war and the demands that it made. *Unnatural* demands for peace-loving people. Expecting them to kill, and to do it over and over again with little rest in between. He was part of a bomber crew; they were there to drop bombs on the enemy and Jimmy's responsibility would be a hard one for him. His was the hand that directed the lethal blow. She thought of those Luftwaffe bombers that had devastated Biggin Hill, killed all the airmen in the air raid shelter. Remembered the first dead body that she'd seen, Elizabeth, lying in the bottom of a bomb crater, twisted and bloodied. Being bombed was a terrifying thing. No wonder Jimmy had changed. Being the one who dropped the bombs must be a dreadful burden to bear.

'You seem a little preoccupied,' he said.

'Oh? Not really. Just wondering how much fun we can fit into a forty-eight-hour pass,' she fibbed.

'Forty-eight for you, maybe. Not all of us get to laze around like you WAAFs.' He winked.

'I'll have you know we run the air force, mister. You'd all be looking for another job if it wasn't for us,' she said, and punched him playfully on the arm.

'I don't doubt that for a second! And you deserve your two-day pass, but they've only cut my leash for a day.'

She watched him shrug, could see the frustration behind it.

'All the same, we could still get up to some mischief in twenty-four hours,' she said.

'I believe we could,' said Jimmy, and he wrapped his arm around her waist as they headed for the beach.

When they got there, Anna kicked off her shoes and they walked together along the pale blonde sand, watched the waves gently glide to the shoreline. Others were strolling there, many in uniform; some reclining in deckchairs, as if it were the middle of summer and there was no war.

No barbed wire invaded the beach here, or stark signs with skulls and crossbones warning of mines, no gun emplacements on the cliffs. It seemed remote from war, this place, so tranquil, that as they walked, hand in hand, she found herself imagining that it had all just been a nightmare.

She shivered with the cold and allowed him to pull her into

the warm comfort of his body. 'They're hardy,' she said, nodding
to the water and the swimmers out there, heads bobbing about
in the ocean like seals.

'Do you swim?' he asked.

'I do, but not today, not in the cold. I'm not that brave,'
Anna said.

'I think you're very brave,' he said, and planted a light kiss
on her mouth.

'I've missed those. But that one was a little cautious, don't
you think?'

'Cautious, eh? I can do better than cautious, but I can
hardly ravage you in front of all these people, now can I?' He
laughed.

'Maybe later. Let's put the ravaging on hold, shall we?' she
said. It was enough that his laugh was back and that his lips held
a promise of things to come.

After their walk on the beach, they bought hot chocolate
from a man selling drinks from an ancient, green, military-
looking van. A spiv, she supposed. There were lots of them
making money from the war. It was the way of the world. They
sat on a stone wall and drank and warmed their hands on the tin
mugs. She told him about her time with his family, his mother
teaching her to cook. About Harry, guarding the canal.

He laughed again. 'I know Mother's proud of him – of his
promotion,' he said.

'She is. And you must be too. Your father's a wonderful
man. Not all fathers are,' she said, and sighed.

'Right, up you get. Follow me. No sad faces allowed,' Jimmy
warned, jollying her along.

And there it was in front of them. A strange, awesome sight.
A magical, enchanted place, like nothing she had seen before. A
tiny island, a high rocky cliff high above the beach they'd just
been walking on. Stretching out over the ocean but connected
to the land by a long suspension bridge.

They walked over the bridge onto the strange, miniature island and she felt as if she were weightless, drifting in the air. She tried to imagine it in a sea mist, floating above the beach, connected to the sky. It took her breath away.

The only thing on the island was an old Edwardian house, elegant and elaborate, something you wouldn't expect to find in that surprising place.

'You're right, it's incredible,' she told him.

'Towan Island, it's called. Some local aristocrat built the house for his family.'

'Imagine it in a high wind or a storm,' she said, and shivered.

'It's cold up here, shall we move on?'

'And what will we do for the rest of our twenty-four-hour escape?' she asked.

'That depends on what you'd like to do,' Jimmy said.

'I don't mind what I do, as long as it's with you. Maybe somewhere quiet on our own? My billet's a bit too far and Lowenna would be there anyway...'

'Maybe we could go and have a drink somewhere,' he said.

'Or...'

'You have something else in mind?'

'A room somewhere. We could spend the night. You've got till the morning to report,' she said.

'A room together – are you sure?'

'I'm sure,' she said. 'I'm *very* sure.'

'Maybe we should wait till after we're married,' he offered.

'Sergeant James Armstrong, I've waited long enough for this day. Don't you dare ask me to wait a minute more.'

Jimmy smiled, his eyes twinkling once more. 'I've waited for something special too,' he said. 'Before we cross over the bridge and leave this extraordinary place, I wanted to ask you something.'

She followed his eyes as he pointed to a bench, inclined his head – an invitation. So, she sat, intrigued, and furrowed her brow in a question. Then he sank to his knees on the grass. And that's when she knew what he was about to ask. She imagined him rehearsing it in his head many times, practising taking the ring from his pocket. He wouldn't have fumbled it then, as he did now. But he finally prised open the black velvet ring-box and she could feel his relief, and tried not to smile because it made him even more endearing. It was a solemn thing he was asking. And she wanted it to be perfect for him.

'Anna Golding,' he said, 'will you do me the extreme honour of becoming my wife?'

She let go of the breath she'd been holding and stretched out her hand in reply. 'I will. Nothing could make me happier,' she said, and waited for him to put the ring on her finger.

He slid it on her finger and then looked up at her. 'Is the ring okay? It's not a real diamond, but the silver is the finest. I wanted to get you something special, except the jeweller said this was the very best he had – with there being a war on. Is it good enough?' he asked, anxiously.

'It's an incredible ring,' she assured him. It was a square shaped solitaire diamond on a beautiful silver band. It was a thing of beauty, and even if the diamond wasn't real, what did it matter? It was *his* ring – and that meant everything.

'And does it fit?' he asked.

'It fits *perfectly*,' she said. *Well, almost*, she thought. A little big, but she wouldn't spoil his moment. She could always put an insert in to keep it snug. And safe. The last thing she wanted was to lose it.

A look of relief passed over his face, replaced with a wide, beaming grin. '*She said yes!*' he roared, as loud as he was able, and a passing stranger looked at him oddly, as if Jimmy had lost his mind.

Slowly, she pulled him up off his knees. 'A proper proposal,' she said, 'that's impressive. But you only needed to get down on one knee.'

'I know,' he said, 'but I didn't know if I could make it. Not as athletic as I used to be,' he said and beamed again.

'No? Well, why don't we go and see?'

'Anna Golding, you're a wicked, wicked woman!'

'Wasn't it you who mentioned *ravaging* first?'

They left the island, arm in arm, both of them laughing.

29

'This place is quite swanky,' Jimmy told Anna as they walked into the fancy hotel on Cliff Road.

He was right, she thought. The Beachcroft was certainly opulent. Lots of RAF personnel were billeted there, but officers only, it seemed.

'So, you think they'll let us have a room? We're hardly officers,' she said.

'I *know* people,' he said, and tapped the side of his nose like a secret signal. *Trust me*, it said.

The room was old-fashioned, heavy with drapes and dark, imposing furniture; ornate and over-stuffed armchairs and a luxurious chaise-longue dominated the space. Anna tried to imagine some Victorian lady of high breeding lounging on it, giving orders to her maid.

'Very fancy,' she said.

'I intend to pamper you. Only the best. And I've ordered us some wine.'

She smiled, could see what he was trying to do. But she

didn't need to be wrapped in luxury or wined and dined, although that was always acceptable, of course. She would have followed him into a tent as long as they could be together.

They sat on the end of the bed, holding hands, both of them looking a little nervous, she thought. And when the wine arrived, she allowed herself just one small sip, remembering the last time she'd drunk wine with him in the restaurant. She'd got tipsy so easily then, didn't want to do that again. Today was a momentous day, one she'd been waiting for and dreaming about. She didn't want to spoil it or blur its memory with wine.

She took a picture of his face in her mind. A keepsake to remember when she was alone and needed the assurance that this day was real. The way his eyes had softened once again to the ones she knew and loved. How the small hollow of his neck met his collarbone. His jawline, not square or jutting, but still well-defined. The faint shadow of a beard beginning to show again. They were images she knew she would recall.

Then she felt his hands on her, exploring her body, and she helped him, guiding them to places that she knew would send a thrill of pleasure through her. She'd felt the first awakening of these shivers of delight when he'd touched her before in those same places, but she'd pulled back then, frightened of the responses of her body, their intensity. She'd vowed never to do that again. Fear would not stop her this time.

The book she'd read on making love had told her that it was something meant to make you feel good, not ashamed. But she knew that already, looking into his face. *Making love.* Was that simply an acceptable way of saying that troubling word *sex*? Were people who made love actually *in love*? she wondered. Not all of them, she surmised. But *she* was, and she was convinced Jimmy was as well.

She felt her clothes being slowly peeled away. It was tender and seductive. Anna knew nothing about lovemaking, but something told her that he would be a gracious and gentle lover. The

tingling sensation she'd felt before in that place that marked her
out as a woman – it was there again as his hands moved over
her. His touch aroused her, but this time she welcomed it, found
herself rocking her pelvis to and fro, which felt natural, an
instinctive thing to do, as if the pattern for this act was already
written somewhere deep in her mind.

And then her body felt as if it were on fire. He was there,
she thought, and had found the entrance to her Aladdin's cave,
a cave of wonder. At first it hurt a little, as his body joined with
hers, as she'd thought it might, but the pain was worth the
ecstasy that followed. Powerful, erotic sensations rushed in to
fill her body and her mind. Her body shook with the pleasure of
it, and small flashes of light passed before her eyes. Blood
pounded at her temples, and all her muscles seemed to clench
at the same time. But it wasn't frightening, it was pleasurable
and exhilarating. Then, suddenly, a shudder ran through her,
and her muscles relaxed, her legs felt numb. Her whole body
shook with the sensation and then, afterwards, a strange feeling
of peace and rapture wrapped itself around her.

Later, she watched Jimmy sleep, fascinated by the way his
body seemed to rid itself of tension, leaving it as relaxed and
free as a child's. She moulded her body into his until it was hard
to see where he ended and she began, and, pressed into his
sleeping form, she found herself breathing with the same
rhythm until the soft mist of sleep descended and carried her to
a place of dreams.

Jimmy had been sad to leave. Had said they should stay in their
room forever, or better still, run away together, where no one
would find them or make them go to war. But he didn't mean it,
she understood that. Still, it was a measure of his weariness and
disillusion with the war and what he had to do. She loved him

even more for that. The fact that, although he hated the killing and destruction he'd become a part of, he would never take the coward's way out and disappear. He was an honourable man, who took the hard road because it was what his country asked. They were other things she loved about him – his code of honour and his valour. Things that went hand in hand.

It would be another four weeks before he would get a pass again. It seemed cruel of the universe to inflict that kind of pain on them but it wouldn't help to say that, so she'd waved him off cheerfully and made him laugh. He'd pointed to the ring on her left hand. It still felt new, as if it hadn't yet become a part of her, but she was thrilled and proud to wear it; to have found such a man, such a love.

The train didn't take long to get her close to home, to the station at Perranporth, where she'd left her bike. The hardest part was getting up St George's Hill. She pushed the Beast for some of the way and remembered the struggles of Old Pop Truscott, trying to coax his ancient van up there. The hill felt more like a mountain now and, halfway up, the heavens played a trick on her. The rain started slowly at first, just a small drizzle that found its way inside the collar of her greatcoat, and then the sky opened up in all its fury. Rain slanted across her path. It ran off her cap in rivulets and found its way into her eyes no matter how she tried to bury her head. Then a howling wind built up, pushed hard against her, pulling the bike off course, tipping her over. Her cap flew off and she hurried after it into a field at the side of the road. Missing uniform could be replaced, but the price was usually docked from your pay.

A crack of thunder rumbled in the distance and the rain took it as a signal to come down even harder. She tumbled down the side of the embankment, managed to grab hold of her cap, but ended up covered in mud.

'What? Why did you do that?' she shouted, shaking her fist at the sky, a vengeful look on her face.

Then she sat back in the mud and laughed. Giggled, the way they all had playing those games that night in Mary's house. She was tired and wet, with mud on her face. But it was funny. She imagined Jimmy would laugh when she told him – especially at her getting angry over such a stupid, petty thing. That's when she climbed out of the field and grabbed hold of her bike.

The road was much flatter now, at the crest of the hill. Up ahead was the entrance to the airfield. She could always go in and have a hot cup of char before tackling the rest of the journey home. She imagined it would make Corporal Landry's day to see her in such a mess. *Demerits from the house captain!* That's what the corporal always struck her as. The thought made up her mind. Anna plumped the soggy cap back on her head, turned up the collar of her greatcoat and got back on the bike. The pedals squeaked and the tyres splooshed noisily through puddles in the road. Only a couple of miles to go and she could warm herself in front of the stove at home, and Lowenna might even have something edible left over to eat.

She couldn't help but smile. Jimmy and she had enjoyed an incredible twenty-four hours, she was happy, really happy. Couldn't the rest of the world join in and be happy too, and forget all this madness? But they wouldn't, would they? It had all gone much too far for that.

Lowenna was waiting for her in the front porch: she must have heard the bike coming. She looked a little flushed, Anna thought, and her hair was in disarray. She watched the young woman adjust the baby on her hip and tuck a strand of the unruly hair behind her ear.

She had marvelled at Lowenna's hair when they'd first met. A glossy, lustrous waterfall, so black it held shades of blue and an unusual luminescence. It seemed to her, though, that this lovely young woman was unaware of it – or of the natural beauty that resided in her, starting on the inside and working its way out. Anna thought her kind, and other-worldly too, like a princess from a fairy tale. She fitted her surroundings perfectly, here in this fairy dell.

She'd told Anna that her husband – a young sailor serving in the Merchant Navy – had called her a *comely wench*. A joke between them, it seemed.

'Quickly, quickly!' said Lowenna, grabbing Anna's arm. 'You got a visitor.'

'But I'm not expecting anyone...' she said.

'She's in the kitchen and she don't look no better'n you!'

'*She?*' Anna asked.

'The woman's a sponge waiting to be wrung. 'Spect she got caught in the rain. Least she t'int all muddy like you.' Lowenna laughed.

'I see.'

'Cummas 'zon! Can't keep 'er waiting no more.'

'What's her name, this poor, soggy wraith?' she asked. But it was no good, Lowenna had gone. Anna left her bike in the porch and followed.

It was warm in the kitchen, which she was grateful for. She'd already started to shiver in her wet, muddy things. The black leaded Cornish stove had the door to its firebox flung open wide to heat the room while something bubbled away on its hotplate above. She noticed a coat hung over the back of a chair, steam rising from it as it dried. This must belong to their visitor, she thought. But there was no one there, unless of course it really was a wraith, a blithe spirit – a waterlogged one.

'She's gone to the water closet,' Lowenna explained. 'She'll be back dreckly, I'm sure.'

'I was beginning to think she was some kind of strange

apparition or a Cornish pisky, maybe.' Anna smiled. 'But I see that she's real. Unless piskies wear overcoats.'

'Now don't you be dismissing the piskies,' Lowenna said, seriously. 'But they stick to the moors, you'll not find them here.'

Anna looked at the discarded coat again. She'd hoped the visitor was Mary, an exciting idea, as she hadn't seen her good friend in a while, and they had a lot to talk about. Like the ring on her hand and a wedding to plan. But it couldn't be Mary, otherwise it would have been an air force greatcoat drying there.

Another notion struck her: Edna was a civilian now, the coat could well be hers. *Was Edna here? Had she travelled from Liverpool?* Her old friend had been wretched, her life turned upside down. There had been a sense of melancholy and desperation clinging to Edna's letter that she'd received over the summer. Anna had been grief-stricken just reading it, remembering the spirited and fun-loving woman that used to be. She had written to Edna several times since, had heard nothing back. She'd been thinking of going to see her – maybe now she wouldn't need to. Now she could console her friend face to face, let her see that no problem was too hard to tackle if they took it on together. The old team.

The kitchen door opened, and a woman walked in. It wasn't Edna.

30

They'd shaken hands, introduced themselves; though no introduction was needed, since it was obvious who the visitor was. Anna had seen the woman once before. Had chased her through the streets of Stockport.

Lowenna made them all tea. 'Good for frayed nerves,' she'd said. Anna needed it, but maybe they all did. It was a strange situation, but intriguing just the same. Perhaps now a part of her past would be explained, and she could come to terms with that complicated idea of family. What it truly meant.

Jimmy was her family now, not because of bloodlines or necessity, but because he *chose* to be. And Mary too. And Gladys and Harry – they'd all taken her seamlessly into their lives.

'Well, ain't you a pair of peas in a pod!' Lowenna said.

'Are we?' Anna asked the woman sitting in the chair opposite.

'Are we what?' asked Jane Walker.

'Peas from the very same pod,' she said.

The woman's hair was different now, much longer than she remembered. They had looked more like twins then, but now she could see there were subtle differences between them. The other woman was slightly smaller than she was, a little younger maybe; and her eyes were different, more almond-shaped – they were green, like Jimmy's. And those eyes were smiling.

'In a way,' Jane Walker said.

'I've no idea what that means. But you are her, I suppose?' she said.

'Her?'

'The woman who wrote to me. The woman who ran away in Stockport that day.'

'It's hard to explain why I didn't stay,' said Jane. 'I wanted to. You can't imagine how much I wanted to stay – how I'd dreamt of that day.'

'Then why did you run?' asked Anna.

'I was a coward; afraid I might frighten you away. I'd pinned all my hopes on finding you, of not being alone any more. Of having family...' she said.

'So, we *are* family then? I'd... I'd thought we might be twins,' Anna said.

'No, though how wonderful that would have been! But we're not twins, or sisters. Your ma and pa only had one child and that was you,' Jane said.

'But how do you know these things?' Anna asked.

'My mother finally told me, just before she died last year. She wanted me to know I wasn't alone, I suppose. Or it was the guilt, maybe. But I knew nothing about you, until then.'

'I don't understand. How did your mother know about me – and why do we look alike?'

'It's a tale of two sisters, you were right. But not us,' said Jane.

'Who then?' asked Anna, impatiently.

'Your mother and my mother were sisters, twins. It seems they looked very alike,' said Jane.

'I've seen a photograph of them when they were young.

They were identical copies of each other,' Anna said, excited now. 'Except...'

'What?'

'They seemed like very different people. My mother was smiling, and your mother was serious and—'

'—Looked a bit stuck-up and snobbish? Don't worry, I'm not offended. She was always haughty.' Jane smiled.

'So, you're my cousin.' Anna smiled. 'How incredible that sounds! It's hard to take in. Are there any more of you – brothers, sisters?' she asked.

'No, I'm an only child too,' said Jane, sadly.

'It's lonely, being the only one. At least that's how it was for me,' said Anna.

'Still, it makes you a little tougher, don't you think?'

'Exactly. But you were lucky,' Anna said, deep in thought. 'You had your mother right there.'

'Hmm.' Jane looked at her. 'She was certainly there, but Mother wasn't the nurturing type.'

'Like my Aunt Beatrice. But you and I both survived and now we've found each other. I'm glad,' said Anna.

'Me too.'

'What was your mother's name?' she asked.

'Kathryn. Kathryn Walker,' said Jane.

'Elizabeth and Kathryn. Women from another age. They sound rather grand,' said Anna.

'Mother liked to think so. She called herself an aristocrat,' Jane said, rolling her eyes.

Anna laughed, and then said: 'I've gained a cousin. What an amazing, extraordinary day!'

'I think so too,' said Jane.

'But why have we never met – it's peculiar, don't you think? What age are you? When were you born? Where have you been living all this time?' asked Anna.

'So many questions, but I understand!' Jane smiled at her

cousin warmly. 'I felt just like you when I first knew. We're almost the same age. And there are things you need to know. We'll get around to it all in good time. But for now, shouldn't we celebrate?'

'More tea?' asked Lowenna. 'And maybe I can find a drop of something to put in it – if the piskies haven't had it all,' she said, and winked.

Anna's teacup rattled in the saucer. She stared at her traitorous hands, willed them to stop shaking. Trying to take in everything Jane had told her so far. 'So, you're telling me that your mother knew about me all along. Knew that my mother had died, that my father had abandoned me, and I'd been palmed off on Beatrice. Yet she never came to see me?'

'Yes, and I'm sorry. If I'd known about you before, I'd have done something. Both you and I were caught in a family feud. But you know what families are like,' said Jane.

'Well, I know what *my* family's like. Luckily not all families are the same,' said Anna. 'Some of them are happy.' She thought back wistfully to the time she'd spent with Gladys and Harry and the warm welcome she'd had.

'My father was kind, thoughtful and generous,' said Jane. 'A gentleman in every way and I loved him so much, idolised him. He loved me too, and he tried to love my mother, but she wouldn't let him get past her anger. She was cruel to him at times.'

'I don't understand. Why did she marry him then?' Anna asked, confused.

'She married him because the man she *really* wanted rejected her for someone else.'

'Where's your father now?' she asked. But as soon as Anna said it, she regretted her words. Wished she could take them back as sorrow registered on her cousin's face and the mist in her eyes spelled a warning of waiting tears. But they didn't materialise, and Anna was relieved. She hadn't meant to make her cousin sad.

'He's gone,' said Jane, a tiny shudder moving through her. 'He died when I was six years old.'

'Life can be cruel, at times,' said Anna.

'Like my mother,' said Jane, without humour.

'And my Aunt Beatrice. She told me I had no other family. That your mother had died many years ago from the Spanish flu. She lied to me.'

'So, we're a matching pair – in lots of ways.'

'And are you a WAAF, as well?' asked Anna.

'A WAAF? No – I'm a civilian,' said Jane.

'But you work at the Air Ministry?'

'I do. I'm a civil servant – just a plain old clerk, I'm afraid – in a dingy, basement office. I shuffle papers and file requisitions for stores from RAF stations.'

'You're still doing your bit, though,' said Anna.

They both fell silent and the only sounds in the room were the crackle of logs in the firebox of the Cornish range and the rain outside as it bounced off the ancient window frames.

Anna wrestled with her thoughts. It was a strange story, this tale of her cousin's early life, with a father who'd loved her but died, and a mother who seemed to have struggled to be fond of her own child. Jane's family history was complicated and sad, a little like her own. It was tangled and unhappy in places and so curious and unlikely that she found herself believing it.

'A tale of two sisters,' Jane had told her. She tried to imagine their mothers, how it might have been. Twins growing up together, doing the same things, wearing the same clothes, close perhaps – affectionate, maybe. Until they both fell in love with the same man. But her aunt had been rejected, thrown aside in favour of her sister, who eventually married that man – William Golding, her father. That was the most disturbing part of the story, at least to Anna. When she'd first heard it, her body had recoiled with the shock, her hands tightly gripped to stop them from shaking, but she could do nothing about the sick feeling in her stomach. She thought about Jane's mother, Kathryn, who had then married on the rebound, but had never loved the father of her child. Had never been kind to him. She'd married in anger and haste, to spite her sister.

Their mothers had become estranged from each other. She thought then of the photograph on her father's desk. Her mother had looked kind, not a woman who could hate or cast her sister aside. Maybe she had tried to heal the rift between them. But neither Anna nor her cousin Jane could ever really know. The sisters were gone, and they only had Kathryn Walker's side of the tale.

Anna tried to understand how her aunt must have felt. The misery of being rejected, thrown over for your own flesh and blood. It could have made her a bitter woman. She tried to find sympathy for her Aunt Kathryn's plight, not to feel angry with her. But it wasn't easy. *Why hadn't this aunt ever come to see her?* She'd known of her birth, how her mother had died and that she'd been handed over to Beatrice. A young child alone and yet *not once* had this woman come to offer friendship or family kinship.

Her cousin Jane had been as much a victim of this family feud as she was. If Anna's family had been more kind and forgiving, she might have met her cousin many years ago.

Real life could sometimes be more incredible than fiction, she thought. Both she and Jane had somehow become trapped between the passion and bitterness of unrequited love. But at least their unusual upbringing gave them something in common, pulled the two women together. She had felt a connection as soon as they met; an attachment that marked them out as kindred spirits.

She couldn't wait to tell Jimmy about it, how she had

someone else in her family now, a cousin whose life had been similar to hers and whose path she had finally crossed. Her cousin seemed warm-hearted and understanding, might even become a friend. Jimmy would be pleased for her, she thought, had encouraged her to get in touch with Jane Walker in the first place.

She had a good feeling about Jane, believed what the young woman had told her. She seemed genuine, Anna thought, and they'd been easy in each other's company.

That's why Anna had done something unusual and out of character. Something instinctive: later, as she saw Jane off at the station, she had hugged the young woman affectionately. It had been a spur-of-the-moment thing that surprised them both, especially Anna, who didn't usually give her trust so rapidly.

And as she hugged Jane Walker, Anna had noticed that her cousin had tears in her eyes as well.

31

RAF ST EVAL

16 NOVEMBER 1940

He couldn't remember the last time he had smiled this much. His face hurt with it. *But that was good, wasn't it?* Some knowing looks had come his way from the rest of the crew and a smirk from one of the WAAFs when she handed him his tea. How did they know about the miracle that twenty-four hours with Anna had brought about?

He knew what some of the chaps in the mess would say – that he'd finally got himself 'sorted out' and that was why this invigorated and optimistic version of his old self had suddenly reappeared. Maybe they'd be right, because making love with her had been incredible, all that he'd dreamed it might be.

He would have waited, done the proper thing, and carried on acting like a monk until they could be married. But he wouldn't lie to himself or pretend the struggle had been an easy one. He was no different from every other man – he had urges and needs, and it had been a welcome relief to know she understood. That she had been brave enough to make the decision for both of them. Because when it came down to it, she had needs too – he could see that now.

The next thing to think about would be a wedding, but he wasn't to worry about that, she'd told him. There would be a perfect time and place for it, and fate might just take a hand. It seemed she believed in fate, and Jimmy was beginning to think that perhaps he did too.

'Sorry to burst your bubble, old thing, but Squadron Leader Blake's requesting your company,' said George.

'Really?' he said, surprised, forcing his mind back to where it had to be.

'Shouldn't keep him hanging on if I were you. He had that hungry look in his eye... waiting for his next victim, I shouldn't be surprised.'

'Can't think what he wants with me,' said Jimmy.

'You been a naughty boy, Ginger?' George packed his voice full of innuendo.

'Never!' he said and laughed. Whatever the S/L wanted him for, it couldn't be anything he'd done, at least nothing serious. His conscience was clear. Maybe George was playing a trick on him, setting him up. Still, best not keep the man waiting.

Even so, Jimmy stopped off at the barracks to change into his best blues. If he *was* in for a reprimand – and he couldn't think why – it was always better to be properly dressed and not stroll in wearing any old assortment of flying kit. That would only put the squadron leader's back up, for he was one of the old brigade: a career man who'd been in the air force for most of his adult life. He always struck Jimmy as fair, but serious all the same, and he had no time for fools.

It was a long way to station headquarters, so he borrowed a friend's bike, which bought him some time and sent his mind travelling back to when he'd been steering that heavy old tandem, with Anna on the back, fiercely pedalling away. It had been a happy time. They'd had fun and he was looking forward to when they could do that again. *The captain and his tail-gunner*, he thought. They made a perfect team.

He was ushered into the squadron leader's office as if he were expected. Even so, he waited another ten minutes for the door to swing open again, by which time he'd run through all kinds of scenarios in his head: things he might have done or *not* done, perhaps. But he'd done everything he was supposed to, had reported back for duty on time. The only thing he could come up with was that time in the mess when he'd almost drunk himself into a stupor, before Freddy had saved him.

He heard a warning cough, so he sprang to attention and saluted.

'Morning, Sergeant Armstrong. Stand easy.'

Jimmy's eyes latched on to the officer's face. The man didn't look angry with him or about to have him thrown in the guard-house, so he did as he was told and relaxed – as much as he could, standing in front of his commanding officer.

'How was your break, Sergeant?'

'Fine, sir. Thank you, sir. Ready to get back to the job, though,' said Jimmy. His brain was like a corkscrew, twisting and turning through all kinds of possibilities. Was it something he'd done on leave? But then the officer was smiling, not frowning. He wanted to breathe, to inhale the deepest breath he could find, but instead, there was a tightness in his chest.

'Good, good. You chaps need a break now and then.'

'Yes, sir,' he said.

'We're compiling an emergency roster, Sergeant – mostly of all you old hands, as it were. Some of the new chaps are having trouble getting into the swing of things. We need experienced flight engineers, navigators and gunners able to fill in with other crews if necessary. We'll be putting your name on the list as navigator.'

'Sorry, sir – I don't follow... you're splitting up our crew?'

'No, not quite. Obviously, you'll still be with your own aircrew, but if you're not on standby and an emergency comes up, you may be called on to complete a mission with some other chaps.'

'I see.' But he didn't, of course – and neither would the rest of the crew, or the other chaps who might be put on this list. Airmen were superstitious, taking good luck charms on missions and crossing their fingers going over the St Eval runway hump. Some would see this as bad luck – being shuffled around like so many cards in a pack. Despite what the squadron leader said, Jimmy knew exactly how crews would feel about having to fit in with chaps they didn't know. It took time to work together, to gain each other's trust, especially when you might be putting your life in their hands. No, Jimmy couldn't see this working at all.

'Sergeant Armstrong?'

'Yes, sir?'

'It may never happen. It's simply a belt and braces thing. Just giving you a heads-up, that's all.'

'Thank you, sir,' he said.

'Dismissed,' said the officer.

He saluted and got ready to leave. Then the door swung open and a young WAAF corporal came through, one of the squadron clerks. Her salute was brief, and she smiled in Jimmy's direction. He thought he detected some sympathy in her greeting.

'Sir, before Sergeant Armstrong leaves, there was a communication for him.'

'Fine, Corporal, you may give it to him, then.'

'I'll just need to check your service number to make sure it's you. Then you can sign for it, Sergeant,' the WAAF said.

'You might bring me in a cuppa, if you get a chance,' said Squadron Leader Blake.

Jimmy noticed a weariness in the officer's voice and

although the man had smiled at his clerk, it struck him as an exercise in politeness, nothing more.

Of course, he got it now. This list he was about to become part of, it wasn't about sharing his experience with newbies at all. It was about the stark truth they all knew, but few of the airmen spoke of. Planes were often shot up, bringing back dead and wounded aircrew. Aircraft could be replaced; it took time of course, but not as long as it took to train aircrew, so slotting in missing fliers might make sense to some.

Not to Jimmy, though. Stepping into dead men's shoes? It was a sobering thought.

Still, he put it to the back of his mind and followed the young WAAF. She reminded him of Anna, and Mary. *We run the air force,* Anna had told him, and she was right, of course: without them, the RAF would be struggling. They took on all kinds of jobs that men had done before and did them quietly and efficiently, without complaint.

He checked his service number on the WAAF's clipboard and signed his name. 'Thanks,' he said, as she handed him the telegram.

'I hope it's not bad news,' the WAAF said.

He looked at the telegram in dismay and confusion, then hurried away to read it in private.

32

ANNA

What a miraculous week that had been.

First, that incredible day with Jimmy, visiting the beach and walking across the bridge to that wonderful fantasy island in the sky, high above the shore. His heartfelt marriage proposal. It all felt a little like a dream now, and part of that magical dream, the image she kept replaying over in her mind, was the two of them making love. She had let him lead them, but her body had replied to his urging in a way that astonished her and satisfied a need within her. She had felt exhausted but happy afterwards and *replete* – yes, that was a good description of the wonder of the act. She had been filled up with love, sated to the very brim of her being. She couldn't wait for when they would do that again.

Four weeks seemed a lifetime to wait, to be without him.

To add to that most thrilling day alone with him, there had been one more extraordinary surprise: finding her cousin. But more than that, discovering that they liked each other. Life couldn't get much better, she thought – until she stepped out of the cookhouse and there he was.

She watched in surprise, a mixture of delight and amazement on her face as he parked his bicycle in a rack and then turned and smiled at her. Except it didn't seem like his normal smile.

'You're here!' she said and ran at him, almost knocking him into the collection of bikes and taking the wind out of him.

'Steady on,' said Jimmy. But his voice held a tremor that she didn't recognise.

'My hero,' she said, excitedly. 'I can't believe you're here so soon – and the bike…'

'Borrowed it from one of the chaps. I had to see you right away,' he said, quietly.

'What's wrong? Something's up, I can tell. They're not posting you away, are they? No! Don't tell me that – not now when we're together at last,' she said, fear tugging at her lips until they trembled, her eyes wide with shock.

'No, not that,' he said and took her arm, guiding her back towards the cookhouse.

'What then?'

'Can we get tea in here? I think we both might need some,' Jimmy said, and slipped his arm gently around her waist, holding her up.

She could feel his strength joining with hers, their bodies melting into one. His touch was powerful, yet gentle, and he held her like a lover, she thought. But then that's exactly what he was. She looked in his face, at his eyes, expecting to see their softness, but there was only despair.

She went up to the counter and brought them back mugs of tea: black, thick like treacle and bitter. *Good for what ails you.* She watched as he took a small hip flask from his jacket and poured some of the contents into each one.

'What's in it?' she asked.

'Emergency rations – contributions from some of the gang. They thought we might need it.'

'But why?' she asked, her voice sombre now.

She saw him stare at the flask in fascination, as if it was the first time he'd seen it. 'Da gave me this, you know,' he said, 'when I first went to flight school. Had it engraved and everything. He was so proud.'

'What does it say?' asked Anna.

'See for yourself,' he said miserably, and held it out for her to read.

The inscription was plain, no flowery letters or swirls. Simple and honest like the man Harry Armstrong who'd bought it and had it engraved. It read: *To James Armstrong, our hero. Love from Ma and Da.*

Her lips silently mouthed the words and she could feel his eyes on her while she turned the silver flask over in her hands. It must have cost quite a bit, but then Harry and Gladys Armstrong were proud of their children, would want to show it in any way they were able.

She looked up at him, saw tears in his eyes that he didn't even try to hide, and a look of desperation.

'What's happened?' she asked. 'Is it your ma? Is she sick?'

'Ma?' he said, looking dazed, his voice barely above a whisper. 'Not Ma. I have to go up there. I'm leaving now. I didn't want you to find me gone and worry.'

'Not your ma,' she said. 'It's Harry, then...'

'Killed,' said Jimmy, his voice cracking. 'I should get going.'

'God, no!' She leaned across the table and grabbed his hand. 'Right, I'm coming with you. We're a couple, aren't we? And they're my family too. I want to be there.'

'They'll never let you go.'

'Just let them try and stop me,' she said. 'Compassionate leave – everybody's allowed that!'

'You'd do that for me?' said Jimmy, a weak smile finally breaking through.

'For us,' she said. 'We're an *us*!'

. . .

They cycled together the few miles back to the airfield on their bikes, side by side, holding hands. One hand to steer and the other comforting each other. A different kind of tandem, this time, she thought – two bicycles made into one. They cycled slowly and on the way he finally told her what had happened.

She'd been horrified and saddened at the same time when she heard about Harry. The trauma of war had found her before and sometimes in her dreams she still relived the nightmare of the bombing at Biggin Hill. But this was different. Harry Armstrong had been a man so full of life and purpose that she found it hard to think of him gone. She could hear that booming bass voice of his in her head and she wanted to cry. How could it possibly be silenced?

A house in the next street had been bombed and some of the family had been trapped inside. They'd asked for volunteers to dig for survivors. Harry would have been one of the first, she thought. He was that kind of man, happy to help out his neighbours and ready to lend a hand, without making a fuss. She pictured him there, getting stuck in, pulling at the rubble, listening for the cries.

Then an unexploded bomb had gone off and killed most of the rescuers.

'Your father's a hero,' she said. It sounded hollow and glib. Meaningless, but then what else was there to say? War news was often bad, but this was the worst kind.

'Maybe Ma would rather have a live coward than a dead hero, don't you think?' he said bitterly, his voice brittle.

'Sorry,' said Anna, and squeezed his hand.

'No – *I'm* sorry,' Jimmy said. 'It's not your fault.'

'It's not anybody's fault. Or if it is, then it must be Hitler's. But then again, it wasn't him who dropped the bomb. Or the bomb aimer's fault that it didn't explode right away,' she said. But she knew it wasn't helping. Nothing would help wipe out the pain Jimmy felt.

'Some of those high-explosive bombs have timed fuses set to explode anything up to seventy-two hours after they're dropped. They're meant to kill bomb disposal teams,' he said.

'But that's monstrous,' said Anna, appalled.

'You'd think so,' he said. 'But then we do it too.'

'I didn't know,' she said, shaken.

'It's war,' Jimmy said, wearily.

They'd both gone quiet after that, and she'd left him waiting at the barrier, by the guard hut. She promised to come as soon as she was able, and they'd travel to London together.

But would Section Leader Garvey grant her compassionate leave for the funeral? She hoped so. She could only try, and it was something she had to do. The rest of the family would surely be there: Mary and Alice and Tom. And she needed to be there too, not only for Jimmy, but also for Glad. And *especially* for Harry.

They'd left Cornwall hours ago, but their progress on the train had been torturously slow. The carriage had been crammed with people – so many of them in uniform now. They'd sat opposite each other, sometimes catching the other's eye, sometimes staring off into space, or pretending to look out of the window, as if there was something interesting out there.

Now, they'd finally arrived in the darkness of the blackout, both of them weary. Grief sat heavily on Anna like a thick, cloying blanket. She felt exhausted with it, and she imagined Jimmy felt the same. It made the last few miles to the house in Peckham the hardest she'd ever walked. They were holding hands. She couldn't remember taking his hand. Or how long they'd been walking like this. She wasn't sure if she was holding him up or the other way around, but either way it was comforting, a barrier against the pain. They hadn't talked of death again; as if some unspoken agreement had been made between them. It would be forced on them soon enough at the funeral, and well-meaning people trying to think of comforting things to say.

They walked on in the silence of the night, broken only by the sound of shoes striking pavement and a bicycle bell as an air-raid warden rode by, checking on the blackout.

Silence, Anna thought. Silence was comforting. Words could be enemies now; they would only get in the way. Trying to put the right words together, so they didn't cause any more pain, would be too difficult, she thought. It wouldn't help either of them. It wouldn't help Gladys or perform the miracle of bringing Harry back.

Harry Armstrong, the hero. *Harry who'd been doing something gallant and noble.*

The thought led her on to another chilling one. It made her panic. Her head whirled with the fear of it and her hands felt clammy, and suddenly there didn't seem enough air to breathe. *Like father, like son.*

Please, please, please, she begged whoever was out there in charge of answering prayers – *please don't let him try to be a hero too.*

33

Funerals weren't meant to be fun, she supposed. They were meant to be solemn and grim. Not that this one was, but it was sad, of course. The service had been short. Harry hadn't been one for flowery words or speeches, Gladys had told them all. It helped that the day wasn't grey, that yesterday's rain had disappeared. Today, the sun paid an unexpected visit, its weak rays finding their way through the stained-glass windows, sending colourful traces of light across the church floor. *Some might call it heavenly light,* Anna thought.

It was the first time she'd seen Alice up close – a pretty girl in her WREN's uniform. She had thought that the last time too, when she'd watched Jimmy and his sister in the restaurant, and assumed they were lovers. *What a jealous fool he must have thought her.*

Jimmy sat in the front row of the church, his arm linked with his ma's the whole way through. They'd hoped to see Tom, but no one had been able to find him. He was somewhere with his regiment, but it seemed that things were complicated in North Africa.

She hadn't seen Mary in such a long time and their reunion
had been filled with smiles and tears as they'd grabbed each
other fiercely, both reluctant to let go. She sat beside Mary in
the church and they held each other's hands, the scent of
flowers and floor wax floating in the air. Then she put her arm
around her friend's waist and helped her walk the final cruel
steps behind her father's coffin, through the ancient churchyard. She heard Mary's stifled sob as Harry descended into the
newly turned earth.

She watched Jimmy and Alice each drop a single flower
into the grave, saw them leave together and wondered why –
didn't know if she was meant to follow. But then Mary's hand
tensed and gripped hers in a vice, sending a small shockwave
through her, so she stayed.

The service had been modest and the coffin a plain, wooden
one, roughly hewn, with no fancy brass handles or frills. From
what she knew of Harry, he would have been happy with his
send-off, pleased that none of them had made too much fuss.
He had been a man of simple needs, an honest, forthright man.
That's when she thought about her father and the difference
between the two of them. When she had lived with him, her
father had surrounded himself with adornments, with people
who had bowed and scraped to him, danced attendance, and yet
Harry, a kindly man, had been the one who died.

'Da would've been pleased you've come,' Gladys said,
breaking into Anna's thoughts.

'Glad, I don't know what to say. No words seem good
enough. He was a lovely man,' said Anna.

'Then those are the *right* words,' said Gladys, as she patted
Anna's hand. The deep lines of sorrow on Gladys Armstrong's
face seemed to slowly melt away and a weak smile tugged at her
lips.

Anna was moved by the woman's courage – if Jimmy was
taken from her like this, would she be able to find that same

gentle valour in herself, or would she be bitter and rail at the world in anger?

'Thank you for letting me come,' she said. 'I know it's a family time.'

'You *are* family... oh, and Anna...' said Glad, eyeing the new engagement ring.

'Yes?' she said.

'Now that you're to be my daughter-in-law, maybe you'd like to call me Ma?'

'Oh, Glad! If you're sure.'

'I am.'

'*Ma*,' said Anna. 'That feels nice.' But it was more than just a word, of course. It was a symbol of her new family.

'I'm glad. I'm so happy you've taken my Jimmy on. You saved him, you know. I worried he would never find someone kind, someone who truly loved him as you do.'

'I'm not sure who's taken who on. He saved me too,' Anna said, and smiled. 'We've both known loneliness, at times.'

'And now he's trying to save me from my Alice,' Gladys said with a heavy sigh, her eyes searching the churchyard.

Anna could see Jimmy and Alice standing together by a sloping grey headstone. They seemed to be arguing.

'We'll leave Da to settle in now,' Gladys said. 'I'm happy we could get him in so close to home.'

Anna remembered the first time she'd seen the church's steeple. *Practically in their back garden*, Mary had told her.

'St Luke's is a fine old church, Ma. He liked it here,' said Mary.

'But I'll not leave him here alone. I'll come every day and have a chat,' Gladys said.

'He'll like that, Ma,' said Mary.

'Right. We'd best be off home and leave that pair to sort themselves out.'

All heads turned back to Jimmy and Alice. They were still

having a serious discussion, but now Jimmy had his arm around his sister's shoulders, looked to be comforting her.

'What's that about?' asked Mary.

'Alice wants to move back in and treat me like an invalid. Thinks I can't fend for meself. Jimmy's puttin' her right.'

'Alice can be bossy at times, but she means well,' said Mary, diplomatically.

'She has a good heart.' Gladys sighed again.

'You all right, Ma?' Mary asked.

'Good enough. Now you and Anna can walk me home. The neighbours have put on a tea for us, we'll not keep them waiting. After that, we'll make plans.'

'Plans?' Mary asked.

'You kids can't stay here forever. Da wouldn't like it, not when you got a war to win,' said Gladys.

'But Ma, you'll need a hand,' Mary said.

'Got two perfectly good ones of me own. Now, what about that tea?'

Anna had learned a lot about Jimmy and his family in the last few days. A shared grief bound people together, she thought. But each had their own way of dealing with it. Some lashed out, like Alice, looking for someone to blame. She had watched Jimmy move quietly through his sorrow, standing firmly at his mother's side. Mary had retreated to some distant place in her head, hardly speaking, her grief trapped inside her. Anna was worried for her; had urged her to cry, but it seemed that her friend could find no tears.

Gladys herself had wept when she spoke of the man who had walked through life with her. Now, she would take those memories and carry on. Da would have wanted her to, she told

Anna, as they'd sat in the parlour together and shared their tears. Grief wasn't pretty, Anna thought, at least *hers* wasn't. It had been noisy and messy, but Gladys was different. Gladys Armstrong, Anna decided, was an extraordinary woman who grieved with dignity. But now she had shooed them all away, wanted to start learning to cope with a different kind of life, she'd said. A life on her own, visiting neighbours, helping folk where she could.

So, they had all left Glad to her new life and her daily chats with Harry in the ancient churchyard. It struck Anna as a happy prospect, not a depressing one – talking to the one you loved and *still* love, even though you can no longer touch them. Memories could be powerful things and happy memories were protection in hard times. They could fend off sadness. She intended to make lots of happy memories with Jimmy.

Once again, they were both on a train, swapping the dust and rubble of war-torn London for the wide, open spaces of Cornwall. In a way it was a relief to be heading back there, a place where she felt she could breathe. She pictured the acres of fields and the high Cornish hedges by the roadside, planted as windbreaks. The wind in the place could be fierce. It made people *teasy*, the locals claimed. 'Teasy' seemed a more friendly word than 'grumpy'. She thought she might start to use it.

Cornwall was somewhere she felt at peace, even though the notion might seem strange in the middle of war. War was still there, of course, with camps everywhere around and people in uniform. Gun batteries and airfields abounded, and barrage balloons bobbed in the sky over places like Falmouth Docks. But the Luftwaffe hadn't dropped as many bombs there as they had in London.

They both still had another four days left of their leave and in her mind, she'd planned a few quiet hours with Jimmy, somewhere they could take a break from the sadness of the funeral.

She wanted to remember the good things they had, before the madness of war pulled them back in again.

But it wasn't to be. They were short of crew, he'd told her. She could see the struggle written on his face, so she hadn't asked him to choose between *them* and his job. That would have been cruel, and there was enough cruelty in the world right now.

She watched him sleep, his head nodding sometimes with the rhythm of the train. His eyelids were smooth and almost translucent, like a child's, she thought, and the light ginger eyelashes lay casually on his cheek, as if they too were resting.

They had so little time left now before they reached the station and they had to go their separate ways. She wanted so much to wake him, to hear him speak, to see him smile. But she didn't have the heart. He must be exhausted, for he had hardly slept these last days. His father had just died, and he'd been doing all the things a son should do to help his ma. He was a good son, she thought. And, someday, he would make a very good father as well, she believed. After all, he had a fine blue-print to follow in Harry.

So, Jimmy was going back to St Eval, and she would return to the magical dell in Trevellas, to bike rides that took her to the ocean. Unlike him, she'd decided to take all her leave, as who knew when the chance might come again.

She thought about Mary and their sorrowful farewell. Her friend had gone back to Lincolnshire to the bombers that took off daily from RAF Binbrook, but Anna had read the pain in her eyes. Eyes that had glistened with unshed tears. She hadn't wanted to go back, would rather have come with them both to Cornwall. Anna knew a little about the effect of trauma, had seen it first-hand at the hospital when she'd been there. Some people seemed to get stuck in their sadness, she thought, couldn't find a way through. Mary struck her as one of those right now. And the worst bit was that there was nothing she could do to help her friend, apart from think of her.

She hoped Mary would find someone to love her, someone who fitted her and brought her the kind of joy that she and Jimmy shared.

34

ST EVAL

Jimmy hadn't been away for long, yet things felt strange, as if he'd returned to an alien place. It was an odd, unsettling feeling, nothing he could pin down at first. The strain of the funeral, he supposed, the shock of losing his da and the battles with Alice. Then having to say goodbye to Anna all over again, when all he wanted was to run away with her, to some exotic island where no one had heard of war. Was there even such a place?

He handed across his papers at the main gate, watched the guard check them and raise a quizzical eyebrow.

'Aircrew, eh? Been on leave?' the airman asked.

'Funeral,' Jimmy said, the weight of the word falling heavily on him once more.

'Ah. Your living quarters at the station here, are they?' the young man asked.

'Of course, why? Is something wrong with my papers?' asked Jimmy.

'No, they're fine. But you missed a bit of a show, that's all. You'll see,' the guard said as he handed back his ID card and finally lifted the gate barrier.

Jimmy shrugged his shoulders and walked on but it didn't take long to work out what kind of *show* had happened when he'd been gone. Part of the aircrew living quarters had turned into rubble, while some of the building doggedly clung on, refusing to fall.

'You missed it,' a voice behind him said. 'We had a raid.'

He recognised the young man, one of the pilots from the air-sea rescue crews.

'A raid? The station's been attacked?' he said in disbelief.

'Guess the *Luftwaffe* thought it was our turn. Not too many casualties, though. They bombed a couple of hangers and these crew quarters, took out a workshop as well. Could have been worse.'

Jimmy went off to look for his crew. Freddy would fill him in. He was a reliable source of information, had an 'understanding' with one of the WAAFs in Operations. In fact, he wouldn't be surprised if Freddy had an understanding with more than a few of the WAAF. Not him, though: he was a one-woman man and happy for it.

He looked for Freddy in all the usual places, but his friend was nowhere to be found. The same for the rest of the crew. That's when the fear assailed him and he started off at a run towards the stark grey headquarters block. He told himself he was being stupid; obviously the crew was somewhere, perhaps taking a break, like him. They'd be in town some place, enjoying themselves.

The thought calmed him down, as well as the long, slow breath he forced himself to take as he walked into the office.

The woman at the desk looked up. She was the WAAF who'd given him the telegram about his dad. She recognised him, he could tell by the expression on her face, but it was replaced with a look of confusion.

'Sergeant Armstrong. We weren't expecting you back for another few days,' she said.

She looked flustered, he thought. 'Well, Corporal, you know what they say – you can't keep a good man down.'

'I've heard that. How can I help you?' she asked.

'I'm trying to locate my crew, wondered if you might know where they are,' he asked.

'We've been rather busy here, reassigning personnel, finding new billets for aircrew. I haven't got time to go checking on every airman on the base.'

'No, of course not and I'm sorry to add to your load, but I'd be grateful for any information you can give me. I don't mind waiting,' he said, politely.

'I'll see what I can do,' the corporal relented and pointed to a chair.

She seemed edgy and embarrassed, and didn't look him directly in the eye. He watched her disappear into the squadron leader's office and wondered what was going on.

How can everything change in the blink of an eye? It seemed to Jimmy that the universe he knew had suddenly been spun around and tipped on its head. His crew had been caught in the explosion. One of them had 'bought it', the WAAF had told him. *Not Freddy, please! Surely not Freddy.* Freddy had nine lives, didn't he? He felt the pain of it overpower him. But when he got to the hospital in Newquay, Freddy was lying in bed, nursing a broken leg and a snapped collarbone. His friend had been lucky, very lucky. Relief flooded through Jimmy like a drug.

'You hear about the skipper?' asked Freddy, his voice breaking.

'What about Andy?' he said, the dread of it tugging at him, the sorrow a massive stone sitting on his chest.

'His luck ran out. The bastards got him,' said Freddy, angrily.

'What about his wife? Have they told her?' asked Jimmy. He imagined the pain of Andrew's wife, to hear such shocking, savage news.

'She came to see me, you know.'

'Who?' asked Jimmy, confused.

'The skipper's missus... Evelyn. Funny that, I'd no idea what she was called, did you?' Freddy asked.

'No. He hardly ever talked about her. Didn't want to jinx himself, I suppose.' Jimmy frowned.

'Didn't work! She asked me to tell her about it. How it happened. Did he suffer, that kind of thing,' Freddy continued.

'And did he—? Suffer, I mean?'

'How the hell would I know? The blast blew him yards away, the fire crew said. Still busy trying to collect bits of him, I shouldn't wonder,' said Freddy, and his voice collapsed into a coughing fit.

'Should I get a nurse?' Jimmy asked.

'No, I'll be fine. Not fine, obviously, but better than poor, bloody Andy will ever be again.'

'I'm sorry,' he said.

'What for?'

'I wasn't here with the rest of you.'

'Your father had died. Life kicks you in the teeth some-times,' Freddy said, and sighed.

'What about George? I couldn't find him. Did he get injured too?' he asked.

'Not a scratch. But you know our Georgie, always an eye to the main chance. Got the quack in sick-bay to recommend two weeks' leave – psychological scars!'

'Sounds like George,' said Jimmy.

'He'll either end up a politician or a millionaire,' Freddy said, and smiled for the first time.

Jimmy left the hospital in Newquay, housed in the very grand Victoria Hotel. It had been built in an age of masters and servants, when opulence was expected, and visitors took the gilded lift down through a tunnel to the beaches below. Nobody did that now.

Of course he was sad. He had never thought of death as glorious, like some, and now, in war, it was inevitable. Death had reached out its grubby hands and found him once again. His father dead, and now Andrew. But he wasn't alone. Lots of people had been killed in the last year, not only servicemen and women, but civilians too. Thousands alone since the Blitz had begun, plus scores of his fellow airmen had unselfishly given their lives. Sometimes, your country asked an unconditional love of you and most gave it willingly without counting the cost. Their pilot Andrew had been one of those. But what about Andy's wife – had she willingly signed up to the contract too? His heart went out to her. The grief she must feel, left with such sorrow; a husband she would never see again and her life with a gaping hole at its centre.

He thought about Anna. They'd never discussed the idea that he might be killed and her left alone, although she had definitely been against wartime marriages at first and maybe that was why.

But you didn't go out on a sortie expecting to be blown out of the sky. Nobody could afford to think like that, otherwise no one would have left the runway. Not that he considered himself invincible, but you couldn't afford to dwell on the danger. *Just get on with the job*, that's what he'd always told himself. And, so far, they'd all been part of a winning crew, a lucky crew. The irony of it, he supposed, was that Andy hadn't been killed in battle or had a chance to fight back. Would the way he died make a difference to his wife, though? Either way, it still made her a widow.

He wandered the streets of Newquay, trying to shrug off the sadness that had sought him out. He was surprised to find himself high above Towan beach once again, looking out towards the island. He thought of it as *their* island now after the magical day he'd spent with Anna. Some internal navigation must have taken him there. *It's a sign*, he thought, if you believed in such things. An arrow pointing the way. Not that he was superstitious, but it looked as if the fate that Anna wanted to believe in was out there somewhere – guiding him towards her.

35

Anna didn't think that a person could ever be this happy, could smile this much – especially after the last few terrible days. Jimmy had taken her totally by surprise, arriving on that old wreck of a bike that she supposed he'd borrowed again. He'd been clever to find her, to find the old stone cottage of Lowenna's, but then, he was a navigator.

'I came to talk,' she heard him say, his voice breaking over her like one of the waves she'd watched down at Trevaunance.

'Later,' she said, as she took charge and led him to the bedroom.

'We alone?' he asked.

'Lowenna's taken the children to the village. We're quite alone,' said Anna, her voice husky with desire.

'Yes – but you don't understand. We really need to talk.'

'Later,' she said 'First things first.'

If their lovemaking had been good before, it was even better now, she thought. It had been gentle then, almost tentative. He'd seemed shy and reserved that first time, as if he didn't want to frighten her away. But now there was a sort of desperation to how they both held on to each other, how they relished each other's bodies as if this might be the last time.

The crescendo when it came was something she could never have imagined, not even in her most delicious fantasy. They both crested the peak together, their eyes full of wonder, their gaze locking on to each other. *This is how it will be for us from now on,* she thought. Cherishing each other every time, like treasure newly found, but familiar all the same. She sighed with contentment.

But when she searched his face for the happiness that she knew must be written on hers, she couldn't find it there. She listened to his sigh – not contentment like hers, but a melancholy sound – and watched a shudder work its way through him. *Was that regret?* she wondered, fear taking the place of her smile that had fled.

His head sunk onto her chest and she let it rest there, stroking his hair, trying to comfort him, although she didn't know what for. Small sounds of pain came from his throat, like sobs that couldn't find their way out.

'Is it your father?'

He didn't answer her. But *of course* it was his father; Harry had just died. She'd watched him try to be brave for his mother, holding back his pain so that he could help with hers, carrying her burden as well as his. She'd never doubted Jimmy was courageous but now she saw that he was selfless too.

'The pain of loss,' she said. 'People say it gets less with time. Your da was a strong man, he wouldn't want you to grieve forever for him.'

'It's not about my da,' Jimmy said, and he raised his head to look at her.

She could see only misery in his eyes. 'What, then?' said Anna. 'What's made you this sad?'

'It's about us,' he said.

'*Us?*' she said, dumbfounded.

'Us,' he repeated again. 'Can't you see it's all wrong?'

She watched him drop his head again and she took it gently in her hands, caressed his cheek. She wanted to make it better for him, whatever it was. But she was at a loss. How on earth could it be anything to do with them – especially after what they'd just done together?

'What's wrong with us?' she asked, a little too loudly.

'Nothing. We're incredible – *you*'re incredible. *That* was incredible,' he said, and fell back on the bed.

'Well then, what? I don't understand what you think is wrong,' she said.

'There can't *be* an us. There *mustn't* be an us,' he said. 'It's hard to explain.'

'Well then, *try!*' She heard the anger in her voice, fought to pull it back. 'Maybe you should start at the beginning,' she told him, a little more gently.

They sat together on the bed as he told her about how his skipper had died and Freddy had been injured. But the strange thing, she thought, as she listened to his litany of sorrow, was the way he kept returning to the pilot's wife. Andy's wife was a widow now. It was a phrase that she could see disturbed him as much as the sudden death of his friend.

'You know how much I love you. You're my world,' he said, and his eyes seemed to shine with the words.

'And I feel the same, you know I do. That's why I'm wearing this,' Anna said, and she held her hand high in the air so he could see the ring.

'But can't you see, it's all different now? I can't hold you to that. I have to release you, and you must let me go. We have to go our separate ways. There's only one way out – you have to forget you ever met me. I won't leave you in the same state as the skipper's wife.'

'Just like that,' she said, her voice cracking.

'No, not just like that – with a great, all-consuming pain,' he said. 'Like my life is being ripped apart. But it's the only way.'

She ran his shocking words around in her head. They felt brittle and harsh. Going their separate ways? How could she ever do that? How could she forget she knew him, or wipe out the love she felt? It was impossible and of course she wouldn't do it. But she could see how troubled he was, could feel his despair.

'And I'm to have no say in this?' she said.

'There are two of us, of course you have a say,' said Jimmy.

'Are we not brave?' she asked him suddenly.

'Brave?' he said, confused. 'Yes, you certainly are, and I suppose I am, in my way.'

'Well then, here's what I say. Not only will we NOT split up or lie to each other and ourselves and pretend we've never met. You'll be getting a marriage licence as soon as you can, and we'll go into Truro to the registry office, and you'll make me a married woman and you a married man.'

'I will? But what if something happens and you're left on your own?'

'Then you've made a decent woman of me.' She laughed and pulled him into her arms. 'Besides,' she said, suddenly serious, 'I would treasure all the time we have together, sharing our lives, completely, fully. I want the world to know we are a family.'

There had been no guard of honour standing outside the registry office. No hordes waiting to throw confetti. No family, either. There wasn't even a wedding dress, but Anna didn't mind. She was proud to be married in her best blues and Jimmy wearing his, and his hair slicked down as if he was going to a dance. Nothing could have made the day more perfect, even if the sun had come out, which it didn't, because it was winter already and Christmas only weeks away.

It felt miraculous, the way the registrar had magically changed her from Anna Golding into Anna Armstrong – and them both from *man and woman* into *husband and wife*. A little like the miracle that Jimmy had performed, she thought, to get the licence sorted in only three days. The registry office had had a sudden cancellation and they'd both agreed they should take it right away. It meant there was no time to get Gladys down for their special day, and they both felt bad about it. But Anna would write to Ma and send word of the wedding, try to explain. They would have a proper family celebration when-ever they were able. After all, she was truly part of the Armstrong family now.

Their commanders had both given permission for the wedding to take place and some accommodating officers had provided 48-hour passes for a honeymoon. Even in wartime, it seemed to Anna, people could be kind and sentimental.

She had no idea where they were going for the honeymoon; it was a surprise, Jimmy had told her. But they couldn't be going far, she assumed, as they'd both be back on duty again soon.

An airman from Jimmy's squadron picked them up from Truro in an old rickety van. It was festooned with a makeshift banner saying 'Just married' and dragging along empty corned beef cans behind it. It moved so slowly and made such a racket that pedestrians stopped and stared, but most of them smiled. Some even waved and cheered and wished them good luck as they passed by. *Strangers*, she thought, *who didn't even know their names, yet had been happy for them.* Newlyweds seemed to have that effect on people; the optimism of a couple starting out on a new life, perhaps, and their downright joy. She'd done the same thing herself – waving at a couple she'd never seen before, wishing them luck.

Not that she and Jimmy needed any. She already felt the luckiest woman in the world.

36

If she could have chosen anywhere for a honeymoon, it would have been here. It was the place where they'd first made love and although it wasn't the same room in the fancy Beachcroft Hotel, it was still special. She couldn't believe she hadn't thought of it. Jimmy was a romantic, something that surprised her a little, but delighted her as well.

They had enjoyed a meal in the plush restaurant when they'd first arrived and since then, they had hardly come up for air. *But that was allowed*, she thought naughtily, as they walked down the street now, hand in hand. *Otherwise you could hardly call it a honeymoon.*

However, the time seemed to have evaporated, and soon they would need to get back to a very different kind of life. She took his arm and wound it through hers. They were like an old married couple, she thought. And how momentous that was.

They walked to their enchanted island and crossed over the bridge, stopping halfway to marvel at the incredible ocean below, to watch the tide as it came in and swirled around the island. It washed over the rocks, changing their colour, washing them clean. The ocean was unstoppable, would always be – it wasn't just water, but a powerful force with a life of its own.

They bought hot drinks from the same food wagon as before and sat on the wall again. And she grinned at him because some things were even better the second time around.

'Déjà vu,' she said.

'Yes. And we'll have lots of times like this, but...'

'But what?' She noticed a small frown arrive on his face, and the way his mouth had suddenly turned down. 'What's wrong?' she said.

'Something important I need to say. I didn't tell you before, didn't want to spoil this amazing time we've had.'

'Tell me!' she said, her voice serious now and a tiny quiver tugging at her lips.

'My squadron's been given new aircraft,' he said.

'But that sounds like good news.'

'It comes with a temporary posting to a training field, somewhere up north,' he said.

'You're going away?' she said, stunned.

'Not long – only two months,' Jimmy said, and dropped his head.

'Two months,' she said. 'Starting when?'

'A matter of days.' His voice choked up.

'Up north, you said? Everywhere in the country is north of Cornwall.' She smiled ruefully and shook her head. It wasn't fair, but then life wasn't always fair – she could tell he felt exactly the same way, so she tried to ease the tension and make it easier on him. She took his hand and said, 'You'll send a postcard?'

'You don't mind?' he asked, surprised.

'Of course I *mind*! But what can you do; run away or disobey an order? We're both in the air force, we knew what we were getting into. And we knew all that when we married too. We'll get through.'

'You know I think you're marvellous, don't you?' said Jimmy.

'That's because I *am* marvellous.' She smiled again, even though it was the last thing she felt like doing. But she wouldn't send him off with a heavy heart – what was the point in that?

She heard his sigh, and felt his body relax beside her. Relief, she thought, and realised he'd been dreading this moment of breaking the news.

'Two months,' he said. 'Only two months and we'll be back at St Eval again. But they'll be months of purgatory, pure hell, without you.'

'You mustn't think like that. Just concentrate on your job. I need you to be safe,' she said.

'Don't worry, I will be. Why don't you go to Ma's for Christmas? She'd like the company,' he said.

'I'd like that too, especially since she missed the wedding. But I've only got a day, not enough time to get there and back – you know what the trains are like. Still, at least Mary's going to see your ma.'

'But you'll be alone, what with Lowenna going away,' said Jimmy.

'I've been on my own before,' she said, evenly. 'I'll be okay.'

'Why not ask that cousin of yours down – Jane, isn't it?'

She hadn't even thought of it. Instead, she'd pictured her and Jimmy in the cottage, spending their first Christmas together; him bringing in logs for the fire, her trying to unravel the mysteries of cooking. A cosy little hideaway, a proper love nest.

But those were joys that had to be put on hold. They'd get to them someday, she was sure of that – as sure as she was that this awful war would eventually come to an end. But how many lives would it wreck before that? How many families would be left with holes in them where people used to be, like Harry – and Jimmy's skipper?

She took a deep breath, and the smell of the ocean filled her head, the salty, tangy perfume carried on the breeze. She shivered.

'You're cold,' Jimmy said, and put an arm around her. 'And you look a little sad.'

'Not sad, exactly. Just thinking about how this damn war has changed things. If I had Hitler in my sights right now, I'd make him pay.'

'I believe you would, Mrs Armstrong. I really believe you would,' said Jimmy with a rueful smile.

'*Mrs Armstrong*. That sounds good,' she said. It was the first time she'd heard it from his lips. His wife, she truly was his wife now and he was her husband – and, one day, she hoped, he'd be the father of their children. What an extraordinary thought that was. And how Gladys would love it.

'So, Anna Armstrong,' he said, 'what shall we do with these last few hours?'

'I think I should perform my wifely duties one more time,' she said with a grin. 'Seems a shame to waste that excellent four-poster bed.'

They ran back quickly to the hotel, laughing like a couple of naughty children caught in the act.

37

TREVELLAS

20 DECEMBER 1940

Lowenna and her children had left the cottage and gone to Plymouth to spend Christmas with her husband for his week's leave. It felt strange without her there and her raucous three-year-old. She missed the baby too, even though its wails sometimes kept her awake.

She'd been lonely at first, but she wasn't a stranger to loneliness: living with Aunt Beatrice meant she had often felt alone. Anna was learning new skills every day, like chopping wood and coaxing the Cornish range into life. But saying goodbye to Jimmy had been especially hard. He'd been gone for almost three weeks now and she was counting the days till she would see him again. Two months, he'd promised. Then he'd try to get them a place in St Eval's married quarters. She wondered how that might work – her getting up at the crack of dawn to cycle to the airfield at Perranporth. But she'd decided to worry about that later. *Cross one bridge at a time*, she told herself. That way she wouldn't get her feet wet.

It had been a hard, emotional time on her shift in the operations room that day. The WAAFs couldn't afford to get personally involved in missions, not if the plotters or wireless operators were to do their jobs efficiently and calmly, without distraction. But sometimes that wasn't easy, listening to the crews taking off on sorties, wondering how many of them would return.

Today had been a terrible time for Anna. She had a Spitfire on her plot, had watched his progress coming back from a sortie over the Channel in the French port of Brest. He had engine trouble, at least that's what his frantic radio transmission seemed to suggest. One of the WAAF wireless operators had tried to guide him to an emergency landing strip. Everyone in the room had held their breath, had willed him on those last few precious miles. But he hadn't made it and had crashed into cliffs.

That was the worst bit, she thought. *When you could do nothing to help except plot their positions on the operations map and move flags around a board.* But behind those plots on her grid were pilots, young men starting out in life. The casualty rate among fighter pilots was high; they all knew that. It was even worse for bomber crews, although she always tried to block that from her mind, because Jimmy was part of a bomber crew and one in seven of those planes never made it home.

The sadness of today's shift had made her weary, her legs heavy and reluctant to push the bike those two miles to her cottage billet. But she had to do it because sometime tonight she was expecting a visitor and she would need to warm the place and sort out the bedding in the tiny back bedroom. Her cousin Jane should be on her way.

At first, Anna had been excited when her cousin had said she would come. She'd even managed to organise a lift from the station for Jane with Old Pop Truscott. But now, between the sadness of Jimmy's departure and the trauma of losing a pilot today, she felt her enthusiasm for the visit start to wane. It might be difficult, the two of them living so closely together in the same house for a week; after all, they were practically strangers. True, when they'd spent time together before they'd got on well, and there were no sharp edges between them. Jane seemed an easy-going type, so hopefully things wouldn't be too awkward.

When she got back to her billet, Anna was surprised by the welcome that greeted her. The kitchen was warm, and something was cooking on the hob. Just as it sometimes was when Lowenna was home. But there was nobody there. The piskies had been working their magic, she thought, and the impossible notion pulled a smile from her lips. Then the back door swung open, and her cousin Jane came in, logs piled high in her arms.

'You're here,' Jane said, cheerily. 'I found the key where you said. Fancy a cuppa? I expect you've had a long day.'

'You'll have had a hard one too,' said Anna, slightly flustered. 'The train takes forever – and yes, I could drink a vat of tea right now.'

'Coming right up. Oh, and thanks for sorting the lift out. The old chap's a character and terribly kind, though not much of a talker,' said Jane.

'You'll find that a lot around here. The old folks, I mean. They're all real gems, but they measure their words, only speak when there's something important to say,' Anna said.

'I know some who could take a lesson from that. Now, how about that tea? And I found some leeks, so I've made leek and potato soup for us. Hope you don't mind,' said Jane.

'Mind? It's brilliant! How long can you stay?'

She could get used to this, to being waited on and spoiled. Anna had woken only moments before and a breakfast of scrambled eggs was already on the table.

'You're a chef,' she told Jane.

'Hardly,' said Jane, and laughed.

'Compared to me you are,' said Anna.

'Just plain food, I'm afraid. I had to learn – Mother wasn't much of a cook.'

'About today... I thought if you'd like, we could take the bikes,' she said, 'and I could show you around. I've got the early shift, so I'll be finished by two.'

'Sounds perfect. But don't think you've got to fuss over me. I'll be fine while you're working. Might even go for a walk,' said Jane.

'When you're back, take Lowenna's bike and, a couple of miles up the road, you'll find the main gate. Meet me there. But watch out for the wolves on the barrier.' Anna winked.

'Wolves I can manage,' Jane said darkly, 'but thanks for the warning. It's the nice ones I've had to worry about.'

The eggs had given Anna an energy boost: fuel to push the pedals around. Today felt different, her muscles didn't protest, and she patted the cumbersome old bike with affection. Jimmy would have understood if he was there. She pedalled with the wind behind her, pushing her on, and she started to hum that silly old song – *their* song now, she supposed. The one about the tandem.

The thought that she would have some company for a while cheered her, and, best of all, she wouldn't be alone on Christmas Day. That would have been misery. It would still be hard to spend it without Jimmy, though, and she wondered what they would all be doing, him and his crew up there – up north. She hadn't asked where.

Her thoughts turned to what Jane had hinted at, about her and men. Had she been let down? Left at the altar perhaps? That was a cruel thought. She remembered the pain Jimmy had gone through, how his first love had been false and it had left him scarred. Even now at times she could see that pain in his eyes, the fear that something bad might happen again. He was a courageous man, but he still had the shadow of rejection written deep in his memory. He would never have to worry about sadness like that again – not with *her*, Anna had said. 'Shackled to me for life,' she'd told him, when they'd been fooling around in that magnificent four-poster bed. And she'd meant it. He was her 'forever love' and there could be no other.

Those were the positive thoughts that guided her to work; and it was a much kinder day in the operations room than yesterday had been. Today, nobody died. In fact, nothing much happened at all, but some days were like that. She sat by the board with her headphones around her neck, waiting for plots from the radar rooms or instructions about height and aircraft numbers of enemy planes from the Observer Corps. But today, nobody came. And none of the Spits took off from the airfield at Perranporth. Too much wind for take-off and landings would be even more hazardous. No point in losing any more fighters to the dangerous cliffs or crashing into the ocean.

The waiting time, that's what the WAAFs around the plotting table called it. Women were good at it – at least that was their commanding officer's theory. So the periods of waiting that were interspersed with the nail-biting stress and hours of patient concentration were nothing unusual for the WAAFs in the ops room. Many of them brought their wool, knitting socks and mittens for the chaps at the front. Dropping it in an instant when the urgent voices of pilots suddenly crackled from the speakers and the war found them again.

Today was one of those magical days in Cornwall when the air was sharp and keen. The ocean breeze felt bracing and sometimes made her feel a little giddy. She imagined it was pure. Certainly, purer than the air that Ma had to put up with in London, after all the bombing. She remembered the city's streets filled with severed water pipes and broken bricks and rubble of every kind. People's homes were blasted to pulp nightly and thick plaster dust hung in the air, its smell mingling

with the sickly aroma of gas from ruptured mains. Other smells
were there as well, ones it didn't help to think about; corpses
that used to be people, trapped among the debris.

She wished both Mary and Ma could see the marvels of this
mystical land. Maybe one day they would have a chance. But
for now, she would ride out to the gate and meet her cousin,
Jane. She would show her the sights and the scenery that made
this place on the coast so special. The wind would be whipping
the ocean today, she thought, sending foam up on the beach of
Perranporth, sculpting the sand into patterns. Sometimes, it
seemed like a giant had randomly drawn pictures there.

The fine sandy beach had always looked enticing to Anna,
but no one could walk there now. No children would trawl in
rock pools or make sandcastles or play pirates or swim in the sea
any more. A huge barricade made from steel and acres of
barbed wire barred the way and concrete pill boxes –
machinegun posts – stood like sentinels on either side of
the bay.

The trappings of the conflict had found their way into the
village of Perranporth, tried to make the bay look ugly, but it
was still beautiful in Anna's eyes. Nothing could take away
from the majesty of the ocean. Not even war.

Today, she wanted to cycle to the very top of the hill, to the
plateau that overlooked the western side of the bay. She needed
to feel the rush of the wind, to be closer to the sky, and the view
from the clifftop at Droskyn Point was stunning. There was a
hotel up there, Droskyn Castle. Not a real castle, but made to
look like one with its medieval turrets and battlements. It was a
folly conjured up by an eccentric owner from long ago, a Bavar-
ian, trying to replicate a German castle on the Rhine, maybe.
Ironic, she thought, that a German, an enemy, should have
modelled the fantasy hotel and now the RAF were billeting
senior officers from the airfield there.

It would be a bit of a climb to the top, but she'd cycled it once before and when she'd told Jimmy that she'd conquered it, he'd called her his *warrior queen*. She could see his face now as he'd said it, hear the laugh in his voice again. She held on to the vision in her head, reluctant to let it go, even though thinking of his absence made her sad, filled her with longing.

'Over here!' someone shouted, breaking into her wistful daydream.

'Ready for an adventure?' she asked Jane.

'Ready to take on the world, but the bike – it's a little strange.'

'Does it work?' she asked.

'It's better than walking,' Jane said, 'but I've never seen one like it before.'

She looked at the bike. Unlike her own heavy black one, Lowenna's bike was blue and smaller, almost like a child's. There was a contraption in front of the handlebars, made out of tin: a container for carrying shopping. It had an image of a fairy on the front, a pale creature with silver gossamer wings, the paint fading now and flaking in places. But there was no mistaking whose bike it was.

'It belongs to a fairy queen,' said Anna, 'a very kind, extraordinary one.'

The ride to the top of the cliffs had been gruelling, but worth it all the same. Seals were swimming close to the shoreline, a whole group of them – she had never seen that many in one place before. They seemed to be playing together, having fun in the Atlantic's rolling waves.

She stood on the edge of the plateau and watched the ocean rush in and crash over Chapel Rock out in the distance. The huge rock stood alone, stranded just offshore, a jagged rock formation, with the Union Jack flying from a mast at its summit. Before the beach barrier was erected, people had walked to it when the tide was out. Hollowed out inside Chapel Rock was a secret, hidden swimming pool. Anna had never swum there, but she'd heard of it. It was a massive square rockpool and twice a day, when the tide came in, the sea flooded into it, making it a deep saltwater swimming pool.

She heard a contented sigh from Jane, beside her and they smiled at each other.

'It's beautiful,' said Jane. 'So peaceful. I could stay here forever.'

'I know, I feel the same,' Anna said.

The two of them rode their bicycles back down to the village, had tea in the Beach Tea Rooms and watched the parade of servicemen and women walk by, some arm in arm, eating ice cream as if everyone was on holiday. It felt like that to Anna, a small respite from the worry of the war, but she didn't go as far as buying ice cream – she would wait until Jimmy could enjoy one as well. The thought of doing it without him, of having *too* much fun, felt like being disloyal to him. He would claim that was foolish, of course – but some pleasures she wanted to share only with him. They were things to look forward to.

'We should think about getting back, I suppose,' said Anna.

'Thank you for this,' Jane said, smiling. 'It's been a smashing day and such a change from being in London.'

'I'm glad you enjoyed it, but the best is still to come. Look at that wonderful sunset beginning out there.' Anna pointed towards the ocean, where the nightly miracle would soon take place, when the blood-red orb of the sun slowly bled into the water of the bay. At that moment it was the prelude, when the clouds were painted with vivid red and orange streaks.

'Incredible,' Jane said.

'Yes, we're lucky here. And if we start back now, we should be able to make it home before full blackout. It's still quite a push up St George's Hill, but it's harder in darkness.'

'Still, we won't lose sight of each other. This bike must glow in the dark,' said Jane.

'Oh, why's that?' asked Anna.

'It's sprinkled with fairy dust.'

They both laughed and set off on the long trek back.

38

Anna had had the graveyard shift from midnight until 8 a.m., the one everyone dreaded. Some called it the witching hour, the time when bad things happened, but she wasn't superstitious about that – bad things happened at different times of the day. You couldn't stop them by crossing your fingers or asking for another shift.

Her cousin Jane had left earlier, heading in the direction of St Agnes to do some exploring, looking for the relics of tin mines. She'd made them both cheese sandwiches for lunch and had ridden off on Lowenna's bicycle, which she'd christened 'the fairy-express'.

Anna had just finished washing her hair when the postman came to the door, carrying a small parcel. He smiled at her, his elderly face falling into well-worn ridges and lines. Proof of a lifetime of smiling at folk and someone who laughed easily, whatever the joke.

'Birthday is it, my bird?' he asked her. ''appy returns for the day.'

'Birthday?' she said, confused, her hair dripping around her.

'The parcel, like,' he said. 'Thought it might be a present.'

'Oh, no, nothing like that. But thank you all the same,' she said, and closed the door with a hurried smile.

At first, she'd been excited, all fingers and thumbs trying to open it. Maybe it *was* a present. But it wasn't from Jimmy, as she'd hoped, as the writing was in a hand she didn't recognise, with lines of capital letters, large and deliberate. As if the author had been careful, wanting to make sure that it reached the right place.

She took off the brown paper. It was covering a box with a letter balanced on top, her name on the envelope. The writing was from the same careful hand as the wrapping. A cold feeling ran through her and she picked up the brown paper jacket again. The postmark said Liverpool, the northwest of England. The cold turned into a shiver, a trembling in her body that wouldn't stop. A feeling of foreboding and doom.

He'd gone somewhere up north – that's what Jimmy had told her. But then wouldn't the package be addressed to Mrs Armstrong, not Miss Golding? Still, her hands trembled with fear, but she made herself drag up some courage and read the letter that now fluttered like a live thing in her hands.

Mr Ted Edwards,
Foreman, Royal Ordnance Factory,
Kirkby,
Merseyside

Dear Miss Golding,

It is with deep regret that I must inform you of the death of your friend, Miss Edna Evans. As a munitions factory, we produce a range of explosive and propellant products. Your friend Miss Evans was filling fuses when one acci-

*dentally exploded and she was one of three women on
the assembly line who sadly died from their injuries. The
fuse exploded because of a defective striker and was not
the fault of any of the women in this factory.
I knew Miss Evans a little and considered her a decent
and upright woman and one of my best workers. She left
the enclosed package in my care some time ago to be
passed on to you, should anything happen to her. I
promised that I would. However, I have no notion of
what is within and can only hope that it won't cause you
any more grief than you must already feel over the unexpected death of your friend.*

I remain, yours faithfully,

T. A. Edwards

Edna – dead? She couldn't be! *She's barely a year older than
me,* thought Anna. How could she possibly die at only twenty
years old? It was madness. This chap had made a hideous
mistake, had mixed her friend up with somebody else. But she
read the letter again and again, until she could almost recite it
blindfolded. The sickening truth was that it had to be real, this
news that made her stomach churn and the blood pound in her
ears. He sounded like a normal, decent chap this foreman,
hardly likely to make up such a monstrous thing.

The dreadful letter fell from her hand, and she collapsed
into the chair, shaken and pale with shock. Guilt mingled with
her grief, made her look for reasons and rational explanations.
Why hadn't she gone to see Edna in Liverpool? She had
promised herself that she would, but the chance had never
arrived. Maybe she should have tried harder. It might have
made a difference. But that was foolish, of course. There was no
way she could have saved Edna from an accident like that and

such a terrible, futile death. Being blown to pieces – she couldn't bear to think of it. The shock, the pain she must have felt. But perhaps there had been none of that. Just blackness, nothingness. One moment you're alive and the next you're catapulted into an awful, senseless void. She tried to imagine it but couldn't.

She wailed in protest. She wrapped her arms around her, gently rocking to and fro. It was a motion that seemed to comfort and soothe. Her lips released a moan, a sad, keening sound of mourning that turned into a sob. Tears flooded her face and she cried until she was weary, till she could cry no more, till her eyes were red and swollen and coated with salt from the streams of pain.

She didn't remember falling asleep, but woke suddenly with Jane shaking her shoulder. Anna pointed at the letter on the floor and watched her cousin pick it up and solemnly read it. Then neither of them spoke, but Anna could hear the sound of running water, a kettle being filled and the noise of teacups rattling. She let herself be looked after, a rug tucked around her legs, a cup of tea put into her hand. It was as if shock had stripped her free will away and emptied her of feelings until she was a dry, desolate shell.

'You've had a bit of a shock, but this is where you buck up.'

'What?' asked Anna, aghast, her voice hardly a whisper.

'You heard. It's dreadful, of course. I'm not saying it's not, but how will this help your friend, Edna? It won't bring her back, will it?' Jane said.

'That's more than a little hard.' The words had been difficult to push past the huge lump of grief in her throat.

'Of course you shouldn't forget her, that's not what I meant. But we've all lost friends to this awful war. All we can do is remember them. What was she like?' asked Jane.

'Edna? She was kind – and funny too. She believed in romance, dreamed of meeting that special chap who would care for her more than he cared for himself. I don't think she ever found him.'

'Those chaps are a little thin on the ground but she sounds like a fine sort.'

'She is. She *was*,' Anna corrected herself, sadly.

'And what about the box she sent you? You've not even opened it yet. It must have been important to her that you have it, don't you think?'

'I don't think I can. Would you open it?' she asked.

'Only if you're sure,' said Jane. 'It might be private.'

There was a letter inside the box, written in Edna's sprawling hand, and something else wrapped up in old newspaper: a small container of some kind.

'I don't think I should read the letter,' said Jane. 'It seems very...'

'What?' asked Anna.

'Personal,' said Jane, and handed it across.

If the letter from the factory foreman had been bad, this one shook the ground beneath Anna. It left a dark, threatening chasm with her hovering on its brink, trying not to be sucked into the blackness of its poisonous heart. She barely tasted the small glass of brandy Jane had placed into her hand. She must have drunk it though, because when she looked at the glass absentmindedly, it was empty.

'It's bad, then,' said Jane.

'Unbelievable, but I have to believe it. Why would she lie about something so horrific? Something she knew would be the worst, most cruel thing I could ever imagine? It's why she begged for my forgiveness, don't you see?' said Anna.

'I'm sorry,' Jane said gently, 'but I don't see. And maybe this is something you shouldn't be telling me.'

'I have to tell someone,' Anna replied, 'otherwise this will turn to hate inside me. I don't want to hate anyone,' she said, miserably.

She didn't want any hate in her life, especially not now, when she had so much joy to look forward to with Jimmy.

'Some time ago,' she said, remembering, 'Edna wrote me a strange, garbled letter. It sounded as if she'd been with a man, that she was pregnant. She begged my forgiveness, which didn't make sense. She didn't need my forgiveness, I thought. She was a grown woman, could make her own decisions...'

'And was she – pregnant, I mean?' asked Jane.

'She was, but she says here that she lost the baby. She asks me to forgive her and to forgive the father as well, because he had no idea that she was pregnant,' said Anna.

'I see. It's sad, of course, especially since she lost the child, but I still don't follow...'

Anna looked down at Edna's letter lying innocently in her lap, and picked it up to read part of it to Jane. Her voice shook, but she forced herself to speak the awful words.

Anna, I beg of you – I hope you can come to understand and forgive us both. Not that it was his fault. I'm the one to blame. He didn't want to make love to me, but I was lonely, and I could see that he was lonely too. He tried to do the honourable thing, but I gave him no choice. I seduced him, so what could he do? If you can't forgive me, please try to forgive him. He's not the wicked man you take him for but has some kindness in him. Please, please understand that when I went to see my ma at your Aunt Beatrice's house, I had no idea he would be there. He was visiting his sister.

I've enclosed a gift for you. I give it to you in love and hope you'll understand. Don't be too harsh. I admired these when he wore them, so he gave them to me as a keepsake – and now I pass them on to you. Please take them with my love. You will always have my love, my dear, dear friend. Friends for life, remember?

Anna tossed the letter aside and hastily pulled the gift Edna had sent her from its newspaper wrapping. She had no idea what it was, but if it was *his* then she wouldn't want it.

Memories came tumbling in on her, hovering like birds of prey. The cufflinks were his special ones, silver, emblazoned with some kind of family crest. As a young child she'd had a curiosity about them, but she'd never asked. Her father wouldn't have answered anyway, she thought. Before she'd been sent to Aunt Beatrice, for the first eight years of her life, Anna had lived in her father's large house in Reigate. Not that William Golding had ever taken much notice of his daughter. He'd never been affectionate towards her or given any kind of hint that the two of them were related. They'd never even shared a meal together, for Anna was expected to eat with the staff in the servants' kitchen.

'Your friend and your father – is that what we're saying here? She was pregnant with your father's child?'

'It's what Edna says, and I don't see why she'd lie, especially when she knew how much the thought would sicken me.'

'Good grief! No wonder that brandy disappeared,' said Jane.

'He's thirty years older than she is. You think he'd have learned to keep his passion in check by now,' Anna said with contempt. She'd said she didn't want to hate anyone, but if anyone deserved her hate it would be him. Her father.

'So, you can't do what your friend asks – and forgive him?'

'Forgive him?' she spat in disgust. 'Would *you* forgive him?'

'No, I don't suppose I would. But then I don't think I'm nearly as nice as you,' Jane said, and smiled.

39

The next few days went by in a fog of gloom and depression. Anna had thrown the cufflinks into a corner of her kitbag, didn't want to see them again, but was surprised at her cowardice – her reluctance to throw them straight in the bin. One part of her mind told her that she should have done, for they were proof of her father's sickening actions.

The two upsetting letters she treated with a measure of reverence. They were the last echo of her old friend, and it didn't seem right to destroy them. She folded them both with care and tied them in a yellow ribbon of Lowenna's, putting them safely in a drawer with her belongings.

Since receiving them, she'd managed to cycle to work and had done her job in the operations room with surprising precision, but as soon as her shifts had finished, she sank back into a bubble of doubt.

How could she not have seen this? Why had she not saved her friend?

Today, she had a full day off. Before, in a different world, she'd have been looking forward to it. It was Christmas Day and she and Jane had cycled up to the cookhouse in Trevellas for a special lunch. An Australian squadron was operating out of RAF Perranporth now. They were a lively bunch and there were rumours they'd organised crackers and party hats for the day's celebration. But she didn't want to celebrate. It didn't seem right to be enjoying herself when Edna would never see another Christmas.

Everyone bustled about in the cookhouse. WAAFs came in from the kitchen with loaded trays and officers laid the massive tables for the airmen and airwomen. It seemed odd to her, the tradition that on this one day senior officers would turn into waiters and waitresses, standing by with food, waiting on the enlisted men and women. But others seemed happy with it, treated it as a novelty, a chance to get their own back on authority.

She took an end seat at one of the long trestle tables, next to Jane. An end seat was easier for a quick escape if all this enforced jollity overwhelmed her.

Section Officer Garvey came up to her, smiled and wished her a happy Christmas. 'I'm glad I've spotted you,' the officer said, 'because I've got something for you.'

'How mysterious,' said Anna. She didn't want to talk or be sociable. Not now. But the woman was her commanding officer and she'd been understanding and sympathetic over these last few horrible days.

'A mystery. That's exactly what it is,' said the officer with a smile. 'I've had it for a while – one of the visiting pilots delivered it from a crewmember of a bomber squadron, but I'd been sworn to secrecy.'

'But...'

'Never mind all that, just follow me.'

Anna watched her walk away, then followed on the officer's heels.

How can one small moment in time change everything around it? It was nothing short of a miracle, this Christmas card she held in her hand. Jimmy had gone out of his way to get it to her – that and the small red velvet box that went with it. Nestling inside its sumptuous case was the most exquisite thing she had seen in a long time: a tiny, golden, heart-shaped locket.

A smile started in her eyes and spread over the whole of her face as she held the precious keepsake in the palm of her hand. She closed her hand around it, almost afraid that it wasn't real, that it might vanish if she didn't keep it safe.

She read the card. The message inside was typical of Jimmy. She wanted to laugh and then she wanted to cry, but instead she kissed it.

> *I hope you're impressed. I even had my hair combed for the photograph inside so you don't forget what I look like. Now you need to put a picture of yours on the other side of the heart, so that they can talk to each other. No chain, I'm afraid. That's my very next project. Happy Christmas to my most lovely, delectable, beautiful, and badly missed wife. We'll be together soon.*

'When do we eat?' Anna asked one of the junior officers, a young man who seemed to be out of his depth waiting on tables.

'Soon,' he said, and hurried away.

'You've changed your tune,' said Jane, a look of relief on her face. 'Thought you weren't going to eat a bite.'

'I'm ravenous,' she said. *Had she eaten anything over the last two days?* she wondered. It was hard to remember.

'No turkey, I'm afraid,' said Jane. 'But the chicken and roast potatoes look edible.'

'I'd eat anything right now as long as it isn't cabbage,' Anna said, and tried for another smile. It was getting easier.

'There's a lot to be said for cabbage. All those vitamins.' Her cousin laughed.

'Not the way the air force cooks it. During training, they

gave us cabbage sandwiches – the cabbage was limp, and boiled until it gave itself up.'

'Sounds like some kind of secret weapon. But it doesn't seem to have done you any harm.'

'No, Mary and I got quite sentimental over the memory of those awful sandwiches.'

'So, this should be like a feast.'

A feast it was. She enjoyed every bite without once feeling guilty about Edna. Or even wishing her father ill. It was as if a veil had been drawn over all the sadness. Jimmy had done that; reminded her that while bad things happened in the world, good things did as well. He wouldn't have wanted her to be unhappy, especially not today.

Bit by bit, she found parts of her happiness restored.

After lunch, the two of them scrounged a lift from an RAF transport travelling into Newquay, and loaded their bikes into it.

Anna had decided there was no better way to end this fine Christmas Day than by going somewhere special. 'You'll be amazed by this place,' she told her cousin. 'It's unique, and if you get it at the right time of day, when the tide's coming in, it's quite magical.'

The town was flooded with cheerfulness. People were laughing and joking and if it hadn't been for so many military uniforms around, sandbags piled up outside shops and windows smothered in ugly blast tape, it might have been Christmas in peacetime.

'The pubs are open at this time of day? How did that happen?' Jane asked, surprised.

'I expect it's just for today. They've been shutting them down in the afternoon and watering down the beer. The chaps at the station are always moaning about the weak beer now.'

A bunch of sailors passed them by, singing loud, bawdy songs, and she thought about Lowenna and her sailor husband, wondered how they might be getting on. The man was in the Merchant Navy, a gunner on a ship guarding convoys. Would it be easy for him to slot back into normal, family life, she wondered, after the mind-numbing fear of waiting to be torpedoed in the icy waters of the North Atlantic? The thought made her shiver with cold.

'Why don't we pop in and have something to warm us up?' asked Jane.

'What, in the pub, you mean?' said Anna.

'Why not? Christmas doesn't come every day. Just the one.'

'But the bikes...' Anna replied.

'Shouldn't think anyone would want to steal either one of them.' Jane laughed.

'All right then, seeing as it's Christmas. But if we're booked for being drunk in charge of a bicycle, I'll blame you,' Anna said, and couldn't help but grin.

It was noisy and busy and there was an almost manic air of desperate celebration in the pub, so they both had one small glass of watered-down beer but didn't stay.

Afterwards, they walked across the suspension bridge, out to Towan Island.

'I can see why you like it here. It's a special place. Fancy having your very own bridge. Who owns it?'

'I'm not sure – some aristocrat or other. But I don't think they're living there now.'

'Look at the sea down there,' said Jane, looking over the edge. 'It's wild.'

'It's rough today. It can be savage, but sometimes it's calm as a millpond. It's got so many moods, and the colours change all the time. It feels alive. That's why I love it,' she said passionately.

'I understand. It's something primal, something that man can't control.'

'I never thought of that, but you're right,' said Anna.

'Perhaps we'd better be making tracks, though.' Jane looked at Anna regretfully. 'It's been a long day and I take it we'll have to pedal the whole way home. But I'm glad we came here, and I'll picture this place in my head when I'm back in my stuffy closet of an office in London.'

She would miss her cousin when she went back to London and Anna had thought of a gift she could send her. Something to put up in that tiny basement office of hers in the Air Ministry. *A small present; still, it wasn't the size of a thing that mattered but the thought behind it.* She would buy some post-cards of Cornwall to send her. One from Newquay and another of an image of the bay at Perranporth, if she could find them. She had a feeling Jane would like that.

40

TREVELLAS

20 FEBRUARY 1941

It was lovely to see Mary, of course. But it was worrying too, for Anna knew that the air force didn't hand out two weeks' sick leave for no reason. Still, her old friend had denied she was ill, had dismissed the idea with an airy wave of her hand. She needed a change of scene, that was all.

But Anna could see the difference in her, from the gaunt, sunken cheeks that used to be round to the anxious look in her eyes. Gone was the fun-loving friend she'd known when they'd stood on the parade ground and laughed at that comical gas mask drill.

At first, she'd assumed it was because of Harry, but there seemed to be something else as well. The pressure of her job, maybe. Or the harrowing effects of war. Whatever the reason for this dramatic change in her friend, she had decided not to try and pry it loose, but to let Mary talk about it in her own time. Meanwhile, she hoped that the freedom and rugged beauty of Cornwall would help ease her friend's anxiety.

There were no spare rooms in the cottage now that

Lowenna and the children had returned, so the pair of them were sharing Anna's bedroom. It was like old times, when their beds had been side by side in that ancient, creaking building in Leighton Buzzard and they'd told each other ghost stories. More innocent times, she thought, before people they knew were killed or Mary's father had died.

They were cycling through the countryside, down to the village of Perranporth. She'd promised to show Mary the Stork Club, a small café close to the bay. It had a great view of the sea and the dunes, but was often busy, especially at night when troops came from miles around and it turned itself into a bar.

'When's Jimmy coming home?' asked Mary when they'd settled in, cups of tea in front of them.

'He said he'd be back at the start of the month,' she said, a sharp edge to her voice.

'Did you truly think he would?' said Mary.

'He promised faithfully,' she said.

'You angry at Jimmy?'

'Not Jimmy, no. It's not his fault. But I've a right to be angry with *somebody*!' said Anna.

'They move us around like puppets, but I don't suppose it's anybody's fault. Remember when we ended up scrubbing pots instead of going on our plotters' course?' asked Mary and laughed.

It was the first time her friend had relaxed since she'd arrived a week ago. Maybe Cornwall was finally working its magic, Anna thought.

'They're making me a corporal,' she said, hesitantly. Mary was the first one she'd told. She wasn't even sure how she felt about it yet – she'd been quite happy being a plain ACW 2nd class.

'Since when?' asked Mary, surprised.

'As soon as I take my next shift, I suppose.'

'Well done, you! Ma'll be so proud, and so am I. Does Jimmy know?'

'I've only just found out myself. Haven't even sewn the stripes on yet. Not sure about it all.'

'Why not? More pay and a better billet,' said Mary.

'I'm very happy with my billet,' she said.

'So, straight from ACW2 to corporal – what happened to leading aircraftwoman in between?'

'I seem to have leapfrogged over leading aircraftwoman.' Anna laughed.

'Imagine trying to leapfrog over our leading aircraftwoman at RAF Wilmslow!' said Mary.

'*Nobody* could have leapfrogged over LACW Dutton! Remember when the girls stole her sticky buns for our celebration?' Anna said. 'She almost blew one of those gaskets she was always on about.'

The memory was a happy one and made them both smile again.

When they'd finished their tea, Mary pointed to the dunes: 'Fancy a quick walk before we mount our steeds?'

'The dunes are off limits, they're mined. Some trainees from the camp at Penhale cut across there one time after a drunken night on the town. Blew themselves to smithereens,' said Anna, and swallowed hard.

'Back home then?' asked Mary.

She nodded. They wrapped up again. It was especially cold, even for this time of year. They looked like Egyptian mummies, she thought, covered from head to toe with greatcoats, woollen hats and gloves, with grey scarves wound tightly around their necks. But they'd been lucky: the snow that had covered most of the country hadn't reached there. The worst blizzards in memory had driven people indoors and grounded aircraft, especially from RAF stations in the north. It had been a relief to hear that. It meant that Jimmy probably wouldn't have to fly; it would keep him safe. She didn't mind how cold it got if it meant he might be saved from harm.

Anna pedalled so hard up the monster hill that Mary battled to keep up. But still Anna pressed on as if something urgent awaited her. She couldn't explain to Mary why she felt this. She didn't know why herself, just that an odd, unsettling feeling of foreboding had suddenly lodged itself in her stomach and refused to let go. She tried to shake it loose: it was totally irrational. *Perhaps something has happened at the airfield*, she reasoned – even though reason and logic played no part in such a superstition.

She pushed on relentlessly, each muscle straining, fighting the exhaustion, watching her warm breath escape in front of her. She saw it transform into a miniature cloud of white mist as it hit the cold air, pulling her onwards. At the crest of the hill she looked around to see Mary still there, pushing hard, staying doggedly on her heels. It felt like they were both struggling to keep up this frantic pace, but soon the road flattened out and Anna stared across at the entrance to the airfield. She'd imagined that this is what had guided her, that something important waited there. But instead of cycling up to the barrier, she stayed on the road. It was as if the old bike had taken charge and was taking her home.

Anna slackened her pace a little and thought of the warm fire in the kitchen that waited for them, along with the chicken stew Lowenna was making. Her brain fooled her into believing she could already smell its wonderful aroma.

Mary arrived beside her, panting with the effort. 'What was all that about?' she asked.

'Call it a rush of blood to the brain,' she said and smiled.

'Don't ever ask me to do that again!'

'Nearly there. Only about half a mile to go and then you can put your feet up and pretend to be a lady of leisure.'

That's when she heard it. The frantic screech of an engine; a tortured sound that she'd heard before at the airfield at Biggin Hill. It sounded like an aircraft in distress, a Spitfire out of control trying to gain height. A pilot who'd misjudged the runway, perhaps.

'Let's go,' she shouted at Mary. 'Somebody's in trouble and the end of the runway's opposite Lowenna's house. We need to warn her!'

They got to the stone cottage just minutes after the deafening crash, when the fighter plane ploughed into the side of it. Gouts of flame sprouted from the cockpit and leapt up to the roof of the house, taking hold of the rafters.

For a second Anna sat on her bike in shock, until she heard Mary's bike beside her clatter noisily on the cobbled path. In a dreamlike state, she pulled Mary behind her, and they made their way to the side of the cottage, around the plane and towards the cockpit that was enveloped in fire. It had embedded itself in a wall, gouging a massive hole. Tumbling masonry covered it.

'We need to try and get him out!' Anna screamed, hysterically. In her mind she imagined Jimmy in there. They had to at least try and get to the man.

'It's no good,' Mary said, and tugged her away. 'Can't you see he's a goner?'

The whole front of the Spitfire was a massive fireball now, sending plumes of flames and smoke into the air, cascading sparks setting the surrounding trees alight. She shook her head in despair. What Mary said was true: no one could live in that furnace. But what about Lowenna and the children? They could be trapped inside the house, the little ones screaming with fear.

'Lowenna,' Anna cried at the top of her voice.

But there was no answering call. No cries or screams.

'Follow me,' she told Mary. 'We'll get to the other side. She locks the back door at night, but we can break the kitchen window.'

That's when she heard the wail of the siren as the fire engine from the airfield made its way to the crash site. But she didn't wait for it, and neither did Mary. There was a kind, generous, sweet girl trapped somewhere in the cottage with her two beautiful children.

41

He was Australian – from Adelaide, Anna had heard – the poor young pilot whose life had ended two nights ago in a Cornish field; far away from his home, miles from his family and friends and the people who loved him. Fighting for a country that wasn't even his. The mood at the airfield had been sombre, but his squadron had given him a proper farewell, with drinks in the pub to send him on his way. There was to be a memorial service in the village church and the local blacksmith was making a plaque to mark the young man's sacrifice.

He'd been a stranger, but still Anna felt sad about his loss, and the futility of his death made it more poignant. His life thrown away in a tragic accident. He hadn't been killed in battle but was a freshly qualified pilot, new to the airfield, and had overshot the runway, trying to land. But the horror of that night might have been even worse if she and Mary hadn't been able to break in and help get Lowenna and her children out.

A lot had changed since then. Anna had lost her billet and was now living at the station in the room that used to be Corporal Landry's quarters. The corporal had been urgently posted elsewhere, no one knew the reason. Still, at least now

Anna understood why she had been suddenly promoted to corporal, leapfrogging the ranks of ACW1 and leading aircraftwoman. She thought about how Mary and she had joked about that, and she managed to smile.

There hadn't been a lot to smile about lately. Mary had been allowed to share these new quarters with her, a tiny room the size of a monk's cell, but they'd managed to fit another mattress on the floor.

Lowenna and her children were safe, and a family nearby had taken them in at their farm. People from Trevellas had been kind, donated clothes, and a few simple toys for the little ones because most things in the cottage had been destroyed. The fire had rushed in through the collapsed wall and rapidly taken hold. Even the roof was gone. Anna had sat on the ground with Lowenna and wept.

But the whole sorrowful tragedy seemed to have had a peculiar effect on her friend. She'd been upset of course, like the rest of them, but now Anna could see some of the old Mary coming back. She walked a little taller now and that positive, confident WAAF whose plotter's skill was second to none was looking forward to returning to her old station in Lincolnshire.

That night, Anna went straight to her quarters after her shift. It was early, only eight in the evening, but she felt weary after the emotional turmoil of the last days, wouldn't mind having an early night. She was still getting used to being a corporal, to being set apart from the other ranks. It came with its problems as well as its privileges. She was still deciding which of those outweighed the other. True, there was a small increase in salary, but having to pass orders down the chain of command came with its drawbacks. The WAAF friends she'd had before now saw her in a different light and she couldn't mix with them as easily, not if she wanted credibility or her orders to be taken seriously. It could mean that she would be lonelier. Only time would tell.

Mary was waiting for her, a grin of expectation on her face. 'Thought we'd have a treat,' she said.

Anna looked at the cake in wonder. 'Chocolate cake, how did you wangle that?'

'Don't get excited, it's not chocolate. It's brown, yes – but it's only boiled raisin cake. Better than nothing, though.' Mary laughed.

'And what's the occasion?'

'I'll be off in the morning, but I wanted to finish on a happy, cheerful note,' said Mary.

'Amen to that,' Anna agreed. 'But why so soon when you've got a few more days before you report back?'

'Thought I'd go and see Ma. Couldn't do it before – didn't want to take my troubles with me, and Ma can see right through me,' she said.

'Because she loves you,' Anna said.

'She loves you too,' said Mary.

'I know and I feel the same, that's why I was sad I hurt her.'

'The wedding, you mean? She understood, and Ma's tougher than that. She was pleased with your letter.'

'I'm glad. Now, what about you? What's happened?'

'I came here with the idea of asking for a transfer from Bomber Command...'

'But why? You're good at your job.'

'It's just that – we have such a high attrition rate up there. So many crews getting killed. You get to know most of them, wave some of them off at the runway and they don't come back for supper. It wears you down. And that last raid that went out...'

'You were especially fond of somebody, is that it?' asked Anna.

Her friend nodded but didn't speak.

'A special chap. I understand,' Anna said.

'He'd asked me to go out with him when he got back. But he never came home, you see,' said Mary, her lip trembling now.

Anna hugged her friend to her. 'I'm sorry, Mary. So, what's changed now? I mean, you look different from when you came.'

'Well, I was hoping to move down here where it was easier...'

'It's not easier, it's just different,' said Anna. 'And we still lose people we know. We had a chap miss the runway and dive into the sea. Another never made it home and crashed into a cliff. And that awful crash at Lowenna's place...'

'I know,' said Mary. 'I get it now – that's the point. Nowhere is free of it. The war gets to you wherever you are. So, I've decided to stay at RAF Binbrook and just get on with it.'

'You're very brave – I've always known that,' said Anna.

'Brave? Maybe. Maybe we're both brave. Or stupid. You'd no idea what was on the other side of that window when you broke the glass to get in and find Lowenna and the children. Maybe we'll get a medal, and they'll call us heroes,' Mary smiled.

Anna absentmindedly looked at the bandage on her hand. It hadn't been that bad – six stitches after putting the window out. 'Heroes?' she said. 'Well then, I'm in trouble for sure.'

'Why on earth?' asked Mary.

'Jimmy – he'll give me what for! I promised him I'd never do *anything* heroic again.'

Gladys was tickled pink: she'd said so in her last letter and Anna could just picture her face, proud that her daughter Mary had been called up to Bomber Command Headquarters and handed a medal. It had been a real fancy ceremony, Ma wrote – she'd even bought a new hat. And why shouldn't she be proud? Anna thought. It was about time the war had given Gladys Armstrong something back. She'd lost her husband to its tyranny and her oldest son Tom had been wounded in North Africa. The family had thought he was dead, but he'd turned up in a military hospital in Egypt. Glad maintained that she'd always known her boy was alive even when all the others had given up hope. A mother knows when one of her children is dead, she wrote. Anna hoped that was true. Especially when she thought about Jimmy and the danger that these bomber crews faced daily. Sometimes, she tried to pretend that he was somewhere safe, behind a desk. It was often the only way she could make it through the day without him – lying to herself.

Now both she and Mary had a military medal each. They'd given Anna a new ribbon to add to hers. But there had been no ceremony and she was relieved no one had made a fuss. After all, what had they really done that terrible night? It wasn't as if either she or Mary had managed to pull the pilot from his plane. But she doubted anyone could have done that; not even the rescue truck from the airfield could have got to him in time.

But maybe it was fair to say that she had rescued Lowenna. She'd found her in a bedroom, hugging her two small children to her, protecting them. Stroking their hair. Singing them a lullaby. It had been such a loving picture in the midst of all the madness, Anna had wanted to cry. Instead she had given them a way out, and guided the poor distraught girl and her family through the smoke and gathering flames.

42

NO. 15 FLYING TRAINING SCHOOL, RAF
LECONFIELD, YORKSHIRE

MARCH 1941

So many new things to absorb. So many changes to get used to: a
new pilot, a smaller crew – only three this time – a different
plane, and an airfield he'd been unfamiliar with. But it was war
and Jimmy understood that their Blenheim bomber, along with
others from his squadron, was the tip of a lethal spear. At least,
that's what Squadron Leader Blake had said in that rousing
speech of his.

Two months of training, that had been the original plan;
and he'd promised Anna he'd be home by then, but he'd been
wrong. They'd be going back to St Eval, eventually, except no
one had told them when. No one had told them much, but that
wasn't unusual – the less you knew, Jimmy thought, the less you
could give away.

The training in Yorkshire had been arduous and several
aircrew had already failed to make the grade. But he and
Freddy were still there, still called the lucky crew, the blue-eyed
boys, although he didn't know why, for his eyes were green.

Only him and Freddy were left from the old crew. George

had never returned from leave, and no one had heard from him again. Posted elsewhere, Jimmy supposed – maybe a cushier job at headquarters and George had always been one to fall on his feet. Their skipper Andy was no more than a memory now and sometimes, when Jimmy forced his brain to flick through its images, he couldn't even recall Andrew's face. It was a sad, unsettling thought – but then, he supposed, people moved in and out of your life. You couldn't hold on to them all.

He was still getting used to their new pilot. The man seemed competent enough, but he was a little edgy, with a slightly superior chip on his shoulder that Freddy had tried to dislodge. It hadn't worked and Freddy had already ticked off the man by calling him Charlie when he insisted his name was Charles.

Their new aircraft were Blenheims – light bombers – and they only carried a crew of three, whereas Jimmy had been used to four of them. Now all the crew, except the pilot, had to double up with other jobs. It was easier for him because his roles hadn't changed – he was still navigator and bomb-aimer – but now he sat right up next to the pilot, in the very cramped space of the cockpit, which he had to get used to. When it was time for him to drop the bombs, he would slide his seat back to get to his controls. Freddy was having a harder time getting used to his extra role as wireless operator, for in their other aircraft that had always been George's job. Now Freddy had to learn a new skill as well as operate the dorsal gun turret between the cockpit and the tail.

But they were getting there, and it was rumoured that soon they'd be made operational again. A Freddy rumour! But then Freddy could often be relied upon to latch onto a reliable source – usually a WAAF.

Jimmy smiled. It was hard not to think about his own very special WAAF, but often he had to force himself to put Anna to the back of his mind. His wife. His wonderful, incredible, clever, and definitely brave partner in life. The thought of her always managed to lift his mood, to make him smile. Not a bad thing, of course, but right then it would be far safer for him and the crew for his mind to have no such warm distraction, cheering though it might be. He had to take the memory of her, the feel of her, the love that she wrapped him up in, and tuck it away safely in a pocket at the back of his mind. But its echo still left a warm glow behind.

Freddy had been right: the squadron had been lined up for a raid, with six other squadrons as well as theirs. Fifty-four Blenheims in all, so not a massive show, thought Jimmy, but enough to make it worthwhile all the same. A sort of test, he assumed, to check their operational readiness before they were sent back to St Eval.

There had been an excited buzz in the air of the briefing room and everyone jumped expectantly to their feet as the wing commander in charge of the operation entered the room and uncovered the large map.

Cologne, in western Germany, centred on the west bank of the Rhine, was a heavily populated city and a busy industrial one. An important target, Jimmy thought. His job tonight was to get his aircraft there, drop his bombs on a power station and get them safely home.

He listened intently to the briefing and made his notes fastidiously. When he looked up at their squadron leader, he noted an odd expression on the officer's face. It only lingered for a second and then it was gone, but Squadron Leader Blake's face had seemed to go grey. Maybe just the light in here, Jimmy told himself.

The Blenheims were to assemble over the Netherlands, coming in at a very low level for the attack. It would take precision flying, the wing commander had warned, but he'd been enthusiastic about their chances, had wished them 'happy hunting'. It was an audacious, daring raid, he'd told them all.

Jimmy didn't know if that was true, but it felt good to be on a proper mission at last. So far, all they'd been doing were dummy runs, playing at them for the past weeks. At least this was finally real.

He settled into his seat in the cockpit, his home from home. His navigation took them to the spot over Holland where they met with the Spitfire escort, there to protect them. He heaved a sigh of relief. It was always good to know you were in the right place. *Maths*, he thought. *A magical tool.*

But the Spitfires didn't have the range to get closer than 100 miles from Cologne, and then the bombers were left on their own. To face the flak. Without any fighter cover, large anti-aircraft concentrations around the power plant could pound the vulnerable bombers. Small, tell-tale puffs of black smoke hung in the air surrounding their formation – an early warning that they were in range of the deadly German flak cannons. Jimmy heard the explosive rounds as they screamed through the air and he tensed, clamped his lips tightly. He saw their lethal metal fragments rip jagged holes in the British Blenheims. He shuddered as two of them went down in spirals, spinning in the air like roman candles.

Then the swift and agile Messerschmitt fighters began buzzing all around them, sending fiery tracers into the wallowing bombers. Fat and easy targets, Jimmy thought sourly, as another British plane fell from the sky.

He tamped down the fear, forced himself to slow down his breathing, bringing his heightened emotions under control. Jimmy dropped his bombs calmly, methodically, determined that someone should pay for the loss of his fellow airmen. He watched them blast their target and shouted for the pilot to take them home – far away from these savage, murderous skies, towards sanity.

It was only then that Jimmy noticed the tremor in his right hand. But when he looked at the pilot sitting next to him, he could see that Charles was shaking too. The plane climbed swiftly higher, its altitude increasing urgently, far above where the brutal flak could reach them.

Neither of them spoke until the Blenheim was safely back flying once again in friendly skies. *Home*, thought Jimmy, relief cascading through him.

'Low-level flying?' said Charles, breaking the silence. 'You know what?'

'What?' asked Jimmy.

'You can keep it! "An audacious raid", that's what they called it. Know what I call it?' asked Charles.

'What's that?'

'A suicide mission. That's what that was,' he said, a quiver in his voice.

And although Jimmy wouldn't have said it aloud, he thought maybe the man was right.

43

ST EVAL

His squadron had been back at St Eval for the past few weeks, although not all of them had returned from the raid in Cologne. The losses had been high: twelve of the fifty-four bombers had failed to make it home, two of them from Jimmy's squadron.

Almost a quarter of the aircrews who took part that day didn't come back. The mood in the mess was subdued. Friends were missing and the number of casualties high. They'd heard in training that the sustainable loss rate was five per cent. *Sustainable* – what a ridiculous word, he thought, angrily. As if it was fine for people to keep on dying. *Who had decided that?* he wondered. *And why?* The crews all knew about the high casualty rates, especially the bomber crews, but it wasn't something discussed in the mess. *What was the point when it would only give you the jitters?* Jimmy thought. Especially when it reduced people of flesh and blood, and friends, to numbers on a casualty list.

They'd been promised a week's leave any day now, but as far as he could tell that day was moving farther away. There was nothing to be done though, no matter how frustrating it was that he hadn't been able to see Anna for so long, not since their wonderful honeymoon. Remembering it kept him going. They weren't the only ones who'd been separated by this terrible war and there was no point getting bitter over things you couldn't control. Jimmy had learned that by now. The country was running out of trained aircrew, so they were all having to make sacrifices. Everyone in the squadron was getting tired but there was no way around it. As far as Jimmy could make out, you flew until you were so exhausted that you couldn't fly any more.

Even so, he was thrilled to be back in Cornwall. To a place where he would be happy to live once this damn madness dragged itself to an end. He was sure Anna felt the same way too, though he hadn't come right out and asked her yet. He'd been trying to get them a place to live, somewhere they could be together – but there was a shortage of spaces in the stations' married quarters. He'd put their names down on the waiting list, but the list was long, especially after the raid that had knocked out a lot of the accommodation.

Meanwhile, they were writing letters. Hers were funny and often uplifting and his were – more like essays, he supposed. But then she'd always been good at raising his spirits; seemed to find the right words, while he sometimes struggled to put down his heart on paper. She seemed to know what was in there, anyway. That was just her. But when this leave of his finally materialised, he was going to make it up to her. He was planning something truly special, a sentimental visit that he had an idea she would love just as much as him.

Right now, he was back on daily patrols, along with Freddy and Charles, sometimes acting as referee between the pair of them. But he understood that at times it was a game they played – goading each other on. A valve to release the pressure of the job. But as soon as they all got into their plane, that's when the game ended in a truce. Jimmy was no longer surprised at the smooth way the three of them went through their familiar routines, getting the bomber into the air, coming together like one person. Each one knew what to expect of the other, as if they could look into each other's minds, he thought.

One important part of Jimmy's job with Coastal Command was anti-shipping patrols. It was good to be on the offensive; to be the hunter for a change and not the hunted. These sorties along the coast of France and occupied Europe were crucial, attacking German shipping, cutting off their supplies. Taking away their ability to fight. It felt good. He'd never imagined he would feel that way, but after the way those Messerschmitt fighters had mercilessly killed his fellow airmen in Cologne, he had no sympathy for them. Now, his enemy truly felt like an enemy.

He sat in the mess, still in his flying kit, a mug of cocoa going cold on the table in front of him. He'd been thinking about Anna, remembering the times they enjoyed their hot chocolate after a walk on the beach. Cocoa – on the posters they called it a fighting food. Encouraged folk to drink it if they could.

He'd been expecting to go up today: the three of them and their kite had been at readiness. But the weather had come in, blanketing the runways and the airfield in a thick layer of fog. Sometimes it was like that: the weather could be just as fierce an enemy as the Germans.

'Here you are! Thought we'd lost you to the group captain's birthday party,' said Freddy.

'It's Group's birthday?' asked Jimmy, surprised.

'Everybody's got one,' said Freddy, laughing. 'Even him.'

'I've just been sitting here, cogitating,' said Jimmy, with a smile.

'Thinking, eh? Shouldn't do too much of that, old bean – not good for the old noddle, you know. You get the message from the WAAF I sent to find you?'

'Nobody came to find me,' Jimmy said.

'No? Well, there's something waiting at the front gate for you. I offered to take it, but they need your I.D. You know how puffed up with power these blokes can be.'

'Thanks, I'll get on down there.'

'You leaving that cocoa?' asked Freddy.

'Have it,' he said. 'It's yours.'

At the gate, Jimmy told them what Freddy had said.

'Right,' said the guard, 'where's your F1250, mate? Can't give you nothing without proof. You might be some agitator for all I know.' The man winked.

Jimmy handed over his RAF I.D. card and waited, intrigued.

The airman checked it and went inside the guard hut, came back with a brown paper parcel. He was holding it gingerly by a finger and thumb. 'Glad to get shot of it, mate. We been taking bets as to what died inside,' the man said, and laughed.

Jimmy watched the gate guard hold his nose theatrically and then cavalierly toss the small paper package towards him. As soon as he caught it, he understood. The smell was overpowering, and he wondered what on earth could be inside and who had sent it. Maybe Freddy had done it as a joke. It was like his childish level of humour. He wanted to know what was in there but he refused to rip it open with the airman looking on.

Jimmy laughed when he opened it. The tin had been punctured in the post, he supposed, and the contents had leaked a little, but it didn't matter. He laughed and laughed. The look of it, the thought of it, transported him to another place and time. A miraculous place that had started a whole new life for him. He wrapped it up again, took it back to the mess. Laid it on the table. Ordered a beer. A proper celebration. He bought one for Freddy too.

'What in the name of all that's holy is that smell? What's in the packet?' Freddy asked.

'A very special gift,' he said.

'Strange sort of gift, if you ask me,' Freddy said, and wrinkled his nose.

But Jimmy just smiled. He understood, even though there wasn't a note attached. They didn't need it. Anna was trying to remind him of the first time they'd met and what it had meant to the two of them.

'I don't get it,' said Freddy. 'Fish?'

'A tin of sardines,' he said.

'Who on earth would send you those and why? You're not going to eat them! They smell disgusting,' said Freddy.

'A fragrance sweeter than the scents of Arabia,' Jimmy said, and laughed. 'I might just eat them, but that's not what they're for.'

'No?' said Freddy, shaking his head in confusion.

'These, my friend,' he said, as a wide grin took hold of his face, 'are a love letter.'

44

20 MAY 1941

Jimmy had asked Anna to organise a week's leave to fit in with his. It hadn't been easy, and she'd had to pay for it by taking on extra shifts and making herself useful by showing some new WAAFs the ropes. But it would be worth it to spend time together at last.

She still couldn't believe she was free. A whole week of getting up when she wanted to. Of sleeping in, if that's what took her fancy. Of staying in bed. There'd be quite a bit of that, she imagined, and not all of it sleeping, she thought, as she looked at Jimmy and smiled. After all, they had a lot of catching up to do.

He was taking her on a mystery tour, he'd said. She wasn't to ask where, but so far, they'd been travelling for most of the day. They'd changed trains twice since leaving Cornwall and now it seemed they were finally getting close to their destination. She could see it by the excitement on his face. Like a small boy waiting impatiently for Christmas to come. Knowing that it would and willing it on.

The train came to a noisy, fussy halt. There were no station signs, but she could see it was a busy terminus, with lots of platforms and bustle and folk changing trains.

'This is us,' Jimmy said with a grin, and helped her off with her kitbag. 'We'll be staying the night here.'

'What – at the station?' she asked, mischievously. 'Thought you said you were going to pamper me.'

'And I'm a man of my word.'

'Never doubted it,' said Anna, and reached across and planted a small kiss on his cheek. 'A down payment,' she said.

'Are you trying to corrupt me, Mrs Armstrong?'

'Is it working?' she asked.

'Let's get to this fancy hotel and see. It's not far.'

They walked arm in arm, and so many memories flooded over her. Now they would make new ones. That's what he'd told her. This wonderful, carefree week would be a holiday, their first proper one together, a time for doing special things.

'It's certainly fancy,' she said, when she saw the ornate station hotel.

'Only the best for my wonderful wife.' He smiled. 'Queen Victoria used to stay here on her way to Scotland. I've booked us the same room. Imagine that,' he said. 'We'll be sleeping in the same bed as Queen Victoria.'

'I expect they've changed the sheets since then,' she teased him.

It turned out they didn't do much sleeping.

Early next morning, they left the stylish luxury of the Crewe Hotel and their room with its pleated satin wallpaper and elaborate beaded headboard. The bed hadn't been Queen Victoria's, after all, but Anna wasn't disappointed. It wasn't the bed you were in that mattered, but the man sharing it with you, she thought.

They headed back over the road to the station. She had an idea where Jimmy might be taking her on this trip down memory lane. There were only a few places it could be, especially as they'd come back to Cheshire, but she didn't want to spoil his fun, or ruin the surprise.

An hour later, they arrived at Wilmslow railway station and made their way to the RAF camp. It hadn't changed: the replica Spitfire still stood out front, and the guard hut was right where she remembered it. But the most important landmark of all, she thought, was waiting for them, exactly where it should be. Such a simple thing – just a small patch of grass outside the gate barrier. A very special picnic had taken place there once, Mary sitting on her blanket and Jimmy next to her. It was the first time she'd seen him and that welcoming smile of his. Her mind had taken a snapshot of it and kept it safe for all time.

She felt his arm around her shoulders now, and that same smile took over his face.

'Well,' he said, 'is it a good surprise?'

'Ten out of ten,' she said.

'And we haven't finished yet. Stay there, we've got a friend waiting for us,' he said excitedly.

She watched him, puzzled. *A friend?* She saw the duty guard inspect Jimmy's I.D. and lift the barrier immediately, as if he were expected. Then he vanished from her sight around the back of the guard hut and that's when something wonderful happened. Something so improbable that it took her by surprise, overwhelmed her with such feelings that she didn't know whether to laugh or cry.

'But how's that possible?' she asked, when he'd wheeled Daisy over.

'A pal of mine found her in a shed. He's been fixing her up.

We can have her for as long as we're here,' he said, a triumphant look on his face. 'You pleased?'

'Pleased?' she said. 'If you'd given me the Crown Jewels, I couldn't be happier.'

'Think we can still manage it? It's a long time since we first took this thing on her maiden run.'

'It was the twenty-ninth of October, 1939. Not far off two years now.'

'You remember the date?' he asked, astonished.

'Of course. I'm a woman,' she said. 'We remember all sorts of things.'

'Okay, clever clogs, but can you still remember how to be a tail-gunner?'

'If you can remember how to steer.'

'Don't forget – no putting your feet up, expecting me to do all the work,' he said and laughed.

'It's just like riding a bike,' she said, cheekily. 'You never forget.'

Even so, she noted they *both* wobbled a bit as they tried to get their balance. But it felt good. The sort of feeling that made her eyes sparkle. Could anything, she wondered, be more perfect than this trail of memories that he'd laid out for them to follow? It felt like another honeymoon, a kind of romantic pilgrimage, and she loved him so much for it. For taking the time to organise this incredible sentimental journey for them, especially when she knew how hard it had been for him at the base lately. He'd tried to save her from some of the worry and sadness; she understood he felt it was his job – as her protector. But they were a couple now, and they could face their troubles together.

She listened to his shout of 'Chocks away!', just like the first time. And it wasn't long before his whistle floated back to her again, as tuneful as she remembered, but then maybe memories are mysterious things that improve with time. Well, this one couldn't be bettered, she thought, and if she was right, she knew exactly where they were headed now. She hoped the hotel in Stockport would be just as magical as the first time around.

She thought about their glorious steak and kidney pie, hoped its miracle would be possible again. Or they might have to make do with that miserable Woolton pie with its tasteless, mushy vegetables beaten into submission. But it wouldn't even matter. It wasn't what you ate that was important, or even how plush and exotic the surroundings were. What truly mattered was the person across the table from you. And if his eyes said he loved you.

At least this time they would stay overnight together. Things hadn't turned out that way when he'd had to go and rescue Freddy, but that hadn't been so bad, and at least it showed how much Jimmy was prepared to do for his friends. It hadn't just been a sacrifice for her, she thought, as she remembered his face, downcast with disappointment.

'You okay back there?' he asked.

'Sublime,' she said. 'But all this exercise is making me hungry.'

'Maybe we can do something about that. Hold on and no slacking. We're coming to the hard bit, that pesky hill.'

'I remember, and so does Daisy. This is where she starts to groan,' said Anna.

But Daisy's chain didn't protest this time, and their feet flew around and around with the pedals, as if the old bike was pleased to see them again.

They hurtled down the hill with the wind at their backs and she heard his triumphant cheer. This time, instead of that piercing whistle of his, she heard him start up a tune, singing at the top of his voice. *Their song – and Daisy's too.* She remembered what he'd said, that night back at his family's house: that his voice was like a bullfrog with a head cold. She smiled to

herself. Singing was a kind of miracle, she thought, and it didn't
really matter how it sounded. She laughed.

'What's up?' asked Jimmy.

'I've never heard you sing before,' she said. 'Mary said it was
like a cinder under a door, but it's really not that bad. At least
you found the tune, which is more than I can do.'

'C'mon then,' said Jimmy. 'As loud as you can. Nobody's
listening and we can look for the tune together.'

45

It had been a thrilling, intoxicating time, as if she'd been drinking something potent, but it must just have been her brain working overtime, she thought, telling her to be happy.

Well, it was working: over the past few days her brain had made her face ache with smiles when she thought back on it all.

The White Lion Hotel hadn't changed much since the last time she'd been there. Except, when they'd first arrived, she'd been confused when the receptionist stared at them and coyly lowered her eyes. Then the manager had come out to greet them. He'd coughed discreetly, asked if they would prefer to take dinner in their room.

Later, she laughed when Jimmy explained that he'd done a wicked thing and told the manager they were newlyweds on honeymoon. It had been a marvellous idea, she thought. They'd spent a lot of time in that wonderful room. Not all of it in bed! It had been the perfect chance to rediscover each other, to make each other laugh. He'd always been able to make her laugh, she thought.

They'd reminisced about the good things they'd shared. She hadn't spoken of her fears for him, or her nightmares. Or talked about the airmen she'd known who'd lost their lives. Or when her station at Biggin Hill had been bombed. It would only remind him of his own danger, and neither of them wanted that. He hadn't told her about the raid on Cologne either, although he didn't need to. They were in the same air force and negative rumours flew around, no matter how much those in charge wanted to keep up morale with positive propaganda. Many of them knew when things went wrong. 'Gone pear-shaped,' she'd heard some of the pilots say, when things didn't work out as planned – like when one of them tried for an aerobatic loop in the sky, and it came out shaped like a pear instead of a circle. *That was as close as any of them got to a pear right now*, she thought.

She sensed him behind her, could feel his warm breath on her neck.

'How's the old posterior?' he asked, moving his hands slowly down her back as if he was making an appraisal.

'That's a little personal, don't you think? Besides, it's not old, my rear end. It's in the best shape of its life.' She laughed. 'All this constant biking.'

'So – you up for another trip today? Thought we'd get in one last push before we have to get old Daisy back.'

'So, where...?'

'Remember that odd little village we stopped at when Freddy and George muscled in on our trip that day?'

'Something to do with flowers, as I recall. Or buds, maybe,' she said.

'Ah, ha! So you don't remember *everything* then. Thought you said that women were superior to us poor chaps,' he said, pointing an accusing finger at her.

'Never said that. We remember all sorts of things, that's what I said.'

'Well, *I* remember,' he said, smugly. 'Great Budworth, and I think we should go there again.'

'Sounds lovely. And you're clever to remember the name.'

'I asked the woman on reception,' he confessed. 'Even *she* had to look it up.'

Everything had been so perfect, so idyllic, as if they were both living in a dream, she thought, including this trip today. She liked it there, not as much as she loved Cornwall, for there were no beaches, or rugged cliffs and tempestuous seas. Still, the whole countryside seemed to be in bloom, and she'd asked Jimmy to stop along the way to feast her eyes on the view. Spring was a colourful time, and Cheshire had put on its best clothes today – just for them, she told him. He'd laughed at that but hadn't disagreed.

The quirky teashop was still there in the picturesque village, and they stopped for tea. Nothing about it seemed to have changed, as if the place had been holding its breath waiting for their return, she thought. A romantic notion, of course, but then this whole trip of theirs had been surrounded by romance, had at times felt a little surreal. Reality was out there waiting for them, the war and its brutality hadn't gone away, but meanwhile, she intended to enjoy every second of this incredible time of theirs as runaways.

There was a telegram waiting for them at the hotel on their return. Back in their room, she watched him open it, anxiously; looked at the contours of his face for surprise, or pain. Grief often made its way in telegrams.

But he put it aside with only a smile. 'It's from Bertie,' he said.

'Bertie?'

'The chap who picked us up in his motor the day we were wed.'

'I see,' she said.

'Says he'll give us a lift from Truro when we get in. There's a bit of a flap on, it seems,' said Jimmy.

'But everything's okay?' she said, a frown on her face.

'Everything's totally fine,' he assured her. 'Although it looks like the end of our little hideaway.'

'So, they're calling you in before your leave's over?'

'You know what it's like... some bigwig gets an idea for a mission, and everybody has to jump.'

'If it's the end, let's make it perfect,' Anna said, and planted a passionate kiss on his lips. The prelude, she hoped, to something more.

She had a feeling about tonight, that it would be an extra-special one. If it was to be their last act of love for a while, then... it should be memorable. There was something else, as well. Although she hadn't mentioned it to him, today was an anniversary of sorts. It was the twenty-fourth of May and six months to the day that they'd been married. He wouldn't have thought of it, she supposed: men were hardly likely to take note of such things. Women were the sentimental ones; but it didn't matter, she would remember for both of them.

There was a knock on the door and the barmaid arrived with a bottle of wine and two elegant crystal glasses.

'You ordered our best wine, sir,' she said.

'Thank you.'

'You bought us champagne?' said Anna when the barmaid had gone. 'How romantic.'

'Special wine for a special day and a remarkable woman, who is all mine,' he said. Anna saw the desire in his eyes and the intensity of his kiss that followed left her breathless. When they came up for air, she watched him pop the champagne and pour them each a glass. But neither of them drank more than a mouthful.

It was one of those times, Anna thought, when passion overcomes everything else – even the best wine in the cellar.

She was right about it being a momentous night. At times it seemed as if the room might explode with their passion. Two bodies had never been closer than the pair of them, as if they were one being, one life. She couldn't imagine anything would ever be more extraordinary. It was as if they had conquered heights that had never been climbed before.

Afterwards, they collapsed into each other's arms, and that's when she knew. She'd been given this precious time tonight for a reason; not a farewell, exactly – but a parting. Something told her that she must be brave and hold on to its memory.

She didn't know how she knew these things – that the pair of them might not be together for some time. Maybe it was just the fear of it. But she didn't think so. She had a premonition of danger coming for Jimmy and she wanted to protect him, the precious man she loved. But in her heart, she knew that their separation would not be for all time. He would survive. She knew that with the same certainty that Gladys had known her son Tom was alive.

She looked down at her husband and kissed his cheek. His sleeping face held a hint of a smile.

46

26 MAY 1941

The train journey home had been long and dull with no chance, this time, of a leisurely overnight stay in some fancy hotel like the one in Crewe. Tiresome and boring, he'd thought. Jimmy had never been good at doing nothing; sitting on his hands and letting others take charge. But train trips were often tedious, and he could see Anna felt the same. Boredom didn't suit her either. His incredible wife was a firebrand. He looked at her now, her head resting easily on his shoulder, for she'd finally given in to the tiredness of the last days and was sleeping peacefully. He felt rather proud of that, the thought that she felt so safe that she trusted him to keep her that way.

It had been an amazing leave but it was time to return to whatever madness they'd cooked up for him now. Not that he minded getting back to it all, pulling his weight. You couldn't let others put themselves on the line for you. It didn't feel right. He'd learned that from his da and from his brother Tom, both men he looked up to.

He didn't want to wake Anna out of her peaceful sleep, but

any minute now they'd be pulling into Truro. Then Bertie would drop them back to their RAF stations. Different stations, but soon, if the gods took pity on them, his application for base housing would move to the top of the list. They would still be ships that passed in the night, but at least they'd be sleeping in the same house, their kitbags hanging from the same hooks. He tried to picture it. Her toothbrush next to his, her shampoo in the bathroom. Those blue cotton stockings of hers hanging up to dry. It was a picture that made him smile.

'You look happy,' she said, drowsily, rubbing the sleep from her eyes.

'I was thinking of you, that's why – and those awful stockings they make you wear.'

'And that made you smile?' she asked.

'Take pity on me,' he said, grinning this time. 'I've led a sheltered life.'

The train pulled into the station and people in the compartment began milling around, pulling luggage from overhead racks. As he watched them it suddenly hit him that this was a moment he would never have again. An end of a magical interlude. He grabbed Anna suddenly from the seat and embraced her, felt her tall, lithe body melt willingly into his. He kissed her, the way he knew she loved to be kissed. They stood, linked together, blocking the way, seeing only each other as if they were the last two people left on earth.

'Oi, mate – save it for later. You're not the only one's got a woman. Mine's waiting at home,' grumbled a soldier, dumping his kitbag noisily at their feet.

'I'm very sorry,' said Anna contritely, an innocent look on her face, 'only we're newlyweds, you see.'

Jimmy watched in silence as the soldier's expression changed from anger to a grin.

'Congratulations to the pair of you,' the man said. 'Hope you'll be as happy as me and my old dear.'

Jimmy led her from the train onto the crowded platform and neither of them said a word. He was the first to burst into laughter when they were safely outside the station doors. By the time Bertie found them, they were both laughing uncontrollably.

'Something I should know?' asked Bertie.

'Nothing to worry about,' said Jimmy, trying to gain control.

'Just the strangeness of life,' said Anna. 'It'll get you every time.'

Jimmy was glad his last memory of Anna had been such a happy one. She had been the first to leave, blowing him a kiss before she walked through the guard gate to the airfield at Perranporth. It was a small station compared to his, but a busy one, it seemed. It had started out with only one squadron, she'd told him, and now there were three. Fighters only, of course, because the runways were much too short for any of the larger kites like his. Night fighters too, she'd said. He didn't think he was a coward, but all the same, he didn't know how brave he'd be taking off in the dark from a runway with steep cliffs below him and a massive, unfriendly drop to the sea.

Afterwards, he closed his eyes and tried to recall some of the images from the incredible days they'd just spent together. They would keep him in a positive frame of mind. Especially if what Bertie had said was true and there was some sort of flap on.

'What's this about, do you know?' he asked.

'The group captain wants us for a briefing first thing tomorrow, so at least you'll be able to get some sleep before then. Don't suppose you've had much of *that* lately,' said Bertie, pointedly.

He didn't answer, just smiled to himself. Let them think what they like, the blokes in the mess would make it up anyway.

But it was all in good part – there wasn't one of them in the squadron who wouldn't have your back if you were in trouble, he thought. That's what sharing danger did. It was a club you joined, and you just knew that the other members would be there when they were needed. With that reassuring thought he closed his eyes and nodded off. He didn't wake until Bertie had pulled his old rattle trap of a van to a halt and shaken him.

'Wake up, Sleeping Beauty, it's time to go to bed,' Bertie said.

'See you in the briefing room and thanks for this – for the lift,' he said, as he stumbled off into the night towards his billet. The last thing he heard was Bertie's laughter. He wondered what his friend knew that he didn't. Whatever it was, he was sure to find out tomorrow.

After the morning briefing, Jimmy wandered off on his own to let the new information he'd been bombarded with sink in. Some of it was troubling – not that the air force cared much if he was troubled; he was just a small cog in a wheel. And it wasn't about doing the job, for the raid seemed straight-forward enough.

The Germans were building new submarine pens over on the west coast of France at a port called La Rochelle, on the Bay of Biscay. The RAF had already tried several unsuccessful attacks on these U-boat bunkers, dropping tons of bombs, but the pens had double roofs made of reinforced concrete and they'd survived the onslaught from above. Now, it was the turn of the torpedo bombers. Beauforts, like the aircraft he used to fly.

That had been the unwanted surprise. To see his name up on a list of aircrew taking out one of the Beauforts. He was to be a substitute for another navigator. He supposed it made sense, at least to the air force – if not to him – that he should be part of a crew of a torpedo bomber again. It was all because of this phantom *list* he'd been put on. The one that Squadron Leader Blake had warned him about but said should never happen. Just a 'belt and braces' thing, Blake had told him.

So, here he was, thrown in with three other blokes he knew nothing about, that he'd never flown with before. He was making up numbers because their navigator/bomb aimer was in hospital – had broken his damn arm playing football. He felt like breaking the bloke's other arm for him... but the feeling didn't last. It was an order. Refuse it and he'd end up in a far worse place than flying with chaps he didn't know.

He thought he knew why he'd been chosen; he was part of the successful crew that had scored that kill on a U-boat. It was his calculations that had worked out the height and speed needed, his hand that had dropped the aerial torpedo. But it had been their pilot Andy who had lined the plane up for the torturously slow bombing run-in, had kept it there, unflinchingly. This time, they would need to get in close enough for him to launch their torpedo straight into the pens and there was sure to be flak from anti-aircraft guns. Would this pilot, whose name he didn't even know, be just as skilled and brave as Andy had been? He hoped so, for all their lives were in his hands.

47

LA ROCHELLE, WEST COAST OF FRANCE

28 MAY 1941

It was good to be back in the air again, to hear the thrum of engines, feel the familiar vibrations beneath his feet.

He missed Freddy, of course, but this crew he'd joined for the raid didn't seem like a bad bunch. Eager, if a little green and inexperienced. The pilot's name was Edward. 'Call me Ed,' he'd told Jimmy earnestly. He still had that new-pilot's sheen on him, Jimmy thought. But, so far, the man had calmly done his job and got them to the port of La Rochelle.

Now the fun would start. They could expect some 'light resistance' from anti-aircraft guns, the briefing notes had said. But in his experience, flak was rarely light and after the murderous flak in the raid on Cologne, Jimmy had his own idea about what 'resistance' meant. The Germans may not have finished the submarine pens yet, but they certainly wouldn't leave them open to attack.

He'd calculated the height and speed needed to get their torpedo on track. He'd called it through to the pilot but wanted to make a dummy run. He didn't know how anxious the rest of them would be about doing the whole thing twice, but while it was all very well looking at photographs in briefings, he wanted to see for himself. To make sure. What was the point in coming this far if they didn't get the job done right?

The pilot hadn't sounded too horrified, had lined up for the run, agreed that if they didn't get it this time around, he'd go round again.

It hadn't been simple, at least not as simple as the briefing implied. But operations were often like that, he thought. Still, he quickly got the lie of the land and decided to concentrate on the middle bunker when he launched their torpedo. There were ten of the pens in a row – standing like vast concrete sentries, Jimmy thought.

'Keep your airspeed steady, this time,' he warned. 'These tin-fish are a swine if they run too shallow – they're temperamental.' He felt bad as soon as he'd said it. He hadn't meant to teach his grandmother to suck eggs; then again, he didn't know how many eggs this young pilot Edward had sucked so far. Not many, he guessed.

'Got it!' Ed said. 'Steady as she goes, so our fish can hit its mark.'

The breath Jimmy had been holding on to came out in one long, slow release of tension as soon as he fired the torpedo. As if he and the aircraft were one.

That's when he felt the plane lurch and buck violently in the sky, and Jimmy instinctively knew why. He'd been through it before. They'd been lucky so far, had escaped the flak from the anti-aircraft guns, but now the flak had finally hit them.

It was like something from a nightmare. The terror of the detonation as one of the explosive shells punched a hole in the plane's skin, shredding it and filling the air with shrapnel right next to the dorsal gunner. It had started a fire. Jimmy had gone to help, but his gloves had caught alight, burning his hands as he frantically put it out, trying to save a man he didn't even know. Now, he never would. The gunner had bought it. Not an ounce of life left in him. The wireless operator, on the other hand, looked very much alive. The man was hunched over his Morse key, stabbing it in frustration, trying to transmit although the bulky radio equipment in front of him was damaged. Jimmy left him to it.

He made his way forward to the pilot, could see the young man's hands wrestling with the controls, fighting to keep the plane in the air.

'We've lost power,' said Ed, 'but I'll hug the coastline, take us out of Biscay and into the Channel. Communications have gone too. Radio took flak.'

'Can I help?' asked Jimmy.

'Take care of the others – they're newbies, might get the wind up.'

'Wireless operator looks fine,' Jimmy assured him, 'but the gunner's had it, I'm afraid.'

'You're sure?' shouted Ed, shocked.

'Sorry. He's definitely bought it,' said Jimmy, trying to keep the fear and panic from his voice. It wouldn't help.

'My God! His wife – how will I tell her?'

'We'll tell her together. Now, let's get this old girl back home,' said Jimmy and patted the cold metal skin of the Beaufort affectionately.

He went back to his charts, to something he knew, and plotted an alternate course for home. They would make it back – they had to. His hands felt clumsy where he'd burned them and he tried to ignore the pain, and the alarming protests of the aircraft: the creaks and groans of air rushing in through the flak-peppered holes in its skin.

They were losing height, he could feel it, and the air

currents had the poor old plane at their mercy, buffeting her all over the sky.

Suddenly, a voice came over his headphones. Loud and urgent, with an edge of desperation to it. A man trying to hold it together, Jimmy thought. The pilot seemed like a decent chap, willing to give it a try, but he sounded as if he was losing the battle.

'Channel's coming up. I'll hold her as long as I can, but she's fighting me,' the pilot said. 'When I give the word, get ready to jump,' he ordered.

'Jump? I'm not jumping. Promised my wife I wouldn't get my feet wet!' Jimmy laughed. Not that it was a laughing matter. He was trying to help Ed relax, to keep the young man's spirits up. The English Channel wasn't that wide, he thought, willing the aircraft on. Surely they could limp to the other side?

'The pair of you need to get ready to bail out. Don't worry, I'll follow. Just want to give you a stable platform and enough height to open your chutes,' said Ed.

'What, into the drink?' said a nervous voice over the inter-com. The wireless operator, Jimmy thought. The man sitting in front of a useless instrument with shrapnel holes in it.

'They'll pick us up. Air-sea rescue patrols come out here all the time. It's either that or go knocking on the Germans' front door. Could have put down in Brest. Don't know about you chaps,' the pilot said, 'but I don't fancy spending the rest of the war behind prison wire.'

Bravado, Jimmy thought. The young pilot had some of the right stuff about him. Maybe they'd make it after all. That's when he thought about Freddy. Freddy, joking about his water wings. Freddy, who had always warned that he couldn't swim.

He pictured the parachute. Thought about those safety drills he'd been through; was glad he'd paid attention. Still, he'd never been happy about making a jump. The thought of falling through the air and hoping you wouldn't break anything important in the landing. And getting the damned thing off. It was all very well in theory, but he wasn't that keen on putting it to the test.

But at least there was one good thing. Something he was pleased about now. At least he'd learned how to swim – he wouldn't need those water wings of Freddy's.

It all happened so quickly. The aircraft tilted dramatically, and the pilot yelled an order that they were both to leave, Jimmy and the wireless operator.

'My plane, my rules,' shouted the pilot. 'I'll be right behind.'

Jimmy helped the other chap, checked that his parachute harness was secure and then guided him to the escape hatch. 'Once you're out, wait a few seconds before you pull the ripcord – until you're totally clear of the plane. If you pull it too soon, your open chute could get caught. Nod your head if you understand,' he chivvied the wireless operator, who seemed frozen with fear.

He watched the young man reluctantly nod his head and then suddenly disappear through the open hatch. Jimmy checked his life vest and parachute harness – and followed on behind.

48

RAF PERRANPORTH

18 JUNE 1941

Anna had been sitting in the cookhouse gazing off into space, thinking about those amazing days – and nights – they'd shared. She could still feel the glow of it, even though they'd both been back for more than three weeks. She knew that the memory of it, its traces – no matter how faint – would be there in her mind for the rest of her days. Did her wonderful husband feel the same? She hoped so, although she hadn't had a letter from him in a while.

She pulled herself out of her pleasant, cosy daydream. It wouldn't do either of them any good to dwell on distracting thoughts, no matter how incredible they were. Losing focus would be dangerous to them both in their jobs. She couldn't afford to let her mind wander when she was working at the plotting table and Jimmy – well, Jimmy needed intense, prolonged concentration when he was flying. Not that he discussed missions with her. She just knew. You couldn't be around aircrew, the way she was daily, and not understand the constant strain they were under and the terrifying things they were expected to do. They all tried to mask it, of course, putting on a happy-go-lucky, plucky front, especially when pals were shot down. No one ever *died*, she thought, instead they *bought it*; but it came out the same: another young man killed when he had barely started to live.

'Section Officer Garvey wants you,' said a WAAF, who'd suddenly arrived in front of her.

'Did she say why?'

She watched the young WAAF's face go through a thoughtful change, as if the task of recalling an order was a painful mental process for her. ACW Courtney was one of the new intake of WAAFs and a silly, giggly sort of girl, Anna thought, who never seemed to take anything seriously.

'Come to think of it, she asked me to pass on a message, so maybe she doesn't really *need* to see you,' said the WAAF.

Anna was off duty, but if the officer wanted her, perhaps something important was in the works and she'd pulled an extra shift. 'So, this message you were supposed to pass on...?'

'I remember now – you're to come to the guard hut. There's an airman waiting for you. Yes, that's it,' said the WAAF.

'Courtney...'

'Yes, ma'am?'

'I'm not *ma'am*, only officers are ma'am – I'm *Corporal*!'

'Yes, Corporal,' said ACW Courtney.

'Courtney, try to remember messages in future. We're at war. One day you may have to relay something important so try to act as if you know what you're doing!'

'Yes, Corporal Armstrong.'

She watched the young WAAF scurry away and tried to keep from smiling. The girl wasn't military material, *but then maybe none of us are*, she thought. It reminded her of Mary and herself and the others who had piled into that RAF transport together. Innocents, with no idea of what was ahead of them.

But they'd all had to learn, and this young woman would as well – eventually.

She forced herself to walk slowly outside, to take in measured breaths of air, to be calm. Excitement threatened to swamp her. She could feel it building up like a fog in her brain and her heart rate was already climbing. Her palms had become damp with sweat, and she rubbed them on her jacket before mounting her bicycle.

An airman was waiting for her! She couldn't believe her luck, to see him again so soon. She immediately started planning what they would do, where they would go for so short a time. She had to be back on duty tomorrow night for the graveyard shift, but at least that gave them a whole glorious day together. Could life really be that kind?

It turned out that life had a few tricks up its sleeve.

It wasn't Jimmy, but his friend Freddy. She'd only met Freddy a couple of times, but she'd heard he was a bit of a prankster, a practical joker. Jimmy had told her stories about some of Freddy's escapades and how he kept their spirits up. But he wasn't smiling now as he came towards her.

His face was a mask of despair.

That's the moment she knew that something in her world had shifted. What it was, or just how bad, she couldn't tell, but if the look of anguish on Freddy's face was a clue then something was wrong with Jimmy.

'What's happened to him?' she blurted in a voice that was harsh and abrasive and sounded nothing like her own.

'Can we go somewhere to talk?' asked Freddy quietly, nodding towards one of the airmen on guard duty at the gate.

'Tell me, Freddy – please,' she pleaded.

'I borrowed a friend's jalopy to get here. It's right there, we could talk in private.'

When they were both sitting in the car, she turned to him. 'Just tell me,' she said. 'You don't have to sugar-coat it. I promise

I won't faint or scream. But it couldn't be any worse than I'm imagining.'

She watched Freddy take a gulp of air and brace himself. 'I came, because – well, for one, I know that Jimmy would want me to. He's a pal. And I didn't want you to hear it from one of those God-awful telegrams.'

'No!' She covered her face with her hands, in shock. She didn't scream or cry, didn't seem to have the energy. Instead, she slumped down in the seat as if her body had been drained of life and feeling.

'Nobody knows for sure where he is or what happened. His plane's missing. They think it might have gone down in the Bay of Biscay, that's the last time they had radio contact. Air-sea rescue has made a couple of flyovers there, but nothing yet.'

'But if the plane's missing, how are *you* here?' she asked, confused.

'That's what I keep asking myself. I feel so guilty,' said Freddy.

'Well then, why? I don't understand,' she said.

'He shouldn't even have been on that raid. Only the usual crew's navigator ended up in hospital and they put Jimmy in as a substitute. But they can't kill the bloke that easily. You know him – he's stubborn as a mule, a contrary pig-headed mule.'

'So, he's listed as missing?' she asked, her voice hoarse, fighting back despair.

'Yes,' Freddy reluctantly admitted. 'He's finally been listed as missing. You know how it goes – they leave these things for a while, hoping crew will turn up at some distant airfield, a smirk on their face and a story to tell in the mess.'

'But he hasn't yet,' she said, almost to herself. 'How long's he been gone?'

'A while. Three weeks. Since he got back from leave,' Freddy said.

'That's a long time to be missing,' she said, quietly, trying to mask the fear. A scream was building in her throat and she swallowed it. What good would it do?

'That's why I came. You'll have the telegram soon, I expect. But you know what those things are like, full of doom and gloom,' said Freddy.

'I don't believe he's dead,' she said. 'If anybody can make their way home, my Jimmy can. It's what he does.'

'Best damn navigator I ever flew with,' said Freddy with a smile.

'You'll tell me if you hear anything, Freddy? Please! Good or bad – I need to know.'

'I'll let you know the minute I hear. And don't go worrying over any damn telegram, people turn up all the time.'

'You get back now, I'll be fine,' she reassured him, and tried for a smile. It was just as fake as Freddy's was.

She watched the car pull into the distance. It was true that she wanted him to go, to be left on her own for a while. But as for being fine? Her lies were every bit as obvious as Freddy's were. She was a long, long way from being fine.

Her tears blocked her eyes so that Anna could barely see the road ahead, but then her old bike had travelled this route so many times, it was automatic, like an inbuilt radar, she thought. It must be how Jimmy felt at times, working not just on his complicated mathematics but on instinct as well.

That instinct would bring him home. She had to believe that. She refused to think of him as anything other than alive and vibrant; the funny, clever, loving man who was one half of her being, her own body.

But if that was really so, she chastised herself, why hadn't she felt it when something awful had happened to him on a sortie? Surely she would have known, would have felt the pain deep in her core. There had been no clue, nothing that spoke of disaster. She took that as a sign, a positive seed of hope in the midst of all this doubt that had suddenly crept up on her. There was no need for sorrow or anguish, because no matter what had happened to that aircraft, he would survive. Despair wouldn't help him. Together, their optimism and positive thoughts of love would bring him through.

She pulled on her brakes, forced the bike to a messy halt. She didn't know why she had come. Other than to be on her own. She would have to face them all at the station sometime, but right now she couldn't bear to see the pity in people's eyes.

A lush carpet of purple stretched in front of her as she dropped her bike on the grass. She remembered what Lowenna had told her about the stately yellow daffodils standing tall, and the bluebells and snowdrops. But there were none there now. She had missed them all, for they were spring flowers, she supposed. But there were masses of these majestic purple flowers hanging like delicate bells from their tall, green spines; purple and pink, standing out against the green of this fairy dell.

She went up close to one of the incredible blooms and bent her head to smell its scent. There was hardly any perfume. How strange, she thought, that something that looked so beautiful would have no sweet smell.

'Don't touch them,' an urgent voice warned from behind. 'They're poisonous, they'll make you ill.'

'Lowenna, what are you doing here?' she asked, surprised but happy to see her again.

'I used to live here, remember? I visit from time to time. Didn't want the old place to feel sad,' said Lowenna.

Anna watched the younger woman gently touch a bald patch of earth, scorched from the crash.

'Maybe it'll grow back,' she said.

'It will, eventually. Nature's a kindly mother,' Lowenna said. 'But the cottage is ruined now. We'll need a new roof, and those walls will fall in dreckly. Still, I'll be back one day.'

'Have they said so?' asked Anna.

'No, but it's what I want, and what I've prayed for, so it will happen one day. Maybe after the war.'

'Then I hope you get your wish,' she said.

'And what's your wish? You came here today to wish too, Anna.'

'How do you know that?'

'I saw it in your eyes. You know these foxgloves?' said Lowenna, gesturing towards the purple flowers. 'They have a chemical in them that can cure heart disease but their poison can also make you ill if you touch them. Bees love them and they're kind to the bees. So you see how strange life can be? The old folk used to say that these beautiful foxgloves could "raise the dead and kill the living".'

Anna watched Lowenna smile. It was good to see there was still a sparkle in the young woman's eyes.

'That's extraordinary. But still, they're the most amazing colours I've seen,' said Anna.

'So, this wish you came here to wish today. Look at those pretty flowers and say it out loud.'

She couldn't hold on any more, being brave like this, trying to pretend that everything today was the same as yesterday. She sank to the grass and sobbed. She cried until her face hurt with it, and the pain that had been inside had finally overflowed. Then, as suddenly as the weeping had started, it stopped.

'You see, that's much better. Now you can get on and think about him and shout your wish out loud.'

'How did you know it was about Jimmy?' she asked.

'What else could bring you so much joy and so much despair? Now, say what you need to say, and someone will hear, will listen to your special prayer. That's how it works. It's mystical,' said Lowenna.

Anna couldn't explain why, because it didn't make any

rational sense, but it felt right all the same. If she sent up this prayer, it would be heard. He would be safe. He would return.

She sat on the ground and, as loud as she could manage, she shouted the words, until they reverberated around the dell: 'PLEASE COME HOME. PLEASE COME HOME. *PLEASE* COME HOME. JIMMY, COME BACK TO ME.'

49

THREE WEEKS EARLIER

It was an odd, almost dreamlike feeling – this falling through the air, as if his body had no weight of its own. Even quite pleasant, a little like being drunk, he thought. Until his brain stopped playing tricks on him and he remembered that, if he didn't do something soon to stop the descent, then he would hit the sea below with a speed that might kill him.

The ripcord, pull the ripcord! his addled brain screamed at him. He couldn't believe that after the lecture he'd given the poor, frightened wireless operator, he'd forgotten to open his own parachute. Another time it might even have been funny.

He thrust his hand through the ripcord handle and pulled savagely. The canopy unfurled above him and a sudden violent motion jolted him upright. It made him feel sick and the webbing of his chute bit painfully into his shoulders.

Think, he told himself. *Think logically without emotion or fear*. He needed to run through a checklist of things he should do that would keep him alive. Life vest! He needed to inflate it, but should he do that before or after he hit the water? He mustn't panic. Panic was his enemy – it would raise his heart rate as well as making it hard to breathe and weakening his ability to think.

The first priority, he supposed, would be getting the parachute off before it became waterlogged and dragged him under with its weight. Then, he could do something about the life jacket. The safety drill had recommended one long breath into the inflation tube of the life vest around his neck. He wasn't convinced that one breath would be enough, at least not one of the breaths he might only just manage after plunging headlong into the cold waters of the English Channel.

Everything happened so quickly that he had no more time to think or plan. He hit the water with such force that the breath was punched from his body. Automatically, he went for the quick-release clasp on his chute, and he could feel it slacken straight away. The next part was harder as his clumsy hands battled with the harness, but somehow it all floated away instead of pulling him down to the depths of the sea as he'd feared.

The life vest was like a waistcoat, except it was made of rubber. Yellow, so they could spot you when your rescuers arrived. That was a calming thought. A wave caught him, and saltwater invaded his mouth, made its way into his throat. He coughed it up, struggling to stay afloat until the wave released him. Then he lay on his back, taking stock, fighting the fear, and a few slow deep breaths later, he had gained control.

Jimmy managed to locate the long tube snaking from the life jacket and, holding it away from the water, fed it into his mouth. The taste of the rubber made him gag, but he forced his breath into it and waited.

One thing he promised himself he would do when he got back home was write a strongly worded complaint to the manufacturers. They were optimistic in their claim that one long breath would inflate the thing. It took him four, and by then his head was swimming with the effort. But it worked, and when the jacket finally inflated, it kept his head out of the water, as it was supposed to do.

He floated aimlessly for a while. Getting used to being a tiny object in a vast expanse of sea. Gradually, his sense of self-preservation took charge, and he began to assess his situation. It would soon be getting dark, but before that happened he should search for the rest of the crew. He hadn't heard the plane come down, couldn't see any wreckage, so he assumed it had carried on flying. Maybe the pilot had tried to make it across to the other side of the Channel.

The wireless operator had jumped before him, and he wondered if the airman had been able to get off a Mayday with their position before the radio packed in. There was no trace of the young man or his chute but he had to at least try and look for him, so he struck out where his instincts led him. His swim stroke wouldn't win any medals for style, and he didn't know how long he could keep it up, but he refused to just give in: there was always hope of rescue.

Coastal Command had rescue floatplanes flying over shipping lanes and when there were RAF raids on, air-sea rescue planes would fly over the Channel in case aircrews had to ditch. There were high-speed launches too that patrolled, looking for downed airmen, ready to pick up survivors before the elements got to them. If luck was on his side, somebody would find him. He just had to hold on.

Although Jimmy tried to ignore it, the cold was getting to him now. And his hands were beginning to look like claws. He looked at them in surprise, for he'd forgotten they'd been burned. Strange, but they didn't feel painful, only numb with the cold.

Then something miraculous happened. At first, he wasn't sure if it was a mirage, but then those only happened in the desert, didn't they? In a heat haze. *What wouldn't he give for*

some of that desert heat right now. But it wasn't anything mysterious, just metal, and his head connected with it, sending a
ringing noise through the obstacle and a pain reverberating
through his head.

It looked like a small boat. Painstakingly, he moved around
it, tracing the shape from front to back. *Or should that be bow to
stern?* From verging on despair, his mood swung to deliriously
happy. *He was saved.*

Still, one part of his brain advised caution. Whose boat was
it? British or an enemy's? What was it doing out here in the
middle of the Channel?

It was an amazing sight, especially to someone clinging to
hope – looking for a way home. But the strange thing was that it
was uninhabited: not a single voice came from it. There was
something that looked like a bridge, but with no glass or port-
holes in it, and when he swum around to the stern again, he
could find no means of propulsion – no propellor to move it
along. It seemed to be moored. Two stout chains were attached
to either side of it, anchoring it, holding it fast in the current.

It was definitely some kind of vessel and had an odd
entrance at the back, as if it had been designed for people to
climb aboard from the water. It was sloped, like a ramp, with
narrow steps leading up to the deck and guard rails to hold
on to.

He summoned the last of his strength, and climbed up and
out of the sea, shaking himself like a dog, water flying off him.
The metal was wet and slippery, battered by the waves, and he
held doggedly on to the guard rails; but once he got to the top of
the slipway, there was a metal doorway on deck that led to
inside the hull.

There'd been rumours about a new kind of air-sea rescue
vessel that Coastal Command were trying out. They were
anchored in the Channel, he'd heard. Boats with no engine or
steering. Just a floating steel platform, like a large buoy, meant to

house airmen who'd had to bail out of their kites. A safe haven, somewhere to wait and recover until they were picked up.

Still, he'd dismissed the idea for it had seemed like a myth. Yet here he was. Standing on one. Safe. Waiting for someone to find him.

But how would they know where to come?

50

RAF PERRANPORTH

25 JUNE 1941

There are different kinds of courage, Anna supposed. The kind where you know the danger and are terrified, but still go headlong into it. That was how she imagined it for those men who must meet the enemy day after day with pounding hearts, and still carry on. Then there was the bravery of the civilians who faced the bombing night after night and the consequences of war when loved ones didn't make it home.

The one she had to summon up was a less dramatic sort of courage – the ability to go on every day, forgetting her grief, concentrating on her job. It was draining and exhausting at times, but she carried on, putting her misery on hold, until she was alone. When she fell into bed, spent, bone-tired, that's when courage evaded her, and she cried it all out into a pillow, where no one could hear.

People had been kind. Some of the WAAFs had offered words of comfort. Others were too embarrassed to look her in the eye. Or maybe too afraid to show their feelings of relief that the telegram had her name on it and not theirs.

It came a week ago. Officer Garvey had led her to the WAAFs' tiny kitchen, had ordered her to sit. She'd watched in silence and disbelief as the officer made tea for her, then handed over the telegram and offered to leave, so she might read the venomous thing in private. But she'd asked her officer to stay. What did it matter? She already knew what it would say; Freddy had warned her.

She'd thought that nothing could shock her any more but then she'd read those awful, hateful words from the Air Ministry – *missing, presumed dead*. She'd promised herself she wouldn't weep. Instead, something inside her seemed to ball into a fist and punch its way up her throat. She'd rushed to the sink, right there in front of her officer, and was violently sick. She was mortified. But her body had turned traitor and she'd kept on retching until there was nothing left in her stomach. Until it felt as if she'd been turned inside out.

She'd been doing a lot of that lately: feeling queasy and being sick.

Now, a protective coat of numbness surrounded her. Freddy had told her that airmen turned up all the time, arrived on their mother's doorstep even after the family had received the dreaded telegram.

Anna clung to that belief.

~

Anna had been called to the flight office and told to wait. It had never happened before and her imagination plunged her into a spiral of despair. When the station commander's secretary came in, Anna studied the WAAF's face intently, especially her eyes. She saw a friendly face, not grim like someone about to hand out bad news. The young woman had brought her tea and a biscuit as well, had delivered them both with a smile.

'They shouldn't keep you waiting much longer, Corporal,'

she said. 'Only sometimes the communication would be quicker and easier if we just shouted instead of using the telephone.'

'The phone?' asked Anna.

'Yes. Didn't they tell you? There's a call for you from St Eval.'

'But who...?'

'Sorry, I don't know. But it must be important if they pulled you out of operations. That phone on the sergeant's desk' – she pointed – 'I'll put the call through when it comes.'

Anna drank the tea automatically, but it all tasted sour and metallic in her mouth lately, so she hadn't been drinking it. The biscuit was an unexpected treat, but she finished it absentmindedly, hardly tasting it. How was she supposed to do anything normal, now? Sitting like this, waiting for a call that could change her life.

The loud, harsh ring made her nerve-ends scream, even though she'd been expecting it. She rushed to grab it before it stopped. She had no idea whose voice would be on the other end of the line. All her hopes said it would be Jimmy, but she knew sometimes hope was a false mistress, leading you on.

'Hello, can you hear me? This is an awful line,' said the voice.

'Freddy – is that you?' asked Anna.

'Yes,' he said. 'And I've got news.'

'Please tell me it's good news,' she said.

'Well now, that's the thing...'

'What's the thing? Has he turned up like you said – smirking and with a story to tell in the mess?'

But she could tell by the silence that hadn't happened. Finally, she heard a cough, and the words began to pour from Freddy as if a stopper had been pulled from a bottle.

'There's been a bloody mix-up, I'm afraid, excuse my French. The pilot of Jimmy's plane's only just been found,' Freddy said.

'The pilot's alive?' asked Anna, dazed. 'But where's he been all this time?'

'That's the rub. He's been in a hospital in Plymouth. He's been unconscious and they hadn't been able to wake him. There was confusion about which lot he came from – they thought he was with Bomber Command, so nobody contacted St Eval.'

'So, what's changed?' she asked.

'He's out of his coma and he's started remembering. He's badly beaten up, but they think he'll make it. Sounds like a bit of a hero. Brought the kite down in Plymouth Sound – God knows what he was doing there. Trying to get home to St Eval, I suppose. Landed her like a damn sea plane – a miracle he managed to survive,' Freddy said, in awe.

'But *Jimmy*,' she said frantically, trying to pin down the story, 'was Jimmy there?'

'Only the pilot. But the good news is that he's told Coastal Command where to look for the other two.'

'Two?' she said, holding her breath.

'Jimmy was one of them. Him and the wireless operator. They both used their chutes. The gunner bought it over the French coast, and I suppose he's still in the plane, somewhere beneath the waters of Plymouth Sound.'

'Freddy, that's *wonderful!*' Then she realised what she'd said. 'About Jimmy, I mean. Not that the gunner's dead.'

'I knew what you meant. And you're right, of course. There's a chance that he's out there somewhere – maybe a fishing boat picked him up from the drink. You can never tell. But at least now the rescue launches will be looking in the right place. He'll have come down in the Channel somewhere and not in Biscay, floating out into the Atlantic.'

'So there's still hope,' she whispered.

'Of course there's hope,' Freddy said, cheerfully.

'You'd say, wouldn't you – if they'd found him already, or if he's ended up in some German prisoner of war camp?'

'Certainly, I'd say.'

'Thanks, Freddy – for what you've done and the phone call and everything. Hope you don't get in trouble.'

'You know me,' Freddy laughed, 'always land on my feet.'

'I'm glad,' she said. 'It's just that four weeks is a long time to be missing...'

'We're talking about Jimmy here!' She could hear the laugh in his voice.

'So, what should I do? Should I try and see this chap in hospital in Plymouth, or come over to St Eval...?' Her head felt like a balloon with too much air pumped in, as if it was about to burst. It wasn't like her, struggling to find her way through a maze of jumbled-up feelings like this. In the ops room, she was known for her calm, organised approach, leaving emotion at the door, to be picked up only when she went off duty. She sighed.

'I should leave the pilot to come round for a bit,' Freddy said, hastily.

'So – I'll wait, then?'

'They'll let us know the minute he's found.'

'And he's *sure* to be found,' she said, forcing her voice to be cheerful, like Freddy's – as if she truly believed it.

51

Miracles, Jimmy thought, *come in steel measuring thirty feet long and brightly coloured in orange and yellow.* That was the outside, where there was also a red cross painted on the deck. The inside was even better. There were flares, and a signal lamp to hang on the masthead, and a torch and bunks and sleeping bags and fresh clothes and a large flask of fresh water. And *biscuits.*

His grin widened the further he explored the strange vessel. He read the notice on the bulkhead: 'Welcome to Air-Sea Rescue 9, a vessel designed to keep you safe. This ASR will be supplied at least once every month, so if you are not picked up immediately, rest assured you will be home as soon as the service is able to locate you. May your stay be short. Meanwhile, rest and relax. Help is on the way.'

There was an inventory that listed a radio, joy of joys – he couldn't believe it. He would be able to contact air-sea rescue. But when he searched the inside space, he found that the wireless was missing, and a note told him it had been taken to be serviced. Still, it was an improvement on how he'd been hours before, exhausted, floating in freezing water.

Jimmy changed into clothes that smelled of mildew, but they were better than the ones he was wearing. The first aid kit was basic, but at least he managed to bandage his damaged hands. His optimism knew no bounds. Soon he would be home, then surely they would give him a short leave? They usually gave you a few days off if your kite got pranged and you had to ditch. Then there was the reorientation bit, getting back to the squadron, larking around in the mess. He thought about all of that, but mostly he thought of Anna. Getting back to her. Of how she must be suffering to think him gone. Thoughts of her would bring him safely home.

He drew up a plan, made himself a timetable, a schedule to get through the day. How many days would he be stranded here, though? That was the first question he'd asked himself and, of course, it was impossible to say, but the worst case as far as he could tell would be a month. It could be less, because he had no idea when ASR-9 had last been supplied.

He rationed his resources. Four packets of biscuits. One packet per week seemed quite generous at first, but turned out to be only two biscuits per day: one for breakfast and one for dinner. He found himself dreaming of that steak and kidney pie that he and Anna had enjoyed. Still, the lack of food wasn't nearly as bad as his sparse supply of water. He forced himself to be frugal – a few sips every couple of hours – but even with such a small ration, his supply of fresh water wouldn't last that long.

He stuck to his plan, staying warm by keeping mobile, moving around the limited space of his claustrophobic 'cabin' inside the hull and doing some of the dreaded PE that he remembered from basic training. At different times of the day, he struggled outside and fired off one of the flares, but he hadn't seen a ship or a launch in the week that he'd been there. There'd been several planes overhead, but their altitude had been far too high to spot any of his safety flares. So, he'd decided to ration those as well – only use them if he spotted a vessel.

The struggle to fix the signal lamp to the mast hadn't been worth it. The red lamp, fuelled by paraffin, didn't show up during the day, so he decided to save it only for darkness.

He made a simple calendar of the time that went by, scratching tally marks on the wall. He scratched his name there as well. Didn't think his hosts would mind! When his tally totalled two weeks, he celebrated with an extra biscuit and an extra sip of water for breakfast. *Damn the consequences*, he thought. They'd be coming to get him soon anyway, the people who came out to replenish his floating home.

The worst part was the loneliness. So much time alone, with no voice but his own to hear. Too much time to consider, to think. Not that he was much of a thinker. He'd always been more of a *doer* than a *philosopher*, but so much silence forced him inside his head. It sometimes drove him out onto the deck and into the bitter cold, but at least out there was the sound of the sea and the waves that crashed against the hull.

For the whole of the following week, a storm in the Channel tossed his small platform about until he feared it might be swamped. The misery of seasickness held him firmly in its grasp, even when he managed to struggle outside to get to fresh air.

His water ran out. He tried to remember the woman he loved. Her name was buried deep in his mind. So deep that it was a part of him, like his own name, but he couldn't even remember that. Daisy! Of course, that was it. He started to sing a song about the woman he loved called Daisy. The voice he heard surprised him. It was his, not exactly musical, but certainly robust, far louder than he imagined it would be.

It was strange, but he couldn't feel the pain in his hands any more, and his brain began playing tricks. His eyesight started to blur, and he shivered and boiled at the same time until he threw himself down on his bunk. But it didn't help because strange visions piled in on top of him, things that part of his brain knew couldn't be true. Chaps in the squadron who had died on missions came to visit him. He could hear them now: their chatter noisy above him, their feet clattering across the deck.

He hoped Daisy wouldn't mind if he didn't come back. He had tried, but he didn't think he could make it. He was tired. Very, very tired.

So, he closed his eyes and fell asleep.

EPILOGUE

RAF PERRANPORTH

27 *JUNE* 1941

Freddy met her outside the gate, picked her up in the same ancient jalopy that looked as if only a miracle had brought it this far. Eyes stared at her as she got in beside him. But she didn't care – let them think what they like. There was only one man for her, would only ever be, and that was Jimmy.

'We'll go to the pub for a drink,' said Freddy, 'if you wouldn't find that uncomfortable.'

'Will I need one?' she asked. She clasped her hands together tightly in case they might shake and give her fear away.

The fear that Jimmy might not find his way back to her.

'Only to celebrate!' Freddy told her.

'Celebrate?' she said, faintly. The word felt strange on her lips and her mind struggled to believe there could be anything to celebrate. Her head went light, and she grabbed hold of the dashboard in front of her, afraid that if she wasn't pinned down, she might float to the ceiling. It was a most peculiar feeling. 'Celebrate?' she said again.

'Yes. We've all got reasons to celebrate,' said Freddy, beaming.

'They've *found* him,' she said. 'Are you sure?' Her voice was trembling now, and she'd forgotten how to swallow.

'I wouldn't be that cruel. They've definitely got him and he's in hospital in Dover. Don't worry – he's not that bad. Just a bit of exposure and some dehydration from seasickness, the medic said. And a couple of burns on his hands, but nothing that time won't heal.'

'My God, Freddy. He's alive! I'll sort out a travel warrant and get there soon as I can.' She wanted to scream and cry and laugh and babble all at the same time.

'Tomorrow. That'll be time enough. We'll stop off in the pub in Perran and raise a glass to the air-sea rescue lot that found him. They said he was delirious with fever. Apparently, he was singing, can you believe that?' said Freddy.

'According to him, he's got a voice like a bullfrog with a head cold,' she said, rapturously happy.

'Sounds like him.'

'Do you know what he was singing?' she asked. Not that it mattered. He was alive, that was all that mattered now.

'Something about somebody called Daisy. Do you know her?' he asked.

She smiled and then she laughed. She kept on laughing, picturing it. She laughed until she had no more laughter left in her, and then she finally cried.

Anna had agonised over whether or not to tell Gladys the news. She hadn't told her that Jimmy had gone missing, hadn't wanted to worry Ma, not after all the sadness the poor woman had already been through. Still, now that he was safe, it didn't seem right to keep her mother-in-law in the dark.

So, she sent her a telegram, telling Glad where Jimmy was and that he was fine. It was a happy, encouraging one; not the cruel kind that the Air Ministry had sent *her*. *Missing, presumed dead*, that one had said, as if her remarkable Jimmy could die so easily. But he'd proved them wrong and in her heart she'd always known he would, that he'd survive. She remembered her desperate prayer in Lowenna's garden. Had somebody heard?

Getting to Dover proved a complicated business of hours spent on trains, but her WAAF officer had been enterprising and found her a billet in the town: a guest house with three other WAAFs billeted there, and the bliss of a bath with hot water.

A whole day's travelling to get there had left Anna anxious and impatient when all she wanted was to see Jimmy as soon as she was able but in the end she'd given in and fallen into bed exhausted, but with a smile on her face. Tomorrow she could make her way to Buckland hospital. Maybe it would be better this way, as she'd have a chance to wash away the travel and frustration.

The hospital wasn't at all grim, as she'd expected. It had been an old-fashioned workhouse infirmary, but you wouldn't have guessed it from the pretty grounds out front. The day was warm and patients who could walk on their own were strolling. Some men were being pushed in wheelchairs by cheerful-looking nursing auxiliaries. Benches had been put outside for patients and visitors alike, she supposed.

When she looked across at one, she had an unexpected but welcome surprise: it was Gladys.

'Hope you don't mind that I came,' said Gladys.

'Of course not! I'm glad. Have you seen him yet, Ma?' she asked.

'No, not yet. You should be first. Thanks for letting me know.'

'I didn't want to worry you before. Nothing either of us could have done,' said Anna.

'Except worry together! What else are families for? A worry shared is a worry halved,' said Glad. 'Haven't you heard that?'

'I have, but I've never known it before, not with mine,' she said, trying not to weep or put a dampener on a wonderful day.

'There, there! No need to cry – you've got a new family now, warts and all,' Gladys said, kindly.

'I love my new family – and real life should have a few warts. There's something odd about perfection, don't you think?' she said and laughed.

'None of us is perfect,' said Glad. 'Not me, not you, not Jimmy, not even my Harry. This family don't do perfection – we do mistakes and forgiveness, and we do noise and fun. We do *real*. But mostly we do love and hugs.'

'I'm sorry you didn't get to the wedding – forgive me?' said Anna.

'Nothin' to forgive. Now, get over here and give me a hug,' Glad told her, patting the bench.

They sat for a while clinging to each other, both of them grateful, Anna thought. Grateful to be alive, to have someone special they both loved and who loved them. Jimmy was the glue that had brought them together and held them now. It seemed a little like magical alchemy, she thought, this chemistry that fixed her and Gladys at this time and place and allowed her to finally have a mother. Not the one she had lost – she could never be replaced – but a kindly woman who seemed prepared to love her all the same.

'I'll go in now,' she said, 'and come and get you later, Ma.'

'No rush. I'm happy here in the sunshine and the gardens. Makes a change from London,' said Gladys, full of smiles. 'Will you tell him now?'

'What? How much I love him?' asked Anna, confused.

'That and you know... the other thing.'

Anna looked down at her stomach and automatically covered it with her hands, as if it needed protection. 'How did you *know?*' she asked Gladys.

'I've had four kids, dear. I know the signs. Congratulations – that's if congratulations are in order... if you're happy about it, seeing you'd have to leave the WAAF an' all.'

Of course she was happy about it. A family of her own. It was what she'd always longed for. But how would Jimmy feel? Would he be as excited as she had been when she'd first realised?

'It's wonderful. I can't believe it's really happening. And you're right, I love the WAAF, but that's nothing compared to my love for Jimmy and the love I'd have for our baby.' *Our baby!* It was the first time she'd said the words aloud and they felt amazing. Anna's face lit up with a smile.

'There now,' said Glad, 'that's the ticket.'

'But what about Jimmy? I can't throw this at him now, can I? Not when he's in hospital,' said Anna.

'He loves you. Now he'll have two of you to love. What could be better than that?'

She didn't know if that was true. Would it be a shock to him, she wondered, after all he'd come through?

Jimmy was sitting in a chair by the bed when she arrived, and the expression on his face when he saw her told her all she needed to know. He hadn't changed – a dip in the sea hadn't stripped the life from his face or the joy from his eyes. She thought him a little thinner, but he looked much better than she'd feared.

'I hear you went for a swim,' she said.

'Come and kiss me,' he told her.

'What, here? Right in front of all these chaps?'

'Let them get their own girls,' he said. 'I've got the pick of the crop!' He laughed suddenly. That same boisterous laugh of his was still there.

She felt relieved. She lunged at him, sat on his lap, smothered him with love.

'You're really okay?' she asked. 'They said you'd burned your hands.'

She felt his arms around her, his hands swaddled in bandages, but still he held her tight and didn't flinch.

'The doctor says I was lucky. There's a place for the poor sods who've been burned. It's called the guinea-pig club, where they fix those blokes up. They've found out that saltwater baths help the burns to heal, and I got one free.'

It was just like him, she thought, to joke about it and keep it light. It was how he always was with important things, but it didn't mean that he took them any less seriously.

'I never doubted you'd come home,' she said.

'I should hope not,' said Jimmy. 'Now, what's up? I know that look.'

'There's something I need to tell you...' She looked around at the others in the ward. 'Is there somewhere we can be alone?' Anna asked.

'There's a day room,' said Jimmy.

'Is it far, will you be able to walk there?'

'I will if you take my hand,' he said, smiling.

They walked beside each other, and Anna remembered the many times they'd done that before and thought of the miracle that had brought him back to her. In the day room, they sat on a couch together: it reminded her of when they'd snuggled up on that threadbare sofa of Ma's. A contented sigh left her lips.

'Happy?' asked Jimmy.

'Couldn't be happier,' she replied.

'Me too,' he said, 'now what did you want to tell me?'

'You're going to be a father,' she said slowly, and waited. She hardly dared breathe.

She studied his face, saw the surprise move across it as the weight of her words settled on him. They sat together, holding hands, motionless, as if they were spellbound. The silence felt thick around her, like a barrier slotting itself between them. She willed him to speak, to breathe.

That's when she saw the tears. They shone in his eyes like shimmering pools until he could no longer hold them and they trickled down his face. They kept on coming and she held him tightly to her, his body shaking. They stayed locked together, until the tremors had ceased.

Were they tears of relief that had poured from his body? she wondered. Like a tap that was blocked and had now been released? The stress of jumping from an aircraft, not knowing if you would die in the ocean. It would take its toll, she thought.

But then the birth of a smile played on his face, and she knew: they were tears of joy. She watched him struggle to speak.

'Are you sure? It's definite?' he asked her finally, his voice cracking.

'Absolutely,' she said, firmly. 'Is it okay? Are you pleased?'

'It's wonderful!' he said. 'I couldn't be more pleased if you'd handed me a million quid.'

'You're right. This is much better than a million quid,' she said.

'If you're sure you'll be fine with it. What about the WAAF? You love your job. Will they let you stay?'

'Shouldn't think so,' said Anna. 'I wouldn't fit in the uniform, and I'd get jammed behind the plotting table. So, you're truly happy?'

'Happy, thrilled, delighted – and terribly proud. There'll be a small part of me left in the world even when I'm gone. Imagine that,' he said.

'Don't say that. You won't be gone, not for a very long time.'

'Certainly not,' he agreed. 'The Luftwaffe just tried and couldn't manage it. So, where will you go to have the little chap?'

'You're sure it's a chap, then?' She laughed. 'That's male pride for you.'

'A girl will do,' said Jimmy and hugged her. 'You're awfully clever, you know.'

'Really? I thought it took the two of us. Remember that last night in Stockport? That wonderful, magical time?' she asked.

'That's when it happened?' he said, surprised.

'I'd like to think so,' said Anna. 'Although there's no way to know for sure. As for what happens next or where I'll go, let's wait and see.'

Ever since she'd known she was pregnant, Anna had been thinking of her strange, lonely childhood. No doubt it had made her strong and independent, and she'd been grateful at least for that. But lately she'd come to realise one important thing. Something that she'd been striving for, an invisible thread she hadn't even known was there. It had pulled her through her life so far, her search for a family to replace the one she'd never had. That, and a sense of belonging. It was why she'd been so happy in the WAAF, she thought. But now she had a real family: Jimmy and her and their baby and his ma, who'd offered her a place in London to come to have their child. *My first grandchild*, Glad had told her proudly.

She wasn't sure where her baby would be born. She loved Cornwall and wanted to stay there with Jimmy, but then he might not always be there. The air force posted you where you were needed, and she had a feeling the war hadn't yet run its course.

But it didn't matter where she went. Now, she knew exactly

where she belonged. It had been mapped out for her the first time she'd seen him, sitting on the blanket with Mary. Eating that awful sardine sandwich.

Wherever Jimmy went was where she belonged. Because her home wasn't just a place, but a way of life. Her real home existed in his heart.

A LETTER FROM ELAINE

Dear reader,

I'm thrilled that you chose to read my book *Please Come Home* and I want to say a huge thank you. I hope you enjoyed joining Anna and Jimmy in their world and if you did and would like to keep up to date with all my latest releases, just sign up at the following link. Your email address will never be shared, and you can unsubscribe at any time.

www.bookouture.com/elaine-johns

I hope you loved *Please Come Home* and if so I would be very grateful if you could write a review. I'd love to hear what you think, and it makes such a difference helping new readers to discover one of my books for the first time.

I love hearing from my readers because it's YOU, the reader, who truly brings a book to life by investing your time and enthusiasm in it. Until you pick it up and get involved with the characters and their lives, the book is only words on a page. So, I'm very grateful to you and if you would like to get in touch, I would be delighted to hear from you via the contact page of my website: www.elainejohns.com.

In writing about Anna and Jimmy, I wanted to highlight some of the positive things that might come out of war. War is a brutal, terrible thing but as well as showing the dreadful acts that we humans are capable of, I also wanted to think about the kindness and humanity that people show to each other. How they help each other through the trauma. Often, good things come out of bad. And there are many examples from both the first and second world wars when folk pulled together and carried on with life courageously and often with humour.

Many relationships were built, and couples found each other; found love. I wanted to think about how someone like Anna could learn to give her trust and discover a new family who took her generously into their lives, giving unconditional love. Did fate move them all into each other's orbit? I like to think it did!

I wish you many happy hours of reading. Stories are the bread of life. Living and working are all very well, but I think that sometimes we need more things like books and music and art and drama and sport – and loving! Let's not forget loving...

Thanks,

Elaine

elainejohns.com

 facebook.com/elaine.johns.79

ACKNOWLEDGMENTS

Many lovely people have been generous with their time and support in helping me research this book and I would like to thank them all. Any errors are mine and not theirs.

Special thanks go to the brilliant folk working at Perranporth Museum for their help and generosity in sharing their Perran wartime files with me. Their warmth and passion, not only for the area but also for history, was great to see.

Several books have been helpful for research and inspiration while I was writing *Please Come Home*, not only about the war and how it affected Cornwall and its people, but also for the insights into those brave and stalwart women of the WAAF (the Women's Auxiliary Air Force). Lots has been written about 'the few' – those brave young men who flew out day after day into hostile skies during the Battle of Britain, and so it should be! However, until quite recently, the WAAF didn't get too many column inches. Much of this, apparently, had to do with the fact that many of the jobs these women did during their wartime service were secret and lots had to sign the Official Secrets Act. The catch-all label of clerk, special duties (as opposed to simply clerk, general duties) was applied to many WAAFs in clandestine roles in intelligence and those like Anna and Mary working in sensitive areas such as radar. These WAAFs considered it their duty to stay silent about their wartime roles until many years after the war had finished, and some information about their sensitive jobs didn't come out into the public domain until as late as the 1970s.

One particular book had a powerful emotional effect on me and I found myself in tears. That was Norman Small's tribute to his wife – a WAAF whom he met and married at RAF Binbrook in Lincolnshire while he was stationed there as part of an Australian squadron of Bomber Command. It was a very human and emotive 'telling' of the story of WAAFs from all over the United Kingdom.

Dr Sarah-Louise Miller's book on the women of the WAAF was also fascinating and although a more academic look at those women, it was very readable and user-friendly.

I'm grateful to all the following authors and their books for their insights into the history of the period and the many happy hours I enjoyed reading them:

- Edwards, Michael. *Perran at War* (Cornwall: Integral Print, 2009).
- Hancock, Peter. *Cornwall at War 1939–1945* (Devon: Halsgrove, 2006).
- Miller, Sarah-Louise. *The Women Behind the Few* (London: Biteback Publishing Ltd., 2023).
- Small, Norman. *Spit, Polish and Tears – Stories of W.A.A.F.s in World War II* (Queensland, Australia: The Pentland Press, 1995).
- Smith, Graham. *Devon and Cornwall Airfields in the Second World War* (Berkshire: Countryside Books, 2002).
- Tait, Derek. *Cornwall at War 1939–1945* (South Yorkshire: Pen & Sword Books Ltd., 2017).
- Turner, John Frayn. *The WAAF at War* (Yorkshire: Pen & Sword Books Ltd., 2011).
- Plus, the very helpful people at Perranporth Museum for access to their wartime files.

My thanks to the many folk who have helped bring this

book to readers: the friendly and enthusiastic team at Bookouture for all their work in guiding *Please Come Home* safely and seamlessly through the publication process. A special shout-out to my editor Natalie Edwards and to Lauren Finger for their hard work and encouragement, and Judith Murdock. Also, to Ellen Gleeson, Hannah Snetsinger, Jess Readett and the super Belinda Jones and Jane Donovan.

Last, and by no means least, to Loll and Matt and Sam for their support and faith and patience.

Elaine Johns

Perranzabuloe, Cornwall

Printed in Great Britain
by Amazon

32988512R00202